P9-CLO-299

SHADOW'S BLADE

Books by David B. Coe

The Case Files of Justis Fearsson
Spell Blind
His Father's Eyes
Shadow's Blade

The Thieftaker Chronicles
Thieftaker
Thieves' Quarry
A Plunder of Souls
Dead Man's Reach

SHADOW'S BLADE

DAVID B. COE

SHADOW'S BLADE

This is a work of fiction. All the characters and events portrayed in this book are fictional, and any resemblance to real people or incidents is purely coincidental.

Copyright © 2016 by David B. Coe

A Baen Books Original

Baen Publishing Enterprises
P.O. Box 1403
Riverdale, NY 10471
www.baen.com

ISBN: 978-1-4767-8125-9

Cover art by Alan Pollack

First printing, May 2016

Distributed by Simon & Schuster
1230 Avenue of the Americas
New York, NY 10020

Library of Congress Cataloging-in-Publication Data

Names: Coe, David B., author.
Title: Shadow's blade / by David B. Coe.
Description: Riverdale, NY : Baen Books, 2016. | Series: Case files of Justis
  Ffearsson ; 3
Identifiers: LCCN 2016004612 | ISBN 9781476781259 (hardback)
Subjects: | BISAC: FICTION / Fantasy / Paranormal. | FICTION / Fantasy /
  Urban Life. | FICTION / Fantasy / Contemporary. | GSAFD: Fantasy fiction.
Classification: LCC PS3553.O343 S529 2016 | DDC 813/.54--dc23 LC record available
at http://lccn.loc.gov/2016004612

Printed in the United States of America

10 9 8 7 6 5 4 3 2 1

Dedication

✳ ✳ ✳

For Alex and Erin,
Who make me so proud, who make me laugh,
And whom I love more than I can say.

SHADOW'S BLADE

CHAPTER 1

They're close, and getting closer by the minute. She's made a mistake by coming inside. The drive-through; that would have been safest, the best way to get food in the kids and return to the interstate before any of the powers pursuing them took notice.

Gracie scans the restaurant, her gaze skipping over garish plastic fixtures of red and yellow, seeking out faces, searching for the tell-tale blur of features. Not here yet. They may be near, but there's still time.

"Mommy, I have t'go potty."

"Me, too."

Panic rises in her heart, and her hands start to shake. Emmy stares back at her, dark eyes framed by dark hair in a face that is warm brown and oval like Gracie's. Her burger is mostly gone, but she's taken only a sip or two of her cola. Smart girl.

Zach's eyes, hazel like his father's, roam the restaurant, his mouth full of fried, processed chicken. His Sprite is gone. A trip to the bathroom now won't forestall the need for another thirty minutes down the road.

She wants to scream, to sob. But she stands and holds out her hands, a mom to the very end.

"Come on, then," she says. "But when we're done we have to get back in the car, understand?"

Emmy nods, wide-eyed and solemn. She does understand. Too well.

1

"I want d'sert," Zach says.

Emmy shakes her head. "Not now, Zach."

His expression darkens, brows gathering like storm clouds. So much like his father.

"We'll have to stop for gas in a while," Gracie says. "We'll get you candy then."

She leads them to the ladies' room—two stalls, and one is taken. She waits while they go, and then, begrudging the time, but hoping against hope they can somehow escape another stop for an hour or two, takes a turn herself. She can hear Emmy coaching her brother on how to wash his hands. They giggle at something, and tears well in her eyes.

It shouldn't be like this.

She finishes, joins them at the sink. Zach has drops of water on his nose and chin and forehead. They both wear impish grins.

"All right, you two," Gracie says with mock severity. "Time to get going."

Emmy's smile slips, and all color drains from her cheeks. "Mommy . . ."

"They're here?"

"Who is?" Zach asks, looking from his sister to Gracie. "Daddy?"

God, no. Don't let Neil be with them. That would be too much for the kids, not to mention what it would do to her.

"Where are they, sweetie?"

Emmy chews her lip before pointing toward the back wall of the restroom. It takes Gracie a moment to orient herself, but when she does, she sags. Of course. Precisely where the van is parked.

The van, which has all their belongings, and which, to those tracking them, probably lights up the desert sky with magic.

"I wanna see Daddy."

"Daddy's not with them, goober."

"I am not a goober!"

"Are you sure, Emmy? You don't feel Daddy at all?"

She shakes her head.

"Mommy, tell her I'm not a goober!"

"Don't call him that, okay?"

Gracie stares at the tiled wall, ignores Zach when he sticks his tongue out at his sister.

All their things. But aside from the booster seats, how much do they really need? And after all, can't they drive some distance without the boosters?

"Okay, here's what we're going to do," she says. "We'll go out the door that's right by the potty, and then . . . then we're going to drive a different car out of here."

Emmy's eyes widen. "We're going to steal a car?"

"We're going to borrow one."

"What about Zeeber?" Zach asks. "And my blankie?"

"You don't have Zeeber?" Gracie asks, voice rising.

He shakes his head. "You always tell me not to bring him to rest'rants, 'cause I'll get food on him."

Gracie exhales through her teeth and rakes a rigid hand through her hair. Zeeber and that stupid blankie. She knows he's right: She hates it when he brings that stuffed zebra into restaurants. But she wants to shake him and ask why he chose this time to listen. The blanket she might be able to replace, but Zeeber . . . Zach's had it since his infancy, and even if this one *could* be replaced, she wouldn't know where to find another. She's never seen a stuffed zebra like it. It's a damn miracle that he didn't drag it into the restaurant with them. A miracle that could get them all killed. Or worse.

A transporting spell might work, but the men who are after them will feel the magic. They would only have one chance at this.

"We can find you another blankie—"

"No!" His voice echoes off the bathroom walls. "No, no, no, no!"

She puts her hands on his shoulders. "All right, all right. Quiet down." Too late she realizes that there is still someone in the other stall. Stealing the car would have been a bad choice anyway, but that leaves them with few options.

"Okay." She straightens, squares her shoulders. "Stay close to me. Do exactly as I say."

"What are we going to do?" Emmy asks.

"We're going to get in the van and drive away."

"Really?"

"Really."

Emmy gives her best "whatever you say, Mom" eye roll, but she keeps her mouth shut, which Gracie appreciates.

"Hold your brother's hand. Don't let go, no matter what."

Emmy takes Zach's hand, as grim as a warrior. For once, he doesn't complain.

"Ready?"

Emmy nods. Zach shoves his thumb in his mouth, something Gracie thought he'd stopped doing half a year ago. Leaving Neil has taken a toll on all of them.

Gracie pulls the restroom door open and ushers the kids out, keeping them close and squarely in front of her. She picks the weremystes out of the lunchtime crowd and they spot her at the same time. Two remain in the parking lot, visible through the glass doors, but less of a threat for now. Two more are in the restaurant, their features blurred, though she can still make out the predatory grins that curve their lips at the sight of Emmy and Zach. She has warded herself and the kids a dozen times already today, and yet she has to resist the urge to waste valuable seconds on still another protective spell.

Instead, she attacks. She doesn't want to hurt the people around her, but she doesn't have time enough to be careful. She lashes out, drawing on the electricity humming in the walls and ceiling of the restaurant. Bolts of magic, writhing and twisting like twin snakes, fly from the palms of her hands. The restaurant lights flicker and then burst. Glass and sparks rain down on them. People scream. And the two men before her are tossed backward like ragdolls. They land on tables, slide across them, and tumble into the laps of diners, eliciting more screams.

Zach lets out a low, "Whoa!"

She pushes the kids to the door, yanks it open and steps onto the sidewalk out front. Two more men face her there. One is young, his magic a soft blurring at the edges of his face. He is nothing.

But the other . . .

Gracie halts, her breath catching. Power like this shouldn't be possible. Not for a mortal. She gets a vaguely familiar impression of sharp, handsome features, silver-white hair and a trim goatee and moustache. He wears dress pants and a button-down shirt. She senses age, wisdom, and all that power.

"Hello, Engracia."

She knows better than to attack him head on. He can defeat any spell she might cast, and she won't have time for a second attempt.

"What have you done with it?"

She tries the unexpected. Her casting lifts the younger man off his feet and slams him into the older gentlemen. Both mystes go down in a heap. For good measure she casts again, dropping a trash can on them. One of those big, rectangular faux stone ones that restaurants keep near their doors. It's full, and it lands with a satisfying crash.

"Run!" she says.

The kids stare at her.

"Run!" She yells it this time. They sprint toward the van.

She pulls the fob from her pocket and thumbs the doors open. She checks again on the two men and casts one last spell—a second garbage can soars at the mystes from several yards away and drops onto them much as the first did. Her head is starting to hurt, and her vision swims. She's going to be in no condition to drive.

She dashes to the van, pulls the door shut, and fumbles with the keys, trying to stick the right one in the ignition.

"Hurry, Mommy!"

Gracie glances back through the rear window. Already the older man is stirring. She shoves the key in place, starts the car, and backs out of the space with a squeal of rubber on pavement.

She hits the curb as she turns onto the street, has to swerve to avoid being hit by a pickup. The driver hollers an obscenity.

But Gracie is watching through her rearview mirror. The silver-haired man is on his feet by now. A young woman emerges from the restaurant and glares after her. The gentleman lays one hand on the woman's shoulder and holds the other out toward the van.

"Mommy!" Emmy says, her voice rising.

"I see him."

She casts a warding on the van. Her stomach heaves, and she fears she might be ill.

An instant later, his spell hits. The van swerves again, tips onto its right wheels. Emmy screams. Zach starts to cry. She fights it, trying to hold the steering wheel steady, and at the same time casting another warding, an answer to the silver-haired myste's assault. And still she fears it will not be enough. She feels faint; her grip on the wheel slackens. But then the van rights itself, dropping back onto all four tires with an impact that jars her and the kids.

She chances one more peek at the mirror and sees the silver-haired myste release the woman. She crumples to the pavement.

Gracie runs a red light, barely missing an SUV. Horns blare at her, but she ignores them, steers the car down the ramp toward the interstate.

The myste will have seen her take the southbound ramp. That can't be helped. But she'll leave the interstate at the next opportunity and strike out into the desert. He won't expect that, and by the time he figures out what she's done, she and the kids will be far away, sheltered somewhere he doesn't know, laying low until it's safe again.

That's the plan, anyway. But even as she hurtles down the freeway, headache building behind her eyes, she glances at her mirrors, expecting to see the dark ones coming for them.

CHAPTER 2

I sat low in the leather bucket seat of the Z-ster, my silver 1977 280Z. The driver's side window was open, a camera balanced on the top of the car door, its lens trained on a motel room door some twenty yards away.

This wasn't any old camera. It was the latest high-end Canon DSLR, with a twenty-plus megapixel APS-C CMOS sensor—1.6 crop factor—mounted with a four-hundred-millimeter "L"-class telephoto lens and a 1.4-times teleconverter. In short, this was a ridiculously nice piece of equipment with some serious magnification. There was no way I could have afforded to buy the thing; I'd rented it for a few days, at the expense of my current client.

I knew that there were professional photographers working out in the Sonoran Desert with set-ups a lot like this one, snapping amazing photos of the Southwest's stunning wildlife.

Me? I was sweating in my car, waiting to get a shot of a cheating husband as he emerged with his mistress from the Casa del Oro Motel near Phoenix Sky Harbor Airport. Another day in the glamorous life of a private investigator.

In all honesty, I could hardly complain. Over the past few months, I had brought down the Blind Angel Killer, the most notorious serial murderer ever to haunt the streets of the Phoenix metropolitan area, and I had battled a cadre of dark sorcerers and the necromancer who led them. That was more excitement and glamor than most PIs experience in a lifetime, and I had crammed it all into one nearly fatal summer. I should have been grateful for work that wasn't likely to get me killed.

Instead, I was bored out of my mind, which probably makes me sound insane.

But what else is new? I sound insane on a regular basis. In fact, I *am* insane on a regular basis. I'm a weremyste. For three nights out of every month—the night of the full moon, and the nights immediately before and after—I lose control of my mind, even as the magic I wield is enhanced by the moon's pull. What's more, these *phasings*, as they're called, have a cumulative effect; sooner or later—I have a strong preference for later—I'll go permanently nuts and will suffer from the same kind of delusions, hallucinations, and neuroses that plague my father. He's a weremyste, too.

The full moon, though, was still seven days away, and for now I had a case to work on, distasteful though it was.

I hated these kinds of jobs. Of all the work I did as a PI—which included uncovering corporate espionage, finding teen runaways, even investigating insurance claims—nothing was worse than these trashy failed-marriage cases. I'd started my business well over a year ago, after losing my job as a homicide detective with the Phoenix Police Department. And in the months since, I'd come to realize that regardless of whether I was hired by the disgruntled husband or the wronged wife, when all was said and done, I could find fault in both of them.

I like clarity in my cases. I like there to be a good guy and a bad guy. Helping one slimeball duke it out with another slimeball was not exactly my idea of the perfect job.

But as owner and president of Justis Fearsson Investigations, Incorporated, and as a guy with a mortgage, I was glad to have the work. My client, Helen Barr, was paying me well to track her tomcatting husband, whose name happened to be Thomas. The Barrs lived in one of the wealthier sections of Scottsdale and she could afford my new prices: $350 per day plus expenses. To be honest, I was a little disappointed by Tom's choice of this motel for a tryst. It wasn't as though he couldn't have sprung for a room in one of the fancier downtown hotels. Then again, if the woman he was sleeping with—one Amanda Wagner—didn't mind, who was I to complain?

Most cheating spouses are far less clever about concealing their affairs than they think, and Tom was no exception to this. He and Amanda had been smarter than others, but that really wasn't saying much. They used more than one motel for their rendezvous, and they tended to arrive at the motels on foot, after parking some distance away.

But they met the same days of the week, at the same times. And they made no effort at all to confine their displays of affection to the privacy of their rooms. I wasn't prone to squeamishness, but I really didn't need to see Tom Barr sticking his tongue down the throat of a woman half his age.

I'd gotten a few pictures of them going into the room about an hour ago, and by themselves those photos were pretty incriminating. But, in the interest of being thorough, I wanted to get them coming out of the room as well. It wasn't like I needed to protect Helen Barr's feelings. She knew what her husband was up to. At this point she wanted the photos so that she could wring as much as possible out of him in the divorce settlement. I couldn't blame her. And since she was paying me, and providing me with this fine camera equipment, I figured I should give her her money's worth.

The door to their room opened and I put my eye to the viewfinder. The happy couple emerged into the desert sunlight and I depressed the shutter button. The autofocus whirred and the camera started to click away—eight frames per second burst rate. Returning this camera was going to be difficult.

I got a couple of good ones. One with Amanda's hand resting on his chest; another with Tom patting her butt and grinning. As I said, Helen was no saint and I knew that neither she nor Tom was blameless in the collapse of their marriage. But Tom was a sleaze, and I'll admit that I was enjoying myself a little bit knowing how much these pictures would cost him.

And then, with a suddenness that made my heart thump, I wasn't enjoying myself at all.

Magic brushed my mind, dark, hostile, and too damn close.

Neither Tom nor Amanda was a weremyste. In all the time I'd been on this case, I had sensed no magic in them, and I saw no sign of the blurring around their faces, necks, and shoulders that I could usually see in other sorcerers like me. So, being a fool, I hadn't taken the time to ward myself from magical attacks. One day being stupid was going to get me killed.

Since my battles with dark sorcerers during the summer, I had been the target of one magical assault after another. As far as I could tell, none had been meant to kill me. Saorla of Brewood, a centuries-old necromancer who commanded these so-called weremancers, had her reasons for wanting me alive, at least until she herself could savor the pleasure of killing me. But that didn't mean the attacks were a picnic.

Now here I was, unwarded, in my car with the engine off, holding a camera and accessories worth more than I made in a given month, my Glock 22 .40-caliber pistol hidden under the driver's seat. Stupid. I would have liked to toss the camera in the back seat, but I had a feeling the rental place would be less than pleased.

I set it down on the passenger side, while simultaneously reciting a warding spell in my head and scanning the street for the weremystes I had sensed. The warding would have to be general, which meant that it wouldn't be as effective as a spell matched to a specific assault. But it would be a hell of a lot better than no protection at all. I conceived the spell in three elements: myself, a sheath of power surrounding me, and whatever magic my stalkers might throw my way. The words and images didn't matter much. They were what I used to focus my conjurings. These days I was working on casting with a mere thought, without having to resort to the three elements thing. But this didn't seem like the time to put my training to the test. On the third repetition of the spell's components, I released the magic building within me, and felt it settle over me like an invisible cloak.

Tom and Amanda had returned their room key and were walking away from the Casa del Oro in opposite directions. I started up the car, hoping that I might manage to slip out of the parking lot without having to confront the dark sorcerers.

No such luck.

The first spell hit me in the chest—these damn dark sorcerers always went for the heart, and this guy was no different. I could tell that whatever spell my attacker tried failed to penetrate my warding. Most attack spells hurt like hell, and in recent months my heart had been crushed, cauterized, and shish kebabed by wielders of dark magic. This time the attack merely felt like I'd been kicked in the chest by a mule. I grunted a breath and winced, wondering if my sternum had been shattered. But that was something I could figure out later.

I threw the Z-ster into reverse, only to feel the car shudder, the way it would if I was driving at high speed along a windy stretch of road. It didn't move, though, and before I could ward the vehicle itself, another car—sleek, midnight blue; I think it was the new BMW 6 coupe—pulled in behind me, blocking my escape. I saw two people sitting up front, which I suppose I should have expected. They had been coming at me in pairs and groups of three for some time now.

It was bad enough being trapped in the parking lot; I didn't want to be trapped in the car as well. I opened the door and climbed out, my movements stiff, my chest still aching. For the moment, I left my Glock where it was. No sense giving my new friends something else to attack with their spells.

They got out as well. The driver was a man: tall, athletic, good-looking. At least I assumed he was; I couldn't get a clear view of his face, because the smear of magic on his features was too strong. The suit he wore might well have been as expensive as the Beamer. His passenger was a woman who was about as tall as he, and dressed in business clothes: black skirt, white blouse, a beige linen jacket, and black high heels. Her dark hair was cut short and I could tell through the blur of power on her face that her eyes were pale blue. It was like the two of them had stepped off the pages of *Vogue* and *GQ* for the sole purpose of messing with me.

"I'm not sure you're allowed to park there," I said, nodding toward the Beamer.

"We won't be here long," the woman said, drawing my gaze. "We have a quick message for you from a mutual friend."

"Saorla is no friend."

Her smile was as thin as mist. "Who's Saorla?"

"What's your message?"

The woman darted a glance toward her companion, my only warning.

Their attacks charged the air, like the gathering power of a lightning strike. I did the one thing I could think of. The sheath of magic that materialized around me shimmered and undulated as if made of heat waves and aqua blue glass. Their spells rebounded off the warding. One of them knocked the man off his feet, so hard he landed on the pavement, the air forced from his lungs with a satisfying *oof!* The other casting slammed into the BMW, scorching away part of that lovely paint job in a frenzy of white flame.

"My turn," I said.

I'd learned the hard way that dark conjurers were good at wardings. They almost always had protective magic in place that blocked even the most powerful of my attack spells. Which is why I had long since given up on direct magical assaults. They were figuring this out, of course. Each new team of weremancers sent after me was better prepared than the last for the quirky spells I threw at them, but I was adjusting as well. And I was nowhere near running out of ideas.

With *GQ* Guy knocked on his keister, he and *Vogue* Woman were too far from each other to share wardings, and that was fine with me. Under normal circumstances, I would never dream of committing any act of violence toward a woman. But for these dark sorcerers, I was more than happy to make an exception. I threw a spell at her first. Three elements: my hand, the heel of her shoe—the left one—and a good hard twist. I heard the heel snap off her shoe. Her ankle rolled and she lost her balance. As she went down I kicked out, catching her flush on the chin so that her head snapped back. She was out cold before she hit the ground.

I spun toward GQ, who had gotten to his feet.

Once again, my casting took advantage of the sartorial splendor of my opponent. His tie, my hand, and an abrupt yank. He stumbled forward, and couldn't defend himself from the fist I dug into his gut. I hit him again, an uppercut that connected solidly with his jaw and should have put him down on the pavement. It didn't. He staggered, fell back several steps, but then he righted himself. Blood trickled from his lip, and even as I saw it, I cast.

His blood, his face, and a magical fist to the jaw. This punch put him down, but not out. He tried to get up, but I closed the distance between us in two strides and kicked him in the side. He folded in on himself, deflating like a balloon. I hit him once more, a chopping blow high on his cheek. He collapsed to the ground and didn't move again. My hand throbbed from the punches I'd thrown, and I was breathing hard, but they hadn't hurt me. I'd been lucky. Again.

"Tell Saorla to leave me the hell alone," I said. I didn't know if either of them could hear me. On the other hand, I wouldn't have been surprised to learn that Saorla herself was nearby, unseen, watching and listening to all that had happened.

I fished in GQ's pockets for the keys to the Beamer, and finding them, moved the car out of the way so that I could back out. That I happened to ram the front grill of the BMW into a dumpster was purely accidental, all three times.

As I walked back to the Z-ster, though, I spotted out of the corner of my eye a large dog padding in my direction.

Except it wasn't a dog at all. Silver and black fur, golden yellow eyes, and paws as large as my hands. A wolf. A were, no doubt. I froze. The wolf slowed, bared its teeth, hackles rising. It continued in my direction, placing one paw in front of the other with the grace of a dancer.

Hurting weremancers was one thing. They were sorcerers, just like me, and they were fully capable of choosing for themselves which side they fought on in the magical war that had descended on the Phoenix area. Weres—werecats, werecoyotes, and, yes, werewolves—often didn't have any choice. They were conscripts, controlled by Saorla and her allies. I didn't want to hurt any of them, this one included. I held my hands at waist level, palms out.

"Good doggie," I said, trying to keep my voice level.

The wolf growled deep in his throat. Belatedly, it occurred to me that it might not like being called a doggie.

I pointed at Vogue and GQ. "Those are the ones you should be angry with. They're the ones controlling you."

The wolf didn't so much as glance at the unconscious weremystes. He remained fixed on me, and his expression hadn't softened even a little. My, what big teeth he had.

I eased toward my car, my hands still open in front of me. And I made a point of not breaking eye contact with the were, of not doing anything that the creature might construe as submissive behavior. He tracked me with his eyes, growling again and padding after me, matching my movement.

As I neared my car, however, he took three quick steps, cutting in half the distance between us and snapping his massive jaws.

I cast: my hand, his snout, and the magical equivalent of a two-by-four. The wolf yelped and backed away.

I ran to the car. But before I could get in and close the door he recovered, lunging at me and forcing me back. I tried swatting him on the snout again, but it only made him angrier.

Vogue let out a low groan. I knew that if I didn't find a way past Rin Tin Tin, and soon, I'd have her and her partner to deal with as well. I didn't want to hurt the were, but I couldn't allow him to delay me anymore.

"You can understand me. I know you can. I've faced weres before, and all of them retained some trace of their humanity, even after they turned."

The wolf stared back at me, teeth bared, a snarl on its thinned lips.

"I don't want to hurt you."

Then do not. Defend yourself.

The voice echoing in my head was not my own, but rather the rumbling baritone of Namid'skemu, the runemyste responsible for my training. He was the reincarnated spirit of a shaman from the K'ya'na-Kwe clan of the A'shiwi or Zuni nation. The K'ya'na-Kwe, also known as the water people, were an extinct line, unless one counted Namid, who was, for lack of a better term, a ghost.

I am not a ghost!

He hadn't actually spoken to me, but after training under his guidance for longer than I cared to remember, I could hear his voice in my sleep.

For the past two months he and I had worked on wardings and assault spells, ignoring other castings with which I also needed practice. Like transporting spells.

But this seemed as good a time as any to practice.

This was a more complicated casting, requiring seven elements: me, the wolf, the weremancers, the pavement on which I stood, the distance between myself and the front seat of my car, the glass and metal of the car door, and the car seat itself, where I wanted to be. I held the elements in my mind, repeating them to myself six times as the power gathered inside me. On the seventh repetition, I released the spell.

Cold and darkness closed around me like a chilling fog, and for the span of several heartbeats I felt as though I was suffocating.

And then I was in the car, heat radiating off the black leather seats and steering wheel. I rolled up the window, dug in my pocket for the car keys, and started her up. The wolf threw himself against the car door.

"Stop that!" I yelled, though I knew it wouldn't do any good. If I got home and found that he had put even the smallest dent in my door, I was going to drive back here and kick the crap out of him, weres and ethics be damned.

I backed out of the spot, taking care—against my better judgment—not to run over either weremancer, and pulled out onto the street. The wolf ran after me, but I accelerated, leaving him behind. The last I saw of him in my rearview mirror, he was loping off the street, vanishing between two buildings. I exhaled and rolled down my window, my pulse pounding and my hand slick with sweat. Autumn air flooded the car and I savored the caress of the wind on my face.

One of these times, my luck would run out and Saorla's weremancers would get the better of me. But not today.

I steered onto Interstate 10 and headed back to Chandler, where I have my office and home.

My office is on the second floor of a small shopping complex. It's nice as offices go: wood floors, windows overlooking the street, and an espresso machine that cost way, way more than it should have. The computer, in contrast, is ancient, which I suppose says something about my priorities.

I switched it on and while I was waiting for it to start up, I also fired up the coffee machine.

When the computer was functional, I removed the memory card from the camera and downloaded the photos I'd taken. They were as clear as I would have expected from such fine equipment. I chose the best dozen or so and copied them onto three compact discs. One copy I hid in my desk. The other two I intended to take with me: one to keep at home and one to give to Helen Barr.

Once the discs were burned and I had a cup of espresso in me, I called Missus Barr and asked if I could come by. She agreed, and I left the office once more and drove up to Scottsdale, fighting traffic all the way. It wasn't yet what I used to think of as rush hour, but in Phoenix these days "rush hour" began at dawn and continued past dusk. It took way too long, but eventually I reached the Barr home, a Spanish Mission-style mansion in the Scottsdale Ranch Park area. The front lawn was perfectly manicured and along both sides of the house were rocky gardens filled with ocotillos, prickly pears, chollas, and golden barrel cacti. A cactus wren sang from atop an ocotillo stalk, and a pair of thrashers chased each other around the base of one of the chollas.

I followed a winding flagstone path to the front door and rang the bell. Within the house, a small dog began to yap, its claws scratching on the floor on the other side of the door.

A moment later the door opened, revealing Missus Barr. I had met her in person once before. She looked younger than I remembered, perhaps because she had her hair down. She was petite and tanned, with dark blue eyes and shoulder-length blonde hair.

"Mister Fearsson," she said, a tight smile on her face.

"Thank you for agreeing to see me."

"Of course. Come in." She waved me into the house and closed the door behind us. "I was about to have a glass of wine," she said, leading me through the living room. "Can I pour one for you?"

I followed her into an enormous kitchen, complete with granite countertops, cherry cabinets, and every small appliance I could name, plus a few that I couldn't. The kitchen alone was probably worth more than my entire house.

"Water would be fine."

She filled a glass with ice and water from the refrigerator door and handed it to me. Then she poured herself a massive glass of white wine and led me over to a breakfast nook that offered a view of the back lawn—also flawless—and yet another rock and cactus garden.

"So, you have news for me," she said, fixing a smile on her lips.

I pulled out one of the discs I'd burned. "I have photos."

Her face fell. She stared at the disc for a few seconds, then got up and walked out of the room, only to return moments later with a laptop computer. She set it on the table and held out her hand for the disc, which I handed to her. She inserted it in the slot and, after a few clicks of the touchpad, began to scroll through the photos I'd taken.

"She's pretty," she said, after the second or third picture. "What do you know about her?"

"Her name is Amanda Wagner." I kept my voice low, my tone devoid of inflection. And I kept my eyes on the screen, not on her.

"She works for a temp agency, and was assigned to your husband's office for a few weeks back in February."

Missus Barr had continued to work her way through the images, but at that she glanced in my direction. "February? That's when this started?"

"I haven't been able to determine exactly when their affair began. The earliest date I've been able to confirm is in the first week of April, but it's possible that they started meeting before then."

"How old is she?"

I lifted a shoulder. "I'm not sure of her exact—"

"Of course you are. How old?"

I hated this part of my job. "Twenty-seven."

Her nod was jerky. "Tom has always been a handsome man. And I suppose the money helps."

I said nothing.

She clicked through a few more images, stopping at the shot of her husband with his hand on the young woman's rear.

"Damn," she whispered.

I chanced a peek at her, and regretted it right away. Tears ran down her cheeks from eyes that were red-rimmed and swollen.

"I'm sorry, Missus Barr."

She swiped at her cheeks, the gesture impatient, angry. "It's not your fault, it's his. And mine. I told you to find out everything, didn't I? I thought it wouldn't bother me, that I'd sue the bastard for divorce, take him to the cleaners, and be happy to walk away. It's not that easy, is it?"

"In my experience, it never is."

A small breathless laugh escaped her. "Am I that much of a cliché, Mister Fearsson?"

I dropped my gaze, cringing on the inside. "Forgive me. That's not what I meant."

"It's all right. That was an attempt at humor." She closed out of the program she was using to view the photos and ejected the disc. "You have more copies of this?" she asked, holding it up.

"Yes, ma'am. That's yours to keep, and if by some chance you lose it, or he finds it and destroys it, I can make a new one. And I'll see to it that the photos are available for the divorce proceedings."

"Good. What do I owe you?"

"I can send you a bill."

"Don't be ridiculous. You're here now. Let me pay you. Or rather, let Tom pay you. I like the irony of that, don't you?"

"Yes, ma'am," I said, grinning. "But I had some expenses that I need to tally up. And I was wondering if you might want to keep me on retainer in case you should need more information."

She hesitated. "I suppose that might be a good idea. How does that work?"

"It's very easy. We've already signed an agreement, and it remains in place until we both agree to terminate it. The difference is, I'll be taking on other clients and will only charge you for those days when I work on your case a minimum of three hours. And in the meantime, I'll bill you for those days I've worked thus far."

"Yes, all right. Thank you, that's . . . I find it reassuring knowing that I'll have your services if I need them."

"Yes, ma'am."

She led me back to the front foyer, seeming more composed than she had when looking through the pictures.

"I'm sorry to have been the bearer of bad news," I told her as she opened the door.

"You weren't, not really. I hired you because I suspected Tom was up to something. Now I know beyond a doubt. Thank you for that."

"You're welcome."

"Don't worry about me, Mister Fearsson. I'm fine. Or if not, I will be soon."

"Yes, ma'am."

"I'm going to call my lawyer, then I'm going to take a nice hot bath, and then I'm going to go out and get laid."

I laughed.

"You didn't expect that, did you?"

"No," I said, and meant it.

"Tom won't expect it either."

My cell phone rang before I could respond. I glanced at the screen. The call was from Kona Shaw, my former partner on the Phoenix police force.

"I'm sorry, Missus Barr—"

"No apologies. Go answer your phone. And be sure to bill me soon. That's one check I'm going to enjoy writing."

I shook her hand and started back up the path to my car. As I walked, I flipped open my phone. Yes, I'm still the somewhat-less-than-proud owner of a flip phone; I try to keep away from gadgets that are smarter than I am, which these days is almost all of them.

"What's up, partner?" I said. "Please tell me you have work for me."

"Private investigating business slow these days?" Kona asked, her voice sounding paper thin through the phone. Our connection buzzed with all the noise in the background, not only the din of voices one hears at any crime scene, but also a prominent hum. It sounded like she was standing by a race track.

"Yeah, a little. Where are you?"

"Just off the interstate. Feel like eyeballing a couple of corpses, maybe telling me if you see magic on them?"

"Sick as it might sound, I can't think of anything better right now. As long as the case has nothing to do with broken marriages or cheating spouses."

Silence.

"Kona?"

"Sorry, Justis. Meet me at the burger place, exit 162 off of Interstate 10. I'll explain everything."

CHAPTER 3

The Interstate was already filling up with end-of-work traffic, but I made decent time through the city. The burger place wasn't too far from where I lived in Chandler. I felt a little like a yo-yo, driving up and down I-10.

Even before I left the freeway, I saw the crime scene. There must have been a dozen police cruisers in the restaurant parking lot, all of them with their lights flashing. I exited and crawled through the crowded roadways until I reached the lot. One of the cops there tried to stop me from pulling in. I took out my wallet and opened it to my PI license. But once the cop got a good look at my face, he waved me in without bothering to check the license.

Fame had its perks.

Since late spring, when I killed Etienne de Cahors, the reanimated spirit of a medieval druid from Gaul, who had been responsible for the infamous Blind Angel Killings, I had been something of a celebrity here in Phoenix. My role in solving a second set of murders this summer only served to cement that status. A part of me wondered if at this point I could have gotten myself reinstated as a detective in Homicide. But the problems that first convinced the higher-ups in the PPD to fire me—the phasings, and the fact that I lose my mind for three days out of every month—hadn't gone away. I was still a weremyste, and thus still subject to the moon's influence on my mind and my magic. Plus, I had come to enjoy my work as a PI, despite its

21

many drawbacks. Mostly I liked being my own boss, and with wealthy clients like Helen Barr now seeking me out, I was starting to make decent money.

I parked and soon spotted Kona and her new partner, Kevin Glass, standing by the doors to the restaurant. Kona raised a hand in greeting and then beckoned me over with a waggle of her fingers.

No matter where she was, Kona stood out in a crowd. She was tall and thin, with skin the color of roast coffee, the cheekbones of a fashion model, and tightly curled black hair that she wore short. With her thousand-watt smile and her tasteful fashion sense, she might well have been the most beautiful woman I had ever met. Predictably, though, she wasn't smiling now. Neither was Kevin, who was also African American and attractive. Together, they were every bit as stunning as the weremancers who had attacked me earlier.

I passed a body as I walked to where they waited for me. It was covered with a white sheet, and a pair of uniformed officers were keeping people at a distance. I slowed as I walked by. A woman's hand, with nails painted bright pink, peeked out from beneath the sheet. I continued to where Kona and Kevin were waiting.

"Thank for coming, partner," she said, her expression grim, her voice flat. "I'm sorry if I pulled you away from something important."

"I can't even begin to tell you how you didn't. Hey, Kevin." I held out my hand and Kevin gripped it.

"Good to see you, Jay."

I glanced around the parking lot and then tried to see inside past the reflective glare of the restaurant's glass doors. "What have you got?"

"Two dead, three more wounded, one of them critically, and a whole lot of frightened people who can't make up their minds as to what it is they saw."

"What do you mean?"

Kona scanned the lot before tipping her head toward the door. "Come inside and we'll talk."

"You don't want me to take a look at the body over there?"

"Oh, you will. But I want you to see the one in here first."

That didn't sound good at all.

I followed Kona and Kevin inside, and halted, taking in the

damage. The place was a mess, the floor littered with half-eaten burgers and torn ketchup packets, french fries and plastic utensils, paper wrappers and brightly colored cardboard, all of them soaking in spilled sodas and shakes. I took a step and heard something crunch beneath my shoe.

"Careful," Kona said. "There's glass everywhere."

I examined the windows, frowning. None was broken. "From what?"

She pointed at the ceiling.

Craning my neck, I saw that the recessed light bulbs above us had been blown out. All of them.

"Geez," I whispered.

"No kidding. Any idea what might do that?"

I shook my head. "None."

"I was afraid of that. Follow me. There's something else I want you to see."

We walked around a condiment station and a trash can, placing our feet with care. I was wearing tennis shoes, and didn't much care that I was walking through a shallow lake of cola, lemonade, and root beer. But I could tell that this was killing Kona, whose love of nice shoes was exceeded only by her love of bright, dangly earrings.

She led me to a table that was as much a wreck as the floor. A body lay beside the table and its fixed chairs, the sheet covering it soaking up the spilled drinks.

"They wanted to move him," Kona said, reaching down to pull the sheet away and wrinkling her nose, "but I insisted they keep him as he was until you could see."

"Thanks, I think."

I squatted to examine the corpse more closely. He was a big man, tall and broad, with nondescript features. His eyes remained open, and his teeth were bared. Forced to guess, I'd have said he died in pain. He might have been a runecrafter in life, but I couldn't be sure. The blurring effect that I could see in the faces of weremystes died with the sorcerer.

I could tell, though, that magic had killed him.

The front of his shirt was blackened and there was a hole in the cloth where the spell had hit him. The skin beneath was scorched as well. And a sheen of glowing magic clung to his shirt and blistered flesh, warm reddish brown, like the color of the full moon as it creeps above the desert horizon.

All spells left a residue of magic that manifested itself in this way, allowing a trained weremyste like me to do a bit of magical forensic work. Every sorcerer's power expressed itself in a different color, and faded at a different rate. The more powerful the runecrafter the richer the magic and the faster it vanished. The russet I saw on this corpse was a powerful hue; having not seen the spell when it was first cast, I couldn't determine how much it had faded, but I was guessing that it had been a good deal brighter an hour ago.

"Well?" Kona asked, watching me.

"Yeah, he was killed with magic." I pointed to his chest. "It hit him there."

"I could have told you that," Kevin said.

"I don't know what kind of spell it was."

"People described it as bolts of lightning," Kona said. "They say it flew from her hands, like in the movies. That's what one guy told the uniforms who took his statement. 'It looked like something out of the movies.'" She chuckled, dry and humorless, and shook her head. "That's not all, either. When she attacked them—"

"Them?"

"Yeah," Kona said. "John Doe here had a partner. The second guy was hit by the same magic, but somehow he survived, at least so far. The EMTs couldn't say why. He was in bad shape when they took him; they said the odds of him recovering were no better than fifty-fifty."

I nodded. "Okay. You were going to tell me something else—something that happened when he was attacked?"

"Right," Kona said. "That was when the lights blew. They flickered and then popped. People said there were sparks everywhere."

I eyed the broken light bulbs again. I'd never heard of magic drawing upon electricity, but there was a first for everything, right? "Tell me about the woman."

"Dark hair, dark eyes, most agree that she appears to be Latina. About five feet, five inches and one hundred and twenty pounds. Witnesses say she's attractive. And every one of them confirms that she has two little kids with her: a girl of about eight, and a boy of four or five."

I straightened, my eyes never leaving Kona's face. "A mom did this?"

"A magical mom, from what you're telling me."

"Damn." I rubbed a hand over my face. "You called this guy John Doe. He had no ID on him?"

"None. And neither did his companion."

I gazed down at the body again, taking in the expensive clothes and shoes, the nondescript features. "Well, this is a little weird."

"This is nothing," Kevin said. "Wait until you see the woman outside."

We left the restaurant and walked to where the second body lay.

"Accounts of what happened out here are a little sketchier," Kona said. "Apparently our magical mom brought her kids out of the restaurant and they were confronted by two people. One was young, blonde, about five-ten. The other was older—mid-sixties, maybe—silver haired with a trim beard and mustache. From what we were told, it seems he's our second killer."

Kona bent and pulled back the sheet covering this second corpse. The woman on the pavement was perhaps in her mid-thirties. She was heavy, with light brown curls and a wedding band on her left hand. She wore jeans and a Diamondbacks t-shirt. I could see no obvious cause of death, no marks on her face and neck, no tears or cuts in her clothing, no blood trail from a wound on her back or head. Her facial expression was as different from that of the first victim as one could imagine. Her eyes were closed, her features so composed she could have been sleeping.

One mark on her t-shirt did catch my eye: a stain on her left shoulder, about the size of a fist and located at the seam where the sleeve began. The shirt was red, so I couldn't be certain, but it might have been dried blood. Not a lot—not enough to have killed her—but enough to draw my attention.

"What's that?" I asked, pointing at the spot.

"That's what we want to know, too," Kona said. "It's the only wound on her."

"So there is a wound under there."

She nodded. "But not like one I've ever found at a murder scene."

"Can I look?"

Kona glanced at Kevin, who was already watching her. He shrugged.

"Knock yourself out," she said. "But don't do anything stupid to my crime scene."

Right.

I didn't have gloves, but I did have a pencil—the one I used to take notes when questioning clients and witnesses. I took it from my pocket and gently slipped it under the dead woman's sleeve. Using the pencil as a lever, I lifted the sleeve and peered beneath it. I couldn't see the entire wound this way, at least not without allowing the pencil to touch the victim's skin. But I could see enough.

The skin hadn't been broken, but it was discolored. At first glance I thought it nothing more than a simple contusion, darker than most, but not strange enough to draw my notice. If Kona hadn't mentioned how unusual it was, I wouldn't have given it a second glance. But as I examined it, I saw that she was right. The skin on and around the "bruise," for want of a better term, was raised and puckered, and the subcutaneous darkening was uneven, almost dotted, as if . . . Well, I didn't quite know how to finish that thought.

"Witnesses?" I asked, still examining the injury.

"Several, but their accounts don't help much. Our silver-haired perp laid a hand on the woman's shoulder, kept it there for maybe half a minute, and then let go of her. When he did, she fell to the pavement and didn't move again."

I frowned. "He did this with his hand?"

"That's what they say. I'm assuming there was magic involved," she said, dropping her voice.

"None that I can find."

"Say that again."

I eased the pencil out of the sleeve and straightened once more. "There isn't any magical residue on the woman at all. If the perp was a weremyste, he didn't use a spell to kill her or direct any magic her way."

"Well, damn," Kona said, staring down at the body. "I didn't see that coming."

"Do you have any idea what the cause of death was?"

She shook her head. "That's what I wanted you to tell me. Now we're going to have to wait for the coroner's report."

I didn't answer at first. I faced the restaurant and surveyed the parking lot and sidewalk, trying to reconcile what I had seen inside with the wound on this corpse lying at my feet. The restaurant grounds were as much a mess as the interior. Two large trash containers had been overturned, strewing garbage everywhere. I walked to the nearer of the containers and squatted beside it. Rust-colored magic danced along the edge of the faux-stone plastic, bleached by the afternoon sun, but obvious now that I knew to look for it. The same magic shimmered on the other container as well.

"The woman with the kids was trying to get away," I said.

"She *did* get away."

I faced Kona. "I get that. What I mean is, these other guys came after her. The dead guy inside and his friend, the silver-haired man out here. They were after her for some reason. She attacked the two inside directly. Out here . . ." I gestured at the mess. "For some reason she didn't go after the older man and his partner in the same way."

"You know this, or are you guessing?"

"I'm guessing," I said. "But there's magic on these trash cans."

Kona's eyebrows went up. "All right. So why wouldn't she use the same mojo here? It worked well enough the first time."

I considered the question. "There are a number of possible reasons. Maybe she didn't want to hurt or kill the guys outside. Maybe she knew them, cared about them, and so she held back."

"That's one possibility. What's the other?"

"I can think of two others. The first is that the casting she used inside wouldn't work out here. It seems like she found some way to tap into the restaurant's electrical system, and she might not have been able to replicate the spell once she was outside. But that reasoning breaks down pretty quickly. A sorcerer powerful enough to use magic like that inside would be able to come up with some other attack."

"All right, then what about third?"

"Well," I said, "if I found myself face-to-face with a sorcerer I knew I couldn't beat, someone so powerful that any attack spell I tried was bound to fail, I'd go to a different sort of attack, something that a normal warding might not stop."

"Like dropping a garbage can on him," Kevin said.

"Exactly."

My eyes met Kevin's, and apparently Kona didn't like what she saw pass between us.

"The woman killed a man," she said. "At least that's what my witnesses are telling me. For now at least, she's as much a murder suspect as the guy with silver hair."

"Even if she was protecting herself and her kids," I said.

"Even if. And what's more, you know I'm right. You haven't been off the job that long."

She was right. For the most part.

"Not that long, no. But the fact is, I don't have a badge anymore."

"Aside from the PPD, you don't have a client, either."

"The PPD isn't a client, and you know it. I do this to help you out, and because, sick as it is, I still love working a crime scene. But I'm not bound by the same rules."

"Justis," she said, a warning in her tone.

I stepped closer to her. "Think about it, Kona," I said, my voice low. "Procedure might be telling you one thing, but your head and your heart are telling you another. The woman had kids with her, little kids. She wouldn't have gotten into a magical battle unless she had no choice."

"That a new magic you've learned?" she asked. "You can listen in to what's going in my head and my heart?"

I held her gaze, saying nothing. After a few seconds of this, she rolled her eyes.

"Fine, it might have been self-defense. Be that as it may—"

"You invited me in," I said, "but I have no official role here. So wouldn't it be helpful to you if I dug around a little bit?"

"That depends."

"It's not like I'm going to help her slip out of the country. But the magic is pointing me in a clear direction: She's a victim, or would have been if she hadn't gotten away. So let me work that angle. Maybe I can find her. And maybe through her I can find your silver-haired killer." I pointed at the second corpse. "And figure out how he killed that woman."

For a long time, Kona didn't respond. She pursed her lips, her eyes trained on the ground in front of her, and after a while she began to shake her head, which told me that I had won.

"She's driving a minivan, silver, late model. We have conflicting reports on whether it's a Toyota, a Mazda, or a Honda. She was last seen turning onto the southbound entrance ramp." I thought she might say more, but after a moment she closed her notepad.

"What else, Kona?"

"It's probably nothing."

"Probably?"

She raised her eyes to mine. "A couple of witnesses said that her van nearly tipped over as she sped away. And one of them was convinced he saw the silver-haired guy hold his hand up, like he was pointing at the van. This was before the woman he was holding died."

I felt the blood drain from my face. I went back to the corpse and again used the pencil to uncover the wound on her shoulder. There was one possibility that explained the wound and what the silver-haired man might have been doing. It might even have explained why there was no trace of magic on the dead woman. The problem was, I didn't believe what I was contemplating could be possible. Didn't believe it, and didn't want to.

"What's on your mind, Justis?" Kona asked from behind me.

I shook my head, and stood once more. "Nothing. I'm . . . nothing."

"Uh huh." No one could pack more sarcasm into two syllables than Kona.

"I'll let you know what I find out," I said. "You'll do the same?"

"As much as I can."

It was, I knew, the best she could offer.

"All right. See you around, partner. Kevin, take care."

"Later, Jay."

I made my way back to the Z-ster, got in, and started her up. After idling for a few seconds, I pulled out of the parking lot and steered onto the interstate. But rather than heading back north into the city, I drove south. I couldn't say why. I didn't think I could track the woman by her magic, though to make sure I cast a spell that, at least in theory, might have worked.

Seven elements: the woman, her minivan, her kids, her red-brown magic, the freeway, me, and a magical trail connecting all of us. I felt the power of my spell dance along my skin as I drove, but I saw nothing.

Still, I drove for a while, emerging from the sprawl of Phoenix into the flat open desert of the Gila River Indian Community. The reservation covered close to six hundred square miles, and had been, since the middle of the nineteenth century, home to the *Akimel O'odham* and *Pee-Posh* tribes, also known as the Pimas and the Maricopas. As with so much Indian territory in the state, there wasn't much to look at on this land. Even back in 1859, the Federal Government had already gotten very good at picking out the least valuable lands for the tribal nations. There were few landmarks along this stretch of highway beyond a small airfield about three miles south of the restaurant.

I tried the tracking spell a second time, but was no more successful than I'd been before. And yet I couldn't bring myself to turn around. I drove forty miles through the heart of the territory and beyond its southern boundary, until I reached the outskirts of Casa Grande. There, finally, I took the exit and reentered the freeway heading north.

I'd wasted some gas and some time, but I didn't mind that. What bothered me was the sense I had after starting back toward Phoenix that I was now heading in the wrong direction. My spell hadn't worked, and I couldn't explain what I was feeling. But I had been a cop and a weremyste for too long to dismiss it.

I resisted the urge to head south again, and made my way back into the city. The one blessing in all of this was that I was driving against the worst of the traffic. Before long I had pulled up in front of Billie Castle's house in Tempe.

Billie and I met during my investigation into the last of the Blind Angel murders. The killer's final victim, a girl named Claudia Deegan, was the daughter of Arizona's senior U.S. Senator, Randolph Deegan, who had established himself as the most powerful politician in the state. He was about to be elected governor in what everyone, including his opponent, knew would be a landslide, and many believed he had presidential ambitions. Among those who believed this was my girlfriend. Billie was a journalist. To be more precise, she was what many in the business call an opinion shaper. She maintained a blog called "Castle's Village," which attracted a wide readership throughout the Southwest.

When we met, she was digging up information on Claudia's murder, and I was less than forthcoming with what I knew. Eight years on the Phoenix police force had left me with a healthy aversion to the press.

But in addition to being tenacious and smart as hell, she was also charming and beautiful, and for some reason surpassing understanding, she wound up being drawn to me as powerfully as I was to her.

Notwithstanding a few preliminary bumps, our relationship had been developing steadily ever since. It took her a little while to believe in the magic I wield, and a bit longer to accept that my ability to cast spells was worth the cost of the phasings. To be honest, I'm not sure that she's convinced of this yet. There are drugs that a weremyste can take—they're called blockers—that would blunt the effects of the full moon and probably keep me from going insane later in life. But they do this at the expense of my runecrafting, and that's not a trade I'm willing to make. At least not yet. But I was convinced that if Billie had her way, I'd be taking them.

Aside from that, though, things have been great.

Well, mostly. Being involved with me did almost get her killed during the summer, when Saorla threw the magical equivalent of a bomb at a Mexican place in which we were having lunch. Billie's injuries were severe: broken bones, concussion, a collapsed lung. But she's better now.

Yeah.

I have no idea why she is still with me. If I had been in her position, I would have run screaming from this relationship months ago. I was a lucky man.

I parked out front, pulled the Glock from beneath the seat and slipped it into my jacket pocket, and approached her front door. Before I was halfway up the path, the door opened and she came outside looking none-too-happy.

"Thank God," she said. "I've been calling you, texting you; I even tried email."

"I was driving. What's up?"

"Your friend's here. He's doing that silent immovable thing and it's driving me nuts."

CHAPTER 4

My "friend," as she put it, was Namid, the runemyste. And it was a measure of how much time Billie and I had been spending together that Namid would choose to wait for me here as opposed to at my home or office.

I walked the rest of the way up the path and halted in front of her. The sun shone in her eyes, making them gleam like gem-cut emeralds. I kissed her, drawing a reluctant grin.

"Hi."

"You should have told me you had a pet before we got involved."

I laughed. "I don't think Namid would like being called a pet any more than he likes being called a ghost."

"Like I care. He should have thought of that before he started sitting like a statue in the middle of my dining room."

"At least he doesn't eat much."

She smiled again, even as she shook her head. "Get inside, and get him out of my house."

"That might take a while."

"The sooner he's gone, the sooner you have me to yourself."

Well, there you go. That's called motivation.

She pulled the screen door open and I stepped past her into the house. As she'd said, Namid was sitting cross-legged on the floor of her dining room, as still as ice.

Namid and his fellow runemystes were created by the Runeclave,

33

an assembly of powerful sorcerers, centuries ago, in an act of sacrifice and self-abnegation so profound I can barely comprehend it. Namid and the others were weremystes, like me, but far more skilled. At the time, the magical community was split between those who believed runecrafting ought to serve the greater good, and those who saw in their talents a path to domination of the non-magical world. Thirty-nine weremystes were put to death and then brought back in spirit form to be eternal guardians against practitioners of dark sorcery.

Namid, who had been a Zuni shaman, was one of them. He had once been my dad's mentor; now he was mine. On some level he believed he had failed my father, and that his failure had led to my dad's early descent into insanity. That, it seemed to me, more than any inherent promise I possessed as a runecrafter, explained why Namid had taken such an interest in me.

He could be an exasperating teacher. He was terse to the point of rudeness, he expected me to master with ease spells that I knew were beyond my meager talents, and he was reluctant to answer questions that weren't relevant to what we were doing at any given moment. But he was powerful and wise, and on more than one occasion he had saved my life.

He was also the the most beautiful being I had ever seen. No doubt because he had been in life a member of the K'ya'na-Kwe clan, the water people, his spirit had taken a form appropriate to that ancestry. He stood as tall as a warrior, muscular and broad in the shoulders and chest. But he was composed entirely of faintly luminous waters. Often, as now, he appeared clear and placid, like a mountain lake at dawn; at other times his surface roughened, leaving him roiled, impenetrable, and steel gray, like the sea in a storm. Always, though, his eyes shone from his chiseled face, as bright and clear as winter stars.

He peered up at me now as I crossed into Billie's dining room, his expression unfathomable. "You are late in getting here. Where have you been?"

Let me tell you, it was a little disconcerting having a centuries-old watery ghost talk to you like he was your mother.

Billie had followed me into the room and was watching me, expectant, also waiting for an answer.

"Kona called me," I said, more to her than to the runemyste. "She needed me to swing by a crime scene over near the interstate."

"Needed you. As in, someone used magic?"

"Yes. Two people were killed at a fast-food burger place. The restaurant wound up looking like a magical battlefield."

I could tell she wanted to ask me more, but Namid cut in with his usual charm and social aplomb.

"These matters can wait. Ohanko needs to train."

Ohanko was a name he had given me years ago. In his language it meant something akin to "reckless one." I didn't mind it; in his own way, I think Namid used it with affection. And I could hardly argue with what it said about me and my behavior over the years.

"Fine," Billie said, turning her back on us and seeking sanctuary in her kitchen. "Train as much as you like. But try not to make a mess of my house this time."

"Have we made a mess?" Namid asked, his liquid brow furrowing.

I pulled off my leather bomber jacket, and the shoulder holster I wore beneath it. "You have a tendency to throw things at me: books, silverware, CDs." I took my Glock from my bomber pocket and secured it in the holster. Then I lowered myself to the floor opposite him.

"I am trying to teach you to defend yourself from a variety of assaults."

"I know. But they're Billie's books and silverware and CDs, and this is Billie's house."

The runemyste stared after her, seeming to contemplate this. "I see. I will try to make my attacks less . . . disruptive."

"I'm sure she'd appreciate that."

"Clear yourself," he said.

Clearing was a technique runecrafters used to focus their thoughts and enhance their spellcasting. In truth, the most skilled of my kind didn't need to work on such things, and even I didn't take the time to clear when I was out on the street, casting to save my life or to attack an enemy. But Namid tended to push me hard in our training sessions, and the act of clearing had become a ritual of sorts, one that allowed me to set aside possible distractions—Billie, my father, whatever work I was doing for clients, and, on days like this one, whatever investigations I had taken on at Kona's request—and concentrate on my runecrafting.

I closed my eyes and summoned a memory from my childhood of

a camping trip my parents and I took to the Superstition Wilderness. This was when I was no more than ten or eleven, before my dad's phasings got so bad that his mind started to quit on him, and before my mother died in a scandal that poisoned my youth and left me essentially orphaned. It was the happiest I could remember being. One afternoon we hiked out to a high promontory, and while we were there, I spotted an eagle circling above the desert, the sunlight reflecting off the golden feathers on its neck, its wing tips splayed. Whenever I needed to clear myself, I focused on that image of the eagle until the rest of the world fell away.

This was what I did now, and when I felt ready to cast, I opened my eyes again, meeting the runemyste's bright gaze.

"Defend yourself," Namid said, his voice rumbling like distant floodwaters.

Namid had never been one to ease into a training session, and true to form, he started me off with a wicked attack spell. I flew off the floor and slammed into Billie's ceiling, my arms and legs spread wide. I couldn't move, couldn't breathe, and had no idea how to get down. It was as if he had strapped me to the ceiling with invisible steel cables, including one that constricted my chest.

Billie emerged from the kitchen holding a towel and damp bowl, no doubt drawn by the noise I'd made when I hit. Spotting me suspended above her dining room, she rolled her eyes and walked back into the other room.

I had learned that the images I called to mind when envisioning Namid's attacks often held the secret to defeating them. I'd thought of myself being strapped to the ceiling with cables, and so that was how I conceived of my warding. Me, the steel ropes holding me in place, and a magical cable cutter to slice through them.

It was only when I felt the spell tickle my skin that I remembered one crucial detail. And before I could do anything about it, I was falling.

I landed on my stomach in front of Namid and let out a grunt and then a groan.

"Your predicament required a more nuanced solution," the myste said, so calmly he might have been talking about the weather. "If you had been held one hundred feet above the street rather than nine feet above this floor, you would be dead now."

"In my defense, I realized that right after I cast the spell."

He lifted an eyebrow but offered no other response.

I sat up, my movements stiff and painful, not only from the fall, but also from my earlier battle with GQ and Vogue. But I repositioned myself so that I was facing the myste again, sitting cross-legged as he was, and I waited for his next assault.

"Defend yourself."

For the next hour, Namid attacked me with an array of spells, some of them familiar, some of them new and terrifying, including one that ripped gashes in my wrists, so that abruptly blood was gushing onto Billie's oak floors. I didn't think that she would be any happier about massive bloodstains on the polished wood than she was about the scattering of her books across her living room, but I also didn't think Namid would want me fixating on that while I bled out.

An instant later, my situation grew far more serious. Even as I started to grow light-headed with blood loss, Namid hit me with a second casting, this one a fire spell. I was not only bleeding, I was burning, too. I didn't know if the flames were real enough to threaten Billie's house, but they were hot enough to sear my skin and to scorch my lungs every time I inhaled.

Panic gripped me. Which was the greater threat: flame or blood loss?

I couldn't think of a single spell to combat both attacks, and so I went for the flames first. Me, the fire, and a dousing of water.

The flames sputtered and went out.

But another spell struck at my chest. It felt as though the blaze had rekindled inside my body, charring my heart, heating my blood to a rolling boil. This was all too familiar, though not because Namid had ever used the spell against me. Back in the spring, Etienne de Cahors had tortured me with a similar attack; he had very nearly killed me with it.

I tried to sheath my chest in a magical shield that would block the pain, but it didn't work. I was growing dizzy and weak. The flow of blood from my wrists was slowing, not because I had done anything to heal the wounds, but because I was dying. I sat in a pool of my own blood. If Billie had come out into the dining room at that moment she would have screamed.

The blood.

I tried the spell again, but with a twist this time, and seven elements rather than three. Namid, me, my heart, his attack, the pain, a magical warding within my chest, and all that blood to fuel the casting. The room seemed to hum with power. Namid's eyes widened. But the pain stopped. Relief flooded me, brought tears to my eyes. It was several seconds before I realized that the blood around me had vanished. I cast another spell. In recent months, Namid had taught me some healing magic, and I used it now to repair the arteries and close the gashes on my arms. When I finished I raised my gaze to meet Namid's. His features seemed to have turned to glass.

"You cast with blood," he said, an accusation in the words.

"Yes, I did. And I'd do it again if it meant saving my life, or Billie's, or my dad's. Or yours, for that matter."

"That is dark magic, Ohanko."

"Why? Because my intent was evil?"

He blinked. I couldn't keep a small smile from my lips. It wasn't often that I managed to render the runemyste speechless.

"I was protecting myself by using every magical tool at my disposal. Including my own blood. I didn't take it from someone else; you know I would never commit a murder to strengthen my magic. I didn't even have to cut myself. The blood was there, a consequence of your attack on me. How can my use of it be dark?"

"Because it is," he said. He had recovered from his surprise at my initial question. "Blood magic is dark magic. This has always been true."

"But—"

He held up a finger, stopping me. "I cannot argue with what you have said. Neither your intent nor your means of harvesting the blood was evil in any way. And I will even admit that as an act of desperation a blood spell might be forgiven. But the fact remains that blood magic has always been the province of the dark ones."

"I used blood to fight Saorla and her weremancers. That day when we fought them on my father's land."

"I remember."

I stared hard at him, trying to read the thoughts lurking behind that impassive clear face.

"This is why you cut my wrists. That wasn't some random choice.

You were trying to tempt me with all that blood and those other attacks."

"We should have spoken of this long ago," he said. An admission. "Weremystes who use blood for spells soon find themselves relying on blood. It strengthens their runecrafting, and so spells cast without blood begin to feel weak. With time it becomes like a drug, something they cannot do without."

"An addiction," I said, my voice low.

"Just so."

I started to say that I hadn't used blood to strengthen a spell since that evening out in Wofford, when my father and I, joined by Jacinto Amaya and his men, fought Saorla and a number of her dark sorcerers. But I stopped myself because I had used blood in a spell only a few hours ago, when I fought the weremancers outside the Casa del Oro motel.

"You have used blood to cast recently," Namid said, perhaps sensing my hesitation or reading the doubt in my eyes.

I considered denying it, but I knew about addiction. In addition to being well on his way to madness by the time I was fifteen, my dad was also an alcoholic. These things were genetic. I'd been halfway to becoming a drunk myself before Namid came into my life and took responsibility for my training. And I had the sense that addiction to drugs or booze couldn't have been so different from an addiction to blood magic. More to the point, I knew that lying about problems like these made matters worse.

"Yes," I said. "I did earlier today. I could tell you that this was the first time since our fight with Saorla, but I don't know if that's true. To be honest, I can't remember if I've done it other times or not."

"It is good that you did not lie to me."

"I guess I'm not that far gone down the path to hell. Not yet at least."

Namid frowned.

"Blood spells are more powerful," I went on. "They allow me to do things my magic might not otherwise do."

"Then you must continue to train, and thus refine your runecrafting. A true runecrafter does not require blood to cast. He knows that power resides in all things. Blood is a crude source."

I thought of what Kona had said at the restaurant, about the mom drawing power from the building's electricity. "When you say power resides in everything—"

"I mean precisely that. For a long time now, I have wanted you to cast without reciting elements, without having to put your purpose to words. When you cast by instinct, you are more apt to draw upon the energy around us, and, as a result, less apt to rely on other sources of power for your runecrafting."

"Like blood."

"Yes."

"I've never suggested that blood spells can replace training," I said. "I even understand what you're asking of me, what you want for me to do. I'd like to be able to cast that way. But I'm not there yet. And if I'm up against a dark sorcerer, and he's my equal in terms of skill and power, he'll beat me every time, because he's willing to use blood in his castings, and I'm supposed to resist the temptation."

The runemyste considered this. At length he lifted his liquid shoulders in a small shrug. "I cannot argue with this logic. I do not believe you will often find yourself in a battle with a conjurer who is your exact equal in ability, but if you do, then yes, until you learn to harness other sources of power, you will be at a disadvantage. That is the price of adhering to the laws of the Runeclave."

"And you don't see a problem with that?"

"The problem is irrelevant," Namid said. "When you served on the police force you were bound by a set of regulations and laws, were you not?"

"Yes," I said, my voice flat. I knew where he was going with this. I really hated arguing with Namid when he was right, which was most of the time.

"Breaking those laws might have helped you catch the criminals you sought, but still you did not break them. Why?"

"Because to break the law in pursuit of criminals makes me no better than they are," I said, as dutiful as a school boy.

"This is no different."

"All right."

Of all the things I had said this afternoon, this seemed to surprise him most.

"That is all? You do not intend to argue further?"

"Would I have any chance of changing your mind?"

"No."

"Then if it's all the same to you, I'd like to lose this argument and get on with my evening."

"Very well. I will leave you. You trained well today. Each day, I see the improvement in your runecrafting."

"Thanks, Namid."

He inclined his head and faded from view.

I climbed to my feet, my back and chest and legs aching, from my fall, from my confrontation with the fashion models, and from sitting for too long. I noticed that there was no sign of blood or burn marks on Billie's floor. Moreover, my arms were completely healed; there weren't even any scars. No one who saw them would ever guess that I had nearly bled to death a short time before. If I had. Either Namid had healed me and repaired the damage to the floor before leaving, or the magic he had used on me had been nothing more than an illusion. I couldn't decide which option I found more reassuring.

I stumbled into Billie's kitchen, my stomach making enough noise to rouse the dead. I was famished, and whatever she was making smelled great.

Billie stood at the stove stirring a pot of deliciousness. "You're done?" she said, glancing my way.

"For today. Sorry you wound up doing the cooking."

She shook her head. "It was my turn. You've cooked all week."

"How are you feeling?"

"I'm all right," she said. But she wouldn't meet my gaze.

Billie had recovered from the worst of the injuries she suffered when Saorla blew up our favorite restaurant. The compound fracture of her arm had healed, though she was still going to physical therapy, trying to work back to full mobility. And the symptoms of the concussion had vanished for the most part, though she still had occasional headaches and brief bouts of dizziness. The rest of her bruises and cuts were nothing but a memory. But memories were the hardest part of what remained.

We had both been watching for signs of post-traumatic stress disorder, and we'd seen a few. She wasn't sleeping well. When she did sleep, she had terrible dreams, many of them of the explosion itself. And we hadn't eaten out since the attack. We'd gotten food to go, but she admitted to me that she felt vulnerable in restaurants. At my urging, she had started talking to a therapist, but she was struggling still.

I was, too, but in a different way. The explosion wasn't my fault. I knew that. Saorla had used it as a warning, as intimidation. She wanted me to help her kill Namid, and she was willing to resort to threats and torture in order to bend me to her will.

But even knowing this, I blamed myself for Billie's injuries. If she hadn't been with me, she wouldn't have gotten hurt. Plain and simple. The logic of it was as immutable as anything Namid had ever said to me. I had been selfish. She was funny and smart and beautiful and I wanted her in my life. The problem was, my life was dangerous, and for someone like Billie, who didn't possess magic, spending time with me could well prove fatal.

I probably should have told her as much and ended our relationship. Doing so would have broken my heart, but it would have been the best thing for her. Problem was, I loved her. Talk about addictions. I'm not sure I could have given up Billie Castle even if someone developed a twelve-step plan for me.

I crossed to where she stood, took the spoon from her hand and rested it on the edge of the pot, and took her in my arms. "How are you feeling?" I asked again.

She answered with a self-conscious smile and put her head on my shoulder. "It's been a hard day," she said, her voice low. "There was a loud boom earlier—I don't know what it was. And then a few minutes later I heard a bunch of sirens as the fire trucks drove by over on Southern. I haven't been able to do much of anything since. I couldn't work, I couldn't read. I didn't want to leave the house." She pulled back to look me in the eye. "That's why I started cooking. It was the only thing I could do with myself. It was either cook, or curl up in a ball and hide under the covers."

"I'm—"

She held up a hand, silencing me.

I'd made a habit of apologizing for her symptoms, which Billie found annoying and her therapist called inappropriate.

"I was going to say that I'm famished," I told her, "and whatever you're making smells great."

That coaxed a smile. "Liar."

I kissed her. "Best I could do on the spur of the moment. And whatever you're making really does smell amazing."

"I know. Enchilada suizas. They'll be done soon, so make yourself useful and open a bottle of wine."

"Yes, ma'am."

We ate a quiet meal: good food, nice white wine, candlelight. Billie didn't have much to say about her day beyond what she had already told me, and so I wound up describing for her in some detail what I'd seen at the Casa del Oro and then later at the burger place. There had been a time when I tried to hide from her the more distasteful aspects of my job. Not anymore. She wanted to know about all of it, and the truth was, I enjoyed being able to talk about my work without fear of saying too much. We had placed only one condition on these conversations: unless we agreed explicitly that what I was telling her was fair game for her blog, all that we discussed remained off the record.

Billie had grown quiet when I mentioned Saorla and her minions, but now, after a lengthy silence, she asked, "Why would Saorla keep sending weremystes after you? She's not allowed to hurt you; Namid is still protecting you, right?"

"She and Namid have an agreement. I don't know exactly what he'd do to her if she went back on her word, but I'm pretty sure he wouldn't be gentle in whatever it was."

"So then why?"

I hesitated. I had done my best to stop keeping secrets from her, but this was one I'd yet to reveal.

"Fearsson?"

"She's convinced that Namid won't always be so vigilant, and that eventually she'll be able to have her revenge. And until then, I guess she likes to remind me that she's out there and that I shouldn't get too comfortable."

I took a sip of my wine, watching her over the rim of my glass, wondering if this would satisfy her.

It didn't.

"Does Namid know about these attacks?"

Not from me. "I'm not sure how much he knows. He senses a lot of what happens to me."

"But you haven't told him."

I traced a finger along the stem of my glass. "No."

"Why not?"

"Because I can't run to Namid every time some magical kid steals my lunch money." Which was true, as far as it went. "He's not supposed to intervene in our world. The only reason he was willing to step in with Saorla was that she has no more right to mess with us than he does. I can't depend on him. I have to deal with her myself."

"That's not very convincing."

"But it's the truth."

"It's true, but it's not everything," she said, eyes flashing in the light of the candle. "And you know it."

This was the problem with falling in love with someone as smart as Billie. She missed nothing, and she didn't tolerate bull. More than that, she didn't like it when I tried to protect her. She regarded me now, her cheeks bright red, but the rest of her face pale, her lips pressed thin.

I tried to hold her gaze, but I couldn't for more than a few seconds.

"I think Saorla keeps sending her weremancers after me because she wants to make certain I don't forget about . . . an arrangement that she and I have."

"An arrangement? What the hell does that mean?"

"She would say that I owe her a boon."

"A boon," she repeated. "You mean you owe Saorla a favor of some sort?"

"Yes."

She glared at me. "I don't understand. Why would you promise her anything? She's insane. She tried to kill you!"

"More than once. I was there, remember?"

"Then why—?"

She broke off, her eyes still fixed on me. I saw understanding wash over her. Blood drained from her cheeks and her anger sluiced away, leaving her wide-eyed with fear and guilt.

"You did it for me, didn't you? That day she came to my hospital room."

I reached across the table and took her hand. Her fingers were frigid.

Saorla had appeared in Billie's room in Banner Desert Medical Center only a few days after the explosion at Solana's Taqueria, and had threatened to kill Billie if I didn't join her there. I managed to fight the necromancer to a stalemate, but the threat to Billie remained. I begged her to spare Billie's life, and she agreed, but only after I promised that I would owe her a favor as payment for her mercy. It probably wasn't the smartest thing I'd ever done, but at the time I didn't see any other way to keep Billie safe.

"I didn't tell you because I didn't want you to worry, or to feel responsible."

"What will you do?"

I shrugged. "I don't know. Maybe she'll ask for something benign. Maybe she'll want me to pick up her dry cleaning or something like that."

She laughed. "You're a clown, you know that?"

"So you've told me."

"Seriously, Fearsson, what are you going to do when Saorla calls in her chit?"

"I'm going to find some way to fulfill my end of our bargain without doing anything illegal or immoral. And failing that . . ." I shrugged again. I had been planning to say, *Failing that, I'll refuse to do what she wants*, but that would leave me back where I was during the summer, with Billie's life hanging in the balance.

Fortunately, before I could say more, my cell phone rang. I pulled it from my pocket, expecting to see Kona's name on the screen. Instead, there was only a number, though one that struck me as vaguely familiar.

I opened the phone and said, "Fearsson."

"Jay."

At the sound of the voice, my heart seemed to stop beating. The only thing worse would have been a call from Saorla.

"This is Jacinto Amaya."

"Yes, sir," I said, my mouth dry. "I recognized your voice."

"Really? You don't sound glad to hear from me."

To which I had nothing to say at all.

CHAPTER 5

Back when I was on the police force, first working in Narcotics, and then later in Homicide, Jacinto Amaya was the Holy Grail. There was no one Kona and I were as eager to bust. And there was no one who frustrated us more.

As the most notorious drug kingpin in the American Southwest, Amaya bore responsibility, either directly or indirectly, for the trafficking of pot, cocaine, heroine, peyote, LSD, crack, MDMA, roofies, and just about every other illegal drug I could name. All the evidence we could find suggested that he had a financial stake in prostitution, illegal gambling, and human trafficking, and that he'd had a hand in literally dozens of murders, including more than twenty committed right here in Phoenix.

The problem was, we'd never been able to prove any of this. He was smart, ruthless, cunning, and willing to use his wealth, his power, and the threat of violence to get his way. Kona and I were convinced that he had moles in the police departments of Phoenix, Los Angeles, San Antonio, Albuquerque, Las Vegas, San Diego, and at least a dozen smaller cities. And he had developed close friendships with some of the most powerful politicians in the country. That was how he stayed out of jail. Or so I had thought.

He and I finally met in person during the summer, and upon entering his home and seeing the way magic blurred his handsome features, I realized that he was also a powerful weremyste.

He had sought me out not only to hire me, but also to enlist me as a potential ally in his own personal war against Phoenix's weremancers. I soon learned that he had as much contempt for dark magic and its practitioners as did Namid. At first I was surprised by this. I had thought that a man like Amaya, who lived his entire adult life outside the law, would have been drawn to the darker side of runecrafting. But as he explained to me, with a candor that was oddly refreshing, dark conjurers needed blood for their spells, and they tended to prey on the young, the disadvantaged and disaffected: the same people who fueled his drug sales, and who kept his prostitution businesses going. He didn't want the competition, and he didn't want to lose his clientele to blood sacrifices. Hardly admirable, I know. But he was sincere in his desire to defeat Saorla and the weremancers working with her, and at the time I was short on allies. I had some sense now of how Roosevelt and Churchill felt when they agreed to fight alongside Stalin.

If our association had ended there, I would have chalked up the interaction to experience and gladly moved on. But it didn't. After our fight with Saorla and the others out in Wofford, which left my father's trailer in shambles and most of his possessions ruined, Amaya offered me ten thousand dollars. He presented the check as an expression of his friendship and made clear that to reject either one would be a grave misstep, pun fully intended. I had no choice but to take the money. He swore that it was a gift, one that came with no strings attached. He wanted to help with the repairs on Dad's trailer, and he wanted to thank me for work well done. But I knew better and so did he. He had meant that ten grand to serve as a sort of permanent retainer, and he was calling now because he had something he wanted me to do.

It occurred to me that Amaya still waited for me to say something and to offer him assurances that I wasn't as horrified to hear from him as, in truth, I was.

"I wasn't expecting your call," I made myself say, knowing how ridiculous I sounded. I glanced at Billie. "I'm . . . I'm with a friend right now and—"

"Ah, of course," Amaya broke in. "How is Miss Castle?"

I hated it when he did that. It was bad enough that he knew how to contact me and that he and his men had been to my home and to my father's trailer. But every time he mentioned Billie's name, reminding me in no uncertain terms that he knew everything about my personal life, it felt like he had aimed a nine-millimeter pistol at her heart. Too many of my magical enemies were using my love of Billie as a weapon; it was starting to piss me off.

"That's none of your damn business," I said, none too wisely.

"Careful, Jay," he said, his voice silken. "No one speaks to me that way. Besides, you were the one who brought her up."

"I assume you have business you wish to discuss with me, sir."

I could imagine him smiling at my attempt to change the subject. "More than that. I have a client for you. Be at my home in forty-five minutes."

He hung up before I could make an excuse or tell him to go to hell. I stared at my phone for a few seconds before snapping it shut and shoving it back into my pocket.

"Who was that?" Billie asked.

No secrets. Sometimes lying to her would have been so much easier.

"Jacinto Amaya. Apparently he has a client for me, and he wants me to meet this person tonight."

"Your job really sucks, Fearsson."

My laugh was as dry as dust. "So you've told me."

"What isn't his business?" she asked.

"I'm sorry?"

"You kind of snapped at him, which, given that it was Amaya, probably wasn't such a great idea."

"Right. He asked how you were doing."

She blinked, sat back in her chair. "Great. Why are all of your friends so interested in me?"

"You mean Amaya and Saorla?"

"I'm using the word 'friends' loosely."

"I'll say." I lifted a shoulder. "They're trying to find ways to get at me, to control me. And they know I'm in love with you." I said it without thinking, without hesitating. I didn't consider exactly what I'd said until I saw the warm blush seep back into her cheeks.

We had yet to declare our love for each other. It had been there for a while now, smoldering beneath the surface. But until this moment, neither of us had spoken the words. I guess I owed Amaya a thank you.

"You're in love with me?" she said.

"Does that surprise you?"

She shook her head. "You know I'm in love with you, too, right?"

For all my talk of how she would be safer without me, hearing those words made my heart do a little Snoopy dance. Yeah, I was totally hooked on her.

"I do now," I said, taking her hand again.

Her smile promised a very nice end to our evening together. Unfortunately, I had an appointment at Jacinto Amaya's house.

"I have to go."

She canted her head to the side. "I don't suppose you can call Amaya back and tell him to go screw himself, can you?"

"Not really, no. But I'll be back."

The smile deepened. "Good."

I stood and began to clear the table. "In the meantime, don't you dare do any of these dishes. That was an amazing dinner, and you have the rest of the evening off."

She followed me into the kitchen, carrying plates as well, and when we both had set them on the counter, she stepped close to me, put her arms around my neck, and kissed me, her body leaning into mine, her back arching.

"What was that for?" I asked when we came up for air.

She kept her eyes closed. "To make sure you're coming back later."

She kissed me again.

"I think that should do the trick," I whispered, my breath stirring her hair. "But if I don't leave now, I'm not going to leave at all."

I pulled away before she could kiss me a third time. She blew a raspberry at me. I strapped on my shoulder holster, knowing that Billie was watching me, trying not to look her way. She didn't like any sort of firearm, and she really didn't like that, working as a PI, I had no choice but to carry one. When the holster was in place, I grabbed my bomber from the chair, gave her a wink, and headed out to my car. I almost doubled back to tell her to lock her door, but I didn't. This was a safe neighborhood; the only threat to her came from weremystes and beings like Saorla, none of whom would be stopped by a door lock. Besides, she didn't need me scaring her by being overprotective.

Even at night, without traffic, the drive from Billie's place in Tempe to Amaya's mansion in the Ocotillo Winds Estates subdivision of North Scottsdale normally took close to half an hour. Amaya had given me barely enough time to say my goodbyes and get to his house; for all I knew, he had calculated the time and distance using an online map.

Ocotillo Winds was a gated community filled with new Spanish Mission-style homes, all of them huge, all of them protected by adobe walls and wrought-iron gates. Amaya's house sat at the end of a short cul-de-sac. It might have been larger than the houses flanking it, but not by much. On the other hand, the walls surrounding the property were thicker, the paired gates blocking the driveway appeared sturdier. A guardhouse stood beside the gates and security guards armed with modified MP5s patrolled the driveway itself.

The first few times I'd come to the mansion, including one time after the explosion at Solana's when I arrived unannounced and angry, the guards had been a bit rough with me. But I'd been to the house enough times now that they recognized the car and greeted me like an old friend.

Which is not to say that they didn't order me out of the car, frisk me, and take my Glock. But they did it all with smiles on their faces, and though they didn't lay their weapons down, they also didn't have them aimed at the back of my head.

When the guards were convinced that I was unarmed and posed no threat to Jacinto, they pointed me toward the front door. It was open already, and a burly Latino man waited for me there, his black hair pulled back in a ponytail, a smile on his lips.

"*Amigo,*" he said, greeting me with a handshake and a slap on the back.

"Hey, Rolon. How's it going?"

He shrugged, ushering me into the house. "Can't complain. Got a new car. Lowrider, like Paco's." He flashed a toothy grin. "But faster, you know?"

I had to smile. Rolon and Paco were Amaya's . . . Well, I wasn't exactly sure what they were. Henchmen? Bodyguards? Trained attack dogs? Whatever Amaya called them, they were built like NFL linebackers, and I had no doubt that they would kill their grandmothers if Amaya ordered them to. But though they worked for the devil, I couldn't help but like them. The truth was, I liked Amaya, as well. I feared him, and I didn't trust him, and if there was a way I could have handed him over to Kona with enough evidence to put him away for life, I would have done it in a heartbeat. He was, however, a difficult man to hate.

Rolon steered me through the foyer into a grand living room with polished wood floors, exposed beams, and a bank of windows that was incandescent with the glow of downtown Scottsdale. Oaxacan folk art covered the walls and shelves of the room and the air carried the faint, sweet smell of burning sage and cedar, as if someone in another room had lit one of the smudge sticks used by the Southwest's Pueblo people.

A lean man with perfectly styled silver and black hair turned at the sound of our footsteps and strode in our direction, his arms spread wide. He was dressed with elegance in a light gray fitted suit, a black dress shirt, and a sapphire silk tie. I had the vague impression of an olive complexion and dark, almond-shaped eyes, a winning smile and bold features, but until my eyes adjusted, I couldn't make out anything with confidence. The blur of magic across his face was too strong.

"Jay," he said, gripping my shoulder with one hand and proffering the other for me to grip. "I'm glad you could make it."

I shook his hand, hiding my amusement. He had all but ordered me to his house, and now he was treating me like an old friend. Out of the corner of my eye I spotted two other people in the room, an older couple, who had gotten to their feet when Rolon and I entered. I wanted to dismiss Amaya's greeting as something he did for show, to impress these other guests. But he was more complicated than that. The enthusiasm of his greeting, I knew, was as genuine as the menace that had shaded his voice on the phone. They were two sides of the same honed blade.

"It's good to see you again, Mister Amaya."

He nodded, his hand still on my shoulder, and steered me to his other guests.

"I'd like you to meet Eduardo and Marisol Trejo. They're friends of mine, and they need your help. Eduardo, Marisol, this is Jay Fearsson. He's the private detective I told you about."

My first thought upon seeing them was that Missus Trejo was a weremyste. She wasn't nearly as strong as Amaya—the smudge of magic on her face was subtle, though unmistakable. My second impression was that they appeared even more out of place amid the luxury of Amaya's home than I did. Mister Trejo had nut-brown skin and hair as white and soft as a cloud. He was short, barrel-chested, and he wore a rumpled brown suit that fit him poorly. His wife was thin and had probably been a beauty as a young woman. Her eyes were a rich earthy brown, and her features were as delicate as his were heavy. Her hair was steel gray, and she wore what must have been her Sunday dress. It had a floral pattern, and it looked like it had been made for a larger woman. I wondered if Missus Trejo had been ill.

"It's a pleasure to meet you both," I said, shaking his hand and then hers.

Amaya sat in a leather arm chair, indicating that I should do the same. The Trejos lowered themselves onto the couch once more.

"Tell Jay what you told me."

"It's our daughter," Missus Trejo said, her voice devoid of any accent and stronger than I had expected. "Engracia. She has . . ." She shrugged. "I suppose you would say, she has run off."

"I'm sorry. This must be a difficult time for you." I pulled my pencil and notepad from my jacket pocket.

"We're concerned for her, as you would expect. But this is particularly worrisome because she has her children with her. No one has seen either Engracia or the children since early this morning."

I sat forward at her mention of the kids, and I searched Marisol's face once more, taking in that soft blur of magic.

"Is she a weremyste?" I asked.

Missus Trejo glanced back at her husband before facing me again and nodding.

"This is why I called you," Amaya said.

"How old are the children?" I asked, ignoring him for the moment.

"Emily is eight, Zachary is five."

Mister Trejo pulled something from within his suit jacket and held it out to me. I hesitated before taking it from him. It was a photograph. The image was grainy—it had been printed on regular paper rather than photo stock—but I could make out the three faces. Engracia, the mom, was as fine featured as her mother, with dark eyes, dark hair, and a complexion somewhere between her mother's and father's. The little girl was the image of Engracia, though unlike her mother she wasn't smiling. The boy had lighter skin, paler eyes, and a grin that could have charmed a hired assassin.

Naturally, my thoughts had already pivoted to Kona's murder scene: a mom who was a weremyste, with two kids the same age as those of the woman who killed John Doe and sent his companion to the hospital. But I had no proof that this was the same family, and every reason to be skeptical of such a coincidence.

"You say they've been gone since this morning?"

"Yes," Marisol said.

I chanced a quick look at Jacinto. He watched me, something akin to a warning in his eyes.

"Please understand," I said, facing Missus Trejo again. "I sympathize. Naturally they're dear to you, and it probably seems that they've been gone a long time. But—"

"You don't understand, Mister Fearsson. Engracia and the children live with us now. They . . . they had to leave Engracia's husband. She left our house this morning with the children, as she always does. We thought she was taking them to school and then going to work. She's a physical therapist at Tempe Saint Luke's Hospital, and Emmy and Zach go to Carminati Elementary. But later in the day the school called to ask why the children hadn't come in today. And when we called Engracia at work, they told us she hadn't been in either."

"Are any of their belongings missing?"

Missus Trejo nodded. "Yes. After calling the hospital, I went and checked the room they've been staying in. Most of their things are gone."

"Is it possible your daughter has gone back to her husband?"

"No!"

We all turned to Mister Trejo, who shrank back from our gazes, his cheeks coloring. But he shook his head and said, "No," a second time. Even from that single syllable, I could hear the heaviness of his accent. "She no go back to him," he said, eyeing me, his expression fierce. "He . . . he beat her. He's no good, and she know that now. Finally."

I shared a glance with Jacinto before facing the Trejos again. "Were the children beaten, too?"

"Not that we know of," Marisol said. "It's possible, though."

I nodded, saying nothing. An expectant silence settled over the room, broken only by the ticking of a nearby clock. I knew that the others were waiting for me to speak, but I tried to ignore them. How many young mothers disappeared with their children each day in the Phoenix metropolitan area? Probably more than any of us cared to know. But how many of them were weremystes? And how many of those few had a daughter and son of the exact ages given by Kona's witnesses? I wanted this to be coincidence. I had only just met Mister and Missus Trejo, but already I didn't want to have to tell them that their daughter was the primary suspect in a murder investigation.

"What do you think has happened to them?" I asked Marisol.

"They don't know," Jacinto said, his tone derisive. You'd have thought I'd asked the dumbest question he could imagine. "That's why I called you."

I held up a hand, hoping to silence him in a way that wouldn't tick him off too much. But I kept my eyes on Engracia's parents. "What are you afraid has happened? And what do you hope has happened?"

Marisol said something to Eduardo in Spanish. He replied, his voice low, his words coming in a jumble. They spoke for several moments. I caught fragments of what they said, but couldn't make out most of it. Amaya listened closely, and I guessed that he understood all of what they said. I wondered, if I asked him later, if he would be willing to tell me what had passed between them.

At last the Trejos turned back to me.

"The best we are hoping for," Marisol said, "is that Engracia decided the children needed some time away from Phoenix. Leaving their father was hard on them. Perhaps she took them camping. They like to camp. Or maybe she would like to find a new place to live. She has spoken of moving to Tucson. Our other daughter is there. Rosa. We have spoken with her, and she has heard nothing from Engracia."

Eduardo said something else, but Marisol merely glanced at him and shook her head.

Facing me again, she said, "Our worst fear is that Neil has them and is . . . is hurting her as revenge for leaving him." Her voice broke, and a tear slipped from her eye.

"Neil is her husband."

She nodded. "Neil Davett. Engracia took his name, as did the children."

"And where does he live?"

Marisol gave me a street address in the North Mountain section of Phoenix.

I wrote that down, along with Neil's full name and a few other things I wanted to remember from our conversation.

"Is Neil a weremyste, too?"

She hesitated before nodding. "I think that's how they met."

"Is it possible that any of this has something to do with magic?"

Marisol frowned, clearly puzzled by the question. "I don't understand. Do you mean did someone use magic to make her disappear?"

"No, I—" I shook my head, unsure myself of what I was trying to say. I didn't want to alarm her or her husband by bringing up the murders by the interstate. I caught Amaya watching me. He shifted his gaze back to Missus Trejo, but I had the distinct impression that he knew exactly what was on my mind. In the past, I had been shocked, and more than a little bit appalled, by his knowledge of what went on inside the PPD. Chances were he had known about the killings at the burger place before I did.

"What I'm trying—"

"Jay wants to know if your daughter has felt threatened by her husband's magical abilities, or perhaps those of his friends."

Actually, that wasn't what I wanted to know, though it was an interesting thought. It made me wonder how much Amaya already knew about Neil Davett.

"Not that I know of," Marisol said. "I suppose it's possible."

Amaya stood. "I think Jay probably has enough to start his investigation. Don't you, Jay?"

His tone carried another warning. Standing as well, I said, "Yes, I believe so. Does your daughter have a cell phone?"

"Doesn't everyone?" Marisol asked, the ghost of a smile on her lips. "We've tried the number all day, but she hasn't answered. I believe she has it turned off."

As I would, if I were running away and didn't want anyone to find me. "Can I have the number anyway, it might come in handy at some point."

She gave it to me and I added it to my notes. "Does she have a passport, and more to the point, do the children have passports?"

Marisol's cheeks blanched. "I don't know. I don't believe so, but . . . I'm sorry."

I chanced another quick look Amaya's way. He didn't appear pleased. "It's all right," I said. "Thank you both. If I have additional questions I'll be in touch." To Amaya I said, "I take it I can reach the Trejos through you."

Marisol and Eduardo got to their feet, both of them frowning, perhaps at the abrupt ending of the conversation.

"Mister Amaya, you know that we don't have enough money to pay Mister Fearsson. We can't even—"

Jacinto took her hand, the kind smile on his face completely at odds with the glower he'd given me moments before. "It is my expense, *Señora*," he said. "Jay has worked for me in the past." His gaze flicked in my direction. "And no doubt will again in the future."

"But we couldn't—"

"Of course you can. You are in need; Engracia may be in trouble. It's the least I can do for you."

She smiled, though she seemed to be on the verge of tears. "Thank you, Mister Amaya. God bless you."

He kissed her cheek, then shook hands with Eduardo and wished him a good night in Spanish. "Paco," he called.

Paco loomed in the arched entrance to the living room. He could have been Rolon's twin—in size as well as appearance—except for the goatee and mustache he had grown since last I saw him. He nodded once to me before turning his attention back to his boss.

"Will you see the Trejos home?"

"Of course."

"Use one of the SUVs. Take Rolon and check the house before you leave them. Understand?"

"You got it." He smiled at the Trejos and led them out of the house.

Even after they had left the living room, Amaya said nothing to me. Only when the thump of the front door's close echoed through the house did he remove his suit jacket and say, "Drink?"

"A beer, please."

He walked to the wet bar near the bank of windows, took two bottles of Bohemia Stout from the refrigerator, and opened them both. Returning to where I stood, he handed me one and clinked the top of his against the top of mine.

"Sit," he said, lowering himself into the leather chair once more. I sat as well.

He sipped his beer and loosened his necktie. "I would have preferred that you not frighten her quite so much."

"There were questions I had to ask. Otherwise I can't do the job you've hired me to do."

His expression soured, but he didn't argue the point. "So, what do you think?"

"I think you know a lot more about what happened to Engracia than you're letting on."

Amaya glared at me, offering no reply for several seconds. "Gracie," he said at last.

"Excuse me?"

"Her parents still call her Engracia, but she goes by Gracie. Gracie Davett."

"That doesn't sound very Latina."

"How about that?" he said without a trace of humor. "Now answer my question."

"How much do you know about the husband?"

"Very little. I've met Gracie once, and that was a few years ago. Marisol teaches Spanish at the school my daughter attends. She's one of Chofi's favorite teachers—that's how I know her. I saw the magic on her and was interested to know more. I learned that she uses blockers and hasn't cast a spell in years. I don't think Eduardo approves of magic, although he and I have never spoken of it."

"But Gracie casts, doesn't she?"

He drank more of his beer. "You tell me."

"She's wanted for murder."

His eyes widened enough to tell me that he hadn't known this. "Thank you for not mentioning this in front of her parents."

"Why would dark sorcerers be after her?"

"Because she's not one of them. That's all the excuse they need."

"Is her husband one of them?"

"An interesting question. One you should check into as part of your investigation."

I took a swig of beer. It wasn't my favorite, but it was richer than most Mexican beers, and Amaya seemed to like it a lot. It was the only beer he had ever served me.

"I was wondering when we'd get to that. I take it you want me to find Gracie Davett."

"And her children," Jacinto said. "You're to bring them here."

"That might not be possible. If she's wanted for murder—"

"Who did she kill?"

"The police don't know yet. He wasn't carrying any ID."

He quirked an eyebrow. "In your experience, is that often true of the virtuous and blameless?"

"That's not the point, and you know it. I can't get in the way of a murder investigation without making myself an accessory."

"Do you really think that a mother—at least any sane mother—would commit a murder in front of her young children?"

I'd been arguing the same point with Kona only a few hours before. So why did I resist agreeing with the man? Probably because he already felt like he controlled me, and because I felt that he did, too. And I didn't like it. Still, I couldn't deny that he had a point. "No," I said. "But the fact remains, she's wanted for murder, and the Phoenix police are going to be searching for her. Anything I do to get in their way is going to land me in a lot of trouble."

"Then I'd suggest you prove her innocent."

I should have known he'd say something like that.

Another thought occurred to me.

"What do you know about an older weremyste?" I asked. "Silver-haired with a trim goatee?"

"He and I have never met, but I've heard others speak of him."

"Do you know his name?"

Amaya glanced down at his beer. "I don't."

I tried to decide if I believed him, not that it mattered at the moment. I wasn't about to call him a liar to his face. "Did these others happen to mention that he could kill simply by laying a hand on someone?"

He raised his gaze to mine. "Yes, they did. You might want to avoid letting him touch you."

CHAPTER 6

I left Amaya's house a short time later, once we had worked out the details of our business arrangement. He didn't like my new rates, but we both knew that with all the high-profile cases I had solved in recent months, I could charge pretty much anything I wanted. And it wasn't as though Jacinto could plead poverty.

Once I was outside, one of his guards gave me back my Glock. I walked to my car, slowing as I gazed up at the moon. A week until it waxed full, six days until the phasing began, and already I sensed it pulling at my thoughts, like a cat unravelling a ball of yarn.

I opened the car door, but continued to stand there, staring up at the face of the quarter moon. Something about that silver-haired man had bothered me since the moment Kona first mentioned him to me. Something other than the ease with which he could kill. But only now, bathed in moon glow did I realize what it was.

He was that rarest of magical beings: an old weremyste who seemed to be functioning and sane. How could that be?

I knew that Saorla had protected the weremancers who worked for her from the monthly effects of the phasings, and I wondered if she had been guarding this man from the moon's influence for enough years to preserve his sanity. I had also learned from Namid that the more skilled and powerful a weremyste became, the more he or she could resist the worst of what the runemyste called "the moontimes." Perhaps the sheer might of the magic this man wielded was enough to keep him from losing his mind. Either way, I wasn't looking forward

61

to meeting him, particularly if that encounter didn't happen until the phasing began.

I climbed into the car and started back toward Billie's house.

I was about halfway to Highway 101 when I figured out I was being followed. Whoever was behind me didn't have much experience tailing people. I could tell, because I had a ton of experience. He was following too closely, maintaining a short distance between us.

No doubt it was another of Saorla's friends.

I continued past the on-ramp to the highway, figuring I would be safer on surface roads if my shadow decided to attack. I steered myself onto Scottsdale Road, and followed it through the heart of the town. It made for slower going, but I was fine with that. I even took a few extra detours onto side streets, each time making my way back to the main road, so that I could be certain the guy in the trailing car really was following me.

He made every turn with me, sometimes idling at red lights right on my rear bumper. Eyeing him in my rearview mirror, I could nearly make out his features. I knew he was alone, and though I suppose it was possible that this was the silver-haired weremancer, I somehow doubted that such a dangerous enemy would prove to be this much of an idiot. Whoever it was drove a Hyundai sedan, late model, metallic green. Not exactly a muscle car. I probably could have shaken him if I tried. But I wanted to talk to him.

At the next side street, I made a sharp right, accelerating through the curve and speeding down a narrow residential lane. The Hyundai came after me. I made a second right onto another residential street. It was empty except for a few parked cars. I hit the brakes and spun the wheel so that I came to a stop blocking both lanes of the road. Moments later, my shadow slung around the corner and, seeing me, slammed on the brakes. He threw his car into reverse, but I'd had enough of this.

Three elements. His tire, my hand, and a long, sharp knife. I heard the tire blow, watched as the car swerved and slowed. When it came to a complete stop, the driver's side door opened and the man inside got out. Despite the dim light, I could make out the smudge of magic across his face.

I warded myself and climbed out of the Z-ster. For the moment, I kept my Glock holstered.

"You were interested in speaking with me?" I asked. "Or do you just tail strange cars at night as a hobby?"

He was about my height, light brown hair, handsome in a nondescript way. He might once have been an athlete, but he had developed a small paunch that his flannel shirt couldn't quite hide.

"I want to know where my wife and kids are."

I nodded, knowing that I should have expected this. "Neil Davett."

"That's right. Who the hell are you?"

"You followed me without having any idea of who I was. That's pretty dumb, Neil."

"Screw you! I can take care of myself. Now where are they?"

"I had been planning to look you up and ask the same question," I said.

He scowled. "I don't believe you."

I took a few steps in his direction, muttering an attack spell to myself, in case he threw a casting my way. He had some power; I could tell that much from the amount of blurring on his features. And clearly he didn't lack for confidence. But I didn't believe he was much of a threat. Unless, of course, I managed to tick him off.

"So first you follow me, not knowing who I am, and then you call me a liar. You're not the brightest bulb on the marquee, are you?"

"And that's the second time you've called me dumb. Now, I'm going to give you one more chance to answer my questions. Who are you, and where the hell is my wife?"

"My name is Jay Fearsson. I'm a private investigator, and I've been hired by Eduardo and Marisol Trejo to find your wife and children."

He had been coiled, readying himself for a fight. But he straightened at that, his brow furrowing. "They don't have the money to hire a PI."

"No, they don't. But they have a friend who does."

"Amaya."

Maybe he wasn't quite as dumb as I'd thought. "That's right. They say that you've been abusing Gracie. They think that's why she ran away."

His jaw bunched, and I thought for sure he'd throw a spell at me. But he kept his temper in check. "That's between Gracie and me."

"All right, then tell me this: do you have any idea why dark sorcerers might be after her?"

"What makes you think they are?"

I stared back at him, keeping my expression neutral. If he didn't know about the confrontation at the burger place I wasn't going to tell him. But his bearing had changed, becoming guarded, wary. He wasn't bristling with testosterone anymore. If anything, he appeared scared. Talking about Gracie and the kids was one thing; he didn't like the turn our conversation had taken.

"Answer me!" he said, sounding more whiny than threatening.

"I have my reasons," I said. "You been playing with blood magic? Maybe getting Gracie involved in stuff she shouldn't be doing?"

"You don't know what you're talking about. And you don't know anything about Gracie. She doesn't—" He stopped himself and leveled a finger at me. "I don't care what you've been hired to do. You keep away from my family, and you stay the hell out of my way."

I'd had enough. I released the attack spell I'd allowed to build inside of me. I figured that Neil had warded himself, but I also thought that my crafting would be more than enough to get his attention, even through his magical shield. I was right on both scores.

The spell I cast was the equivalent of a fist to the gut, if that fist happened to belong to a magical Rocky Balboa. Neil doubled over with an audible grunt. A moment later he dropped to the ground, landing on his butt.

He raised his eyes to mine and gritted his teeth, giving me warning enough to brace myself. Magic charged the air and his spell hit me full in the chest, knocking me back on my heels. I had hit him in the gut rather than the face because I didn't want to risk drawing blood that he could then use to enhance his casting. Even so, his crafting was more potent than I had expected.

A second spell hit me, much like the first. But though the impact staggered me, my warding held.

"All right," I said. "We've proven to each other that we can cast, and that our wardings work. What now?"

He reached around to his back and the next thing I knew, something in his hand flashed with the cool glow of a nearby streetlight. I grabbed for my weapon and leveled it at him.

"Don't do it, Neil!"

He hesitated, the knife blade hovering over the back of his hand. I didn't want to see what he could do with blood magic.

"You're not going to shoot me."

"I will if you draw blood for a spell. I won't have any choice, will I? And now that you're holding that knife, I can claim it was self-defense."

Doubt crept into his eyes.

"I used to be a cop. I know how these things work."

Still he hesitated.

Three elements. His hand, his knife, my hand. It had been a while since I had worked on my transporting spells, but I'd pulled off a complicated one earlier in the day, and this one was as rudimentary as such a casting could be. One moment he was holding the blade, and the next minute I was. His eyes went so wide I almost laughed.

As a precaution, I warded my hand and pistol. I didn't want him using the same spell against me.

"When was the last time you saw Gracie?" I asked him.

Nothing.

"Believe it or not, you and I want the same things. I haven't met your wife or your kids, but I want to find them. I want them to be safe."

"Her parents hate me."

"Yeah," I said. "They seem to. But what do you expect? You're a gringo, and you married their baby. She goes by Gracie instead of Engracia—"

"That was her choice. Hell, I wouldn't have minded if she had wanted to go by Trejo instead of Davett. It was all her."

"I believe you. But they never will. Especially if you keep hurting her."

I knew as soon as I said it that I'd made a mistake. But guys who hit women piss me off. Always have, from even before I joined the force.

Neil shut down on me, clenching his jaw, murder in his eyes. I half expected him to fire another spell at me.

"When did you see her last?" I asked again.

"Go to hell."

I probably should have seen that coming.

"Fine." I holstered my weapon and dropped his blade where I stood. "I'm leaving now," I said, backing toward the Z-ster, my eyes fixed on his face. "You can try to follow me, but with that flat you're going to ding up the wheel rim. Don't get in my way again; next time we meet, I won't be so easy on you."

I opened the car door and started to ease into the driver's seat.

"It's been almost two weeks," he said. "It'll be two this coming Sunday."

I stopped, straightened once more, one arm resting on the roof of the car.

"Where did you see her?"

"A park near my house. I had the kids for the weekend; she was picking them up."

"Was there anything unusual about her behavior, or maybe about things the kids said while you had them? Anything at all that might explain her disappearance?"

He shook his head. "She was distant, but that's been the case for a while. And the kids . . ." His gaze slid away. "Do you have kids?"

"No."

"Then you wouldn't understand. I wasn't watching for signs, I wasn't trying to read every gesture or guess the hidden meaning behind every word. I had them with me, and that was enough. I was trying to soak up the time. Enjoy them, you know?"

"When are you supposed to have the kids again?"

"I'm supposed to have them every weekend. Those are the terms of the separation agreement. She was supposed to call last Friday to arrange the drop-off. She didn't, and I never heard from her. I went by her parents' house, just to see that they were okay. I saw them in the yard, so I drove off. I didn't want to start a fight. I wanted to see my kids, that's all. But when she didn't call again today I got mad. I went by the hospital where she works, and she wasn't there. I started feeling scared, worrying that they were in trouble . . . So I went to the kids' school. They hadn't been in, either. By then I was really scared. That's when I started trying to track her down."

"You were following her parents. You found me through them."

He faltered, then shrugged. "I didn't know what else to do. The phasing is coming up, and I want them with me for that. It's safer."

I frowned. "You and Gracie are both weremystes, both subject to the phasing. Why should the kids be any safer with you?"

Neil's gaze flitted away, giving me the impression that he wished he'd kept that last remark to himself.

"Unless," I said, "you're using blood magic to protect yourself from the moon."

"I want my kids back," he said, refusing now to look my way. "And my wife. I miss my family. That's the only thing that matters to me."

One of the insidious things about abusive relationships was that abuse and love could exist side by side. The love was twisted by violence and a desperate, almost pathological need to control, but it was there nevertheless. Neil sounded like a guy who loved and missed his wife and kids, and wanted them in his life. I could even believe that his concern for their well-being was sincere. But that didn't mean the abuse wouldn't start up again as soon as he and Gracie were back together.

I didn't know what to say to him. A part of me felt sorry for the guy; another part of me wanted to kick the crap out of him. Once we started attacking each other with magic, he'd been quick to go for his knife. I thought about my conversation with Namid earlier in the evening. It seemed that Neil was used to using blood in his spells, which told me that he had more than a passing familiarity with dark magic.

"I have every intention of finding them," I told him, feeling that I ought to say something. "And I'll do whatever I have to to keep them safe."

He nodded.

I got in the car and drove away, watching Neil in my mirrors to make sure he didn't do anything foolish. Once I had turned off that small lane, I made my way to the highway and headed back to Billie's.

The house was dark when I got there. I parked out front, alarm bells going off in my head. I had my Glock in hand before I was out of the car. I opened the screen door and found that the front door was still unlocked. I turned the knob and then pushed the door open with my foot, both hands on my weapon.

Billie lay curled on the couch, a blanket around her shoulders. I could see that she was breathing. A candle sat in a shallow bowl on the coffee table beside her, cool wax pooled around its base. Everything else seemed to be in order. I started to holster my weapon.

A faint rustling, made me whirl, the pistol raised to fire, my heart in my throat.

I froze.

A small owl sat on the top shelf of her bookcase, yellow eyes gleaming in the dim light cast by the moon and the streetlights. Gray and black streaking, small tufts on its head similar to those of a Great-Horned Owl. I knew it right away for a Screech Owl. But what was it doing in here?

I chanced a quick scan of the room and saw that the screen on one of the open front windows had been slashed. I even thought I saw a few wisps of down clinging to the edges of the opening the owl had created.

I took a slow step toward the bird. It watched me, but didn't flinch or give any indication that it intended to fly. I eased closer.

When I had covered half the distance between us, I spotted the tiny roll of paper attached to the owl's right foot.

"You're a were," I whispered.

It cocked its head to the side.

Weres had long been stigmatized in our culture, portrayed in movies and television shows as vicious, tortured animals that could pass their curse on to normal humans with a single bite. In truth, they had much more in common with weremystes than with monsters. On the nights of the phasing, they transformed into the animal that shared their bodies. But they wielded no magic beyond this, and they could not assume their animal forms at other times.

The spells Saorla and her weremancers placed on them changed this. The dark sorcerers had been using weres as servants—wereslaves, I called them. They claimed to have magic that would free the weres from the moon, and allow them to control when and where they took their animal form. This magic, they assured their victims, was a gift.

In reality, it was anything but. All it did was give control over the weres to those who cast the spells. They could turn the weres at will, and compel them to do their bidding.

Six days remained until the start of the phasing, which meant that this were had probably been forced into owl form by a dark sorcerer, probably for the express purpose of delivering a message to me. Confident now that I wouldn't spook the bird, I crossed to the shelves and carefully removed the note from its leg. Then I held out my arm.

"I'll let you out. It'll be easier than trying to squeeze through that hole in the screen."

The owl clicked its beak before hopping to my arm, its wings opening as it sought to keep its balance.

"You're a beautiful bird," I said. "I wish my father could see you."

I opened the door and stepped outside. At the first touch of the night air, the owl leapt off my arm and flew away, wings beating silently. It flashed beneath the streetlamp, but after that I lost track of it. I scanned the street, but saw no one, and then went back inside, taking care to lock the door.

Billie was awake and sitting up, her hair a tangled mess, her eyes puffy.

"You're here," she said.

"Yeah. Sorry it's so late."

She pushed a strand of hair out of her face and yawned. "What time is it?"

I stepped into the kitchen, switched on the light and checked the clock on the stove. It was only a few minutes past ten, though it felt much later.

"Ten after ten," I called to her.

I unrolled the tiny piece of paper I'd taken from the owl, and read.

You are not to interfere—S.

It was written in a tight, neat script. I had no doubt as to who "S" was. Apparently the circle of people interested in Gracie Davett was expanding by the hour.

Saorla had included no warning in her missive—there hadn't been room on the scrap of paper for much more than what she'd written. But the fact that she had sent the wereowl here, to Billie's home, was threat enough.

"Fearsson?"

"Yeah." I balled up the paper and threw it in Billie's trash.

A moment later she shuffled into the kitchen, squinting against the light. "What are you doing?"

"Nothing. I was checking the time."

She lifted her eyebrows. "You wear a watch."

Even drowsy, she was smarter than me—I?—although I'm not sure that was saying much.

"Does whatever you're hiding from me have anything to do with that big tear in my screen?"

I winced, scratched the back of my head. "Yes, it does. There was an owl waiting here for me when I got back."

Her jaw dropped. "An owl? In my house?"

"It was a were, and it had a note tied to its leg."

"Was the note for me or you?"

It was my turn to cock an eyebrow.

"Yeah, all right. Stupid question. Who was it from?" Before I could answer, she put up a hand. "No, let me guess. Saorla."

"You're getting good at this."

"I don't seem to have much choice. There was really an owl in my house?"

"A wereowl."

She gave a roll of her eyes and pulled the blanket tighter around her shoulders. "I suppose it could have been worse."

"Weresnakes?"

Billie scowled. "I was thinking of Saorla herself showing up. But thanks. Now I'll be scanning the floor for weresnakes every time I walk into my kitchen."

I stepped forward and wrapped my arms around her. She snuggled against my chest.

"Have I mentioned that your job sucks?"

"A couple of times. And that's just today."

"What did Amaya want?"

"He hired me on behalf of an older couple. Their daughter and her children are missing, and they want me to find them."

"That's sad. But as things with Amaya go, it doesn't sound too bad."

"Not of the face of it, no. But I'm almost positive that this is the same woman I told you about over dinner, the one Kona is after."

She frowned up at me. "The one from the burger place?"

"I think so." I described for her my conversation with the Trejos and my encounter with Neil Davett. "And," I said, "I also don't think it's a coincidence that there was a note from Saorla waiting for me when I got back here."

"So the husband's a weremyste, too."

"Yes. And I think he's into dark magic. I'm positive that if I'd given him the chance, he would have drawn blood for a spell."

"Do you think he's working with Saorla?"

It was a good question, one I didn't know how to answer. I had little doubt that the weremancers at the burger place worked for her, the men inside who hadn't been carrying ID, as well as the silver-haired man outside who could kill with a touch. But I had the impression that Neil was on his own. Saorla didn't mess around, and she didn't place her trust in amateurs. Even the couple at the motel earlier in the day had been powerful and professional enough to pose a threat to me. Neil had been careless; Saorla would have said that he was ruled by his emotions.

Billie rapped her knuckles lightly on the side of my head. "What's going on in there, Fearsson?"

I smiled. "You've got me thinking. To answer your question, no, I don't think her husband is working for Saorla. At least not on this. He struck me as a guy who was desperate to find his wife and kids."

"So that he can abuse them again."

I tipped my head, conceding the point.

"You need to find them before anyone else does."

"Yes, I do. But first I need to sleep, and so do you."

She canted her head to the side, the depth of her smile quickening my pulse. "I slept already. I'm not tired anymore." She kissed me. "And I seem to remember somebody letting it slip that he's in love with me."

"I remember that, as well."

"Good. Then take me to bed."

"That's easily the best offer I've had all day," I said. I scooped her up into my arms, eliciting a giggle, and carried her back to her bedroom.

It was a late night.

Unfortunately, it was also an early morning.

I awoke to a faint, familiar chiming that at first I couldn't place. It took three tones before I recognized the sound of my cell phone. It was still in the pocket of my bomber jacket, which lay on the floor near Billie's bed.

I scrambled out from under the sheet and blanket, grabbed the bomber, and fumbled for the phone. The clock readout read "7:12." And the caller ID beneath it read "Kona at 620."

I opened the phone and sat back on the edge of the bed. "Fearsson."

"Billie charging you rent yet?" Kona asked. "I can hardly reach you at your own place anymore."

"No," I said, still trying to wake up. "No rent yet."

"Get your head in the game, Justis. I need your help."

"Yeah, all right. What's up?"

"I'm holding the ME's report on Merilee Guilford, the woman who was killed outside the Burger Royale."

The Medical Examiner's report. That got my attention. "And?"

"Cause of death was blood loss."

I shivered, as if Saorla herself had run a cold finger down my spine.

"Blood loss," I repeated.

"That's what they say. Now how do you suppose that silver-haired gentleman took her blood when we didn't find a cut anywhere on her body?"

I didn't want to speak the words.

"Justis?"

"We need to find this guy, Kona. You've seen what blood magic can do." She and Kevin had witnessed our battle with Saorla and her weremancers during the summer. They had also investigated a series of ritual killings committed in the weeks leading up to that confrontation. "And you've seen that dark sorcerers have no qualms about taking blood from people without their permission."

"Yeah?" she said, seeming to brace herself for what I was about to say.

"Well, I think this guy can take their blood just by touching them. He's like a magical vampire."

For a few seconds, she didn't answer. "You know what?" she said. "I must be spending too much time with you and your magical friends. Because that's exactly what I was afraid you were going to say."

CHAPTER 7

Since my conversation with Amaya the previous night, I had been debating whether I should share what I'd learned with Kona. Professional ethics dictated that I tell her nothing. The same way attorneys maintained a privileged relationship with their clients, PIs were bound morally, if not legally, to keep private our conversations with the people who hired us. And if that had been the only consideration, this would have been an easy decision. But Kona was trying to solve a murder, and had brought me in to help her. I couldn't be positive that Gracie Davett had killed the man in the restaurant, but I would have bet every penny Jacinto was paying me that there was only one weremyste mom with an eight-year-old daughter and five-year-old son running around the Phoenix metropolitan area right now.

It occurred to me that I'd found my out right there: Amaya was paying me. He had hired me, not the Trejos, so technically I wasn't violating any trust by sharing information about their daughter. But that felt like a cheap way around the problem. In the end, I decided that telling Kona was simply the right thing to do.

Neither of us had spoken a word since her last remark, but before I could act on the decision I'd made, she said, "We did get one break. I think we have a line on the magical mom."

"Is that right?"

"This morning a guy came in to report that his wife and kids are

73

missing. The husband and wife are separated and he thinks she's taken the kids out of the city in violation of their separation agreement. Now technically that would be child abduction, and he's willing to press charges in order to get the kids back."

"Yeah, I'm sure he is."

I didn't mean to say it aloud, and judging from the silence on the other end, Kona understood that.

"You have something you want to share?" she asked after a pause.

I sighed. "Gracie Davett, right? Neé Engracia Trejo?"

"And you know this because . . . ?"

"I was hired by Gracie's parents last night. They're worried about her. They're convinced that Neil's been abusing her. They don't know if he's hurt the kids, too, but they think it's possible."

"When were you planning on telling me this?"

"Truthfully? I had just decided to when you brought it up."

"No shit?"

"No shit."

I could imagine her nodding.

"All right then."

"You can't be considering helping this guy, Kona. He's been beating his wife."

"We have no proof of that."

"How much proof—"

"Hold on there, Justis," she said, talking over me. "Yes, she has been admitted to the hospital on three occasions in the past eighteen months with odd injuries. A dislocated shoulder, a broken wrist, and a severe sprain in her elbow. And twice the ER physicians who treated her reported seeing other injuries as well. Scrapes and bruises, some on her limbs, and some on her face and neck."

"Sounds like abuse to me. How much more evidence do you need?"

"You know full well how much more. Abuse is hard to prove. I shouldn't have to tell you that; you were too good a cop for too long a time to be as naïve as you sound right now. She's denied repeatedly that he ever hurt her, and as incriminating as some of those injuries were, none of them was conclusive enough to convince any of the attending physicians to take action. They had a break-in at their house not that long ago. You want me to arrest him for that, too?"

I didn't answer. She was right: proving abuse without the cooperation of the victimized spouse was next to impossible.

"I should also tell you," she went on after a tense silence, "that as far as we can tell the kids have never shown up in an ER, except for one time when the little girl had an appendicitis."

"Well, I suppose that's something," I said. "What are you going to do?"

"My job." She sounded exasperated; I wasn't making this any easier for her. "She's wanted for murder. I have witnesses who say that she killed two men."

"Two?"

"Oh, yeah. John Doe number two died overnight. We still don't have a name for either one of them, by the way."

I wondered if Saorla was listening to this phone call, laughing at our ignorance.

"Anyway, the woman's wanted for murder. And now she's in violation of her custody agreement. That's two strikes against her. I don't have any choice in the matter, Justis. I have to find her, and one way or another, she's probably going to jail."

"Judging from what she did to those guys in the Burger Royale, I'm not convinced you've got a jail that can hold her."

"Well, that's what I want to hear."

We lapsed into another silence. At this point if my life, I felt little residual loyalty to the PPD, but I didn't like the idea of pitting myself against Kona.

"You asked me a minute ago what I was going to do," she said. "I think I'm the one who should be asking that question of you."

"I have paying clients," I said. "They want their daughter and grandkids back, and they don't want them anywhere near Neil Davett."

"Right. I had a feeling you'd say something like that."

"Sorry, partner."

"No, I get it. You have a job to do. But so do I, and anyone who gets in my way and helps this woman is going to be on the wrong side of the law. You understand what I'm telling you?"

"Of course."

"All right then. I guess I'll be talking to you."

"Right. Bye, partner."

It wasn't the most awkward conversation I'd ever had with Kona, but it definitely made the top five.

I closed my phone and looked back at Billie. She was wide awake, propped up on one elbow, her eyes on me, her expression grim. Her brown curls spilled over her bare shoulder, and she had the blanket and sheet pulled up almost to her neck.

"That didn't sound so good," she said.

"It wasn't."

"A magical vampire?"

I cringed.

"You combine that with the wereowl, and I think you could pitch this to a Hollywood agent."

At least she was able to joke about it.

"I should probably get going," I said. "This woman I've been hired to find is pretty hot right now. I need to get to her first."

Billie's eyebrows went up. A grin crept over my face.

"'Hot' meaning a lot of people are after her. It's an investigative term."

"Right," she said, sounding unconvinced. But she was smiling and she caught my hand in hers before I could get up. "I had a nice time last night."

I leaned over and kissed her. "So did I."

She gave me a little push. "Okay, go find this hot woman you're after."

"I'll do my best."

I showered, dressed, grabbed an apple from the fruit basket on her counter, and was out the door well before eight o'clock. The air had grown cool and the sky was a clear, deep blue. Perfect autumn weather and a fine day for a drive into the desert.

But even after I was in the Z-ster with the engine running, I sat staring out the window, watching as Billie's quiet neighborhood came to life. I had no idea how to find Gracie Davett, and I was all-too conscious of the fact that Saorla was probably watching my every move from her magical perch, wherever that might be. The last thing I wanted to do was lead her and her weremancers to Gracie and the children.

In the past, I had used spells to keep Saorla from listening to my conversations. Perhaps I could keep her from tracking me, as well.

The problem was, doing so would tick her off, and she would take out her anger on Billie and my dad, both of whom would be appalled at being used as leverage in that way.

But thinking of my dad gave me an idea.

I pulled away from the curb and drove back to my place in Chandler to pick up a change of clothes and a new toy I'd bought myself with some of the money I'd been earning. It was a Sig Sauer P938 Edge, a new back-up weapon that fit far more comfortably into an ankle holster than my bulky Glock ever had, and more comfortably in my hand than the Smith and Wesson Bodyguard 380 I'd been using as a backup for the past several years. The S&W wasn't a bad weapon—far from it. I liked it at first, but I'd never gotten to the point where I truly felt at ease with it. The trigger pull was too long, and thing just didn't settle right in my hand, and so I hadn't been willing to rely on it. My new Sig Sauer . . . well, let's just say that it was love at first sight, literally.

From Chandler, I made my way to the Phoenix-Wickenburg Highway, which was the quickest route to Wofford, where my old man's trailer was located on a small plot of open desert.

Wofford wasn't much of a town and while I loved desert wilderness I had to admit that my dad's place was not the most scenic spot in the Sonoran Basin. The trailer sat at the end of a short, rutted road on top of a gradual rise. When it was new, the trailer was kind of nice, but it hadn't been new in fifteen years. During the summer, Saorla's weremancers used spells to fracture the cinderblocks that served as its foundation, causing the entire trailer to topple over.

We had managed, using the ten grand Amaya gave me, to prop it back up and repair the shattered windows. We had also replaced most of the kitchenware and picture frames that broke when it fell over. But the place remained tired and rundown, a bit like my dad.

He liked to sit out front on a lawn chair, holding an old pair of Leica binoculars that he trained on every bird that soared past his place. His doctors didn't want him to get too much sun, so a few years back I rigged a sort of covered patio using two-by-sixes and a plastic tarp. That had been destroyed this summer as well, but I'd set up a new one that worked even better than the first.

My father was subject to delusions and hallucinations. He had days when he could barely function, and when even the simplest attempts at communication left him flummoxed and frustrated. And he had others when he seemed damn near normal. He wasn't really a danger to himself or to others, which was why I had been able to keep him out of a mental health facility. But he didn't do well around crowds; he grew confused and quick-tempered. So, I did his shopping for him, coming out to restock his refrigerator and pantry every Tuesday morning, and I only took him into the city on those occasions when he needed to see his doctors.

If he had managed to keep track of the days this week, he'd be surprised to see me. But that was a big if.

These trips out to Wofford were always a bit of a crap shoot. I never knew what condition I'd find him in, what mood. He could be ornery and lucid, or docile and utterly incoherent, or pretty much anywhere else in between those extremes. Today I was counting on him being clearheaded enough to function and help me out, which, I knew, wasn't very realistic.

I drove up to his place, the Z-ster bouncing over the dirt road, and stopped the car. A cloud of red dust billowed behind me, twisting in the cool wind. Dad sat slumped in his chair, long legs stretched out in front of him, the binoculars resting in his lap. He wore an old flannel shirt over his usual t-shirt and jeans, which was a good sign. When he was really out of it, he didn't bother with weather-appropriate clothing. I could also see, however, that he had on tennis shoes but no socks. I muttered a curse. In the many years I'd spent scrying my father's state of mind, I had learned that more often than not, no socks meant he was out of it.

He had looked over at the car as I pulled up, but now was staring out over his land, his eyes fixed on the New River Mountains to the east, an unsteady hand raised to his brow to block the sun, which still hung low in the eastern sky.

"Good morning, Pop," I called, climbing out of the car and shutting the door.

He glanced my way and lifted his other hand in a half-hearted wave, so at least he knew I was here. But he didn't say anything and soon turned away once more. Mixed signals.

I walked to where he sat and leaned down to kiss his forehead. His skin felt cool, and he didn't smell bad, as he did when he hadn't showered for a few days. "How are you feeling today?"

He shrugged, but said nothing, his gaze never leaving the mountains.

"Are you hungry?"

He considered the question and nodded.

"How about a bowl of cereal?"

Another nod.

I stepped into the trailer, filled a bowl with raisin bran, and poured a little bit of milk over it. Dad could be particular about the foods he ate. He only liked a certain brand of cereal, and he could tell the difference if you tried to slip a cheaper brand into his breakfast bowl. I'd learned that one the hard way many years ago. He liked milk on his cereal, but not too much. He had other preferences as well, all of them specific and none of them open to negotiation. But that was okay; at his age, with all that he had been through, he'd earned the right to be a little picky.

I brought him his cereal, along with his favorite spoon—don't ask—and then pulled out a second lawn chair, which I set next to his.

He took a spoonful of cereal and chewed it slowly, following the the flight of a hawk with his eyes. Usually he would have told me the species, but he didn't say a word.

"Have you been sleeping all right?"

He nodded.

"And you've been eating?"

A frown crossed his features, but after a moment he answered with another nod. I guessed that he had last eaten sometime yesterday, but couldn't remember when.

I let him down the rest of his breakfast in peace, wondering if I had wasted a trip. I needed his help, but he wouldn't be able to do anything for me in this state.

It occurred to me that if he hadn't eaten before my arrival, he probably hadn't had anything to drink, either. I went back into the trailer and filled two glasses with ice water. When I walked outside again, his bowl was empty. I took it from him and handed him the glass. He drank deeply, draining half the glass.

"Thank you," he said.

"You're welcome. You're talking."

His brow creased. "Was I not?"

"Not a word."

"Sorry. I thought I was."

"You feeling all right?"

He lifted a shoulder. "I suppose. A little muddled. It Tuesday already?"

I shook my head. "Saturday."

"Was I in bad shape on Tuesday?"

"No, you were fine. I came out today because I need some help."

"From me?"

I nodded.

"Magical?"

"In part."

He sat up a little straighter and took another sip of water. "I don't know, Justis." He and Kona were the only people in the world who called me by my full name. "It's been a while since I cast any spells that matter."

"Since this summer?" I asked. "When we fought Saorla?"

"Yep, I think that would be the last time."

"Well, if you can't do it, I can try to find another way."

"What is it you're trying to do?"

I looked him in the eye. "Hide from Saorla."

He grimaced, ran a hand through his white hair so that it stood on end. "She's not going to like that."

"No, she probably won't."

"Then I'm in."

I laughed.

"Why me, though? You know other weremystes."

"Honestly? Because Saorla knows I come out here a lot. And she thinks you're nothing more than a burned out old weremyste."

"I *am* nothing more than a burned out old weremyste."

"Dad, that's not—"

"It's all right. I think I understand. Going to another weremyste would draw her interest. But she doesn't think much of me, and she doesn't pay too much attention when you come out here."

"Exactly. I need to track down a woman, another weremyste. I think Saorla and her friends are after her, and I want to get to her first, without Saorla knowing about it."

"So what kind of spell would you need me to cast?"

I stood and peered around the far side of the trailer to where my father's 1989 Ford F150 pickup was parked. It was one of those two-tone models, chestnut brown with a broad tan stripe along the side panels. "Well, first of all, when was the last time you started up that old truck of yours?"

He swiveled in his chair so that he could see it. "My truck? What's the matter with your car?"

"Saorla knows it, and so do her flying monkeys."

I could tell he didn't like the idea of lending it to me. He probably hadn't driven the thing more than ten times in the last year, but that truck had been his baby for a quarter century.

"Keys are in the trailer," he said, sounding like he begrudged every word, "on a hook inside the door."

I went inside, found the keys, and walked to the pickup. The driver's side door groaned a bit when I opened it, and the interior had that old-burnt-vinyl smell that's unique to cars and trucks that sit out for too long in the desert sun. It probably could have used an oil change, and the paint had faded over the years. Still, the truck had less than sixty thousand miles on it, and when I turned the key, it started right up. It might not have been vintage, or even "classic," according to the definitions used by car dealers, but if my dad had wanted to sell it, he could have gotten a good price. I almost laughed at the thought; that was never going to happen.

I shut it off and walked back to where he sat. He glared off toward the mountains, muttering to himself. He was cogent, but I'd ticked him off a little bit by asking for the truck.

"I'll be careful with it," I said. "I take good care of my own car, I'll do the same for yours."

"You'd better. That thing's vintage."

"Doesn't vintage mean it's from the Twenties?"

He cast a nasty look my way. "You know what I mean."

"I told you I'd be careful with it. I'll even bring it back with a full tank."

"Fine."

"Thanks."

He nodded, his expression thawing. "Now, what's this magic you want me to do?"

I sat once more. "Well, that's a little more difficult. I've used spells to, in effect, mute conversations I didn't want her to hear. I want to use a similar spell to make it so that she can't find me. I've never cast a spell like this before, and I'm not exactly sure how it would work. But I have a feeling that if I cast it on myself, she'll still be able to track me. She knows my magic. That's not enough for her to overcome the spells I've used to keep her from eavesdropping, but it might allow her to follow me. If you cast the spell, though . . ." I left the thought unfinished.

"Interesting. Have you asked Namid about this?"

"Namid isn't allowed to interfere."

"I know that. But he's allowed to teach, and we need to be taught a spell."

Put that way, it made a lot of sense.

"Namid," my dad said, calling out the name. "We need your help."

An instant later, the runemyste materialized before us, sunlight sparkling on his smooth waters.

"You summoned me, Leander Fearsson. This is something you have not done in many years."

"I know. I'm sorry. But Justis and I need to do a bit of magic, and we're not sure how to cast the spell, or even if it's possible."

Namid glanced at me, but then addressed my dad again. "And what is this spell?"

"Tell him," my father said.

"I want to make it impossible for Saorla to find me. Is there a camouflage spell that would work against someone with her powers? Something that would allow me to come and go as I please, without her following me?"

The myste's waters roughened. "She follows you?"

She follows me; she sends her weremancers after me; she even sent a note tied to the leg of a were. I considered telling him all of this, but in the next instant thought better of it. He would confront her, and that in turn would make her even more angry with me than she was. I was handling her little harassments. I didn't need to tell on her, like some kid in school tattling on the locker room bully. On the flip side, I sensed that she truly feared Namid. If she had been following me today—and I suppose it was possible—his arrival would have been enough to frighten her off.

"She seems to be keeping track of where I go," I said, hoping I could leave it at that.

"How long has she been doing this?"

"Long enough. It's not a big deal. But I don't want her following me today. I'm trying to find a weremyste, and I think Saorla is after her, too. I don't want to lead the dark sorcerers to her."

"She should not be harrying you," the myste said, as much to himself as to me. "I have made this clear to her."

"Namid, it's all right. Just tell me whether or not there's a spell that'll do what I want it to."

"Yes, of course there is," he said, his voice rumbling like flood waters behind a dam. "Have I not told you before that runecrafting is a living art? If the spell has not yet been used, then you must create it yourself, but there is always a way."

"But I'd have to cast it," my father said. "Isn't that right? If Justis does it, and she knows his magic, she might still know where he is, no matter how we cast the spell."

"You may well be right," Namid said, sounding impressed.

Dad jerked a thumb in my direction. "He thought of that, not me."

"Well done, Ohanko." His glowing eyes narrowed. "If you can dampen your magic in some way, you might make yourself invisible to those of us who can sense such things."

"Right. That's what I was thinking. But I don't know the spell."

"Do you?" Namid asked my father.

Dad shook his head, but his gaze flicked toward me, and I had the feeling that he was protecting my feelings.

"Of course you do," I said. "It's all right. Tell him."

"I don't know that I can explain it," he said, an admission of sorts. He frowned, eyeing me the way he might an old broken down car he wasn't quite sure how to fix. After a few seconds, I felt magic stir the air around me. The skin on my arms pebbled.

Namid's eyes widened. "Good, Lokni. Very good. That is a powerful glamour. I do not sense him anymore, and yet there he stands."

"What did you do?" I asked.

Dad shrugged. "I thought of a blanket, one of those silvery thermal ones that the astronauts took to space. And I imagined it covering you so that your magic couldn't be seen or felt." He shrugged again, a small grin playing at the corners of his mouth. "I guess I can still cast new spells when I have to."

I smiled. "I guess."

"I will leave you now," Namid said. His bright gaze lingered on me for a few seconds. "Saorla has done more than follow you. I sense this. You would prefer not to discuss the matter now, and I will respect your wishes. But this is a conversation you and I will have eventually."

I had the distinct impression that he wasn't asking for my acquiescence so much as expecting it. I nodded and watched him fade.

"Sounds like you have a trip to the wood shed in store."

"Yeah," I said, still staring at the spot where Namid had been. "But I can't worry about that now." I faced my dad. "There's one more thing I need you to do. I'm going to cast the spell I've used to muffle my conversations. Between that spell, and my car sitting by your trailer, I should be able to convince Saorla that I'm here with you. But the ruse will work better if you're inside the trailer rather than outside."

A frown flitted across his lined face. I felt much worse asking this of him than I had asking for the truck. Sitting outside and watching for birds was one of the few pleasures he still had in his life. Making him give that up, even for one day, seemed unfair.

He was a trooper, though. After that initial reaction, he fixed a smile on his face. "Sure, why not?" he said. "It's been a while since I used that fancy disc player you got me for Christmas. I think I'll watch a movie or two."

"Thanks, Dad."

The smile faded. "If it helps you with Saorla, it's worth it. At some point you'll tell me more about this woman you're trying to help, right?"

"I'll be happy to. I'd tell you more now, but the truth is I know very little about her, beyond the fact that she's got two kids with her. Eight and five."

The expression in his eyes hardened in a way I remembered from my childhood. "Then you should get going."

"Yes, sir." I stood, kissed the top of his head, and reached for my lawn chair, intending to fold it up and put it away.

"Leave it," Dad said, standing as well. "I'll leave mine out, too. It'll make it seem that there are two of us inside the trailer."

"Good thinking. You don't seem muddled anymore."

He grinned. "You and Namid have that effect on me. Now, go."

He didn't wait for me to answer, but stepped into the trailer, and closed the door behind him.

I cast the muffling spell, hoping it would be enough to fool Saorla of Brewood. Then I climbed into my father's pickup, turned over the old engine, and started back toward the interstate.

CHAPTER 8

The drive from my father's place to the southern end of Phoenix took me through some of the busiest sections of the city. We were past the worst of the morning commute, but still the roads were crowded. Bumper-to-bumper traffic moving at sixty-five. NASCAR had nothing on Phoenix's highways.

I had in mind to go south again, beyond the outskirts of the city. That was the direction Gracie had driven, and I still remembered how the afternoon before my instincts had screamed for me to keep driving past Casa Grande. But first I stopped at the Burger Royale.

The restaurant hadn't reopened, and the parking lot had been cordoned off with bright yellow crime scene tape. I only saw two cars in the lot, both of them cruisers. Only one car had anyone in it; the police wanted to keep people away, but for now at least no one was actively working the scene.

I parked by the expanse of tape and got out of the truck, my wallet already in my hand.

The cop in the cruiser rolled down his window. "Can I help you?"

I held up my wallet, which I had opened to my PI license. "My name's Jay Fearsson. I was here yesterday with Kona Shaw in Homicide. I'm wondering if I can take a quick look at something."

He eyed me, squinting in the sunlight. "Fearsson. You the guy who killed the East Side Parks Killer?" That was what cops had called Etienne de Cahors before the press dubbed him the Blind Angel Killer.

"Yeah, that's me."

"That was a nice piece of work."

"Thank you."

"I can't let you go inside the restaurant. Even Elliott Ness can't get in there. But you can walk around the lot if you want."

"Works for me. I appreciate it."

He raised a hand, acknowledging my thanks, but he had already turned his attention back to his smart phone.

I ducked under the tape and walked to the sidewalk in front of the restaurant, where those large trash bins still lay on their sides, surrounded by garbage and, at this point, covered with swarms of flies and yellow jackets.

I hoped to catch a glimpse of Gracie's magic, but after twenty-four hours, most of that rust-colored glow had faded. The glare of the morning sun on the bins didn't help. I circled them, found a spot that was still in shade and bent lower to get a better view.

Magic residue still clung to the plastic, shimmering weakly, like a candle flame on the verge of burning itself out. I started to recite a spell that, at least in theory, would work as a sort of magical Geiger counter tuned to her magic in particular, so that I could track her and know when I was getting close. After only a moment of this, I stopped myself. It sounded too much like what Saorla had been doing to me. The silver-haired conjurer wouldn't have left this place without attempting something similar. What's more, Gracie probably knew that. In which case, either she had found a way to mask her magic, much as my dad and I had done, or Saorla's friends already had her. I was betting on the former.

She had switched off her cell phone because she didn't want Neil tracking her with the signal. I assumed that she had done something similar with her runecrafting. Which begged the question, how was I supposed to find her? I straightened and gazed southward, my eyes following the interstate to the horizon.

What had her mother said? Gracie had spoken of living in Tucson, and she liked to camp. With the kids with her, she could only disappear so far into the wilderness. She would need bathrooms, food, a safe place to pitch a tent. There were a few spots like that in the Tucson area, but the ones that came to mind were too obvious, too easy to find. Anything Marisol would have thought to tell me Neil would know as well.

That left another choice, one that was more remote, and offered her more possibilities if she needed to run.

I didn't have a tent or sleeping bag with me, but that was a problem for later. I pivoted on my heel and strode back to my father's truck.

"Thanks," I said as I walked past the cruiser.

The cop didn't even look up. "No problem."

I stopped at a nearby gas station and filled the tank before getting on I-10 and heading south. Once clear of the city outskirts, traffic fell away. The truck had an AM/FM radio and a cassette player that might have worked still. But Dad kept no tapes in the car, and I couldn't find anything worth listening to on the radio. I drove with the windows down, the desert air on my face and neck, and I tried to sift through the smells of sage and truck exhaust for the elusive scent of magic, dark or light.

Where could Gracie be headed? She had run away from her husband, and had abandoned the refuge of her parents' home. She had escaped the dark sorcerers at the restaurant, so was strong enough to take care of herself. She had resorted to killing, so she also must have understood how much danger she and her kids were in from the people pursuing her. And after all that transpired at the restaurant, she had to know that the police would be after her as well.

If she was smart, she would leave the country, but without passports for the kids I didn't think she would get past the border police. In her position, my next choice would have been L.A., or perhaps San Diego. Both were big enough that a Latina mother with two kids—even a woman with power like hers—could melt into some quiet, obscure neighborhood without leaving a trace. But moving to either city would require money, and unless she was carrying gobs of cash, she would have to rely on credit cards, which were easily traced.

That didn't leave her with many options.

As I neared Casa Grande, I felt that same impulse to keep driving south. It was almost as if Tucson were calling for me. For a moment I gave serious thought to abandoning my plan and remaining on I-10.

This time, though, it occurred to me that what I'd assumed yesterday was instinct might actually be magic. I wasn't sure how Gracie had done it, but she had left a spell on the road that was making me *want* to keep driving. It was clever, and yesterday it had very nearly worked. But I knew she hadn't intended the spell for me, and though loath to admit it, I had a feeling that the silver-haired weremyste was probably too smart and too powerful to be fooled by such a conjuring.

I exited I-10 at the exchange with I-8, which cut east to west, from Casa Grande through Yuma, and, ultimately to San Diego. Once again, as I left I-10 I felt the road tugging at my head and heart, with the power of a gibbous moon. Even knowing it was magic, I had to grip the wheel until my knuckles whitened to keep from turning around.

Gracie might have thought her spell clever, but it was too strong, too obvious. Rather than putting Saorla's weremancers off her trail, it would serve to keep them on it. I could only hope that they hadn't found her already.

I drove west on I-8 for about an hour, watching my mirrors for any sign of dark sorcerers. During the summer I had been attacked by a weremancer in a sleek silver sedan of unknown make. And I knew every make there was.

Today, though, I didn't see any unusual cars. Lots of semis, and a few campers, but no sedans with smoked windows and ungodly acceleration.

At Gila Bend, I took the exit for state road 85, which headed south toward Ajo and then Organ Pipe Cactus National Monument. I had thought that when I took this exit, I would feel that same spell-induced urge to remain on the freeway. I didn't. I felt nothing at all.

It was enough to make me wonder if I should keep going toward San Diego. I pulled into a gas station near the exit and sat for several moments with the engine idling, wondering what to do. If Gracie's spell at Casa Grande had been an amateurish attempt to throw sorcerers off her trail, then chances were she and the kids were headed toward the California coast. But what if she was more clever than that, more clever even than I had credited? What if that first spell had been a more subtle ruse designed to mask this second exit?

After some thought I decided that if she was on her way to San Diego, there was little more I could do for her. I would never find her there. Earlier this morning I had come up with a plan. I was going to stick with it.

I pulled back out onto the state highway and drove south. I stopped in Ajo to buy a cheap tent and sleeping bag at a sporting goods place, pick up some food, and put more gas in the truck. Compared to the

Z-ster this thing gulped down gasoline, and the Z-ster wasn't exactly a Prius.

Then I continued on to the national monument, the terrain growing more dramatic with every mile I drove. Miles to the west, in the Cabeza Prieta Wildlife Refuge, the Growler range rose from the desert floor, its worn peaks stark against the azure sky, the deep folds in its mountainsides casting dark shadows across the rocky faces.

Closer to the road, huge saguaros grew beside equally impressive clusters of the organ pipe cacti for which the monument was named. They shared the desert floor with brittlebrush and creosote, mesquite and paloverde, chollas and ocotillos and prickly pears, creating a stunning palette of soft earth tones. A woodpecker flew across the road to one of the larger organ pipes, its wings flashing white and black, and a covey of quail ran along the roadside, the curved plumes on their foreheads bobbing comically. Ahead, beyond the entrance gate, the sheer, rugged cliffs of the Ajo Mountains appeared to glow red in the late afternoon sun.

I had been here once with my dad, many years ago, but I had forgotten how beautiful it was. More recently, the monument had been saddled with a bad reputation as one of the least safe of America's national parks and monuments. The monument sits right on the border with Mexico, and since its establishment back in the 1930s, the park service had resisted efforts to put large fences along its southern edge. They preferred to keep the park scenic and natural, and to allow the free flow of wildlife through that section of the desert. I can understand their thinking. But as a result, Organ Pipe National Monument had long ago become a popular place for illegal crossings by immigrants as well as drug couriers. And in 2002, a park ranger named Kris Eggle was killed in a shootout with members of a Mexican drug cartel. That tragedy focused attention on the problem and convinced the service and border security to take more decisive action. They constructed a steel fence along the southern edge of the monument, which had curbed some of the motor traffic across the border.

Still, illegal crossings continue to this day, and the monument's reputation as a somewhat dodgy vacation destination persists. This was one more reason why it seemed to me the perfect place for Gracie Davett and her kids to lie low. The campgrounds wouldn't be crowded, and if they decided that fleeing the country made sense . . . well, the porousness of the border worked both ways.

I paid an entrance fee at the park gate, and drove through the scenic core of the monument, known as the Valley of the Ajo. Those stark cliffs loomed to the east, basking in the golden sunlight. Black vultures circled over the drive, the silvery patches at the ends of their wings catching the light, and lizards scuttled across the road, their tails held high as they vanished into the saltbrush. I couldn't help but smile. At some point I would have to bring my dad back here.

I passed the visitor's center, which was named for Eggle. Soon after, the road wound into the Twin Peaks campground.

For a few hours now, I had been wondering how best to approach Gracie. I didn't want to scare her, but I knew that as soon as she saw the blur of magic on my face she would assume the worst and would throw assailing spells at me. I had confidence in my ability to ward myself against whatever spells she tried. Then again I'm sure the two guys she killed at the Burger Royale had been confident, too.

I eased the pickup onto the campground loop, and followed it to the far end, where the tent sites were located. I didn't figure Gracie was driving an RV. I turned onto the first of the two "tents-only" rows, driving slowly past the sites like any newcomer trying to find a good place to pitch a tent. Some of the sites were taken. Two or three had tents pitched on them but no cars parked on the sites. People milled about on several of the others. But more than half of the campsites were empty. Reaching the end of this row, I had to circle all the way back to the front of the loop to try the second row, which was also the last row in the campground, farthest from the ranger station. About halfway down this road, I spotted what I'd been looking for. A silver Honda minivan sat parked next to a large blue and white domed tent.

At first I didn't see any adults. But as I rolled past the van, I spotted a little girl sitting at the picnic table by the site's fire grate. Pretty and grave, her skin nut brown, her dark hair hanging loose to her shoulders, she watched me, unblinking. I gazed back at her, remembering the picture of Gracie I'd seen at Amaya's. This girl had to be her daughter. After a moment, I smiled, but her expression didn't change. And as soon as I was past their site, she jumped up from the table and ran to the tent.

I hadn't wanted to alarm them. Seems I'd failed already, and I had yet to say a word to any of them or even get out of the truck.

I pulled into an empty site two down from theirs and climbed out of the cab. As soon as my feet hit the ground, I felt the moon. My eyes were drawn to it; it's pull was magnetic. It hung low in the eastern sky, pale and large, paralyzing in its beauty. It was still a half-dozen days shy of full, but its weight on my mind felt as solid and real as the door of the pickup against my hand. Every phasing was bad—I had no reason to think that this one would be any worse than last month's or the one before that. But at that moment, I found it hard to believe that we were still days away from the full. Maybe it was being out here in the desert, far from the city. Whatever the reason, the moon's pull seemed more powerful here, more insistent.

I shook my head to clear my thoughts and walked around the campsite a bit, making it seem as though I were figuring out where I would place my tent. I made a point of not looking back toward Gracie's minivan or that blue tent. The last thing I wanted was to spook them into leaving.

As it turned out, that wasn't the danger.

The spell hit me between the shoulder blades with the force of a cannon ball. I went down hard, my face and chest slamming into the sand and gravel. My mouth throbbed painfully. I could tell I had split my lip; I hoped I hadn't lost a tooth as well.

Before I could get up, a footfall scuffed behind me.

"Don't even breathe," a woman's voice said. If she was scared, she hid it well. "Keep your hands where I can see them. And if I feel the slightest touch of magic, I swear to God I'll blow your head off."

I heard the tentative crunch of another step.

"Are you alone?"

"Yes," I said.

"Who the hell are you?"

"My name's Jay Fearsson." I had trouble forming the words. My lip was already swelling, and I was talking into the ground. But I forged on. "I'm a private detective. Your parents hired me to find you."

She laughed, dry and harsh. "That's bullshit. Did Neil send you?"

"No. I swear, your parents did. I met them at Jacinto Amaya's house. He's paying me, but on their behalf."

No answer. Apparently she hadn't expected that.

"I guess your mom—Marisol—she teaches at Chofi's school. That's Amaya's daughter. She loves your mom; Amaya said she's the kid's favorite teacher." I was babbling, but I hoped that at least some of what I said might convince Gracie I was telling the truth.

"How did you find me?"

"Your mother said you like to camp, you and the kids. And after what happened at the restaurant, I figured you'd want to find an out-of-the-way place to hide, somewhere cheap, something you could pay for without using a credit card. The campgrounds near Saguaro National Park would have been another choice, but it's too obvious, too close to Tucson. So I guessed you were here."

"Crap." She said it in a low voice; I'm not sure she realized she had spoken aloud.

"It was either here or San Diego," I said, still talking for the sake of it. I didn't imagine I could win her trust with this soliloquy, but maybe I could keep her from shooting me. "The spell you put on I-10 around Casa Grande was a little heavy-handed. But then you didn't use any magic at the exit off of I-8, which was smart. I think most people would keep driving toward California."

"You didn't."

"That's because I spoke to your mom. If she hadn't mentioned camping, I wouldn't have thought to come here."

She said nothing, and for several seconds all was silent except for the distant liquid song of a canyon wren. Thinking perhaps I had convinced her to trust me, I moved my hands, bracing them on the rough ground so that I could push myself up.

"Don't!" she said, before I could raise myself off the ground.

I raised my hands off the dirt. "I was just going to get up."

"I know damn well what you were going to do. And I'm telling you not to."

"I'm here to help you, Gracie."

"I don't need help."

"I disagree. I know who's after you."

"What's that supposed to mean. Who do you know?"

"I know Saorla. And I also know the Phoenix police. I used to work for them."

"A weremyste cop? I'm not sure I believe that, either."

"Tell me about the silver-haired man."

She didn't answer right away. "What do you know about him?"

"I know that he can kill with a touch, that he can pull blood for a spell without having to cut someone. Do you know his name?"

"No." She said it with some hesitation, leaving me unsure as to whether I should believe her.

"Had you seen him before the restaurant?"

"Possibly. I don't remember."

"You don't remember? He strikes me as someone I'd have trouble forgetting."

"Well, that's you. Get up."

I planted my hands again and pushed myself up, every movement deliberate, slow. I got to my feet and faced her. She wore jeans and a white tank top that revealed toned brown arms. Her hair was a good deal shorter than it had been in the photograph her parents showed me, barely reaching her neck. It was a good look for her. Magic obscured her features, but I could make out an oval face, and large dark eyes.

I had no trouble at all seeing the silver and black Ruger SR9 she had trained on my heart. She held it with both hands, a standard grip. I had a feeling she knew her way around a pistol and was probably a good shot.

"You shouldn't have come after me. My parents are . . . they don't understand."

A drop of blood fell from my chin. I ran my tongue over my split lip, tasting blood and wincing at how much it stung.

"They're worried about you," I said. "And about your children. Where and when did you first see the silver-haired man?"

"I told you, I don't remember. And even if I did, it wouldn't matter."

"You don't know that. Anything you can tell me might matter."

"I don't know who he is. That's the bottom line. The rest—" She shook her head. "What was that name you mentioned earlier?"

"Saorla?"

"Right. Who is that?"

I licked my lip again. "Do you know what a runemyste is?"

"Of course."

"She's like a runemyste only not. The runemyste I know calls her and her kind necromancers. Their power is similar to that of the runemystes, but they use dark magic, blood spells and the like. She's powerful and she's ruthless and she hates me a lot. I think she knows about you. Right after Amaya hired me, she warned me not to interfere."

"You should have listened to her."

"Well, I didn't, and I'm here now. So instead of trying to drive me away, maybe you should accept that I'm here to help you, and even consider that having an ally might be a good thing."

I cast the spell without hesitation, without bothering to repeat the elements three times. The transporting spell again. Her weapon, her hand, my hand.

Magic electrified the air, and an instant later, I held the Ruger. I didn't aim it at her; I kept it lowered at my side. But I warded myself from attack spells, and cast a second warding to keep her from taking her pistol back.

The glare she threw my way could have flayed the skin from my bones, but she didn't try to cast.

"Not bad," she said, her tone grudging. "I should have been ready for it."

"Yeah, you should have. Just like I should have been ready for the attack that knocked me down."

I walked toward her and held out the Ruger for her to take.

She frowned, but took it. "I don't understand."

"I'm not here to hurt you, and right now I'm not even interested in taking you back to Phoenix. I meant what I said. I came here to help. You've got some powerful mystes after you. I think you could use an ally."

The frown lingered, but she hadn't yet pointed the pistol at me again, which I took as a small victory.

"I'll think about it," she said after some time. She started away from me, back toward her campsite. "For now, keep your distance."

I watched her walk away before making my way to the nearest of the campground restrooms to clean up my lip. Once the blood was gone, it didn't look too bad. It was going to be swollen for a couple of days, but that was the price I paid for turning my back on another weremyste without warding myself.

I retreated to my site, and then, because there was nothing else to do, I pulled out my tent and set it up on a wide expanse of fine dirt and gravel some distance from the road. A hummingbird buzzed around the brush and trees as I worked, its purple throat glistening in the twilight sun. When I finished I walked to the station at the head of the campground loop to pay for my site. I took the long way around when I went, but on the way back I passed by Gracie's campsite.

This time, she and both children were out of the tent. They had a small camp stove set up on the picnic table and appeared to be making some kind of flavored rice dish. Gracie glanced my way as I approached the site, but she said nothing to me. The boy held a smart phone in his stubby fingers and wore ear buds. He seemed completely absorbed by whatever was on the screen.

The girl, though, watched me, as she had earlier when I drove in. I tried smiling at her again, but she didn't smile back. Something occurred to me then—I should have thought of it before, when I was lying on the ground, but my mind had been focused on other things. I considered stopping to ask Gracie more questions, but she had told me to stay away, and I wasn't going to win her trust if I ignored her wishes.

I dug into the food I'd brought and made myself a sandwich of avocado, tomato, and cheese, which was something of a camping tradition for my dad and me.

The sky darkened. The moon climbed higher, bright white against deep indigo. A few stars began to emerge in the velvet, and nearby a great-horned owl hooted, low and resonant. Airplanes passed high overhead, blinking like fireflies, the muted drone of their engines trailing behind them.

I heard Gracie talking to the kids, although I couldn't make out a word of what she said. At one point the boy squealed with laughter, bringing a smile to my face. Soon after, they grew quiet. I thought they must have gone to sleep, but a short time later magic hummed in the ground and the air. Before I knew it, I was on my feet, striding toward their site, my Glock in hand, my pulse racing. I stopped near the minivan. I didn't see any new cars, or, for that matter, anything else to indicate that they were in trouble. I had heard no voices since the boy laughed, but I could make out the rustling of sleeping bags.

I scanned the nearby campsites, but they were still empty.

Now that I thought about it, the magic I'd felt could have been a warding. With only a tent over their heads, Gracie would want to have magical shelter as well. My heartbeat slowing, I made my way back to my site. I would probably be smart to ward my tent before I went to sleep, too.

I sat on top of my picnic table and stared up at the sky again. The moon was too bright for the stars to be truly spectacular, the way they can be sometimes in the middle of the desert, but still it was as beautiful a night sky as I had seen in some time. I needed to get out of the city more.

I heard the high metallic whine of a tent zipper, and a moment later the scrape of approaching footsteps.

Gracie had put on a fleece jacket, and she had put away her weapon, though I assumed she had it on her. I would have in her position. She stopped in front of my site, but remained on the road, her hands buried in her jacket pockets.

"May I?" she asked

"Sure."

She hesitated, then took a step, seeming to think that something would happen when she crossed the boundary of my site. When nothing did, she stepped to the table and sat as far from me as possible.

"I heard you a couple of minutes ago," she said. "You came to our site."

"Yes. I felt magic, and thought you might be in trouble."

"It was a warding. And it's a good thing you didn't come closer. It would have burned you to a crisp."

I let out a harsh laugh. "Thanks for the warning."

She stared back at me.

"Don't you think it would have been a good idea to tell me that before you cast the spell? What if I *had* come closer?"

"I told you before to keep your distance. That's all the warning you should have needed. Either you really are here to help, in which case you would have done as I said, or you're lying to me, in which case you would have deserved what you got."

It was my turn to stare. "Boy, you are a piece of work, aren't you?"

"Do you have kids?" she asked, her tone hard, the words reminding me of her husband.

"No, I don't."

"Then you can't possibly understand. I'll do anything to keep them safe. Anything at all. And I make no apologies for that."

I nodded. I might not have kids, but I had Billie and my dad and Kona, and I knew the lengths to which I'd go to keep them safe. "I understand more than you think I do."

She considered me, her expression unreadable in the pale moonlight. I thought I saw some of the tension drain from her shoulders.

We sat in silence for what felt like a long time. Finally, she stood. "Well, I guess I should get back. Zach doesn't sleep well when I'm not there." She started to turn away.

"Your daughter is already showing signs of possessing magic, isn't she?"

Gracie went still, like an animal unsure of whether it should bolt or attack.

"When you threw that spell at me today, you did it without seeing my face, and without having seen me drive in. After I was on the ground, you told me specifically that if you felt a spell, you'd shoot. She saw the magic on me, didn't she? She told you I was a weremyste."

She jerked into motion, walking swiftly back to her site. "Leave us alone," she said over her shoulder. "If you come near us again, I'll kill you."

CHAPTER 9

I let her go, unsure of what else to do. But I listened for the zipper on her tent, and only when I knew she was back with the kids did I cast a warding over my site and retire to my own sleeping bag.

Before I went to sleep, I checked the reception on my phone. I had a couple of bars and so called Billie.

"Hey there," she said upon answering. "I had hoped to see you tonight. Did you get the message I left you?"

"Did you leave it at my house?"

"Yeah. Where are you?"

I started to answer, but stopped myself. "I'm not sure I can tell you," I said. "I'm fine, I promise. But I have to operate on the assumption that someone's listening in on our call."

"Someone?"

"Saorla. I wanted to check in and let you know that I'm thinking about you."

After a long pause, she said, "I don't like this, Fearsson."

"I know. I don't either."

"Can you at least tell me what you're doing?"

"I'm trying to keep someone safe, although that's not going so well right now."

"That doesn't sound so good. How long are you going to be . . . wherever you are?"

"I don't know. I'm sorry I can't tell you more."

She didn't answer at first. "Well, I guess I'll be talking to you sometime."

"I love you, Billie."

"I love you, too. Hate your job, though."

I chuckled. "Yeah, I get that. Goodnight."

"Goodnight, Fearsson. Be safe."

I closed the phone, folded my bomber jacket into something resembling a pillow, and lay down, shifting every few seconds until I found a position that was comfortable. It had been some time since last I slept on the ground. It wasn't quite as much fun as I remembered.

The owl hooted again, and coyotes howled from nearby, their cries echoing off the cliffs. But I was listening for voices and the hum of car engines. I didn't expect I would sleep much.

The next thing I knew, though, morning sunlight was filtering in through the nylon of my tent. I heard the puttering of a car engine and felt a frisson of magic over my skin. I grabbed my weapon—the Sig Sauer—zipped open the tent, and scrambled out on my hands and knees.

The engine belonged to a small pickup that idled by Gracie's site. The truck had a park service insignia on the door, and a ranger stood on the road, chatting amiably with Gracie, who was making breakfast for her kids.

I placed my pistol back in the tent, where the ranger wouldn't see it. Weapons were allowed in national parks now—not too many years ago they hadn't been—but I didn't want to draw attention to myself by letting him see it. The ranger climbed back into his pickup and rolled toward my site. As he approached, I cast a spell removing my warding from the previous night; the moment I released the magic, Gracie glanced my way. So did her daughter.

"Good morning," the ranger said, getting out of his truck. He held a clipboard and scanned it for a few seconds before looking my way. "You paid for a single night. You leaving us today?"

"I'm not sure. I was thinking of staying on for another night or two. My plans are a little unsettled, so I'm paying as I go."

"Good deal. As you can see, we have plenty of room. But remember to pay again this morning before you go off hiking or something."

"I will. Thank you."

He jotted something down, raised a hand and smiled, and got back in his truck. As he pulled away, I glanced at Gracie. She was watching me still.

She said something to her kids, then started in my direction. She halted several feet shy of my site. Her hands were in her pockets again, and she toed the ground, her gaze lowered. She seemed at a loss as to what to say, and I'll admit that I was in no rush to help her out by breaking the ice.

"Who's Billie?" she asked, which was about the last thing I'd expected.

"Magic that lets you listen in on other people's private conversations. That would be handy in my line of work."

A faint smile touched her lips and dimpled her cheeks. She shrugged. "I told you I'd do anything I had to. Given what that could mean, eavesdropping seemed mild."

A fair point.

"Billie's a friend. She would have been worried if I hadn't called."

Gracie nodded, glanced around the campground. "I'm sorry for . . . I shouldn't have threatened you like that. But I still don't know much about you, and what you said last night . . ."

Comprehension came to me about twelve hours too late. "They're not after you at all," I whispered. "They want the kids."

Tears welled in her dark eyes. After a moment, she nodded again. "They want all of us," she said, her voice dropping to a whisper as well. "But Emmy in particular. She's much more than she should be at this age."

"Does Neil know?"

She flinched at the question, but then lifted a shoulder. "I don't know. I've tried to hide it from him, but it's possible that he figured it out for himself. That's why I left. I was afraid he'd notice, or that she'd tell him."

"*That's* why you left?" I said, unable to keep the incredulity from my voice.

Her lips thinned and anger flared in her eyes.

I was about to say, *You didn't leave because he was beating you?* I thought better of it, though. I wanted to win her trust, and critiquing her approach to marriage didn't seem likely to make that any easier.

"Go back to Phoenix." She said it with such venom, I wondered if she had guessed what I intended to say. "I've already told you, we don't need your help."

A thousand retorts leapt to mind, none of them designed to smooth over our differences. I swallowed every one of them. "I came to do some camping," I said, trying to make it sound like the truth. "So I expect I'll be sticking around for a few days."

Her jaw muscles bunched, and her glare didn't soften even a little. I had the feeling she was swallowing a few choice remarks of her own. At last she whirled away and strode back to her site. I wouldn't have been surprised if she packed up the kids and left, if for no other reason than to get away from me.

As a cop, I had grown accustomed to people responding to my presence with some level of wariness, even resentment. It came with the job. But since leaving the force and becoming a PI, I had run into that reaction far less frequently. These days the people I met who were in trouble wanted me around; they were willing to pay me to do the work. It had been a long time since I'd encountered this much hostility from someone who I was, at least ostensibly, trying to help.

I retrieved the bags of food from my dad's truck and pulled out some dried fruit and nuts—my standard camping breakfast. I wasn't hungry, but I forced myself to eat and washed it all down with some water. Then I walked back out to the campground entrance and paid for another night at my campsite. I made a point of walking by Gracie's site on the way back to my own. The kids were playing some sort of card game and Gracie was washing their breakfast dishes at a water spigot by the nearest bathroom. She glanced at me as I walked past, but I pretended not to notice.

It was going to be a long day. I had brought a book with me, and I could always go on a hike, but I was supposed to be working. I was supposed to be protecting Gracie and her kids. Taking a leisurely stroll through the desert didn't seem right. And sitting here at my site reading a book struck me as pointless.

When my cell phone rang, and I saw Kona's name on the screen, I knew a moment of pure relief.

I flipped open the phone. "Hey, partner. Please tell me you have something for me to do."

"You that anxious to get away from Billie?"

"Not Billie, no. Long story. But I could use an excuse to get away. Something splashy and fun, maybe? What have you got?"

"Nothing good," she said. "I can tell you that much. And I don't need you sounding all chipper, either. It's not even nine a.m. and my day is shot to hell and back again."

"I'm sorry." I tried to sound properly chastened, but I'd always found Kona's moods more entertaining than intimidating. "You know I didn't mean anything by it. I'm fooling around."

"I know what you're doing. And I'm saying that your need for entertainment isn't justification for enjoying other people's misfortune."

Kona didn't usually give me quite so much grief.

"What's going on, Kona?" I asked, all hint of amusement gone from my voice.

"Another double homicide, and I need your magic eyes on this one. It's not entirely clear what happened."

"All right. Tell me where, and I'll be there as soon as I can."

"Well, that's the thing. I'm at Burt Kendall's pawn shop on Glendale, near Thirty-Third."

The air left my body in a rush, as if someone had kicked me in the stomach. "Don't tell me."

"'Fraid so. Burt's one of the victims."

"Damn it. You think it was done with magic?"

"That's my guess, but I need you to confirm it for me."

"Of course. It'll take me a while to get there. A couple of hours. But I'm leaving now."

"A couple of hours? Where the hell are you?"

"Like I said. Long story." I switched the phone to my other hand. "Listen, Kona, I'm sorry about the way I was earlier. I didn't . . . Damn."

"I know. And I didn't mean to get all preachy. I'll see you in a while."

I closed the phone and started toward the truck. Halfway there, I faltered, muttered a curse, and walked to Gracie's campsite. I stopped at the edge of the road.

"I have to leave for a while."

Gracie was at the minivan, piling the dishes and pots into a box in the back. She didn't face me at first, and I wondered if she would ignore me entirely. The kids still played cards, but the little girl paused to eye me and then her mom.

"Where are you going?" Gracie asked, shutting the rear door of the van and turning.

"Back to the city. A friend needs some help with something. I should be back here by nightfall."

She nodded, but kept silent.

"Will you still be here?"

"No idea."

I really didn't need this crap. "Fine."

I stalked to the pickup, got in, and drove away, a part of me hoping that they'd be gone by the time I got back, and a part of me fearing the same thing.

Pawn shops have a lousy reputation. No one wants them in their neighborhood, because by definition they attract a down-on-their-luck clientele. The wealthy and respectable don't usually need to put their stuff in hock, nor do they need to seek out bargains at the expense of those who have.

The truth is, most pawn brokers are respectable businessmen and women whose shops are regulated by state law. Are there bad apples? Sure. I'd guess there are in any profession. But most follow the letter of the law.

And then there are those like Burt Kendall, who are a credit to the business.

Burt was a bear of a man, gray-haired and bearded, with ruddy cheeks and the bluest eyes you ever saw. He told me once that he moved to Phoenix for the climate and got into the pawn business because, as he put it, he didn't have the skills to do anything else. He opened Kendall's Pawn back in the early seventies and had been running the place ever since. Forty years plus. In all the time I knew him, I had never known anyone to complain about his rates, his practices, or his merchandise.

Kona and I often went to him for information, but on the one occasion when I heard someone refer to him as an informant in front of him, he bristled. As far as I can remember, it was the only time I ever saw him lose his temper. He never took money for the information he shared; he believed that he was doing a public service.

On several occasions, Burt contacted the PPD about goods he'd received, even though doing so cost him money.

"I don't want no ill-gotten gains," he'd say, in the Brooklyn accent he never quite shed. "I wanna go home tonight and be able to look Rose in the eye."

Rose, his wife of fifty years, died of cancer two years ago. More than half the detectives on the force attended her funeral.

This was not a man to get caught up in shady business deals. Which begged the question: why would anyone kill him?

I had a feeling that the answer came back to magic. Several years before, he contacted me personally about a magical talisman that came his way. Like the other goods he turned over to the department, he was sure this item—a small jade statue of a chimera—had been stolen, and he brought it directly to me. I never asked him how he figured out I was a weremyste, but I think he knew my dad as well, and after reading about his dismissal from the department, put two and two together. I never saw any evidence that Burt was a weremyste himself, but he knew a lot about runecrafting, and he had an eye for magical objects.

Kona wouldn't have called me if she didn't suspect that magic played a role in Burt's murder. So perhaps he had come across something powerful and valuable, something that would attract the notice of Phoenix's dark sorcerers, and that was why he was dead.

The drive to Burt's shop took close to two hours, and it was only that quick because I ignored most of the speed limits along the way. I knew that Kona would be ticked off at having to wait so long, but in my defense, I had warned her.

"Where the hell were you driving from?" she asked as I climbed out of the pickup. "And whose truck is this? Where's that little silver thing you're so attached to?"

Kevin stood with her, and before answering her questions I shook his hand.

"The truck is my dad's," I said, shutting the door. "My car is at his place. And I can't tell you where I was."

Kona had a way of making her expression go hard, so that her skin appeared to crystalize into ice or stone. I had always envied her that glare. She often directed it at suspects, and I had seen her use it to intimidate the most hardened of criminals. She gave me that look now, and I swear I almost told her everything. I had to remind myself that Gracie was wanted for murder, and I had made myself an accessory.

"Why can't you tell me?" she asked.

I gazed past her toward the shop. Aside from the yellow police tape strung across the door, there was nothing on the exterior that screamed out "crime scene!"

"Want to show me what you found in there?"

She continued to stare at me, until I grew uncomfortable. I glanced down the street and then met her gaze.

"I hope you know what you're doing," she said.

"You and me both."

"All right, come on."

The three of us ducked under the strip of tape and entered the building. I halted a step inside the doorway and surveyed the wreckage, my mouth hanging open.

It was like a magical bomb had been detonated in the middle of the shop. Every display case had been shattered. Pistols, rifles, shotguns, knives of every shape and size, and a dazzling array of rings, necklaces, bracelets, and wrist watches had been scattered across the floor, strewn in a sea of glass shards. Acoustic and electric guitars had been blasted off the wall, their necks broken and twisted, their bodies crushed. Martins, Taylors, Gibsons, Fenders—it was enough to make a guitar aficionado weep.

I made my way into the shop, trying to place my feet with some care. Still, glass crunched under my shoes with each step. I noticed that there were surveillance cameras in the corners of the store.

"What do the tapes show?"

"Nothing," Kevin said. "As best we can tell, the system cut out a few minutes before the killers got here."

That figured.

The rest of Burt's merchandise was in the same state as the display cases and guitars. Cameras, computers, sports equipment, stereos, bikes. Nothing had been spared.

And overlaying all the damage was a sheen of fresh magical glow, purple, like a storm-cloud in mid-summer. There was no apparent pattern to either the destruction or the magical residue. Again, it all reminded me of an explosion. Powerful, random, deadly.

A corpse lay in the center of the shop, covered by a white sheet. I walked toward it, glancing at Kona and Kevin. "May I?"

"Be our guest."

I squatted beside the body and pulled back the sheet to reveal a young man in an Arcade Fire t-shirt and jeans. He had piercings in his eyebrows, his nose, his lip, and tattoos up and down both arms. Still, the art he wore couldn't hide the wound on his upper arm. It was red, puckered, the skin raised and the subcutaneous markings almost like pin pricks. But aside from this wound, and some red marks on his neck, there was nothing unusual about the dead man's appearance. I saw no magic on him, and no other injuries that could have killed him. Not even a cut from flying glass.

"That wound on his arm look familiar?" Kona asked.

"Very. I guess our silver-haired friend was here."

"I hope so," she said. "I'd hate to think that there are two guys running around my city who can kill that way."

"Where's Burt?"

Kevin pointed in the direction of the cash register. "Behind the counter."

I walked around and found the second corpse there, also covered with a sheet. I took a breath, pulled back the cloth, and exhaled through clenched teeth. Burt's face was frozen in a rictus of pain, his teeth bared, his eyes squeezed shut. And he was covered with that same purple glow, as if he had been dipped in magic before he died.

He also had a gunshot wound in his chest, but it hadn't bled a lot, and I would have bet every dollar I had that the magic had killed him, and not the bullet.

I heard footsteps behind me, knew them for Kona's. "Well?"

"There's magic everywhere. It's all over the shop, and it's all over Burt. The only thing not touched by it is that other corpse. The only mark on him is that weird wound we first saw at the Burger Royale."

"And what do you think that means?"

I covered Burt again and stood. "Understand, I'm only guessing here."

"Best guess, then."

I stared at her, saying nothing.

"Justis?"

"It occurs to me, I don't have to guess," I said. "If you'll let me take something from Burt, I can see what happened. I can scry the last minutes of his life."

"This is something new, right?" Kona asked. "There's a reason you didn't do this when you were on the force?"

"Yeah," I said, "it's new. I learned the magic in the last year, and I used it when we were working the Deegan case, remember?"

"That thing you did in South Mountain Park."

"Exactly."

"And why didn't you do it at the Burger Royale?"

"You had enough witnesses for those killings. You didn't need the magic. But there are no witnesses here, and everything I could tell you would be nothing more than conjecture."

"What would you need to take? I don't want you messing with my crime scene."

I squatted once more and took another look at Burt's body. Blood would have been best, but the blood on his chest had dried. "A hair would do it," I said.

Kona wrinkled her nose. "A hair?"

"Just one. I could also use something of his that's lying around, but blood, hair, or bone would work best."

She glanced at Kevin, who was already watching her, an eyebrow cocked. "This is pretty weird," she said, facing me again. "But sure, if you can take a hair from his head without disturbing the body in any other way, go ahead."

I managed to take hold of a single hair and with a sharp tug, pulled it free. "Sorry, Burt," I whispered. Straightening again, I retrieved from my pants pocket the flat piece of polished agate I used as a scrying glass. There was nothing inherently magical about that stone or the sinuous bands of blue and white that surrounded the small crystalline opening at its center. It was nothing more or less than a rock, something I had picked up at a mall long ago. But its beauty was familiar, comfortable. And over the years it had worked as a scrying surface better than any mirror or glass or crystal ball I'd tried.

I coiled the hair around my finger and held it against the bottom of the stone. "This will take a few minutes," I said to Kona and Kevin. "It's best if you don't interrupt me."

Kona lifted a shoulder. "Do your thing," she said.

Right.

Scrying spells weren't particularly complicated; this one took only three elements. Burt, my stone, and this place in the moments before he died.

I stared at the stone, watched as those winding bands of color vanished. An image coalesced slowly in the depths of the stone, and as it did, I heard voices in my head, vague at first, but growing louder until I could make out what they said.

. . . Sources tell me it could be here. The speaker was an older man, with silver hair and a neatly trimmed goatee to match. He stood in the center of the shop, and a younger man, tall, athletic, watched from a pace or two behind him. I assumed the younger man was a weremancer, but because Burt wasn't a weremyste, he couldn't see the magic in people. And with this spell, I saw what Burt saw.

Both the older man and his companion appeared perfectly normal in the scried image; no magical blur obscured their features. The silver-haired gentleman wore a linen suit and a silk tie, and though I knew that he could kill with a mere touch of his hand, I couldn't help thinking that this was how every villain in every Hollywood movie should look: elegant, handsome, effortlessly graceful. *And so I ask you again, Mister Kendall,* he said, *do you have it?*

Even his voice was smooth, a soft tenor tinged with the hint of a British accent.

I told you, already, Burt answered, sounding loud and clumsy by comparison, *I don't know what you're talking about. If you could tell me what it looks like—*

No, I think that would be a bad idea, on the off chance that you're telling me the truth.

I am—

The older man raised a hand, and Burt fell silent.

You, come here.

Burt turned, allowing me to see his assistant—the guy with the tattoos and piercings who now lay dead in the middle of the shop. At that moment he still stood with Burt behind the counter, but at the silver-haired man's summons, he walked out into the shop area. I had no doubt that the older man had used a spell to compel him.

Tommy, don't, Burt said.

The kid ignored him.

Tommy is it? Silver-hair asked. Tommy didn't answer, but that didn't seem to surprise the man. As the kid stopped beside him, Silver-hair drew a knife from his pocket and laid the edge along Tommy's neck. The kid didn't so much as flinch. *Now then, Mister Kendall, I will ask you my questions, and you will answer me. If you refuse, he'll die. If you lie to me, I'll know it, and he'll die. Are we clear?*

Please, I honestly don't know—

Silver-hair quieted him again.

Do me the courtesy of allowing me to ask my questions. Have you had any objects of unusual origin brought in over the last month or so?

Unusual origin? I don't even know what that means.

The older man pressed the blade harder against Tommy's neck. Still, the kid's expression remained blank. *Think, Mister Kendall. Poor Tommy is depending on you.*

You're trying to find magical items, Burt said, his words a rushed jumble. *Talismans, maybe old books, that sort of thing?*

Have you received anything of that sort?

No. I keep an eye out for them. I have a certain clientele that wants to know when magical stuff comes in, and I haven't had anything to show them in months. I swear it.

This particular piece might have resembled a weapon.

You mean like a magic gun?

Silver-hair glanced back at his companion and huffed a sigh. Then he faced Burt again, and when he did, Burt let out a scream that made me flinch.

He collapsed to the floor, clutching his leg. A few moments later, Silver-hair's friend hoisted him to his feet once more.

I'm a tolerant man, but my patience is not without its limits. Where do you keep your magical items?

The pawned ones I keep in back, Burt said, his voice strained. *On a shelf over my desk. If the loans aren't repaid, I bring them out to that case. He pointed at a nearby display case. But aside from what's there now, I've got nothing. I told you, I haven't gotten anything new in—*

His words trailed into another scream. I didn't know what Silver-hair had done to him this time, but I had to grit my teeth against a rising tide of nausea.

You disappoint me, Mister Kendall. I had hoped to avoid this.

I couldn't tell if he said more. Burt's cries drowned out every other sound. I let the vision fade and slipped the stone back into my pocket before closing my eyes and rubbing a hand across my forehead. A headache had started to build behind my eyes.

"Well?" Kona asked.

I shook my head. "I didn't see much. It was definitely our silver-haired friend again, and another guy who I'm sure was a weremyste." I described what I'd seen in the stone and repeated as much of the conversation as I could remember. "I'm assuming that one of the spells intended to torture Burt wound up killing him, at which point they probably shot him in the chest to make make people think it was a robbery gone bad. I'd guess that they searched the place and then used the kid's blood to power the spell that wrecked the shop."

Kona pursed her lips, staring down at Burt's corpse. "Is it possible that the kid saw something Burt missed?"

"It's possible. But I don't think that this kind of seeing spell will work on him. They had him in a . . . a thrall of some sort. During the final minutes of his life, he had no idea what he was seeing or doing."

"So we don't even know if they got what they were after," Kevin said.

I surveyed the shop, taking in the level of destruction. "I'm guessing now," I said. "But I don't think they did. I have a feeling our friend was pretty well ticked off when he cast that last spell."

"Would you know what they were after if you saw it?" Kona asked me.

"I might."

She nodded once. "Then let's take a look around."

A doorway behind the counter drew my eye. The door stood ajar and a sign on it read "Employees only."

"Anyone been back there yet?" I asked.

"We've been all over this place, but we don't know what we're after."

I nodded and followed her into the back. The mess back here was almost as bad as that out front, though the one display case in this part of the building, which stood against the far wall, had not been shattered. It held a few handguns, including what appeared to be an original Colt .44-40 six-shooter. Apparently Silver-hair didn't know crap about non-magical weapons. If he had really wanted to convince anyone that this was a robbery, he wouldn't have left the Colt.

The shelf over Burt's desk was empty, as he told Silver-hair it would be. The desk drawers had been pulled out and dumped on the floor, and with Kona's permission, I searched through the pile of pencils and pens, papers and paper clips. As I expected, I didn't find anything of note. Either Silver-hair found what he was after, or Burt was telling the truth. I was betting on the latter.

"There's nothing here, Kona. At least nothing I can see. I can help you with this one, if you'll let me. You're probably not going to find these guys through the usual channels."

"We could use the help, Justis. Thanks." After the conversation we'd had about Gracie the day before, it felt good to be on the same page with her. Then she had to go and spoil it, at least that's how she would think of it. "If this thing he's after isn't here, where else might it be?"

I met her gaze, and despite the grim surroundings, a grin tugged at the corners of my mouth. "You're not going to like my answer."

It took her a moment, and when it came to her, she rolled her eyes. "Oh, don't tell me."

"What?" Kevin asked, looking from one of us to the other.

"Brother Q," Kona and I said in unison. I was smiling as we said the name. She wasn't.

CHAPTER 10

I first met Orestes Quinley when Kona and I were still working in the Robbery detail of the Violent Crimes Bureau. Back then, he was a small-time criminal who wound up doing a couple of years in Eyman State Prison for burglary. He was also a weremyste of limited power—limited enough that the prison held him for a while, until he earned his parole.

In the years since then, Orestes, who also went by the name Brother Q, had gone straight and had made himself into a sorcerer of some power. He owned a small shop in the Maryvale precinct of Phoenix called Brother Q's Shop of the Occult, which had to be one of the worst names ever for a business. In all my years of going to see Q, I had never seen an actual customer in the place. But the work kept Q out of trouble, and I hadn't seen any evidence to suggest that the guy was starving or on the verge of being evicted.

During my time on the force, and in the year and a half since I had become a PI, Q had been a reliable informant on matters relating to magic. Kona thought he was crazy, and I suppose she had good reason. There was no denying that he was strange. He always referred to himself in the third person, and on occasion, for no reason whatsoever, he spoke in verse. He'd been doing this since the day I met him, and while I'm sure it began as an affectation, I wasn't sure he could have stopped now if he tried.

But the truth was, I liked and trusted the guy, and I think he felt the

115

same way about me. To this day, I was the only cop who had busted him and made the charges stick. I'll admit that was a strange basis for a friendship, but it worked for us.

Often when I pulled up to Q's place he was seated outside in an old lawn chair, sunglasses perched on the end of his nose. Not today. The door to his shop was shut, and a faded "Closed" sign had been placed in a window by the entrance.

I knocked on the door, waited, knocked again.

After a minute or so, I heard someone moving around inside.

I pounded on the door once more, rattling the frame. "Open up, Q."

"Who's that?"

"It's Jay Fearsson. Let me in, will you? I have questions for you, and I have a twenty with your name on it."

No answer.

"Q?"

"Yeah, all right," he said. But I could tell he didn't want to talk to me. He unlatched the chain and an instant later the door swung open.

Q stood before me in ragged jeans and a torn, faded Jimmy Cliff t-shirt. As always, his hair was in dreadlocks, and a gold hoop shone in his left ear. He also had a dark, angry bruise on his cheek, below his right eye.

"What happened to you?" I asked.

"What?" He frowned. "Oh, that. Q had a fight with his woman."

"She hit you?"

He nodded, turned, and walked into the shop. I closed the door behind me and followed.

"You hit her first?"

He rounded on me. "Q did no such thing! Q doesn't hit women. Never has. Q was sorely tempted that night, let me tell you. But Q left instead. Seemed the best idea."

"You're back now."

"Yeah, but she's gone."

"I'm sorry, Q," I said, and meant it.

He shrugged. "Love and marriage ain't for the faint of heart; 'times Q think men and women be better off far apart."

I grinned. "That was a good one."

He led me to the back of the shop and sat in a wooden chair indicating that I should do the same. "What'chyou after, Brother J?"

"I don't know."

His eyebrows went up. "That's gonna make it hard for Q to earn that twenty you mentioned."

"What do you know about a silver-haired weremyste? Dresses well, might be from Great Britain."

"Q needs more to go on," he said. But he averted his gaze as he said it.

"All right. He's into dark magic, blood spells. And here's something that might set him apart: he doesn't need to cut himself in order to access the blood he uses. He doesn't need to cut anyone else for that matter. He can draw it out of people; all he has to do is touch them." I leaned forward, staring at Q, who continued to avoid my gaze. "That ring a bell?"

"He's bad news," Q said, his voice low.

"I think I just said as much."

"Q doesn't know much more about him than you do. He's from England like you said, an' he's as dark as a man can be."

"He have a name?"

"Q's heard people call him Fitzwater, but that might not be his real name."

"Who's he working for?"

Q shook his head. "A man with power like that? People work for him."

That made sense. Chances were that silver-hair—Fitzwater—answered directly to Saorla.

"He's looking for something, Q. A magical weapon of some sort. I don't know more than that. He thought Burt Kendall had it, and he killed him before tearing his shop apart to find it."

Q's eyes found mine. "Burt's dead?"

"Yeah."

"Well, shit. I always liked him."

"Do you know what this guy Fitzwater might be chasing?"

Q got up and walked to the nearest window, his hands in his jeans pockets, his shoulders hunched. Despite his quirks, he was usually jovial—that was his default mood—and I wasn't sure what to make of this quiet, brooding version of my old friend. I couldn't tell if he was broken up about his woman leaving, or just plain scared of Fitzwater. "Q doesn't carry weapons," he said, his back to me. "You know that. It's bad mojo."

Which wasn't at all what I had asked.

"I didn't suggest that you had it here. I asked you if you know what the guy's after. And since you won't look at me, and you won't answer my question, I'm guessing you do."

He shifted his stance enough to let me see the sullen cast of his features. Then he faced the window again.

"Q—"

"This one's different, Brother J. You come to Q all the time with questions like these. Except none of them have been like this. Not even when you were after the Blind Angel dude. This is different."

"So it's going to cost me more than twenty."

He turned at that. "Q's not talkin' about money," he said, shaking his head. "*This is different.* You're not askin' for help to put away some small-time conjurer, or even t' stop a killer. You're askin' Q to take sides in a war."

"A war? What kind of weapon is this?"

Q clamped his mouth shut and glared at me, no doubt wishing he hadn't answered my knock in the first place.

"There's no war yet," I said. "I'd know if there was. But if this weapon is that powerful, then I need to find it now, before the killing starts in earnest. So yeah, I guess I am asking you to take sides. Did you really think you could avoid that choice forever? Was your plan to hunker down and hope that every dark sorcerer in the city ignored you until the fighting ended?"

"How do you know Q won't join the dark ones and help them kick your ass?"

I laughed. That probably wasn't the wisest thing to do, given that I still needed information from him.

"Q's stronger than you think, Jay. There's plenty out there who'd want Q on their side. And there's even more who don't want Q as an enemy. You get what Q's sayin'?"

"I'm not laughing at the idea of you kicking my ass, Q. I swear I'm not. I'm laughing because never in a million years would you join forces with dark sorcerers. That's not your way."

He tried to scowl at me, but wasn't very successful. After a few seconds, a reluctant grin split his face, and the whole room seemed to get brighter. That was the Q I knew.

"That might be the best thing you've ever said to Q."

I shrugged. "I meant it. I understand you not wanting to get in the middle of this. And you and I have done business long enough that you know I would never let slip where the information came from. But I have to know what I'm hunting for."

His smile had faded, leaving his expression solemn and fearful. "It's a knife."

I blinked. "That must be some knife."

"It's old. Really old. Q's never seen it, but he's heard folks talk about it for a long, long time. It's made of stone. Pale, the color o' coffee with cream in it. 'Cept for a streak of red in the blade, like blood."

"In the blade or on it?"

"In it," Q said. "Embedded in the stone."

"You say you've never seen it. Do you know where it is, or who has it?"

"Q don't know any more than he's told you. Not who has it or where, not even where it comes from. Like Q said, it's old. And it's supposed to be powerful, wicked. Some people would pay a lot of money to have it. An' others, includin' Q, don't want it anywhere near them."

"If this thing is as old as you say, why are people suddenly after it now?"

"Q don't know the answer to that either, but it's a good question. A knife like this doesn't just appear out of nowhere. Somebody found it again, or decided now was th' time t' use it."

I didn't like the sound of that one bit. An ancient blade, with what looked like blood embedded in the stone. I had no doubt that the "somebody" Q referred to was Saorla, and that she had Fitzwater and his buddies scouring the city for this knife. Even having no idea what the weapon could do, or what kind of magic it possessed, I was certain I didn't want it falling into her hands.

"Brother J?"

"Yeah," I said, shaking my head to clear my thoughts. "Sorry." I took out my wallet and pulled a crisp twenty from the billfold. "Here you go."

He took it and slipped it into his pocket. "Thanks."

His brow had furrowed, and I sensed that he was wrestling with something. I watched him, saying nothing.

"You might want to ask yourself," he said after some time, "how it came to be here in the first place."

"What do you mean?"

"From what Q's heard, this isn't an Indian knife. It doesn't belong here."

"Do you know where it's from?"

"No idea. But not Phoenix, not even the Southwest. Q heard that a long time, back when he did want to find it an' sell it, back before he knew the dark ones were after it. Understand?"

I nodded. "Yeah. Thanks, Q." I started toward the door.

"You going after this thing?"

I pulled the door open but paused to face him once more. "I'm not sure I have much choice. I don't know who else is trying to track it down. But even if Fitzwater is the only one, I have to find it before he does."

"Q doesn't know what it takes to use it, but that kind of power . . ."

"I'm not sure I'd want to use it. Can it be destroyed?"

"It might be a thousand years old. In all that time, it seems likely somebody's tried. Don't you think?"

It was worth considering.

"Take care, Q."

I stepped back out into the afternoon sunlight and checked the street. A part of me expected to see weres and weremancers coming at me from every direction, led by the silver-haired gentleman. But the sidewalks were empty. I slid into the pickup, started her up, and pulled away from the curb.

"Namid, I need to speak with you."

The last word had barely crossed my lips when he materialized in the passenger seat of the truck, his waters roughened, so that the sunlight shining through the windshield made him sparkle like a tropical sea.

"Ohanko, the glamour your father put on you still protects you. I would not have found you but for your summons."

"That's good to know."

"And yet, you have summoned me again, something you and your father do with entirely too much frequency. I have told you this before."

"What do you know about a magical stone blade?" I asked, ignoring the reprimand.

He stared back at me, his eyes shining, his translucent features conveying enough surprise to tell me that he knew of the knife.

"I would ask the same question of you," he said, his voice like waves pounding a rocky shore. "What do you know of it?"

I trusted Namid as much as I did any person or creature I'd ever encountered, but I had given Q my word that I wouldn't tell anyone where I got my information. Not even Namid. "I know that dark sorcerers are searching for it. They killed a pawn broker, a man I knew, and wrecked his shop. I don't know where their search will take them next, but they're after it." Something occurred to me then, something I should have considered earlier.

"They cannot be allowed to find it."

I put that other thought aside for now.

"Why not? What is it?"

I wasn't sure he would answer me. Namid wasn't always forthcoming with this sort of information. He usually preferred to handle matters of magical intrigue on his own, rather than to involve me. He surprised me, though, and that scared me.

"It is a weapon of unparalleled magical power."

"I get that. But what is it, Namid? What can it do?"

"It is the *Sgian-Bán*, the Pale Knife." He pronounced it as Skee-an bawn.

"That sounds Celtic," I said.

"Very good. It is."

"So I take it this belongs to Saorla."

He faced forward, his expression hardening. "It would be more precise to say that she belongs to it."

I frowned. "I don't understand."

His waters were growing more roiled by the moment. He might have been confiding in me, but he wasn't happy about it. "The *Sgian-Bán* is the blade that was used to sacrifice the necromancers. This blade made Saorla and her kind centuries ago. It is infused with the blood of every necromancer empowered at that time. And just as it preserves their blood, it preserves as well an element of their power.

It is a blade of awesome might, of magic you can scarcely comprehend, all of it dark, perverted by their avarice and malevolence."

He faced me once more. "It is the one weapon in your world that can be used to kill runemystes, and as far as we know, it cannot be destroyed."

I had long since learned to expect the worst where Saorla was concerned, and yet, as dangerous as I had thought this knife might be, I hadn't imagined it could be this bad.

"Why haven't I heard of this before now?" I asked. "During the summer, Saorla and her friends went to great lengths to kill another of your kind. Patty Hesslan and Regina Witcombe put me through that elaborate ritual so that they could use me to kill you. We both almost died. Why didn't they use this Pale Knife instead?"

"It was lost," he said, as if the answer should have been obvious. "Until this moment I assumed it would remain so. You are sure that the weapon is here, in this city?"

"I'm not sure of anything. I'm trying to piece together a story I was told and a murder I all but witnessed. Tell me more about the knife."

"I would not know where to begin. I have told you in the past that Saorla and her fellow necromancers sought to set themselves against the runemystes. They did not approve of the Runeclave's attempts to protect your world against dark magic, and they opposed its decision to sanction the sacrifice that created my kind."

"Was a weapon used to kill you as well? Is there a blade that can counter theirs?"

He shook his head. "Our sacrifice was a ritual of magic. No blood was spilled, which is why we can take the form we do, without the hint of corruption that lies at the core of Saorla's being. But theirs was no sacrifice, not in any true sense. They used their magic and their blood to imbue the knife with unnatural power, and they transformed themselves into demons, powerful, fell, and all but immortal."

"And then?"

A small shrug rippled his waters. "And then the knife was hidden away. It remained an object of power, and they wished to keep it secret from the runemystes and the Runeclave. We learned of it, but only hundreds of years later, as the true nature of what they had done became clear. By then the knife had nearly passed out of knowledge, to become little more than lore. Rumors of it floated on the air, as insubstantial as smoke. It was in the land you know now as Germany. It was in Eire. Some claimed that it found its way to the New World before your nation gained its independence. But all of this was said in whispers. We knew not what to believe and what to dismiss as hearsay."

"But we know now it was more than rumor," I said. "It turns out it was here in America, and we know that the necromancers didn't have it, because they would have tried to use it long ago. So if it wasn't them, who would have brought it here, who would have kept it for all this time?"

"There are those who collect such items," the myste said. "There is a lucrative market for such magical artifacts. Some of these collectors are weremystes, some are not. But all of them would recognize the value of this knife. It is beautiful as well as powerful, and its hilt and blade are marked with carved runes, so that even those who cannot sense the magic in it would know that they held an object of power."

I'd long been aware of the black market in magical goods, and I knew as well of several collectors in the Phoenix area. Strictly speaking, the market wasn't illegal; there were no established laws governing the sale and ownership of such things. But those of us in the runecrafting community tried to keep track of these transactions for this very reason. Among the thousands of old books, carved amulets, ritual blades, and cursed or blessed gems, medallions, and baubles that filtered through this elusive marketplace, one might occasionally find items of true power, items that had no business gathering dust in someone's collection. I had a hard time imagining that an object as powerful, important, and deadly as this knife could have been on display for all these years in the living room or study of some rich magical dilettante.

Because it probably wasn't.

"No," I said.

Namid swung his bright gaze to me, his watery brow creasing in surprise. "No? I do not understand."

"I don't think it's with a collector. At least not the type you're talking about. The man who's after it didn't go to the home of a wealthy collector in North Scottsdale or Paradise Valley. He went to a pawnshop in Glendale."

"Do you believe he found it there?"

"I'm reasonably sure he didn't. But this guy knows what he's doing. He wouldn't be wasting his time, or Saorla's."

Another idea came to me, not necessarily one I liked. It had already been a long day, and if I followed through on what I had in mind, I was going to be racing the sun into the evening.

"I'll do my best to find this blade, Namid, but I might need to summon you again."

"You have my permission to do so," he said without hesitation. "You must tread like the fox, Ohanko. Those who would wield the *Sgian-Bán* will not scruple to kill any who oppose them."

That much I knew already. Namid vanished from the truck, and I started the long, slow drive from the outskirts of Maryvale to a small park on the east side of Mesa.

The park itself wasn't anything special. But at this time of the moon cycle, in the days leading up to the phasing, it was home to what weremystes and magical wannabes called the Moon Market, a gathering of vendors, mystes, and craftsmen who catered to runecrafters eager to ease or avoid entirely the worst effects of the full moon. Much of what was sold at the market was junk: knock-offs of Zuni fetishes, New Age books on Wicca and Shamanism, herbs that smelled great but did little else, carved and polished crystals that had been so over-processed as to rob them of any powers they might otherwise have offered. But occasionally I had found hidden in among the worthless stuff books of real value, raw crystals with palpable power, and herb sachets put together by people who knew what they were doing.

I didn't expect to find the knife here. I was searching for a person, not a thing, and I found him where I thought I would, sitting behind a table covered with genuinely beautiful and potent gemstones. Barry Crowseye was a Navajo who owned a small gem shop in Tolleson. He was tall, with long silver-white hair that he wore tied back in a ponytail. He had skin the color of cherry wood, dark, penetrating eyes, and a chiseled face, that could have come off a coin. In other words, he was the sum of everyone's notion of how a Native American should look. He wore jeans, a gray sweatshirt, and a leather vest.

Seeing me, he smiled and stood, extending a hand across his table of wares.

"How's it going, Jay?" he said, his voice deep. "I haven't seen you since you brought down the Blind Angel. Nice piece of work."

"Thanks, Barry."

Many in Phoenix's runecrafting community had resented me for insisting that the Blind Angel Killings had a magical purpose, and for a while I hadn't exactly been welcome in the market. Barry had been as skeptical as the rest, but he'd always treated me well.

He folded himself back into the canvas chair behind his table. "So what case are you working on now?"

I grinned. "You do that every time I see you."

"Do what?"

"Assume—correctly, of course—that I'm here for information instead of something else."

He made a vague gesture that somehow encompassed the entire market. "You don't believe in this stuff, Jay. I can't say as I blame you, but the fact is, you don't think herbs and crystals are going to keep the moon from crushing your mind in a few nights. So when I see you here, I expect to be answering some questions."

"I've said it before. You'd make a good PI."

"I think I'm better off selling rocks. How can I help you?"

I trusted Barry. I'd known him a long time, and he had never steered me wrong, or given me any reason to doubt his word or his motives. But I couldn't bring myself to ask him about the knife directly.

"Have you heard people around here talking about a magical weapon of some kind? Something old and seriously dark that's only been rediscovered recently?"

He gave a slow shake of his head. "I haven't, and it sounds like I'm glad."

"No kidding. To be honest, I would have been surprised if folks were talking about it in the open. The people who want it aren't exactly advertising the fact, and whoever has it is probably lying low. It was worth a shot though. The reason I came was to ask you about a person, a collector of artifacts, Pueblo culture mostly. I think you mentioned him to me once, years ago, when I was still on the force. Old guy, *Akimel O'odham*, I think," I said, giving the preferred name used by the tribe formerly known as the Pima Indians.

"You're thinking of Lucas Quinn," he said. "He made jewelry for a while and went by Lucas Twofeather, because he thought the tourists would be more likely to remember him." He grinned, exposing a gleaming golden tooth.

"Is he still alive?"

"As far as I know. Last I heard he was still living in the Gila River Community, a few miles north and west of Komatke. He has a place at the end of a dirt road off of Seventy-Fifth. It's not much more than a shack at the top of a small rise, but it's his."

He pulled out a piece of scrap paper and a pencil, and drew a rough map.

"He's not real fond of strangers," he said, handing me the paper. "And he doesn't like white people. The truth is, he's odd and a loner, and he's not some high-powered collector, like some of the rich white people who hire you."

I nodded. This was why I had come in the first place. "I'm not interested in talking to rich white people."

Barry cocked an eyebrow.

"All right," I said. "I'm not interested in talking to them about this."

"You really think Lucas could be sitting on an ancient magical weapon?"

I rubbed the back of my neck. "It's something that vanished a long time ago. It's only recently resurfaced. People seem to think it's in the Phoenix area. And I think that if it had fallen in the lap of one of those rich collectors, he or she would have been bragging about it. But if a loner had it, someone odd, someone who didn't particularly like those other collectors . . ."

"I suppose it's possible. Of course if somebody's trying to find it now—"

"He could be in trouble. Thanks, Barry. I owe you one."

I left the park, got back in the truck, and headed west, toward Komatke. Traffic had started to build on and off the highways, and the sun hung low enough in the western sky to make driving in that direction a battle. But given where I was headed, the freeways weren't going to help me much, and sticking to the surface roads did make the drive a bit easier.

Still, it was after four when I finally turned onto Seventy-Fifth Avenue in the Gila River Community. Barry's map proved to be a lifesaver. Without it, I never would have known Lucas Quinn's road was anything more than a track carved into the desert by dirt bikes and ATVs. Whispering an apology to my father, I steered his truck up the road, bouncing over potholes and jutting rocks, a cloud of brown dust billowing behind me.

I crested the small rise Barry had mentioned, muttered a curse, and stopped to survey the scene waiting for me there.

The shack lay in ruin, its roof caved in, its windows shattered, the wooden planks of its walls twisted and splintered. The front door hung from its bent hinges, swaying in the wind.

I eased the truck forward stopping beside a beat-up white pickup that made my dad's truck look like a marvel of modern technology. It had probably been days, if not weeks, since the damage had been done, but that didn't stop me from pulling out my Glock before leaving the truck. I approached what was left of the shack, my pistol held before me, my eyes sweeping over the structure and the surrounding land.

I pushed open the battered door with my foot and peered inside. The interior was in no better shape than the rest. Shards of broken plates and glasses covered the dusty wooden floor, along with a few books, their pages torn, and the broken remains of a wood table and several chairs.

I had expected to find a body, but I didn't see or smell anything to indicate that Lucas's corpse was here.

But with my back still to the door, I did hear a light footfall behind me, and then the menacing growl of something large and very much alive.

CHAPTER 11

Before I could raise my weapon or ward myself, a second footstep, this one heavier than the first, made the floor creak. That was followed by the unmistakable clack of a round being chambered in a pump-action rifle.

"I think you should put your pistol on the floor and raise your hands." A girl's voice, with the faint lilt I was used to hearing in the speech of American Indians.

I did as she said, then straightened, my back still to the door, my eyes fixed on the shattered window that looked out over the sloping desert behind the shack. "Can I turn around?"

"Not yet. Who are you, and what are you doing here?"

"I'm Jay Fearsson, and I'm a private investigator. I was hoping to speak with Lucas Quinn. I have reason to believe he might know something about an item I'm trying to find. Who are you?"

"Who sent you here?"

"No one sent me. A man named Barry Crowseye told me how to find the place."

"You know Barry?"

"For a long time now."

Another growl made the hairs on my neck stand on end.

"Who's that with you?" I asked.

"You can turn around. Very slowly. I'm feeling a little twitchy, and so is my grandmother."

129

I stepped around, taking care not to make any sudden moves. The girl couldn't have been more than eighteen. She was a bit heavy, with long black hair, dark eyes, and a face that was angelic, despite being partially obscured by the sights on her rifle. Next to her, its teeth bared, its ears lying flat, stood an enormous pale gray wolf with amber eyes.

"That's your grandmother?" I asked.

"Yep. And you're in her house."

That I hadn't expected.

"You're a weremyste," she said.

"If you can tell that, you're a were."

"That's right. I'm a wolf like her." She said it as "woof," but I had no doubt as to what she meant.

"I didn't mean to trespass. I came to talk to your grandfather. You can ask Barry if you want to."

"My grandfather's dead."

Again, a deep growl rumbled through the shack.

"I'm sorry to hear that," I said, breathing the words. "Murdered?"

She nodded.

"By the people who destroyed this house."

"By weremystes," she said.

"Not by me, I promise you. But I'm sure they were interested in the same item I'm after."

"Whatever that is, it's not here. If they didn't find it, it never was."

I glanced around, noticing what I had missed before. There was nothing left in the shack of any value. Whatever remained of Lucas Quinn's collection had been taken.

"They stole it all? Everything he had?"

For the first time, the girl hesitated. "Yes." She said it forcefully, but I could tell she was lying.

"I'm sorry, but I don't believe you. You and your grandmother removed what was left, isn't that right? But then why leave the shack this way?"

Her mouth twisted, making her appear even younger than she had. My guess of eighteen might have been too high.

"I took it all away," she said after some time. "Grandmother hasn't changed back from being a wolf since the night he died. I'm not sure she ever will."

I grimaced. "I'm sorry."

"I left the shack this way," she went on, not responding in any way to my words of sympathy, "because I thought they might come back. People loot stuff all the time, so they wouldn't wonder about that. But if I cleaned it up, they might come looking for us."

"That was good thinking," I said. "What's your name?"

"I'm not sure I want to tell you that."

"All right. Would you be willing to let me see the items they left behind? The stuff you took away?"

"I'm not sure about that either."

I gave a self-conscious smile. "I can't say that I blame you. Truth is, you have no reason to trust me, and I can't make you answer any of my questions. But I'm going to ask anyway. Do you ever remember seeing, among all the things your grandfather had in his collection, a stone knife? It would have been a pale, warm beige, the color of creamed coffee, with a red streak in the blade."

The girl frowned, and I could tell she was thinking about it, which was as much as I could ask. But it was the wolf who answered, with a sound that was half-yelp and half-chuff.

I regarded the wolf and then the girl, a question in my eyes.

"She says he had it."

"You're sure that's what she was saying?" I asked, trying not to sound too skeptical. But grandma, with her big teeth and big claws, responded by making the sound again, which was almost enough to convince me. "But you don't have it now, do you? It wasn't here after your grandfather died."

"No, it was gone by then. I don't remember seeing anything like it."

"How long ago did all this happen? When was he killed?"

"It was early September, so it's been more than a month."

Something didn't make sense. If the grandmother was to be believed, and if we were interpreting her yelps correctly, Lucas had the knife at one point. But if Silver-hair stole it weeks ago, why would he still be searching for it? Why would he have ransacked Burt Kendall's pawn shop? Unless a different weremyste huffed and puffed and blew down Lucas's house in order to take the blade. Too many questions, and too many fairy tales about wolves.

"Did you or your grandmother see the people who attacked the house?"

"No, we were away at a pow-wow. Grandfather didn't come."

Had Lucas's attackers planned it that well, or had the girl and her grandmother been lucky?

"I'm sorry for all you've been through," I said. "And I'm grateful to you for answering my questions. What you've told me has been helpful."

"So why do you look so confused?"

I laughed. "That's part of being a PI. Sometimes it takes me a while to sort through everything I've learned. But you've told me a lot."

She didn't say anything, and I couldn't help noticing that she still had her rifle pointed at my chest, though she was no longer sighting me and her finger was not behind the trigger.

"So are you going to let me go, or are you going to shoot me?"

Grandma yelped a third time.

The girl lowered her weapon. "I guess I'm going to let you go."

She grinned, and so did I. I nodded to grandma. "Thank you."

"What will you do when you find the knife?"

"I don't know yet. I'd like to destroy it. Failing that . . ." I raised my shoulders, dropped them.

"All right." She sounded vaguely disappointed. "You can go now."

I glanced down at the Glock. "I'm going to pick that up. Don't blow my head off, all right?"

"Don't do anything stupid," she said, which was a good answer.

I knelt, picked up the pistol by the barrel and returned it to my shoulder holster. The girl and wolf watched everything I did, and when I eased toward the broken doorway, they backed out of my way.

The sun sat balanced on the western horizon, huge and orange, its glow touching the wolf's fur so that she appeared almost red.

"Be well," I said, walking to the pick-up. "Again, I'm sorry for your loss."

They watched me, but neither of them made a sound. I got in, backed the truck around, and started down the dirt road.

Questions and thoughts churned in my head the whole way back to Organ Pipe Cactus National Monument. The sun set not long after I cleared the boundary of the Gila River Community, but its glow lingered in the sky for a long time, and soft light clung to the desert hills and saguaros and mesquite trees I passed along the way.

There is something eerie and yet calming about driving on desert roads in twilight. Distances telescope, the eyes play tricks on the mind. I saw few cars or trucks as I made my way back to the monument, but when I did see one, time seemed to slow and then accelerate. Headlights appeared on the horizon as bright and clear as the gibbous moon. But always they were farther away than I thought, so that I felt as though I was standing still. Right up until the other vehicle and my father's truck reached each other, at which point the lights flashed by with a rush of air that shook the pickup. And then the desert was plunged into relative darkness once more, at least until the next pair of lights winked into view.

All this time I had been convinced that Saorla, Silver-hair, and their allies were after Gracie and her children because of the power they wielded or might one day wield. Jacinto Amaya had led me to believe as much, as had Gracie herself. And I had been all too willing to believe it. Emmy was manifesting abilities no eight year old should have, and based on what I'd seen in the Burger Royale, Gracie was a skilled runecrafter. All things being equal, Saorla would want them fighting on her side in this coming war.

But I knew now that I should have questioned my assumptions long ago. As powerful as Gracie might have been, Saorla had lots of powerful weremancers at her disposal. Thinking about it, I would have guessed that Gracie escaped Silver-hair at the restaurant not because she was stronger than he, but because she was willing to do anything to get away, and he *wasn't* willing to kill her. He had to have been holding back, knowing that if she got away then, he would find her again eventually.

Gracie might have been a powerful weremyste, but she wasn't so strong as to be worth all this effort. And in the same way, all of Emmy's value right now lay in her potential. Saorla had years to turn the girl to her purposes. Why would she be so eager to take the girl now?

Unless this wasn't about Gracie and Emmy at all. Unless Saorla was really after the knife.

An attack on the home of an old collector in the middle of nowhere. A double murder at a pawn shop in Glendale. And a remark Kona made in passing the day before when we were arguing about Neil Davett. *They had a break-in at their house not that long ago. You want me to arrest him for that, too?*

Could the three incidents be related? Was that why Saorla wanted Gracie and the kids? Because she thought that Neil, or even Gracie herself had that knife? Crazy as it seemed, it made no less sense than the idea that she wanted Gracie and the girl in her army.

Just this very morning, Gracie had shed tears admitting to me that the silver-haired weremancer and his friends were after her kids. Had that been an act, or did she really believe it? Neil Davett had been quick to go for his knife the night he followed me from Amaya's, leading me to believe that he had some dealings with dark magic. But what if he had more involvement with Saorla and the others than I thought? Was it possible that the knife had found its way into his hands? Could he be stupid enough to extort payment or favor from Saorla in exchange for the weapon? Could that have been why Gracie left him?

Too many questions.

By the time I arrived at the monument campground, night had fully fallen, and a hush had settled over the tent sites and RVs. I drove past Gracie's site as slowly as I could, and was relieved to see the minivan still parked there. Whatever her feelings about me, she hadn't used my absence as an opportunity to flee. Their site was completely dark, though, and I didn't dare go near their tent. The last thing I wanted was to be crispy fried by her warding. I crawled into my own tent, set my own wards then slipped into my sleeping bag, and was dead to the world in mere moments.

My cell phone woke me in the morning. I figured it must be Kona, but when I fished the phone out of the pocket of my bomber, which I had once again used as a pillow, I saw Billie's name and number on the screen.

I flipped it open. "Good morning."

"You're alive." I heard relief in her voice, but also a rebuke. Too late it occurred to me that a good boyfriend would have taken time to contact her.

"Yeah, sorry I didn't call. Kona brought me in on another case. I wound up driving all over, from Glendale to the Maryvale precinct, and then out to Komatke, before coming back here."

"Wherever 'here' is."

"Right."

"Was this another murder?"

I sighed. "I'm afraid so. A guy I knew, actually. I'm not sure I want to say more than that."

"I understand. You okay?"

"Yeah, thanks. How are you?"

"Oh, fine," she said, airily. "I'd tell you more, but the NSA is probably listening to my calls, and, well, you know what the blogging business is like. Nothing but intrigue and danger."

"Well, that's what drew me to you in the first place. I needed a little excitement in my hum-drum life."

For a moment neither of us spoke, and I wanted nothing more than to be with her.

"How are you really?" I asked.

"I'm fine."

Not convincing. "Billie?"

"It's just . . . It's harder to sleep when you're not around. And I . . . I need to shop, but I'm afraid to leave the house."

"I'm sorry I'm not there."

"You're not supposed to apologize, remember?"

"I wasn't apologizing for . . ." I swallowed the protest, not wanting to start a fight. "I wish I was there. That's how I should have said it."

"So when are you coming home?"

"I don't know. Whenever this is over, I guess."

"And that will be . . ."

"A while yet, probably. There's a lot I haven't figured out. I'll try to call, but—"

"Sure. Don't worry about it."

It was too abrupt. She sounded angry, scared.

I started to tell her again how sorry I was, but stopped myself. "I should go," she said. "Call when you can. And let me know what I can do."

"I will. I love you."

"Yeah, me, too."

Not the most heartfelt of declarations. I snapped the phone shut, resentful of this job that had taken me away from her, determined to get some answers to all those questions I'd been asking myself the evening before. And yes, I'll admit it: just a little annoyed with her for making me feel guilty.

I flung myself out of the tent into another cool, clear morning.

Gracie and her children were up and eating breakfast. The sound of the little boy laughing tempered my mood a bit. I zipped the tent shut and carried a change of clothes to the nearest restroom. I felt Gracie watching me as I walked past their site, but I ignored her.

She didn't give me the chance to do the same on the way back. As I neared their site, she stepped out into the road in front of me.

"You got back late."

"You my mom now?"

Her smile was thin and reflexive. "I suppose I deserved that."

"I suppose."

I stepped around her and walked to my site. She followed.

"So I was thinking maybe you're right," she said. "Maybe we could use your help."

"That so?"

"I'm trying to apologize, all right? Could you give me a break?"

I turned so suddenly that she had to stop short to avoid walking into me. "Tell me about the break-in at your house."

"How did you—"

"I used to be a cop, remember. I still have friends on the job."

She pushed her hands into her pockets. "The break-in happened after the kids and I left. But from what Neil told me, it sounded like someone went through all of our stuff, the way they would if they were searching for something. A lot of things got broken—picture frames, plates and glasses, some of Neil's stereo equipment. But they didn't take much."

"Did they take anything at all?"

A frown knitted her brow. "I assumed they did. I guess I don't know for certain."

"What do you think they were after?"

"I don't know."

She took no time to think about it, and though she looked me in the eye as she said this, I didn't believe her.

"I think you're lying to me."

"You don't know me well enough to make that kind of judgment."

"They're going to find it, you know. Something like that can't stay hidden for long. And whoever has it is going to wind up dead."

"I have no idea what you're talking about."

She pivoted on her heel and started away from me.

"Did he steal it from them?" I asked, following her now. I didn't want to use Neil's name out loud, because I thought the kids would hear. I figured she would know who I meant. "Is that the real reason you left?"

"I told you yesterday why I left."

"And I'm not sure I believe that, either."

She halted and faced me, her arms thrown wide. "Why would I lie to you?"

"Because you're scared. Because you're in more trouble than you want to admit, and you don't see a way out. But you think that maybe, if you can simply keep your head down for long enough, it'll all blow over. And I'm here to tell you it won't." I glanced past her toward the kids. Emmy watched me, her expression as hard as her mom's. "If Neil's as much a fool as I think he is," I went on in a whisper, "and he did what I think he did, there's no running away from this."

"Neil didn't do anything wrong."

She spun away from me again. Once more I wanted to ask her why she was so eager to defend him. But before I could speak, a sound reached me, one that had no business being here, one that stopped me cold.

Gracie halted in mid-stride, and stood stock still in the road, her head canted to the side, as if she was listening for it as well: the dull chop of a helicopter. I searched the sky. She did the same, even as she pulled the Ruger from her pocket. The chopper was still some distance away, and several seconds passed before I managed to pick it out of the featureless blue sky.

"Mommy?"

Emmy and Zach were running toward us, Emmy pulling her brother along by the hand.

"I know, sweetie." Gracie squatted down and put one hand on Emmy's shoulder and one on Zach's. "I need you both to be brave, okay?"

The kids nodded.

"Get back in your tent," I said. "Maybe if they don't see us—"

"They don't need to see us," Gracie said. "They sense us."

"Is it Daddy?" Zach asked, squinting up at the sky.

Gracie shook her head. "I don't think so, kiddo."

I continued to mark the chopper's approach. "Well, if we're not going to hide—"

"I'm going to blow them out of the sky."

I turned to her. "They could be cops. You don't want the police after you for killing one of your own. And we're not even certain they're here for you."

"I am," Emmy said, eyeing me, her expression grave but perfectly composed. "I can tell."

I didn't want to believe her, but I did. And the truth was, I thought I could tell, too. Everything about that copter felt wrong. It didn't belong here, and appeared to be headed straight for us. Not for the monument, but for us in particular. Even the police wouldn't be that precise.

"My truck then." I ran to the tent to retrieve my Glock and the Sig Sauer.

"What good—"

"It can deal with dirt and gravel better than your minivan," I said.

"Okay, let me get the booster seats."

I gaped at her. "Seriously?"

Gracie's cheeks shaded to crimson. "Mom moment. Never mind." She shepherded her children to the truck. "Kids, we're going in Mister . . ."

"Fearsson."

"Right. Mister Fearsson's truck. And this once you're going to have to ride without your boosters."

Zach's eyes went as wide as saucers, and seemingly for the first time since my arrival, Emmy grinned.

"Really?" she asked.

"Really." To me Gracie said, "I'll be right back."

She ran to her site. I helped the kids into the truck. Gracie came back moments later with an old day pack and a huge stuffed animal—a zebra—that looked like it had been through a war or two. She squeezed in next to Emmy and handed the zebra to Zach. He hugged it to his chest like it was a puppy, even though the thing was about as big as he was. Together they looked like something out of a comic strip.

There was no back seat, and not a lot of room up front, but this was an old truck and it wasn't made with bucket seats. Rather, there was one long seat stretching from door to door. We all fit, though it was snug. I started the truck up, pulled out of my site, and drove around the loop way faster than I should have. As I drove, I put a warding on the pickup, taking care to include the tires.

Zach turned to his mom, panic in his tiny face. "I need blankie, too!"

"This shouldn't take long, kiddo. Blankie will be fine without you for a little while."

His face reddened, and even without knowing much about children, I sensed a tantrum coming on.

I reached across them, opened up the glove compartment, and was pleased to find that my dad still had an old pair of Korvette's brand binoculars in the car.

"Hey, Zach," I said, handing them to him. "Can you hold these for me and keep an eye out for Gila monsters?"

"What are Gila monsters?"

"Really big lizards. Very cool things to see. They might be on the road."

"Yeah, okay! Mom, I'm looking for Hee-lo monsters!"

"I heard," Gracie said. But she was watching me from the far end of the seat, seeming to reappraise me.

"I was a boy once, too."

Gracie and I both rolled down our windows so that we could listen for the chopper. I glanced up at the sky, but didn't spot it.

"It's behind us still," Gracie said. "Coming in fast."

At the end of the campground loop, I hesitated, wondering which way to go. The monument roads were scenic, twisting, and slow; if we took one of them, we risked getting stuck behind a camper. But the only other road was the state road leading north, back toward Ajo, or south toward the Mexican border. It was straight as a string, with few turnoffs.

"Ideas?" I asked.

"The mountain drive is rough," Gracie said. "Lots of up and down. There aren't many places where a helicopter can set down."

"Sounds good to me."

I followed signs to the drive, which was little more than a dirt road barely wide enough for two-way traffic. We hadn't been on it for two minutes before we found ourselves stuck behind a camper. Fortunately, the driver noticed us and used a turnout to let us pass.

I sped up, and though the road was rough, I was able to cut across an open basin filled with saguaros and organ pipes, making pretty good time. On the far side of the basin, the road split into a one-way loop and began to climb into some rocky hills.

"They're right over us," Gracie said, pulling out her Ruger.

"Don't shoot unless you have to. I'd bet every penny I have that they're warded."

She frowned, but didn't raise the weapon.

The drive was growing rougher by the minute, and the kids were bouncing around the cab like rubber balls. I didn't think my dad would be pleased with what I was doing to his struts and shocks.

Something streaked downward into the road only a few feet in front of us, and when it hit, flames erupted from the pavement. I jammed on the brakes. Gracie's left arm shot out, pinning the kids to the seat like one of those metal bars on an amusement park ride.

A second impact behind us shook the truck. I checked the rearview mirror. Fire blocked our way back as well.

"I don't think we're driving any farther," I said over the pounding of the helicopter rotors, which were growing louder by the minute.

Magic brushed my skin. I glanced at Gracie and then at the blaze in front of us. The flames wavered but didn't go out. She tried the spell—whatever it was—a second time. Again, the fire guttered, like a candle in a hard wind. But still it burned, perhaps even a bit brighter than before.

"Damn it!" she muttered.

Emmy shook her head like a disapproving parent. "You owe us a quarter, Mommy. Each!"

Zach actually laughed. I was starting to like these kids.

"Yes, I do," Gracie said. But she was watching me.

I recited a warding spell in my head, the most comprehensive I could think of. I visualized it as a set of domes, one for each of us. Clear, flexible, stretching from head to toe, impermeable to magic and bullets and anything else those guys in the chopper might throw down at us. I held tight to the magic, allowing it to build, until at last I released the spell and felt my shield cover my body. This time both Emmy and Gracie stared at me.

"What was that?" Emmy asked.

"A spell to keep you safe, to keep all of us safe."

A moment later a second spell draped over me.

Gracie eyed me, daring me to complain. "If you think I'm going to put all my trust in another person's warding, you're nuts."

"I've been called worse."

One corner of her mouth quirked upward.

"We're going to get out of the truck," I told the kids. "Stick close to your mom, all right?"

I hesitated, but then pulled my Glock from its holster. In my opinion, firearms and children don't mix; I don't like having my weapon out where kids can even see it. But in this case, I wasn't willing to leave the car unarmed.

"Cool!" Zach said. "Can I see?"

I held it up, well beyond his reach.

"I mean—"

"I know what you meant. This isn't the time or place."

He scowled.

"This way out, kiddo," his mom said.

She pushed open her door. I did the same.

Once again, as soon as my boots hit the pavement, I felt the moon, its pressure on my mind about as light as an anvil.

The helicopter, shiny and black, unmarked as far as I could see, hovered above us. Five blades, a rear horizontal stabilizer with a vertical two-bladed rear rotor, and a smallish pod that might have held four people. I was guessing this was an MD 500, or maybe a 530, given the terrain. Small, fast, agile, and maneuverable enough to track us no matter where we might go.

I couldn't tell from this angle how many people were inside, but at least one guy had his door open and held what appeared to be a high-powered rifle. Even directly overhead, he was too far away for a clear view, but I thought I saw a blur of magic on his face.

We struck out into the desert. There was no trailhead here, but the terrain was open enough that we could scramble over rock and dirt anyway. Unfortunately this also meant that they could see us.

"I think the one with the weapon is a weremyste."

"They all are," Gracie said, speaking with such certainty that I didn't dare question her.

A sharp, flat sound drew my eyes skyward once more. The gunman had Gracie sighted, but he didn't look at all pleased.

"That was a good warding," she said.

"He shot at us?"

"At me. He missed."

"That didn't sound like a—"

"I don't think it's a regular rifle."

Of course. "Probably a trank."

"What's a trank?" Zach asked.

"It's a kind of bullet that would have put me to sleep," Gracie said.

That was a better answer than I would have given. At least we knew they didn't want her dead. Me, on the other hand, they probably didn't care about one way or another.

The helicopter banked away from us, flew a tight circle, and hovered over the road. After a moment it began to descend. It would be a tight fit, but apparently the pilot believed he could land the thing on that dirt track.

"Up there," I said, pointing toward the nearest of the rocky peaks surrounding us.

Gracie's brow furrowed. "It'll be slow going." Her gaze flicked in Zach's direction. "He's just five."

"I can carry him if I have to. But they're going to be on foot, and I want the higher ground."

She faltered, nodded.

"Hey, Zach," I said. "Think you can climb this mountain?"

He stopped to gaze at the summit, an open hand shading his eyes, his disappointment at not getting to hold my pistol seemingly forgotten. "You mean to the top?"

"The very tippity top."

"Yeah, sure."

"Emmy, how about you?"

"If he can, I can," she said. But she was staring back at the copter, fear in her dark eyes. "Mommy?"

Something in the girl's tone stopped Gracie in her tracks. "What is it, sweetie?"

"He's here. The old man."

Even I understood. The silver-haired gentleman. Fitzwater.

"Are you sure?" I asked.

Gracie grabbed both kids by the hand and led them up the hillside. "She's always sure."

CHAPTER 12

Moments later, the helicopter set down on the road. The doors opened and four men clambered out, ran to the side of the road with their heads down and started up the hillside after us. Two of them—one with the rifle and another carrying a pistol—were big, broad as well as tall, with military-style buzz cuts. They wore navy windbreakers over powder blue dress shirts and dark slacks, reminding me of security men I had seen at the home of Regina Witcombe, a billionaire financier who also happened to be a weremancer and a friend of Saorla. Now that I thought about it, Witcombe was one of the few weremystes I knew of who could afford an MD helicopter.

A third man, who I assumed must be the pilot, since the helicopter stood empty, was smaller, wiry. Of the four, he seemed most comfortable blazing a trail across open desert.

The fourth man, as Emmy had anticipated, was our weremyste vampire, the man I had seen in my scrying at Burt Kendall's pawn shop, and, I was sure, the man Gracie had escaped at the Burger Royale. He wore a tweed jacket, a dress shirt and tie, and black slacks. He also had on a fedora that matched the jacket, but I could see that his hair was silver. I thought he also had a neatly trimmed silver beard, but I couldn't be certain. His face was little more than a flesh-colored smudge of magic. I hadn't seen such power on a weremyste in years.

Fortunately, neither he nor the security guys seemed to have anticipated an off-road experience. They wore dress shoes and were having trouble keeping up with the pilot, who appeared more at ease in the wild.

We made good progress for the first five minutes or so, but then Zach started to slow down. Emmy wasn't doing much better. Against my better judgment we stopped.

"I can't carry both of them," I said to Gracie, thinking that my voice was low enough to escape the kids' notice. I was wrong.

"You don't have to carry me," Emmy said, glowering. I wasn't sure why, but she didn't seem to like me very much. "I can walk."

"All right." I turned to Zach, who was breathing hard, his cheeks flushed almost to glowing. "You want to get on my shoulders, kiddo?"

Emmy had taken her mother's hand and was climbing again, but she glared back in my direction. "Don't call him that."

"Sorry." She had already faced forward again, and I don't think she heard me. At least now, though, I understood her hostility: she didn't want me acting like I was their dad. "You want me to carry you?" I asked Zach again.

He nodded. I picked him up, swung him onto my shoulders, and resumed my climb. It was harder with the kid, but not much. He didn't weigh a lot, and frankly having a weremyste vampire at my back was all the motivation I needed.

We were still some distance from the top when another ball of fire burst from the ground a couple of feet in front of Gracie and Emmy. The girl let out a scream, and Gracie halted, clutching her daughter to her.

"That's far enough, I believe," came a voice from behind us.

I stopped, my shoulders aching, sweat soaking my shirt. I wanted to urge Gracie on, but it seemed she had decided to face her pursuers here, and since I didn't know them as well as she did, I followed her lead. At least for now.

The security guys and pilot had stopped as well. The only person moving was the older man, who stepped past his companions and halted maybe ten yards below us on the incline, one foot ahead of the other. He wasn't breathing hard, nor did he appear to have broken a sweat.

Magic stirred the warm air. A few feet to my left, a stone about the size of a television lifted off the ground and flew toward the man.

Several feet short of him, it exploded, as if pulverized by some unseen fist.

"I expected more from you, Gracie," he said, his words shaded with that faint British accent I'd first heard in my scrying the day before. "That's the name you prefer, isn't it? Gracie, rather than Engracia. So very American. In any case, after your performance at the restaurant, naturally we warded ourselves against such a spell."

I lifted Zach off my shoulders and set him on the ground, the motion drawing the gentleman's gaze. Zach sidled closer, until he stood just behind me.

"Mister Fearsson, if I'm not mistaken."

"That's right. Who are you?"

He smiled, and even seeing him through the magic, I marveled at what it did to his features. Under any other circumstance, I would have thought him the friendliest man on the face of the earth. The crooked grin, the crinkling of the skin at the corners of his bright blue eyes, the hat and silver hair and beard. He looked charming.

"Lionel Fitzwater. Perhaps you know of me."

"No, I can't say that I do."

If this disappointed or angered him, he gave no indication. He shrugged and said, "No matter. You need do nothing more than stay out of my way. I have no quarrel with you for the time being. We want Gracie and her children. Whether you live or die is entirely up to you."

"Well, I'm afraid it's not that simple. Because there's no way in hell I'm letting you take Gracie or her kids."

The smile faded. "Very well."

That was all the warning I had. Something hit me in the chest with the force of a bullet, though neither of the security guys had fired a weapon. If I hadn't been warded, I'm sure I would have died. As it was, I was thrown backwards. I landed on top of Zach, who let out a cry.

I felt magic again, but nothing touched me. I rolled off of Zach, my chest aching, and helped him up.

"You okay?" I asked, searching his eyes.

He nodded.

"Good boy."

I stood, moving stiffly. The security boys and pilot were climbing to their feet as well. I assumed that Gracie had retaliated for the attack that hurt Zach, and I had the feeling that whatever spell she used had done nothing at all to Lionel.

Fitzwater smiled again, but this time it didn't reach his eyes, and the effect was entirely different. "I had hoped it wouldn't come to this," he muttered. I'm not sure his companions heard him. But they certainly did when he said, "Michael would you come here please?"

One of the security guys—the one with the rifle—started up the hill.

"No," Gracie whispered. Then, "Kids, run! Straight up the mountain!"

The kids did as they were told. Gracie turned to run as well.

I cast to give them time. The guard, his leg, and the rock in front of him. The rock hit his shin; he stumbled, fell.

That would buy us a few more seconds. I strode after Gracie and the kids.

Another spell brushed past me and hit Zach in the back. He fell with a little grunt. Gracie whirled at the sound. Before she could run back to him, I grabbed him around the waist, picked him up, and tucked him under my arm, barely even breaking stride.

"Get up here!" Fitzwater said, a snarl in the words.

We didn't have much time, and I had no idea where we could go to escape what I knew was coming.

"Halt!" he shouted at our backs.

Gracie didn't slow and neither did I.

"I prefer to take both of them, Gracie, but really it's only the one we want. Her, and the item you took. As far as I'm concerned, the other child is expendable."

At that, she did stop. Emmy took another step, yanking on her mother's arm. But Gracie wouldn't move. I saw her shoulders rise and fall with a deep breath. Then she turned.

I did the same. I set Zach on his feet once more, but then took hold of his tiny, sweaty hand.

My life, I knew, was forfeit. Gracie, Emmy, and the knife were the prizes. *The item you took* . . . If we survived this, Gracie and I were going to have a heart-to-heart. But that was for later.

Fitzwater had already made clear that he didn't give a damn about me. And I had no doubt about Gracie's priorities. She would help me, but only if she could do so without endangering the kids. She wouldn't have stopped had Fitzwater threatened to kill me. To save Zach, though, she could gladly give her own life, much less mine.

By this time, Michael, the security man, had joined the older gentleman and was watching him like a dutiful puppy, awaiting his instructions.

"I can't hold him off if he uses blood."

Gracie said this in a low voice and I knew she was speaking to me, but I wasn't sure what to say in response.

More to the point, at that moment Namid's voice reverberated in my head. *Blood magic is dark magic.*

Maybe. But hadn't he also told me that a blood spell could be forgiven if it was cast in desperation? Well, I was desperate to save the lives of these children and their mother. Could there be any better justification for casting such a spell?

Fitzwater smiled at the security man. "Forgive me," he said.

Michael frowned, canting his head to the side. I think he meant to ask why the older weremancer had apologized. He never got the chance.

As soon as Fitzwater laid a hand on Michael's shoulder, the security man's eyes rolled back in his head, his knees buckled, and the rifle dropped from his hands. Still, somehow, despite the fact that Michael was six inches taller than Fitzwater and had to have fifty pounds on him, the older man held him upright with that one hand.

The other he stretched out toward us, his wrist cocked at a shallow angle so that I could see his palm.

Not good. Not good at all.

I did the only thing I could think of. Power might have been all around us, but blood was right there beneath my skin. I raked the underside of my left arm with the fingernails of my right hand, opening up three ragged gashes. Blood welled in them, and as the first tendrils of Fitzwater's power caressed my skin, I cast.

I clung to that image—tendrils—and imagined my own spell as a thin steel wall slicing down through those leading threads of his magic and blocking the rest.

Fitzwater staggered at the touch of my conjuring, his eyes closing for a second. As the bulk of his assault slammed into my warding, I reeled back and almost fell. I sensed the wall I'd summoned bowing under the force of his casting, and I feared it wouldn't hold. He had drawn more blood, and he was better at this than I was. I squeezed more blood from the wounds on my arm and cast the spell again. I'm sure the second crafting saved us. That and a spell Gracie cast to bolster my warding.

After perhaps forty-five seconds, Fitzwater opened his eyes once more, the look in them murderous. How could I have ever thought him charming?

He released his hold on the security man, allowing him to crumple to the ground, limp as a broken marionette. I noticed a small red stain on Michael's shirt where Fitzwater's hand had been.

"Holy shit, Mike!" the other security man said, running up the hillside to his friend. "What the hell happened to him?" He dropped to his knees beside Michael and felt for a pulse. "Jesus! He's dead." He glared up at Fitzwater. "What the hell was that? What did you do to him?"

"You should not have interfered, Mister Fearsson," Fitzwater said, ignoring the man beside him.

"What are you going to do?" I pointed at Mike's friend. "Kill him, too? Use his blood like you used Mike's?"

The second security man backed away from him, scrabbling on all fours, like a bug.

"If you must know, I was planning to kill you."

I had an idea of what was coming and I cast, hoping that my warding would be enough against Fitzwater, thinking that at least this once he wouldn't have access to blood.

I should have known better.

A small rock flew from in front of him and hit the security man square in the forehead. Sandy Koufax couldn't have aimed it better. Blood gushed from the wound it opened, only to vanish just as quickly.

Twice in the past year, I had been controlled by dark sorcerers, and that was two times too many. Etienne de Cahors had used such magic on me several times, and very nearly made me kill myself with my own firearm. Patty Hesslan, another of Saorla's minions, tried to compel me to summon Namid so that she could kill us both. I hated these spells, and since the summer had been learning magic that would allow me to combat them.

But I was still a long way from perfecting those castings.

Fitzwater's spell crushed my warding as if it were no more than tin foil and fell upon my mind with the weight of a boulder.

"Come here," he said, the words reverberating in my mind.

I started toward him, unable to resist.

"Make him stop," Gracie said from behind me, "or I swear to God, I'll kill him before he gets to you."

I didn't have to see her to know that she had the Ruger aimed at me, which was good because I couldn't have turned even if I wanted to. Fitzwater's control on me was complete. I tried to cast a warding around my mind, as Namid had taught me, but my spells were no match for those of this silver-haired nightmare.

"And why should I care if you do?" he asked.

"Because then I'll have access to his blood, too."

I had covered about half the distance between us when Fitzwater held up a hand, stopping me. I stood utterly still, unable to do more, feeling weak and pissed at myself for still not knowing how to defeat these damn spells.

"What do you propose, Gracie? Are you prepared to surrender yourself to me? Are you willing to tell me where it is? You know that we don't want to hurt you, or your children. We want you to join us, and we want what is rightfully ours. Come back with us, and all is forgiven. I'll even let your friend here live."

"You don't want to hurt us. You want to enslave us."

"What an ugly thing to say."

"Get out of here," Gracie said. "And don't come near us again."

Fitzwater shook his head. He was staring past me at Gracie, his eyes narrowed, and now he smiled again, though his charm had long since vanished. "I don't think you're going to shoot him at all. Even if you were capable of such a thing, he's probably warded, as you were earlier when James fired that dart at you."

He beckoned me forward with a waggle of his fingers. Helpless to do anything else, I started toward him again. I expected a bullet in the back of the skull at any moment, but maybe Fitzwater knew Gracie better than I did. She didn't fire.

Silver-hair ordered me to stop once I was beside him, but he didn't go for my blood right away. Apparently he thought I was more important to Gracie than she was letting on.

"Last chance, Gracie. Come with me quietly, by your own volition, or allow Mister Fearsson to die, and come with me anyway. It's your choice, but my patience wears thin."

I couldn't move—not my hands or my legs. I couldn't use my Glock to blow the bastard's head off. I couldn't even speak, and I'm not sure I would have known what to say if I could. But I could move my eyes—that had always been the case with these spells. For some reason I could direct them where I needed to.

And right now that meant looking down at the gouges I'd made in the skin of my forearm. They were bloody again. There wasn't much, but the scratches had darkened as blood seeped into the rough channels. And I didn't need a lot.

Namid was going to be really ticked at me.

Seven elements this time. Fitzwater, me, his control spell, my mind, a shield around it, Gracie and her kids, who needed me to break free, and the blood on my arm. I knew that a blood spell could defeat a control spell; I'd done this once before, although not against a weremancer as accomplished and powerful as Fitzwater.

As soon as I released the magic building inside me, he whipped his gaze around.

"What are you doing?"

He reached for me, and I jerked away from him. I didn't have full control of my body, not yet. But I had won enough freedom for myself to stagger away, putting a bit of distance between us.

His hand brushed the front of my shirt, but nothing more. He didn't touch *me*, which, I was sure, saved my life.

"No!" He growled the word, his face contorting.

And I felt what remained of his control spell give way. I could move again.

My first impulse was to punch him in the face, or kick him in the groin. But I knew better than to give him any opportunity to grab hold of me. The man took the phrase "death grip" to a whole other level.

But that didn't mean I couldn't incapacitate him. Three elements: my foot, the fine red dirt covering the desert floor, his eyes. My casting was as immediate as thought. A spray of dust kicked up from the ground in front of him, coating his shirt and jacket, dirtying his face.

He let out a strangled cry, his hands covering his eyes a second too late. Emboldened, I stepped toward and threw one punch. I didn't dare hit him anywhere near his hands, and I certainly didn't want to bloody him. So I hit him in the throat. Hard.

He went down in a heap. For good measure, I kicked him in the side, then danced away so that he couldn't grab my leg. I'm not sure I needed to. For the moment, he didn't seem to be a threat to anyone.

A spell surged past me and the helicopter pilot fell back, rolled a few feet down the hillside and slammed into a large rock at the base of a saguaro cactus.

I glanced back at Gracie.

"I think he was going for a knife."

"Thanks," I said. I retrieved the rifle from where the dead security man lay and aimed it at James, the other security guy. "Take him and go," I said, pointing at Fitzwater. "You might want to avoid letting him touch you. And put down your weapon. You won't be taking that with you."

"What did he do to Mike?" he asked, placing his pistol on the ground.

"Ask him."

"I'm asking you."

I hesitated before deciding that telling the guy might pay dividends in the future. "You ever cast with blood?"

His cheeks reddened, but he held my gaze. "Yeah, some."

"Well that's what he did, but he doesn't need to cut someone open to do it. He used magic to suck most of the blood out of your friend."

"With his hand?"

"That's right. For a spell that was supposed to control all four of us. Back away from the pistol." He glanced at the rifle I still had aimed at his heart, and took several steps back. I grabbed the weapon off the ground and gestured for Gracie and the kids to come back down the hillside.

"We're getting in our truck now," I said. "And we're leaving. You can try to stop us, but I think you know we're both more powerful than you are. Together we could rip your head off."

He swallowed, nodded.

I took Zach's hand again, and the four of us hurried down to my dad's truck, giving the pilot a wide berth, though it seemed Gracie's spell had knocked him out cold.

I slowed as we neared the truck, my eyes on the chopper.

"What's the matter?" Gracie asked, voice still tight.

"I'd like to disable that chopper, but I'm not sure how to do it."

"Maybe this'll work."

Magic sang in the air around us and one of the rotors twisted downward with a groan of metal and then a splintering of composite. When she was done, the blade had a ninety-degree bend in it.

I wasn't sure how she had cast the spell, or where she'd gotten the power to do such a thing, but those questions could wait. "Yeah," I said. "That should do it."

She nodded, but I saw sweat on her brow and upper lip where there had been none a moment before. She started toward the truck again, her first step a little unsteady.

"You all right?"

"Fine. Where are we going?" She helped Emmy and Zach pile into the pickup.

"The road's one way," I said, tossing the weapons I'd taken into the truck, in the space behind the seat. "So we'll complete the loop, pack up our sites, and get the hell out of here."

I started the truck, threw it into gear, and peeled away with a splatter of dirt and gravel.

"You know, I was doing fine here until you showed up," Gracie said, glaring at me from the far side of the cab. "Where the hell did you go yesterday? For all I know, they followed you back here."

"Yeah, for all you know, which isn't a whole hell of a lot. It's just as possible that they would have found you regardless. And if I hadn't been here, they'd have taken you, or killed you."

"Whatever. Why don't you drop of us back at our site and go back to Phoenix? We don't need your help. We don't *want* your help. I can keep my kids safe without you."

I swallowed the first response that came to mind. Kids this young shouldn't be exposed to that kind of language.

I eyed the rearview and side mirrors, checking the sky for any sign of a second copter. I didn't hear rotors, at least not yet. But by now I was sure one of our pursuers had radioed for help. I should have done something to the instrumentation. I had no reason to care about James, the other security guy, but I found myself hoping that Fitzwater didn't use the opportunity to drain him, too.

I chanced a look at Emmy and Zach. "Kids, how are you doing?"

Emmy shrugged and said nothing.

"I'm hungry," Zach said, the sullen tone a match for his expression. If it wasn't for the zebra in his arms, he probably would have melted down already.

"Yeah, so am I."

Gracie fished around in the backpack she'd tucked behind the seat back at the campground, and pulled out a handful of granola bars and a water bottle.

She handed a bar to each kid, and, after a moment's pause, held one out for me. I eyed it, eyed her, then took it.

"Thanks."

I'd never liked the sweet bars, but at that moment I would have been happy with Twinkies. The water made its way down to me and I took a few sips.

"You sure they can't fly that thing with only four blades?" Gracie asked.

"Pretty sure."

I saw some of the tension drain from her neck and shoulders.

"But they'll be calling for reinforcements. I don't imagine that Fitzwater gives up that easily."

She looked up at the sky. "No, he doesn't."

"This is the first place they'll look."

She twisted around and I could tell she was about to lay into me again.

"I'm sorry," I said before she could open her mouth. "You didn't need me telling you that."

The anger drained from her eyes, and her entire body appeared to sag. I had a feeling that rage had been the only thing keeping her going.

"I don't know where else to hide," she said, her voice flat.

"Maybe it's time to hit a city. L.A. might work, or Vegas."

She shook her head. "Cities make me nuts. And with the phasing coming, I'd rather not be in a hotel or on a friend's couch."

I understood that.

I stared out at the road, wondering if she was right; had I really led Fitzwater and his pals to them? "I didn't think I was followed," I said, my voice low. "I've taken a lot of precautions the last few days. This isn't even my car."

"You stole it?" Emmy asked, turning wide eyes on me.

Gracie let out a snort of laughter.

"No, I borrowed it."

Emmy's smirk conveyed such skepticism that I had to laugh, too. "Seriously, it's my dad's."

"Oh," she said, sounding disappointed. "I thought stealing cars was a weremyste thing."

I glanced at Gracie, who shook her head.

"Long story." Her smile faded. "I shouldn't have said that before, about you leading them to us. I don't know that, and the truth is you're probably right. They would have found us anyway. They're going to find us no matter where we go."

"Not necessarily. If you can keep moving—"

The laugh that escaped her was devoid of all humor. "Right. That's some way to grow up. Endlessly on the run."

"Not endlessly. Just until we figure out a way to beat them."

She opened her mouth to say more. Both kids were watching her, though, and upon seeing this she clamped her mouth shut again. But I knew exactly what she was going to say. *They can't be beaten.*

"Actually, they can be," I said, responding to the unspoken words. "I've done it before."

"Yeah? When was that?"

"You ever heard of the Blind Angel Killer?"

CHAPTER 13

Gracie didn't respond right away. She was watching me, her mouth open in a small "o." Her expression reminded me of one I saw on Billie's face on those rare occasions when I managed to surprise her.

"That was you," she said in a breathy whisper.

"What was him?" Emmy asked.

"Mister Fearsson—"

"Jay, please. I really don't like being called Mister Fearsson."

"That old man called you Mister Fearsson," Zach said.

I laughed. "You're right, Zach, he did. I don't like him either."

Gracie regarded me for several seconds. "All right, Jay it is. Jay here is a bit of a hero. He managed to . . . to catch a man who had been doing some terrible things to people in Phoenix."

Emmy faced me. "What terrible things?"

I glanced past her to Gracie, wondering how much to say.

"He was killing people, sweetie," Gracie said. "And apparently he was using magic to do it."

"That's right."

Gracie's cheeks had lost some of their color. "I had no idea."

"The police kept that pretty quiet. Some people know." I thought of Amaya. And Saorla. "But it's not general knowledge."

"So he's in jail now?" Emmy asked.

I faced forward again, feeling a sudden need to keep my eyes on the road.

Which, of course, left it to Gracie to tell my lie. "Yes, he's in jail."

155

Emmy eyed us both before giving a little shake of her head "No, he's not." To me she said, "He's dead isn't he?"

Smart kid. Thinking about it, I realized that I should have waited until Gracie and I were alone to mention Cahors. I had a lot to learn about being around kids.

"Is he dead?" Emmy asked, sounding less certain, and more afraid.

Gracie and I exchanged another look.

"It's all right," she said.

"Yeah, he's dead."

"Did you kill him?"

"I had some help, but yes I did. And while it's a terrible thing to kill someone, given the chance I'd do it again. He was a bad man."

"Who else have you killed?" Zach asked.

This was not a conversation I wanted to have with anyone, much less a five-year-old kid. Fortunately, his mom stepped in.

"That's not an appropriate question, Zach."

He frowned, but said, "Sorry."

"That's all right. It's not something I like to talk about, okay?"

He nodded, and for several moments no one said a word. A dry wind blew through the windows and the crunch of gravel and squeak of my father's truck filled the cab.

"Did you kill him with that gun?" Zach asked, breaking the silence.

"Zach!" Gracie sounded mortified.

"I was just wondering!"

"Hey, there's a coyote." The timing couldn't have been better, and I didn't even have to lie this time. I pointed out the front at a coyote slinking along the top of a low ridge, weaving among the saguaro trunks.

"Where? I don't see it."

Gracie spotted it right away and pointed it out to both kids. I slowed, then stopped to be sure they both saw it. I even gave those old binoculars back to Zach.

While they watched it, I checked the sky again. No sign of another chopper.

Once the coyote disappeared from view, I got us moving again. The conversation careened all over the place, which I imagine is normal where five and eight year olds are concerned, but it steered clear of the Blind Angel Killings.

At the end of Ajo Mountain Drive, I turned onto the main park road and headed back to the campground. As we neared the campground loop, though, I saw a white and blue highway patrol SUV with its lights flashing. It was parked outside the ranger station near the campground payment kiosk.

"Damn!"

"Bad word!" Emmy said. "You owe us a quarter, Jay. *Each* of us."

I didn't answer.

"You think they're here for us?" Gracie asked.

"Call it a hunch. I wouldn't be surprised if they got a tip from some anonymous concerned citizen. You are wanted, after all."

"As if I needed the reminder. So what the—" She glanced at the kids and apparently decided she didn't want to lose any more quarters. "What are we supposed to do?"

"I'm afraid that if we go near the campsites, we'll be arrested."

"We? What did you do?"

"I'm with you; they'll assume I've been helping you. Which makes me an accessory after the fact."

She blew out a breath and pushed a hand through her hair. "I hadn't thought of that. I'm sorry."

"I knew what I was doing when I came here."

She dipped her chin, but I could see that her thoughts had already turned elsewhere. "All our stuff is at the site. Including the minivan."

"They'll impound the van. It was spotted at the scene of a crime. And they'll probably take the rest as well." I checked my mirrors and scanned the area for additional police cruisers or cops on foot. We didn't need any more surprises. "Is there anything there you can't live without?"

Emmy peered up at her mom and pointed at Zach, shielding her hand with her body so that her brother wouldn't see.

Gracie closed her eyes and sighed. "Yes, a couple of things. Nothing I want to name right now, but leaving without them could . . . make things unpleasant."

I had an idea of what she meant. As a kid, I'd never been particularly attached to my blanket, but Zach had mentioned his earlier, and it seemed important to him.

"All right," I said. "I have an idea. You know transporting spells, right?"

A smile creased Gracie's face, the first one I'd seen that wasn't tinged with fear or anger, weariness or irony. This was pure smile, and it transformed her face. I'd already known she was pretty; any fool could see that. But when she smiled like that, she was beautiful.

I looked away, made a point of checking the mirrors again.

"That's brilliant," she said. "But at this distance . . ."

"We'll get closer, but I need for all of you to hide."

Just like that the smile was gone, and she was all business. "All right. You hear that kids? We're playing a little hide-and-seek."

Zach grinned. I think Emmy knew better than to mistake this for a game.

They couldn't all fit in the space in front of the seat, and there was no room at all behind the seat. Which meant that before this was over we were going to have to be more creative. But first we needed to find a place where they could hide for a few minutes.

I had the two kids crawl down in front of Gracie, in the passenger side footwell. Gracie put on a pair of sunglasses, poured some water into her hands and spiked up her hair, and then leaned against me as if she was my girlfriend.

Emmy didn't like this at all; Zach giggled.

"Quiet, kiddo," Gracie whispered. "Not a peep, okay? And Emmy, this is only for show. Promise."

"I have a girlfriend, Emmy," I said. "I love her very much."

This might have mollified her a little. I couldn't be certain, and I had bigger concerns. A uniformed cop had emerged from the ranger station. Halfway to the SUV, he spotted the pickup and halted.

Show time.

"Here we go," I whispered.

I pulled forward, slowing when I pulled even with him, but not stopping. I didn't want him coming over to the truck. They were scouring the campground for a mom and her kids; as long as he didn't see Emmy and Zach, we would probably be all right.

"I wasn't sure if we could go through," I called to him.

He took a second to study us both, but then he nodded. "Yeah, you're fine. You have a site in there?"

"Yes, sir."

"What number?"

If I gave him the number of my site, which was so close to Gracie's, he would have questions for me. Instead I gave him a number that would place us at least three or four rows from the end of the campground. I wasn't sure which was the greater risk: that I gave him a number of an unoccupied site, or one with people in it who might show up at any moment. Mostly, I hoped we'd be far from here before the lie boomeranged on me.

He nodded and waved us on.

I steered us along the outside loop past a couple of rows of RV sites and then pulled over within sight of a restroom. I checked the mirrors, looked around, peered down the row. I saw no one.

"Okay, listen up, kids," I said. "I want you to run to that restroom over there. Each of you get in a stall and lock the door. Don't come out until we tell you it's all right. Got it?"

Emmy wrapped her thin brown arms around one of Gracie's legs. "Mommy, I don't like this."

"I'm not sure I do either, sweetie." Gracie said it to Emmy, but she was watching me.

"I can leave all three of you here, but I have no idea what I'm trying to find in your tent. My transporting spells won't work."

A horn blast made all of us jump. An RV had pulled up behind us.

"Crap," I muttered.

I waved a hand at the guy and started forward again. He turned off a few rows later. We kept going, creeping closer to that last row, which, I felt certain, had to be crawling with cops. Four rows from the end, I spotted another restroom near the road.

"We can try this again," I said. I checked my mirrors. They were clear. "Or, if you think you can pull off the spell from this distance, we can try that."

Gracie's brow creased. "This is awfully far. Can't you drive us closer?"

"I can. But if we run into a cop, and he wants to look in the truck, we're scr—we're in trouble."

"I have another idea," Gracie said.

Before I could ask her what it was, she opened the door and hopped out of the pickup. "Turn here," she said. "Having the kids use the bathroom is a good idea. We might have a long drive ahead of us. I'll be back in a few minutes."

I didn't have time to respond. She jogged off the road and onto what appeared to be a dirt trail following the perimeter of the campground.

If they caught her now, I was really in trouble.

I steered us onto the narrow lane and drifted over to the side when we pulled even with the restrooms. Making sure that no one was nearby, and leaving the engine idling, I got out of the pickup, walked around to the passenger side, and opened the door. "You heard your mom. Use the bathroom and then come right back here."

They crawled out of the truck and ran to the restrooms. I stayed by the truck, watching for Gracie, every second feeling like an hour.

Even as I waited for them to emerge from the outbuildings, I pulled out my phone and dialed Kona's number.

"You got anything for me?" she asked upon answering.

"On Burt, you mean?"

"Yeah, on Burt."

"Nothing to speak of, no, and I don't have a lot of time right now. The other day you said something about a break-in at the Davett house. What can you tell me about that?"

The urgency in my voice must have reached her through the thin connection, because rather than telling me she wasn't being paid to do my job, she merely answered. "Not much," she said. "A neighbor called it in after hearing a bunch of noise from inside the house. Glass breaking, things being knocked around, stuff like that. So by the time the husband got home, a squad car was already there. Davett checked on a few valuables and then said nothing important had been taken and refused to file a report."

That fit. Neil didn't want to report it, because he knew exactly what the people who broke in were after, and he didn't want to explain any of this to the police.

"So that was it," I said. "No report, no investigation."

"'Fraid so. Why the interest?"

"I think it's possible the people who killed Burt went to the Davett's place looking for the same item."

"This more than a hunch?"

"I wish. Hunches are about all I've got going for me right now."

One of the restroom doors opened.

"I've gotta go, Kona. I'll call again when I can."

I closed the phone before she could say more. I figured she would still be ticked at me the next time we spoke, but I couldn't worry about that now.

Emmy appeared in the restroom doorway, but waited for Zach. When he came out, she took his hand, but still she remained in the shadows of the building, watching me, waiting for me to signal to her that all was clear.

Like I said, smart kid.

I turned a slow circle, trying to act nonchalant. Seeing no one, I opened the truck door again and gave them a little wave. They ran back to the truck, climbed in, and tucked down into the footwell.

"Where's Mommy?" Emmy asked.

I watched the end of the road for any sign of her. "She'll be here soon," I said. "Transporting spells take a little time."

That wasn't really true—they didn't take any more time than other spells. But I didn't want to scare her. I was concerned enough for the both of us.

"What *are* transporting spells?"

"They let you move things from place to place, or, in this case, they let you retrieve things that you can't get to in any other way."

"Like blankie?" she said.

"Like blankie."

"I hope she remembers to get more of our food."

"Me, too," Zach said, the words muddy.

I glanced into the pickup. He had his thumb in his mouth and was staring at the truck door, his eyes a little glassy. Given the chance, in another few minutes he would be napping.

I heard a car rolling toward us along the loop road, and then the soft crackle of a police radio.

"Shit."

"That's a bad one," Emmy said. I didn't have to see her to know she was scowling. "That's two quarters each."

"Emmy, before this is over, I'm going to owe you a lot of money."

I hurried around to the driver's side, got in, and pulled away from the restrooms. I didn't drive fast, and I had no intention of going far. But any cop who saw me there would be curious enough to stop.

"What about Mommy?" Emmy asked.

"Don't worry, sweetie. We're not going far."

She watched me, her eyes wide. If she objected to me calling her sweetie, she didn't show it.

When I was certain the cruiser hadn't turned down this row, I found an empty site and pulled into it, hoping Gracie would find us.

Minutes dragged by. I started to wonder if I ought to circle around to that last row. If she'd been caught, I needed to know. On the other hand, I didn't want to be arrested, too. Sure, I would probably be able to talk my way out of an accessory to murder charge; and if I couldn't Kona would do it for me. But in this case, my fate was beside the point. As much as I hated the idea of taking the children to Marisol and Eduardo Trejo with news of Gracie's arrest, that was better by far than getting caught ourselves and having the kids wind up back with an abusive father.

To my great relief, Gracie appeared on the road behind us a few minutes later. The kids squealed at the sight of her, and I had to shush them. She walked swiftly, but somehow managed to keep herself from appearing hurried or nervous. And her arms were full of an assortment of children's books, clothes, and stuffed animals, including an old, gray and blue blanket that probably had once been white and blue. I assumed this was blankie.

Upon reaching the pickup, she flashed a crooked grin through the open window on the passenger side. "Sorry. I'd use a spell to grab one thing, and immediately think of something else I should also take. And I had to be careful not to take too much at once. The place is crawling with cops."

"Well, climb in," I said, "and let's get out of here."

"With pleasure."

She passed a blanket through the window to Zach.

"Blankie!" he said, hugging both the blanket and his enormous zebra, and then sticking his thumb in his mouth.

Gracie frowned at this, but got in and handed another blanket and a stuffed puppy to Emmy.

"I know you don't need them," she said. "But I didn't want to leave them behind."

Emmy smiled. "Thanks."

Gracie stowed the books and clothes at her feet, and cast a glance my way. "I wasn't sure if you needed anything from your tent, and I don't know what your stuff looks like. A transporting spell wouldn't have done me much good."

"It's all right. There's nothing in there but a cheap sleeping bag that I bought in Ajo."

I pulled out into the one-way road once more and drove slowly through the campground, doing everything I could not to draw anyone's attention, and hoping we didn't meet up with another cop on the way out. Near the kiosk at the entrance, I saw the same officer we'd encountered earlier. He was leaning on a car with Nevada plates. A couple sat up front; two kids sat in back. I slowed the truck and waved at him. He straightened and squinted over at us. For a moment I feared he might not recognize us from a few minutes before. But then he waved and turned his attention back to the family from Nevada. I steered us away from the campground.

Before long, I had us on highway 85 heading out of the national monument. I had no idea where we were going, but I wanted to put as much distance as possible between us and all those police.

"So here's a question for you," I said, after we had driven for a while.

Gracie eyed me over the tops of the kids' heads, her expression guarded.

"According to what witnesses told the police, and based on what I saw of the scene later, it seems that when you were cornered in the Burger Royale, you were able to cast a spell that drew on the building's electricity."

Emmy eyed each of us, perhaps trying to gauge where this conversation was going.

"What about it?"

I sighed, wondering if she was just naturally defensive, or if I brought this out in her. "I'd like to know how you did it."

"Why?"

"Because I can't and I'd like to be able to."

That brought a smile to her lips. "You're asking me to teach you something about runecrafting?"

I nodded. "Yeah."

"It's not that hard," she said with a lift of her shoulder. "There's power everywhere—at least that's what I was taught. And incorporating it into a crafting is . . . I don't know. It's like anything else."

"I was taught something similar," I said, thinking of Namid. "When you say to incorporate it, do you mean the way you would blood for a blood spell?"

"Yes! I hadn't thought of it that way, but I think it's similar. It's part of the spell. I've done castings that draw on electricity, fire; I even used a running engine once. It makes my spells a lot more powerful." She grinned again. "That's how I bent the blade on that helicopter. I pulled the heat out of the ground and used that."

My eyebrows went up. "That's pretty amazing. So do you do it all the time?"

She shook her head. "I usually can't do it more than once or twice in any given day. And even if I'm careful, I can get one hell of a headache afterwards."

"I wonder why."

"I think it's because I'm using my body as a conduit for other types of energy, and my body doesn't like that."

I had wanted to practice these spells. That was the only way I was going to learn to use them. But we had a lot of driving to do, and I knew we might be attacked by weremancers at any moment. I couldn't afford what might prove to be a debilitating headache.

"Do you want to try one?" she asked.

"I think I'd better not while we're on the road."

"You're probably right. But I think if you approach these spells the way you would blood spells, you'll be able to make them work when you need to."

"Maybe. Or maybe you have talents the rest of us don't."

I said it with a smile, but she merely stared back at me for a few seconds before turning away to gaze out the window.

"Gracie?"

"I'm going to try to get some sleep," she said, without facing me. "Wake me if there's a problem."

"Yeah, all right," I said.

I eyed her, but she had settled in against the passenger side door, her eyes closed. I was left to drive and to wonder what it was I'd said wrong.

CHAPTER 14

Finding another campground, as opposed to a hotel room, would have been the safer course. Paying cash for a campsite never raised eyebrows; paying cash for a hotel room, particularly so close to the Mexican border, along a route used by drug traffickers, was bound to set off alarm bells. And credit card payments were too easy to trace.

But when I mentioned all of this, once Gracie had woken up, she insisted we find an out-of-the-way hotel.

"I need a shower and a comfortable bed," she said. "And we'd need to buy a new tent and new sleeping bags, which means using a credit card anyway. We might as well be comfortable."

She had a point.

Another idea came to me. As I put us on state road 86, which cut across what was known on maps as the Papago Indian Reservation, home of the *Tohono O'odham* nation, I pulled out my cell phone and scrolled through the list of contacts.

"Mommy says people who drive and use cell phones are morons," Zach said, talking around his saliva-soaked thumb.

"Your mom's right, but this is important, and it can't wait."

Gracie's frown returned. "Take your thumb out of your mouth, kiddo."

She reached for his hand, but he jerked out of her grasp with a loud, "No!"

I found the number I was after and pressed dial.

"Amaya," said the voice on the other end.

"It's Jay Fearsson."

"I can see that," he said, sounding impatient. "What news do you have for me?"

"They're safe. They're with me."

"Where are you?" he asked. The impatience had fled his voice, leaving him sounding almost too eager.

I hesitated. "We're outside the city."

"I understand. Where?"

"I'd rather not say. I'm afraid Saorla might be keeping track of my conversations." *And I'm not entirely sure I trust you enough to answer that question.* I wondered if it'd been a mistake to call Jacinto. I wanted to ask him if he would pay for a couple of hotel rooms for us, on his credit card. But now that I had him on the line, I wasn't so certain this was a good idea. I wondered how much he knew about the *Sgian-Bán*?

"Yes, of course," he said. "You're right to be careful. Why don't you go ahead and bring them to me. They'll be safe here."

Yeah, I didn't really believe that either. I had no trouble imagining why Saorla and her cabal were after the knife and wanted to enlist Gracie and Emmy in their army of dark sorcerers. And I had already promised myself that I wouldn't allow that to happen.

But wasn't it possible, even probable, that the other side—the "good side"—was as desperate as Saorla to find the weapon and add the girl and her mom to their ranks? They were all prizes to be won. If Gracie was as powerful as she seemed, and Emmy fulfilled the promise she had already shown, they might not need the knife to tip the balance in this magical war. Add in the *Sgian-Bán* and it might be enough to turn a stalemate into a rout. I wouldn't have been surprised if all these thoughts had crossed Jacinto's mind; I had heard the hunger in his tone. And, I had to admit, on some level I appreciated the importance of doing everything possible to bolster the strength of whatever force was arrayed against the dark ones. Our kind weren't supposed to use blood magic—though once again, I had just now, while battling Fitzwater—and so we needed every advantage we could find.

The problem was, while Amaya might have seen himself as fighting on the side of the angels, I knew better. There were no angels here, and I didn't want to see this family dragged into any war, regardless of which side drafted them.

"Jay?"

"I'm here," I said. How did I say as much without pissing him off? It took me all of two seconds to conclude there was no way.

"You're going to bring them to me," he said, a command in the words. "That's what we agreed to when I hired you."

"That's what you wanted me to agree to," I said. "I told you then, it might not be possible, at least not right away."

"What the hell does that mean?"

"I'll be in touch when I know more, and when I'm sure it's safe to bring them back to Phoenix."

"Fearsson! *Fearsson!*"

I snapped the phone shut, ending the call. But that second call of my name had been so loud, it almost sounded as though Amaya was with us in the truck. Gracie and the kids were watching me.

Zach grinned and pulled his thumb from his mouth. "Fearsson! Fearsson!" he said in a sing-song.

I mussed his hair. "Goofball."

"Am not!" But his grin widened.

"He didn't sound very happy," Gracie said, appearing far less amused.

"He'll have to get used to disappointment," I said, quoting an old movie. She didn't seem to catch the reference.

"Who was that?"

I had a feeling she already knew, but I didn't flinch from her gaze as I said, "Jacinto Amaya."

She quirked an eyebrow, reminding me of Billie. "Not a man you want to make angry."

"No. But I'm not just going to hand you over to him."

Her gaze drifted away, settled on the highway in front of us. "Thank you. But then why did you call him in the first place?"

"We need for someone to put a couple of hotel rooms on a credit card. He seemed like the logical choice, at least until I realized how eager he was to have you under his roof. It was my mistake. I'll be more careful next time."

"That's not . . ." She shook her head, looked out the windshield again. "You're doing fine. We appreciate it."

Another idea came to me. I dug into my pocket for my wallet and handed it to Gracie. "There should be a credit card in this in the name of Leander Fearsson."

She took the wallet but for several seconds did nothing more than stare at it. "Do you really expect me to find anything in this?"

I frowned, eyeing the wallet and seeing it as she would. It was a mess. An overstuffed, ragged, disorganized mess.

"It should be in one of the sleeves behind my driver's license."

She searched the wallet, a frown wrinkling the bridge of her nose. "There are receipts in here from, like, the 1950s."

"I wasn't alive in the '50s."

"Well, clearly the wino you rolled to get this wallet was."

I laughed. Emmy eyed her mom and me, her expression cross.

"Oh, here it is. 'Leander Fearsson,' you said. Right?"

"That's it."

"This an alias?"

I laughed again. "Hardly. Leander is my father's name. I take care of him, and sometimes I need to make purchases in his name. It's tied to a separate account. Someone watching for charges on one of our cards might not notice a charge on his."

"He might notice."

I shook my head, staring straight ahead. "Not likely."

"He a weremyste too?"

"An old one," I said, which told her all that she needed to know. Generally speaking, an old weremyste was a crazy weremyste.

"I'm sorry. My mother took blockers, so I never had to worry about that. But Neil's mother . . . I know what it's like."

I didn't have much to say in response. I drove, and allowed the conversation to die. The reservation included some gorgeous high country, and I was content to enjoy the scenery and figure out where we might stay tonight. At Quijotoa, I cut north on a narrow two-lane that tracked toward Casa Grande. There were quicker ways to do this, more direct routes. But all of them involved spending at least some time on one of the interstates, and now that I had Gracie and the kids with me, the thought of getting on the main freeways set off warning bells in my head. I'd learned long ago to trust my instincts on such things.

"You heading someplace in particular?" Gracie asked, her voice sounding loud after such a long silence.

"Not really. But I was thinking that I want to avoid getting on the freeways if I can help it."

She nodded. "I agree."

"Any idea why?"

"No idea at all," she said. "Just a feeling."

"Yeah. Me, too."

Zach took his thumb out of his mouth. "Mommy, I'm hungry."

"We'll be in Casa Grande in a little while," I said. "We can find some food there."

"Pizza?"

I had to grin. My childhood hadn't been the happiest, and with my mom dying and my dad drinking himself out of a job and going nuts before my eyes, my adolescence was a complete disaster. But in that moment I thought it must have been nice to be five years old and oblivious to the perils dogging us all.

"Sure. Pizza sounds good." I glanced at the fuel gauge. "We could use gas, too."

I wasn't crazy about the idea of putting charges on my dad's card. The money wasn't the issue. I paid his bills for him, and this one I would pay out of my account rather than his. But this was just the sort of "unusual activity" that was bound to draw the attention of the credit card bank. Of course, there were ways around that. I handed my phone to Gracie, had her dial the number on the back of the card, and took the phone from her. After being on hold for a few minutes, I spoke with an agent and told her my father and I were taking a short trip and would be using the card. I answered a few questions, told her the bank could call me at this number if they needed to, and hung up.

One problem taken care of.

I only hoped I was right in thinking that neither Saorla's friends nor Amaya would think to watch my father's account.

Traffic built as we neared Casa Grande, and by the time we found a pizza place, the kids were starved and grumpy. We wolfed down a meal, gassed up the car, and set out again, crawling through the city and its outskirts, past strip malls and car dealerships, chain motels and bars, pawn shops and liquor stores.

Eventually we emerged from the sprawl, passed over Interstate 10, and drove back into more open country. At first, much of it was agricultural, vast tracts of dusty farmland. But at Florence, we turned north toward the dry peaks and high desert of the Superstition Wilderness. I had no intention of taking them too far off the beaten path, but I knew the area and was certain we could find some small motel along the road that would offer a bed and a shower and a hot meal.

Neither Gracie nor Emmy had said much since lunch. Emmy had her nose buried in a book. Gracie was leaning against her door, staring out the window, the desert wind blowing through her hair. Zach had fallen asleep, his head lolling in his mother's lap, her fingers running gently, absently through his light brown hair. I was reluctant to break the silence, and the relative peace we all seemed to be enjoying. But I had a question for her—about a dozen, really—and once they started to worm their way into my thoughts, I couldn't ignore them.

"The day we met," I said, drawing her gaze, "I asked you about Fitzwater. I didn't know his name yet, but I think you did. You told me you weren't sure if you'd ever seen him before the restaurant, and you said it didn't matter if you had. Then you started to say something else, but you never finished the thought. I've been wondering what you intended to say."

"I'm not sure I remember. A lot's happened since then."

"You were telling me for the second or third time that you didn't know who he was. But then you said, 'The rest—' . . . And that was all."

"The rest is unimportant." She said it without hesitation, as if the words had been waiting all this time for her to give them voice. "That's what I was going to say."

"And by the rest you meant . . ."

"Leave it alone, all right? It doesn't matter."

"I think it does matter, more than you want to admit."

"It's not your problem!"

"Seriously?" I said. "That's the best you can do? It's not my problem?" I shook my head. "In case you didn't notice, Gracie, I'm in this now. Up to my eyeballs. You might not have wanted me involved, but your parents did, and so here I am. They're after all of us now, and if I haven't convinced you yet that I'm on your side, I don't know what else I can do, short of getting myself killed."

Nothing.

"I know what they're after. A friend of mine is in the medical examiner's office because of it."

At that she looked my way, her face blanching. I'd tried to be obscure enough not to scare Emmy, but direct enough to get Gracie's attention. For once, it seemed, I'd gotten it right.

"I'm sorry. It wasn't your girlfriend was it?"

"Thank God, no. But still, you have to start trusting me, just a little bit."

She glanced down at Zach, who still slept. "What do you want to know?"

"Fitzwater thinks you have . . . it. He asked about it today."

"Yes."

"Did he also ask about it at the Burger Royale?"

"I can't remember. Everything happened so fast that day—"

"He did."

We both looked down at Emmy.

She remained intent on her book and for a moment I wondered if I was wrong in thinking she had spoken. But then she tipped her face up to her mom and nodded. "He said 'What have you done with it?' I remember."

"Thanks, sweetie," Gracie said.

"He also called you Engracia, which is weird."

"Read your book"

Emmy went back to reading.

"Is that weird?" I asked.

"A little bit."

"Who else calls you Engracia?"

"No one," she said, her voice low. "Aside from my parents, no one has called me Engracia since high school. I hate that name; always have. I've been telling people to call me Gracie for as long as I can remember."

"Apparently he didn't get the message."

"That's so odd. I—" She gazed down at her daughter and shook her head. "She wouldn't get something like that wrong."

"I didn't," Emmy said, still reading.

Gracie's smile was fleeting.

"Is Engracia still your legal name?"

She nodded. "It is. I suppose he could have gotten it through a legal search or something of the sort."

I had more questions, but none that I wanted to ask in front of the girl. Apparently Gracie sensed this.

"Emmy, you want to listen to your music on my iPhone?"

Emmy glanced first at her mother and then at me. "Yeah, okay," she said in a way that made it clear we weren't fooling her for a minute.

Gracie produced the iPhone from her backpack, attached a pair of earbuds and handed them to Emmy. Emmy dutifully put them in and took the phone from her mom.

Once we could hear the thread of her music, Gracie faced me again. "What more do you want to know?" she asked, her tone about as welcoming as a briar patch.

"Do you have the knife?"

Color flooded her cheeks.

"You do, don't you?"

"I know where it is."

"Did Neil steal it from them? Is that what happened? Maybe he thought he could get some money out of them."

"You don't know what you're talking about. You're guessing now, and you're way off the mark."

"Fine, then how did you get it, and where exactly is is now?"

She bit back whatever she first wanted to say and stared out at the road.

"My friend isn't the only person who died because of the knife, Gracie. There was an old man who lived up in the desert on the Gila River reservation."

Her head whipped around. "He's dead?" she said, appearing stricken.

"You knew him?"

She turned away again.

"Fine, then tell me more about Neil."

"Why?"

"Because I think it's possible these dark sorcerers are after you because of him."

"You're wrong."

"I know he's into dark magic."

She scowled, but wouldn't meet my gaze. "And how do you 'know' that?"

"The night I talked to your parents at Jacinto Amaya's, he followed me and we . . . well, I guess you'd say we had a little confrontation."

"Is he all right?"

"He's fine. But I noticed that he was quick to go for a knife. There's no doubt in my mind that he was going to use it to draw blood for a casting. Which is exactly what a dark sorcerer would do."

"Is it?" she said, sarcasm saturating the words. "I couldn't help but notice that you used blood against Fitzwater a little while ago. Does that make you a dark sorcerer, too?"

"That was different!" I heard the defensiveness in my voice and cringed inwardly. She'd come too close to hitting the mark.

"Because it was you and not him?"

"Because it was a last resort against a weremancer I couldn't defeat in any other way. Neil pulled his knife out of habit, not desperation." I offered the distinction with more surety than I felt, but I didn't pause to let her see that. "Maybe he was drawn into the dark stuff," I said, making an effort to soften my tone. "Maybe he had friends who used dark magic, and he started out just experimenting with it."

She said nothing.

My grip on the wheel tightened. "Why are you still so eager to protect him? After all he's . . ." I broke off, shaking my head.

"After all what?" She bit off each word, though I saw that she glanced at Emmy as she spoke.

Emmy gave no indication that she was listening.

"Never mind."

She glared at me. "Stop the truck."

"What?"

"I said stop. Pull over."

I opened my mouth to argue.

"Now!"

Emmy did look up at that, her eyes wide.

We were on an open stretch of road. Another pickup pulling a small trailer followed us at some distance and a pair of motorcycles rode ahead of us. I pulled over and came to a stop, dust billowing over my dad's truck. As soon as we stopped moving, Gracie pushed open her door, slipped out of the truck, while at the same time easing Zach's head down to the seat, and then stalked off into the desert.

Emmy eyed me expectantly.

At last I got out and joined Gracie in the brush and dirt. She stared off toward a distant line of mountains, her fists on her hips.

"Nice spot," I said.

She rounded on me. "I don't know what my parents told you—No, that's not true. I know *exactly* what they told you. And apparently you believed every word. Well now you're going to listen to me. Whatever you think you know about us, it's not true. More to the point, it's none of your goddamned business."

I wanted to tell her that she owed the kids two more quarters, but this didn't seem like the time.

"It's not only your parents," I said, trying to keep my voice level. "You've been to the ER quite a few times, and the police have noticed a pattern to your injuries."

Her cheeks colored, but her eyes held mine. "I hope you were better at this when you were a cop."

Kona had said something similar when she and I argued about Neil and his role in Gracie's disappearance.

"Your parents are worried about you, and I've seen enough cases of abuse to be worried, too. About you and the kids."

She ran both hands through her hair. "My parents don't know what they're talking about," she said. Much of the anger had leached out of her voice. "They don't understand my life, and they never particularly liked Neil. Not because of anything he did, but because of what he represents, and because of who I've become since we married." A faint, sad smile curved her lips. "They want me to be Engracia Trejo." Her accent materialized like magic when she spoke her name. "They don't like me being Gracie Davett.

"But despite what they think they know, and despite what you've decided is fact, Neil has never hurt me. He's never hurt either of the kids. Whatever his faults, he's not abusive."

"Then why did you leave him?"

"What?" she said, her voice rising once more. "I'm not allowed to leave unless he hits me?"

"That's not—"

She threw her hands wide. "I left because it wasn't working. And like I said, anything more than that is none of your damn business."

She started to walk away.

"It's not that easy, Gracie."

She halted, her back to me, her dark hair dancing in the wind.

"For whatever reason, you and your family have drawn the attention of dark sorcerers. Now I'm guessing that's because either you or Neil has been working with them or for them. I'd also guess the break-in is tied up in all of this. They were after the knife, because somehow one of you has come into possession of it. You don't want me accusing Neil of anything, and you don't like it when I question the things you tell me. But there is way, way more to this that you're admitting. To be honest, I don't care if it's Neil's fault or yours. I came out here to help you, and that's what I'll do. But it works both ways. I need you to trust me, just a little bit, enough to help me understand what the hell is happening here. Someone like Fitzwater doesn't simply show up at your door. There's a reason he found you. And I'm still convinced it has something to do with Neil, but if you tell me it was you, I'll believe it."

Gracie turned, squinting against the sun.

"I didn't bring blood magic into our lives," she said, surrender in the words.

"So he *was* casting dark spells."

"Yes. But it wasn't like he had joined with men like that." She waved a hand, and I knew she meant Fitzwater and the guys he'd had with him today. "He was playing around, trying new magic. He never . . ." She gazed back down the road the way we had come, her expression more fragile than I had yet seen. "He didn't like it that I had more power than he did. Some husbands don't like it when their wives out-earn them. Neil made plenty of money, but he was no match for me when it came to spells."

I frowned. "Did you two . . . did you have magical battles or something?"

"No. We used to play around a bit, that's all. I thought it was fun. But after a while he grew frustrated, because I was always better than he was. That's when he started playing with blood spells. One night he insisted on playing one of our old games. We hadn't in a long while. I'd gotten tired of the way his mood soured when he couldn't keep up with something I did. But this night he insisted.

"We did fire spells. That was our usual. We'd set up candles in our room and see who could light them fastest. Sometimes after, with the room all lit up like that . . ." Her mouth twisted and she crossed her arms over her chest. "Anyway, on this night, he pulled out a knife and before I knew what he was doing he had cut himself and lit all the candles with a single spell. There was this *whoosh* of power, and it was like a wave of fire had swept through our bedroom. I swear he almost burned the place down. He was all pleased with himself, but I got angry with him, told him not to use spells like that in the house ever again.

"We got into a big fight. He said that I didn't like being beaten at my own game. The truth was, though, I was scared. I'd heard about blood spells but I'd never seen one. And I didn't want that kind of magic around the kids."

"So that was why you left."

She hiked a shoulder, dropped it again. "I didn't leave right away. He said he wouldn't use blood spells anymore, at least not around the house, and for a while I don't think he did. But we didn't play that game again. Or any others, for that matter. Even that would've been all right. But he stopped talking to me, at least beyond the day-to-day stuff. We didn't laugh anymore. It was like there was this constant tension, you know? After a while, I couldn't take it any more, so I took the kids and went back to my mom and dad's place." A smile ghosted across her lips, reminding me of one I had seen on her mother's face. "That's how desperate I was to get away at the end. I went back to them."

I had no idea what to say.

"The kids don't know any of this . . ." she said.

"Of course. I won't say a thing."

"I'm not in love with him anymore. It got too sad for that. But I still love him, and I want the kids to keep loving him. That's why I reacted the way I did."

"I understand. What about the knife?"

She shook her head. "I'm not ready to tell that story yet."

I suppose I could have pushed her, but she had opened up to me more than I expected, and I thought maybe if I didn't push now, my patience would pay off later.

"Fair enough," I said.

She regarded me for another moment before nodding and turning to walk back to the pickup. I should have followed right away, but for a few seconds all I could do was watch her, feeling a blend of pity and something else I couldn't quite name. Or perhaps didn't want to name.

I had only met her a couple of days ago. This morning I hadn't been sure I wanted anything to do with her. And now . . . Now I had to remind myself that I was here to protect her and her kids, and that the woman I loved was back in Phoenix, probably worrying about me.

I took a step toward the pickup, but then froze as magic brushed my mind.

Justis Fearsson.

I spun, expecting to see Saorla behind me. But I only saw clusters of brittlebush and stunted prickly pear cacti.

I know that you can hear me.

"What do you want, Saorla?"

Where are you? I can speak in your mind, but I cannot see you or find you. What glamour is this? What have you done?

I didn't answer. I was impressed, though, that my father's warding had worked against her so well.

I can always find the woman, you know. I can use her to make you tell me anything, to make you do whatever I wish.

"Not without Namid knowing about it. Now what is it you want?"

I want the woman. Not yours. She is nothing more than a cudgel I can use against you. But this other—you know which one I mean—her I want, and her children as well.

She didn't mention the knife, and I thought better of admitting to her that I knew of it. "Well, that's too damn bad." I said it with enough force, but my heart was laboring, because I knew what her response would be. I should have expected this.

Do not be so quick to refuse me, she said in my mind, as if reading from a script I'd already memorized. *You owe me a boon, and I choose now to demand its payment.*

"I won't give them to you. You can demand all you want, but I won't do this. You want to use them, to make them soldiers in your army, and I won't allow it."

It is not for you to decide! Her words raged in my head like a storm. She might not have known where I was, but she could still lash at my mind with her power.

I winced, raised a hand to my temple.

You will bring her to me, and the children, or I will kill everyone who you hold dear. Your love, the dark-skinned woman you used to work with, your father.

I started to object, but she talked over me, her voice like thunder in my ears. *Namid protects them, I know. He protects you, as well. But he does not know of our agreement, does he?*

I could picture the cruel smile that met my silence.

I thought not. Defy me, and he shall learn of it. And once he does, he will be helpless to protect you or those you love. A promised boon is no small thing, Justis Fearsson. We have a bargain, truly sworn. Uphold your end of it, or face the consequences of breaking your promise to one such as I.

In the next instant she was gone from my head. I sensed her absence as forcefully as I had her presence. Nothing looked different; her voice was gone, of course, but even that wasn't what told me she had withdrawn. It simply seemed that a weight had lifted, that my thoughts were once again my own.

I rubbed at my temple a second time; the shadow of a headache lingered, but most of the pain had vanished with her. I turned eastward. The moon hung low in the sky, white on blue and nearly full. Its pull on my thoughts was more gentle than Saorla's had been, more kind. I'm not sure I'd ever thought of the approach of the full in such benign terms. I had a lot to figure out before the phasing began.

I stumbled back to the truck, trying to clear my thoughts.

"You all right?" Gracie asked as I drew near.

"Sure, I'm fine."

"You don't look fine. You look sick." She stepped in front of me, forcing me to stop. And then she laid the back of her hand against my forehead, the way my mom used to when she checked me for fever. "You feel cold."

"Aren't I supposed to? Cold and wet, like a puppy's nose?"

That earned me a giggle from Emmy.

"Seriously, Fearsson, what's up with you?"

"Don't call me that." I said it more sharply than I'd intended, but right now I really didn't need anything that would make me equate her with Billie, even in the most superficial way.

"I'm sorry. Jay. Now tell me what's going on."

"There's nothing—"

"I saw that you were talking. I couldn't make out what you said, but your lips were moving and you seemed good and pissed. So I'd like to know who you were talking to and what it was you were saying."

I managed not to flinch away from what I saw in her eyes. With the sun shining in them they were a deep, earthy brown. "It's nothing you need to worry about."

"Generally speaking, I like to be the judge of that myself, especially when it concerns my children."

She had a point, I suppose. And being embarrassed at my own fear and powerlessness didn't seem like the best excuse for keeping her in the dark. I regarded the moon again.

"I was talking to Saorla."

"Saorla," she repeated, her eyes narrowing. "You've mentioned her. She's the one . . . like a runemyste, only dark."

"That's her. She wants to know where we are, and she thought she'd try to scare me into telling her."

"Scare you how?"

I met her gaze once more. "By threatening to kill all the people I care about."

She stared back at me, clearly at a loss for words.

"I essentially told her to go to hell. I don't know what the consequences of that will be. I'm hoping she understands that once those people are dead, she has nothing on me, so she's better off letting them live and using the threat again and again. But she's more than a little unhinged and I never know what she might do. So the next time you're feeling sorry for yourself and want to tell me to mind my own business or remind me again of how little I know about you and your life, try to remember that I have a stake in this, too."

Her cheeks colored and her lips thinned to a hard, flat line. But after a second, she nodded once and backed out of my way.

I walked around to the other side of the truck, and climbed in. She had already taken her seat and shut her door.

Saying nothing, I pulled out into the road once more and continued on to wherever the hell we were going next.

CHAPTER 15

We found a cheap motel along one of the state roads on the far side of Florence. The kids were ready to be out of the truck, and so was I. Using my dad's credit card, I paid for two adjacent rooms, which weren't hard to get. We were the only people there.

Gracie and I didn't say much to each other, which was fine with me. I wanted a shower, a nap, and then I wanted to call Billie. Of course, nothing ever goes precisely according to what I want. My shower was short on water pressure and shorter still on hot water. I had a feeling that both rooms were working off of a single water heater, and almost as soon as I stepped into the shower, I heard Gracie run a bath for the kids next door.

And the walls were about as thick as one of my dad's t-shirts, so my attempt at a nap didn't go much better. The truth was, listening to Emmy and Zach laughing with their mom, I found it hard to stay mad for very long.

At least I had no trouble reaching Billie. She answered on the first ring.

"Fearsson?" She sounded worried.

For my part, all the resentment I'd felt after our previous conversation melted away at the sound of her voice.

"Yeah, it's me. I'm okay. How are you doing?"

"I'm fine. Where are you? Or can't you tell me yet?"

"We're in the middle of nowhere. That's probably all I should say."

"But you're all right? No problems?"

"I wouldn't go that far," I said. "I'm all right, but we did have a run-in with some of Saorla's friends earlier today." I didn't mention my conversation with Saorla herself.

"So I guess this woman you're protecting is still hot then, isn't she?"

I knew she meant it as a joke, and that I should be able to see the humor, but just then I couldn't. Her remark dovetailed uncomfortably with feelings I'd been wrestling with all afternoon.

"Fearsson? I was kidding."

"I know. It's been . . . We've had a long day. I wish I was there with you." That was the truth. I wanted out of this whole mess.

"When do you think you can come home?"

"I'm not sure," I said, unable to keep the weariness out of my voice. "We need to find a place where Gracie and her kids will be safe," I said, no longer caring who could hear me. I needed to talk about it. With Billie. "A place where Saorla can't find them." *And I don't know if such a place exists.*

I didn't have to say this last for her to hear it. She was smart as hell, and she already knew me so well. "That doesn't sound like it'll be easy to find."

"No, it doesn't. Amaya wants me to bring them to him, but I don't trust him to take care of them either. They've become these weapons that everyone seems to want. Weapons with a weapon."

"I don't understand," she said. "What weapons are you talking about?"

"There's only so much I can say right now. Gracie is powerful, and the daughter might be as well. She could be the wild card in all of this."

Another squeal of laughter made me look at the wall separating my room from theirs.

"Anyway," I went on. "I'm feeling a bit short on allies right now. And on top of that, I'm pretty certain that Kona still wants to arrest Gracie for a couple of murders."

"Sounds like a fun trip."

"Like a Caribbean cruise, but in the desert."

"Do you need anything?"

"No, I called because I wanted to hear your voice."

"I know that. I'm glad you did. But now I'm asking you: is there anything you need me to do? Anyone I should call, or anything I can bring you?"

As it happened, there were a few things I wished I had with me, but I didn't want to drag Billie into this. Gracie was a weremyste, a skilled one. She was better off with me here to help her, but in a pinch, she could take care of herself and her kids. Billie was strong and smart and capable, but she couldn't ward herself, and in a battle with Fitzwater or someone like him, I'd be so consumed with keeping her safe that I might endanger Gracie and the kids, or even myself.

"That's a generous offer," I said. "One I might accept in another day or two, but not yet."

"All right. Let me know when."

"I will. I love you."

"Love you, too. Bye."

She hung up. I clicked my phone shut, but continued to stare at it for a long time. At least this time we hadn't ended our conversation with a fight. A knock on my door forced me to look up from the phone.

I stood and pulled it open. The room was so small, I didn't have to take a step; I could reach the doorknob from the end of the bed.

Gracie stood before me, her hair damp and smelling of hotel shampoo. She glanced down at my phone, which I still held.

"I'm sorry, I thought you were off."

"I am." I slipped the phone into my pocket. "What can I do for you?"

"The kids and I are hungry; we're wondering if you are, too."

I wasn't, but I knew I should eat.

"Sure. Did you have anything in mind?" I heard the flat tone of my voice. Apparently she did, too.

"I'm sorry about before," she said. "About everything. You were right in what you said. I hadn't stopped to consider that you're taking a risk just by helping us. We're grateful to you. I'm grateful."

I nodded, looked away. "Thanks."

I think she wanted to say more, but I wasn't exactly making it easy for her. I wasn't sure it was in anyone's interest for us to get closer.

"I don't think we're going to find much food around here," I said, making myself face her again. "But we passed a diner about twenty miles back. We can eat there."

She inclined her head toward her room. "I think that if we try to put those two back in the pickup, they'll mutiny. They'll stake us to the ground. We'll be a couple of Gullivers in the motel of the Lilliputians."

I grinned at the image. "I know how they feel, but I'm not sure we should split up."

Her expression hardened a bit. "I've taken care of them for a long time, without any help from you. I think we'll be all right for an hour."

I knew better than to argue the point. "Okay, I'll drive there and pick up a few things. What do the kids like to eat?"

We walked to the next room, where the kids were parked in front of a small television, watching some cartoon. The picture wasn't very good but they didn't seem to mind too much. Emmy had her book in her lap and wasn't paying close attention to the show. Zach held the zebra in one hand and sucked on the other thumb, his eyes glued to the screen.

I took their orders—a grilled cheese for Emmy, a plain burger with nothing on it but ketchup and mustard for Zach. Gracie surprised me by asking for some kind—any kind—of meat.

"A steak, a meatloaf. I don't care. I'm sick of granola bars and pizza. I want some real food."

"I'll do what I can."

I was no more eager than the kids for another drive, and it turned out to be closer to thirty miles each way than twenty. But the folks at the diner were willing to make everything we wanted, including a couple of nice New York strips for Gracie and me. Before long, I was back at the motel. The kids were still watching TV. Gracie was sitting outside the room with the door open, staring out at the road.

"What are you doing?" I asked, as I climbed out of the pickup with my bag of food.

"Keeping watch, enjoying a few minutes of down time, getting away from 'Mister Magoo.' Take your pick. What did you get me?"

"Eight-ounce strip steak and a baked potato. There's even some sour cream to go with it."

"Not bad! If there's a bottle of wine in that bag, you just might get lucky later."

I halted a few strides from where she sat, the smile on my lips dying.

Her cheeks had gone pale. "I'm sorry. I meant that as a joke. It was ... I wasn't serious. I used to say stuff like that to Neil. It slipped out."

"It's all right. Billie and I joke around that way, too." I forced a smile. "Besides, no wine. We're safe."

"Right." She stood, gave me one last awkward look, and stepped into the room. "Dinner's here," she said.

The kids cheered. I followed her inside, wishing I had accepted Billie's offer.

Gracie and I hardly exchanged a glance over dinner. Fortunately, the kids didn't notice. One of the four stations that came in clearly on the television was showing one of those animated movies with the talking toys, and they were content to eat and watch.

I bolted down my steak, wished them all a good night, and retreated to my room. It wasn't fully dark yet; on a normal night I would have been up for another few hours. But I was tired, and I needed time alone. I hadn't been in my room for two minutes, when again someone knocked on the door. Gracie no doubt.

She stood in the cool twilight air, her fleece zipped up to the neck, her arms crossed in front of her.

"Sorry to bother you. I need to know what time you want to be moving in the morning."

"Early," I said. "I think we're safer on the road, as long as we keep our distance from the interstates. And I prefer to stay in a different place each night. That okay with you?"

"It's fine, but give me a time. It sometimes takes a little while to get the kids moving."

"Let's be on the road by eight."

She nodded, and turned away. "Sounds good," she said over her shoulder. "Good night."

A scream woke me from a sound sleep. I'd left my Glock on the night table beside the bed, and in seconds I was at the door with my jeans on and the weapon in hand. But I paused there, listening. Thinking about it, I realized that what I'd heard hadn't been a cry of fear. It had conveyed pain. Agony even. I thought it came from Gracie's room, but all was silent now, and I began to wonder if I'd dreamed it.

A door closed on the other side of the wall, and an instant later a second sound spiked through the cheap plaster, sharp and yet muffled in a way. Someone was trying to stifle a shriek.

I yanked open the door and felt it riding the wind, as distinctive as the smell of burning leaves on an autumn night: magic.

I whispered a warding spell and stepped softly toward Gracie's door, gripping my Glock with both hands. I hadn't covered half the distance, when the door to the room opened and a small figure dashed out. I pointed the weapon at the ground, cursing my racing heart, and the twitch that had nearly made me pull the trigger.

"Jay!" Emmy ran to me and threw her arms around my waist.

"What's going on, Emmy?"

"It's Mommy. I think she's sick again. You need to come right away," She released me and grabbed for my hand. Her hand brushed the pistol and she stopped, stared at it and then at me. "You don't need that."

Right. I unchambered the round and tucked the weapon into the back of my jeans. Emmy led me to their room, pausing on the threshold to put a finger to her lips and point at the nearer of the two beds. Remarkably, Zach was still sleeping.

I nodded and followed her inside, feeling another riffle of magic as I did, this one different from the first. More muffled cries emanated from the bathroom, the door to which was shut.

"See?" Emmy said, sounding frightened. I didn't know the kid well, but I had the sense that she didn't scare easily. "She's sick."

I crossed to the door, knocked once. "Gracie?"

"Go away." Her voice was rough, strained, the way it might if she'd been sick to her stomach. But a magic induced tummy ache? I wasn't buying it.

"You say she's been sick before?" I asked Emmy. "Recently? In the last day or two?"

"She gets sick a lot. But it's been a while since the last time."

"A while . . ." I repeated.

Emmy shrugged. "A bunch of weeks."

Another moan made her grab hold of me again.

A bunch of weeks.

Sweat tickled the back of my neck. "All right." I patted Emmy's back, but then gripped her shoulders and made her step away. "You stay out here, all right?"

I rapped on the door again. "I'm coming in."

"No, you're not," Gracie said, in that same taut voice.

I tried the knob, but it was locked, which I'd expected. I cast a spell. The door, the latch, and a hot blade cutting through it. The metal chimed softly. I pushed the door open just enough so that I could slip inside and closed it again.

"Damn you! Get out of here."

She looked like hell, her face shining with sweat, her hair plastered to her forehead and the back of her neck, her skin so pale that the rings under her eyes were as dark as bruises.

But she wasn't gripping the toilet as she might have had she been ill. Instead, she knelt in the bathtub, her breath coming in shallow gasps. She wore a nightshirt that said "World's Best Mom." The collar and shoulders were damp and clung to her skin. I could see that she was shaking and even as she glared up at me, her eyes huge and dark in the dim yellowed light of the bathroom, she convulsed and gritted her teeth against another shriek.

I winced, took a single step toward her, but was stopped in mid-stride by the realization that there had been another sound as well: the snap of bone.

"Holy shit," I said in a whisper. "You're a were."

She was on all fours now, her head hanging low. "Yes."

"The kids don't know."

She shook her head. "I've managed to hide it during the phasings. But a spell hit me earlier. I was asleep, so I don't know where it came from. It started me changing. I'm trying to fight it, but I don't know if I can."

I was still trying to wrap my head around the fact that Gracie was both a weremyste and a were. I'd never heard of that before. At least now I understood her reaction in the truck when I said something about the rest of us not having talents like hers. The rest of us really didn't. But I thrust those thoughts to the back of my mind. We'd have that conversation another time.

"Dark sorcerers have enlisted weres in their war with the magical community. They turn them in between the phasings and use them as soldiers, messengers, assassins. But I had thought they needed to establish some level of control with an initial spell. That's how it's worked before." Unless, of course, the spell was cast by Saorla. She could do just about anything she wanted with magic. But for now I kept that to myself, too.

"Not anymore, it seems."

Her back arched and even through the shirt I could see her flesh rippling. The crackle of shifting bone echoed in the room. "God!" she screamed, the word ripped from her chest.

"Mommy!" Emmy shouted through the door.

"It's all right, sweetie!" she called, though the rasp of her voice wasn't likely to reassure Emmy.

"Can you ward yourself?" I asked.

Gracie shook her head. "I don't feel . . . the magic anymore." She could barely speak for her panting. "I did. Before. But it's started now. They don't need . . . to use more magic."

"So what can I do?"

"Get out."

"Gracie—"

"The kids need you . . . more than I do."

I shook my head, not wanting to believe that I could do nothing for her. "What are you? As a were, I mean."

Her head snapped up, eyes closed, teeth bared. Teeth that looked a good deal bigger than they had over dinner. "Cat," she managed to say.

Great. I assumed she didn't mean the cuddly domestic variety.

"Get out," she said again. "And make sure . . . I stay in." She swallowed. "They want me. I feel it. I'm supposed to . . . to go somewhere. After. When the change is complete. Don't let me."

"I won't."

She collapsed to her elbows, gripping her head with both hands, which resembled paws more and more. Her fingers had shortened, thickened, and they were covered with a fine coat of tawny, mottled fur. By the time she raised her head again, her eyes has started to lighten toward amber, her face to flatten and take on feline characteristics.

"Don't let me out," she said, in a voice like sandpaper on rock.

"Maybe I can—"

"No. There's—" She was cut off by another spasm and more grating of bone on bone. Her cry of pain skirled upward into a wild screech that was more cat than human. If I'd had to guess, I would have said she was becoming a bobcat, although that might have been wishful thinking. If she turned into a mountain lion, that bathroom door wasn't going to hold her back.

I opened the door once more and backed out, taking care not to let Emmy catch sight of her mom.

The girl stood near the door, clutching a blanket with both hands, tears on her face, her eyes like dinner plates.

"Is she all right? What's happening to her?"

"You were right, she's not feeling well."

"I felt the magic, Jay. When I was outside getting you. I felt it. Now tell me what's happening to Mommy."

The problem with preternaturally intelligent kids, is that they sound rational and mature beyond their years. But they're still kids, dealing with the fears and innocence and vulnerability that comes with being eight years old. Emmy might have known that a spell had been directed at her mom. She might even have been able to process on some level the fact that her mother was a were, and spent three nights out of every moon cycle in the form of a wild cat. But the distance between understanding those things and knowing that her mom was transforming into a bobcat in the next room . . . ? Well, for this night at least, that was a bridge too far.

On the other hand, lying to her didn't seem like a great option either, and so I chose to give her a version of the truth.

"You're right. There's magic involved, and what she's going through is hard for her. But she can handle it, and I'm certain that she's going to be okay once it's over."

"Does it hurt?" Emmy asked, sounding much more like a little girl.

"Yes, it does. But your mom is strong and brave. And in the meantime, I'm going to stay right here with you, all right?"

She only hesitated for an instant before nodding.

I walked to the television and switched it on, bumping up the volume enough that it would mask some of the noise coming from the bathroom.

As soon as the TV was on, Zach woke up. He'd slept through his mother's screams, but his ears seemed to be tuned to the little Sony speakers in that box. He climbed out of bed, blanket in one hand, zebra in the other, and a thumb in his mouth. I'm not sure I could have managed it all, but it didn't seem to phase him at all. He sat down on the floor in front of the TV and his sister joined him there. I flipped through the few channels we had, trying to find something vaguely appropriate. One of the stations was showing an old Western in those saturated tones that Hollywood used when film first flipped from black and white to color, and I decided that was the best we were likely to do.

After about a minute, Zach got to his feet and started toward the bathroom.

"Whoa, kiddo," I said, stopping him. "Um . . . your mom's in there."

"I have t' pee."

I could tell Emmy was watching me, but I kept my eyes on Zach. "How would you like to pee outside, in the middle of the night? The moon's up. You'll be able to see."

A grin crept over his face, and I could tell he liked the idea. But then the smile faded, leaving him chewing his lip.

"I can come with you," I said. "There's nothing to be scared of."

A high snarl from the bathroom, drew his gaze.

"Come on," I said, holding out my hand.

"I can go barefoot?"

"Of course. It's no fun if you don't go barefoot." If he stepped on a piece of glass, Gracie would kill me.

"Okay."

I took him outside, let him take care of his business, and then led him back into the room. He settled back on to the floor. If I'd had wipes or hand sanitizer or something, I would have cleaned his hands, but I had nothing. When he put his thumb back in his mouth, I cringed.

I thought about checking on Gracie, but there wasn't much I could do for her, and I don't think she wanted me to see her in were form. So I sat on the floor next to Emmy. Zach got up, stepped over me, and sat on my other side, the blanket tucked under his arm.

Every once in a while, another growl or cry came from the bathroom, and each time Emmy glanced up at me. But she and her brother stayed with me; neither of them went anywhere near the bathroom door. They might not have known that their mom was a were, but I had the feeling they had been through nights like this before, during the phasings. Kids with two weremystes for parents must have learned early on to entertain and fend for themselves.

After a while, both of them dozed off. And sometime between the credits for the Western and the start of whatever came on next, so did I. The next thing I heard was the opening of the bathroom door.

I opened my eyes and reached for my Glock, more out of habit than any intention to shoot Gracie, whatever form she was in.

But she was human again, naked, holding the tatters of her nightshirt in front of her. She faltered at the sight of us on the floor and her eyes met mine for just an instant. I looked away. After a moment, I heard her start forward again. The whine of the zipper on her bag was followed by the rustle of clothes.

"I'm decent," she said a minute or two later.

I faced her, watched as she bent to pick up Zach. She held him and kissed his forehead before laying him down in his bed. He didn't wake. Emmy did, though.

"Mommy!" she said, her voice thin and sleepy.

"Hey, sweetie."

"You're all right. Jay said you would be."

Gracie eyed me over the girl's shoulder. "Well, he was right, wasn't he?"

"What happened to you? Were you sick again, like you and Daddy are sometimes?"

"Something like that, yes."

"It sounded different this time."

"I know, sweetie. You need to sleep now."

"I'm not tired."

"Well, I am, and I bet Jay is too. So we're all going to sleep. Understand?"

"All right," Emmy said, sounding anything but willing.

I climbed to my feet. "I should go."

"Wait for me outside," Gracie said, her tone leaving no room for argument.

"Okay. Goodnight, Emmy."

I stepped to the door, but Emmy held out her arms toward me. The corners of Gracie's mouth twitched, though I couldn't tell if she was suppressing a smile or a scowl. I took Emmy from her and kissed her cheek.

"Goodnight, pumpkin."

She wrinkled her nose and smiled. "Pumpkin?"

"Yeah, that's what I call all my orange friends."

She giggled. "I'm not orange!"

"Hmmmm. Maybe not. But you look like a pumpkin to me. Now go to sleep, okay?"

"Okay. 'Night."

I left their room and walked halfway to mine before stopping and leaning against the motel wall. The desert air had cooled enough that I could see my breath, silver and insubstantial in the light of the moon. I still didn't have a shirt on, but somehow, after the warmth of the room and the heat of the kids dozing against me, I didn't mind the cold.

The moon's pull was magnetic. It almost seemed like it was drawing the thoughts from my head, leaving me dazed and tired and yet oddly at peace. I had no reason to believe that this phasing, when it began, would be any better or worse than others I had endured, but tonight at least, the moon felt . . . different somehow.

Gracie joined me a few moments later, wearing just a t-shirt and jeans, barefoot like I was. I expected her to yell at me for entering the bathroom against her wishes, but she said nothing. She leaned against the building beside me and tipped her face toward the moon, her eyes closed.

"You all right?" I asked.

"I think so."

"I would have thought you would ward your room. I'm glad you didn't."

"I did," she said. "I just cast the warding in a way that let you in. And I'm glad, too."

I hesitated, then said, "You should have told me that you're a were as well as a weremyste."

She opened her eyes and glowered at me. "I'm not sure I *should* have done anything as far as you're concerned. I never asked for your help, remember?"

I gazed back at her, silent, waiting.

Eventually she looked away and blew out a breath. "Boy, you bring out the worst in me."

"I don't mean to."

"Doesn't seem to matter." She eyed the moon again. "You're right, I should have told you. Most likely that's one of the reasons Fitzwater is after me. There aren't many of us."

"You're the first I've met."

"He probably thinks that Emmy will be the same."

"I'm not sure it matters what he thinks."

Her brow furrowed. "Meaning?"

"Fitzwater is an errand boy," I said, thinking of Marlon Brando and Martin Sheen. "He's dangerous and powerful and he scares the crap out of me. But he only does what Saorla tells him to. If someone wants you and Emmy it's her."

"Fine, *she* thinks Emmy will be like me. What difference does it make?"

"In the way you mean, it makes no difference at all," I said. "But if we're going to find some way to beat them, we have to understand exactly who we're up against. And as dangerous as Fitzwater might be, Saorla's ten times worse."

She eyed me, nodded.

"Tell me about the spell."

Gracie shrugged. "I was asleep when it hit me. But I could tell it was strong, and I knew as soon as I woke up what it was intended to do."

"Was it directed only at you? Could you tell?"

She started to answer, but stopped herself. "Maybe not," she finally said. "There was a . . . a vastness to the casting. I hadn't thought of this before, but it was too big to have been just for me. It was like a huge magical net."

"That sounds like Saorla. I wouldn't be surprised if she turned every were within five hundred miles of here. She's gathering them, hoping you'll answer her call with the rest. And when you don't, she'll have them fan out across the desert to find us."

"So what do we do?"

"We sleep. And then we keep moving."

"All right." But she didn't say goodnight, or walk away from me. "The kids like you. They trust you."

"Zach does. Emmy's still making up her mind."

Gracie dismissed this with a waved hand. "She's slower to trust than he is. She's like me that way. But she's starting to accept you, I can tell."

"Well, I'm glad. They're good kids."

She didn't answer right away. "You could take them back to Neil.

If you're right, and Saorla is determined to make me part of her army, maybe I can go to her and at least give Neil time to get the kids away from here. I can even give her . . . the other thing she's after."

Tears glistened on her cheeks. I had to resist the urge to wipe them away.

"That's a bad idea, Gracie. I understand the impulse, but Saorla won't be satisfied with just you. She wants you, the knife, and the kids as well. And if Neil has any ties to dark sorcerers, they might not be safe with him."

"To my parents then."

I considered my last conversation with Amaya. "That might not be entirely safe either. And once you give yourself over to Saorla, there's no telling what she might force you to do. Your best hope—" I gestured toward her room. "Their best hope, is to keep moving and keep fighting."

"I'm not sure I can. I'm tired . . ."

This last was almost lost in a sob. I put my arms around her, and she clung to me, crying against my chest. We stood that way for some time, until at last she pulled away a little and turned her face up to mine. I was aware, all of a sudden, of the thinness of her t-shirt, the fact that I wasn't wearing any shirt at all.

"I'm sorry," she whispered, her eyes shining with tears and moonlight.

I released her and took a deliberate step back. She ran a hand through her hair, looking away.

"I don't usually go to pieces like that."

"It's understandable," I said. "Some sleep will do you good."

"Right. Goodnight." This time she did spin away, the motion so abrupt she might have been fleeing.

I waited until she was in her room, and I heard the chain lock rattle against the door. I cast one last baleful glance at the moon and returned to my room, desperate for a bit of sleep myself. I should have known that it wouldn't come so easily.

"Ohanko!"

Namid stood in the center of my room, his waters roiled, his eyes gleaming bright, the color of bone.

"You are a fool!"

CHAPTER 16

I closed the door as gently as I could and faced him, resigned to the tongue lashing I knew was coming.

"You offered her a boon?" he said, in a voice that thundered like a waterfall.

Well, maybe not entirely resigned.

"I didn't offer her anything, Namid. You should know better. She wrung it out of me. If you want to yell at me, go ahead. But don't treat me like I'm an idiot. I had no choice."

"Of course—"

"I had no choice! It was all I could do to save Billie's life. And if you dare tell me that I should have let Billie die, I swear, I'll leave now and I'll never speak another word to you as long as I live."

This, of all things, seemed to calm him. "How you came to be beholden to her matters little," he said, his voice dropping. "You owe a debt, and I am powerless to help you."

"You've told me that before."

"I have, but never has it been more true. She has demanded recompense, as is her right. You have refused her once. Do so twice more, and all protections I have promised you are forfeit. It will be within her right to kill you, and I will be unable to intervene on your behalf."

"She wants me to hand over to her the woman and children in the room next to this one."

Namid stared past me, as if he could see through the wall to Gracie and the kids. Hell, for all I knew, he did exactly that. After all the years we'd known each other, I still had little sense of what the myste could and couldn't do.

"I understand why," he said, after a brief silence. "The woman is powerful, and the girl has uncommon promise. The boy is too young to read, but he could be a weremyste of consequence as well."

"The mother is both were and weremyste. Have you ever heard of that before?"

His watery brows rose. "I have, though it is rare."

"I think Saorla wants to add them to her army of weremancers."

"That is likely."

"I also think that the woman or her husband has the *Sgian-Bán*."

"*What?* Does she have it here?"

"I don't know where she has it, and it's possible that it's with the husband, though whether he knows it or not is an open question. There was a break-in at their home not so long ago. I think that Saorla's minions were hoping to steal it."

"This is all . . . unsettling," he said. "The *Sgian-Bán* should not be transported through your world like baggage."

"I know. I'm working on it. But whatever happens I won't give Gracie and the kids to—" I broke off, a cold sweat breaking on my brow. "You shouldn't be here," I said, low, urgent. "She can sense you, and she'll find us."

The scowl he sent my way made me feel like the dumbest rock on the planet. "I, too, prefer not to be treated as if I were an idiot. I have shielded myself. Saorla can no more find me than she can stop the moon from rising."

"She can't do that?" I gave a wan smile.

The myste smiled in response. "She cannot." His expression sobered. "I would never have said that you should let Billie die," he said. "She is dear to you, and so is dear to me."

"I'm sorry. I shouldn't have—" I shook my head, rubbed a hand over my face. "Long night."

"You were going to tell me that you will not let the woman and her children come to harm either."

He offered it as a statement, and I saw no need to answer.

"Which tells me that you mean to defy Saorla, to break your word."

"Would you expect me to do anything else?"

"No. You are a most difficult man. And a most honorable one. So what will you do?"

"I don't know yet. I'm open to suggestions."

"I would suggest you tread like the fox."

I grinned. "Yeah. Thanks."

"Sleep now, Ohanko. I will leave you."

"Do you sense any weres nearby?" I asked.

He raised his chin, like a wolf sniffing the air. "There are some within perhaps twenty of your miles. But none closer than that." He shifted his gaze toward the wall separating my room from Gracie's. "Except her."

I nodded. Twenty miles. And if Saorla had turned them, they were on foot or perhaps wing. We were probably safe for tonight. "Thanks."

"Ohanko."

I watched him, waiting. He appeared to be struggling with something. I wasn't used to seeing such conflicted emotions on his face.

"You smell of dark magic, of blood spells. I have warned you of the dangers. I know you face a difficult time, but you need to exercise more self-discipline."

I couldn't very well deny it. After a moment's pause, I nodded again.

He faded, leaving my room dark, save for the moonlight slanting past the old window curtains. I fell into my bed and was out almost as soon as my head hit the pillow.

It was well after eight o'clock when I woke to a whoop of laughter from next door. I had wanted to be out of here by this time, but given the night we'd had, I wasn't going to complain. I showered, dressed and packed up what little I had. But then I pulled out my phone and called Billie again.

"Good morning."

"Hi," I said. "You up for a road trip?"

"Really? You didn't seem so keen on the idea when we spoke yesterday."

"I know."

"So what's changed?"

"I need some things, and I'd like your help."

"You know that I didn't learn to cast spells since our last conversation, right?"

I laughed, though my chest tightened. I was taking a risk and putting Billie right in the middle of something dangerous, something I still barely understood. "I won't lie," I said. "This might not be such a good idea. But if you're willing, I'll do everything in my power to keep you safe."

"I know that. What do you need?"

I thought of the magical bomb with which Saorla had attacked us; I could still see Billie lying amid the wreckage, bloodied and unconscious. And I knew she still grappled with the emotional aftermath of that day. "It's been hard for you recently," I said. "If you don't feel that you can leave the house—"

"I went shopping for food yesterday."

"Well, good. But this is—"

"It's all right, Fearsson," she said. "When I have a purpose, it's easier. And if I can help you . . . Just tell me what to do. What do you want me to bring?"

I listed several things: the extra handgun I kept at home—the Smith and Wesson Bodyguard 380; extra ammo for that weapon, for my Glock, and for the Sig Sauer; another change of clothes; my tent and sleeping bag; her sleeping bag; another tent and three more sleeping bags for Gracie and the kids; and whatever snacks and drinks she could find at my place. Billie wouldn't like the idea of bringing me a pistol and bullets, and she really wouldn't like what I intended to do with the .380, but that couldn't be helped.

"Anything else?" she asked.

"I'm sorry about the expense of the camping gear."

"Stop it. What else?"

"If I can borrow some cash from you, that would be helpful, too."

"Of course. Where should I meet you?"

"You remember where I took you on our first date?"

"Like I could forget," she said, her voice warming.

I couldn't help but smile. "That's probably the safest place."

"Okay."

"Billie, there's a chance you'll be followed, either by the police, or by Saorla's friends, or both. If you get scared, or decide you can't do this, call me. I'll understand."

"I'll be fine. Anything else?"

I didn't respond right away. I'd never tried to cast a spell over such a distance, but Namid was always telling me that magic was an act of will, and that any spell was possible if I concentrated hard enough and envisioned it properly. Fortunately, my dad had made this last bit possible with the glamour he had crafted before I left his trailer. I envisioned the same metallic blanket he had cast over me, covering Billie, hiding her from Saorla and her weremancers. My father had cast his spell to conceal my magic; I took the spell a step further. I wanted her to be completely hidden. Seven parts to the spell: Billie, her car, her voice, the conjured blanket, Saorla, Fitzwater and his friends, and Billie again, safe and concealed. I repeated the elements in my head six times and once more, releasing the magic on the seventh recitation.

I felt it electrify the air around me, heard a crackling sound in my phone.

"Fearsson?"

"Yeah, I'm here."

"What did you do?"

"Did you feel something?"

"Something happened to the phone," she said. "And yeah, it felt like . . . I don't know. But I got goosebumps for a second, like a sudden chill."

"I cast a spell," I said. "I don't know if it will work, but if it does, you should be safe, or at least safer."

A pounding at my door made me jump.

"Jay? You all right?"

I opened the door. Gracie was there with the Ruger in hand. Seeing that I was on the phone, she frowned.

"Hang on, Billie." To Gracie I said, "I'm fine."

"I felt magic."

"That was me. Everything's okay. I promise."

Her frown deepened, but she seemed to relax fractionally.

"Billie, I'll see you later. I love you."

"Me, too. See you soon."

I closed the phone. "We're meeting Billie, and I had to cast a spell to . . . to shield her from prying eyes."

"Over the phone? You think it'll work?"

"I think it's better than nothing. And she felt something, so, yeah, it might have worked."

"Wait. Did you say we're meeting Billie? You're girlfriend Billie?"

My cheeks burned and I avoided her gaze. "I don't remember telling you she's my girlfriend."

"You told Emmy, in the truck."

"Oh, right. Well, yeah, her."

"You thinking we need a chaperone?"

I gave her a sharp look. She was grinning, although her cheeks were flushed as well. After a few seconds, I chuckled. "I figured a chaperone couldn't hurt."

"Last night was my fault," she said. "Sometimes after changing I'm . . . hungry, in more ways than one."

"It wasn't anyone's fault. And fortunately for both of us, we didn't do anything stupid. Billie's bringing me a few things from my house, and she might be able to help us. She's a lot smarter than I am, and she's not afraid of much."

"She a weremyste?"

"No."

Gracie raised an eyebrow. "Okay." When I didn't say more, she turned to leave.

"Wait."

She faced me again.

"Please don't tell her this, but the other reason I want her here is that I'm worried about her. I know it's dangerous to bring her into this, but like I told you yesterday, Saorla is threatening the people I love. My dad might be crazy, but he's a weremyste. He can ward himself if he has to. My best friend, Kona—she was my partner on the force when I was still a cop—she's not a weremyste, but she's always armed and she knows how to defend herself. Billie's smart and strong, but she doesn't have magic, and she doesn't own a weapon. So I prefer to have her with me, just in case."

Gracie nodded. "You should have said so in the first place."

We turned in our keys at the front desk, loaded up my father's truck, and started down the highway back toward Florence.

The drive to Sonoran Desert National Monument, where I'd taken Billie on our first date, would have been an easy one had I been willing to drive on the interstates. Avoiding them, however, made it a far more complicated trip, one that could have taken us unnervingly close to the city. The route I decided on was convoluted as hell, albeit scenic.

We had to stop for breakfast, of course, and later for lunch. I didn't know when Billie would reach the monument, but as we finished eating, she texted me.

"There. Sunset."

I smiled.

"What?"

"She's in the monument," I said, "at a spot where . . . at a spot I've been to before."

"Why are your cheeks so red?" Emmy asked.

Gracie laughed. "Because we're on our way to meet Jay's girlfriend."

Zach grinned and covered his mouth. Emmy smiled too, clearly pleased by this news. I thought once more of the way she'd responded in Organ Pipe, when Gracie and I pretended to be a couple.

"You have a girlfriend?" she asked.

"I told you I did. Remember?"

"Is she pretty?"

"Emmy!" Gracie said, frowning. "You know there are more important things than that, right?"

Emmy wrinkled her nose and shook her head. "Not to boys."

I stared at the road, doing my best not to laugh. "Wise beyond her years," I muttered.

Gracie sighed. "Tell me about it."

We drove into the monument a short while later. I spotted Billie's blue Honda parked by the trailhead where she and I started our evening hike so many months ago, and pulled in behind her car.

"Where is she?" Emmy asked, sitting up taller and craning her neck to see.

"We have to hike in a little bit."

The kids groused at this, but I promised them treats at the end of the walk, hoping that Billie wouldn't let me down.

As it happened, we didn't have to walk far. And that wasn't a good thing at all.

We were maybe two hundred yards down the trail when I heard footsteps approaching from the opposite direction. I slowed. The Sig Sauer was in my ankle holster, and I thought about drawing it. But then Billie rounded a bend in the trail. She was craning her neck to see back over her shoulder, and so didn't spot us at first. And when she faced forward and saw us, she gave a small, startled gasp. Then she recognized me and hurried forward.

"I think I'm being followed," she said. "Hi," she added, with a glance at Gracie. She did a quick double-take before focusing her attention on me.

"Followed by who?"

"It's not really a who. Or even a whom."

We shared a brief smile. She was chief of the grammar police, and proud of it.

"What, then?"

She shook her head, glancing back again. "You're going to think I'm nuts, but there was some kind of animal—a big one—and I swear it was watching me. I had hiked all the way out to that viewpoint, but I could hear it moving around in the brush and it kind of freaked me out, so I left. I think it followed me the whole way back."

"A were," Gracie said. She had her Ruger out.

"Possibly." To Billie I said, "Could it have been a coyote?" I knew a were who turned into a coyote—or a "ki-yoat" as he would have said it—but I couldn't imagine he was the only one in the Phoenix area, and I certainly wasn't ready to set out a bowl of kibble for this one.

"Maybe. It certainly sounded big enough. To be honest, coyote might be the best option."

I nodded peering past her into the brush. I didn't see or hear anything unusual, but I trusted Billie's instincts.

"Let's get back to the truck," I said.

If only it had been that easy.

A mountain lion slinked onto the trail from between a pair of mesquite trees, blocking our path to the parking area. I looked back and saw a pair of coyotes padding along the trail behind us, their yellow eyes fixed on the kids, their teeth bared. A mountain lion working with coyotes. It was almost enough to make me laugh.

Emmy let out a whimper.

"Fearsson?" Billie said, her voice low and tight.

"I know. Everybody stay still."

"The hell with that," Gracie said. She raised her Ruger, aiming it at the puma.

"No!"

I grabbed her arm, but she shook me off.

"That's a person, Gracie! It could have been—" I had intended to say, *It could have been you*, but at the last minute I remembered that the kids didn't know. "Anyone," I said. "It's not their fault."

I'm sure she knew what I was thinking, what I had been about to say. Still, she had her weapon trained on the cat, her hands steady, one eye closed. I was certain she would fire. But after a moment she muttered a curse and lowered the pistol. Not all the way, but enough. "So what do we do? Talk them into giving themselves up?"

"We cast," I said. "Non-lethal spells."

"They've seen us, and they'll tell their masters where we've been."

"Then we'll have to get far away from here. But we're not killing them."

"Fine," she said, spitting the word. A crafting tickled the air around us, and the mountain lion recoiled, snarling, its ears laid flat. But it didn't leave the trail.

I threw a spell at the coyotes, hitting them with the same magical two-by-four I used against the wolf outside the Casa del Oro Hotel. They reacted much the same way the puma did to Gracie's casting. They didn't like it, but they didn't tuck their tails and run.

Gracie adjusted her grip on the Ruger. "Now what?"

I know where you are, Justis Fearsson. I cannot see you, but I see the woman and her children. I see my weres.

"Saorla," I said. Her timing couldn't have been worse. Or better, I suppose, depending on your point of view.

You will have to kill them. The weres will not leave you of their own accord. You must kill them to escape. And we both know that you will not do this.

"What about her?" Gracie asked.

The cougar advanced on us, its mouth open, its belly scraping the trail. The coyotes crept closer as well.

"She knows where we are."

"I guess meeting your girlfriend wasn't such a great idea."

Billie glared. "Hey!"

"I don't think they followed Billie. They were here already. They were turned last night by that spell. They just happened to follow her, and then I think they sensed . . . others of their kind. Weres can do that, right?"

She cursed again. Emmy and Zach shared a look; their mom was going to owe them some money after this was over.

"If they come any closer I'm firing. I don't care—"

"Whether you kill them or merely wound them, they'll shift back to human form. And then you'll have assault charges to deal with, on top of everything else."

An idea came to me. Three elements. The coyotes, the path they were on, and a magical cage surrounding them. I chanted the elements in my head, and released the magic on the third repetition. Gracie eyed me, as did Emmy, but I kept my focus on the coyotes. They took two more steps toward us before meeting the conjured enclosure and flinching back. They tried again, but couldn't get past the invisible bars of my cage. They tried to go around the barrier, first one way and then the other, growing more frantic by the moment.

"What did you do?" Gracie asked.

"I put them in a cage."

I cast again, trapping the cougar the same way.

"That's not nice," Emmy said. "Animals don't like cages."

I didn't get a chance to respond. Pain flared in my head, as if someone had pierced my skull with a white hot poker. I think I groaned. I know I raised my hands to my head.

The weres are nothing. I demand that you give me the woman and her children. You owe me a boon! You cannot deny me what is rightfully mine!

"And you shall not."

This last I heard, as I would any spoken word. I opened my eyes and found myself on my knees. Saorla stood beside the puma, stroking the cat's massive head. I had a feeling she had done away with my conjured cage.

The necromancer looked just as I remembered her from our previous encounters. She wore a plain green dress of rough cotton, and a gray shawl, held in place by a silver clasp. Brown hair fell in soft waves to her shoulders, framing an oval face that was beautiful and disarming and utterly false. Her eyes were pale blue, like a hazed summer sky, and her lips were full, sensual. She was, I realized in that moment, very much like the moon: beautiful, remote, merciless. She watched me as I staggered to my feet, the smile on those lips conveying cruelty and amusement in equal measure.

"I'm guessing this is Saorla," Gracie said, still gripping her pistol.

"So I am," the necromancer said. "And you would be well advised to put away your weapon. Its bullets cannot harm me, and if you fire you might inadvertently hurt one of your children."

To her credit, Gracie didn't immediately lower the Ruger, but after a moment she did remove her finger from the trigger.

"She is lovely, Justis Fearsson. I see now why you have been reluctant to surrender her to me. Perhaps you thought to make her yours. A replacement for the other woman? Or a second lover? Are you so bold?"

Billie had moved closer to me, and now she bristled, her mouth opening. I touched the small of her back, trying to keep the movement as subtle as possible. When she glanced my way, I gave a small shake of my head, though I kept my eyes on Saorla.

Was it possible? The way the necromancer spoke it seemed she didn't know Billie was here. Could it be that the concealment spell I had cast over such a great distance had worked so well?

Magic is an act of will.

I heard the words as if Namid had whispered them in my ear. He had said them to me a thousand times. But until that moment, I had never truly understood. And though I knew that I loved Billie, I hadn't known how much. Until now.

"No, Saorla. I've kept her from you because you intend to hurt her, and her children, and I won't allow that. And just because you don't see Billie with me, that doesn't mean she's not in my heart all the time."

Gracie stiffened, clearly understanding. Billie gaped at me, but I knew she would understand as well. It was the kids I was worried about.

"Come here, child," Saorla said, speaking to Emmy.

Gracie grabbed hold of her daughter and pulled her close. "No way in hell," she said, snarling much as the mountain lion had.

I thought Saorla would threaten her, or perhaps even attack with a spell. Instead, she said, "I give you my word that no harm will come to her, or to your son, or even to you. And I promise as well that wherever I take her, you will accompany us." She smiled and nodded my way. "He has warned you against me, I know. And by taking that which is rightfully mine, you have given me cause to be angry. Yet still, I make this promise to you. I am not the creature of evil and hate he thinks me. I am very much like you. More powerful, of course, but I have borne children of my own. Long ago, yes, but as you would expect, such memories never fade." Another smile crossed her lips, though only for an instant. "And even if all of this was not true, you cannot hope to stop me from doing as I please." She squatted down, so that she was at eye level with Emmy. "Now, come here. Let me see you."

Still, Gracie wouldn't have let Emmy go if the girl hadn't peeked up at her and said, "It's all right, Mommy. She's not going to hurt me."

Gracie stared down at her and then turned my way. I nodded once, because I believed Saorla wouldn't harm Emmy, and also because I was desperate for anything that would distract the necromancer, even if only for an instant. Gracie stared daggers at Saorla, but she released Emmy.

Emmy walked to where Saorla stood, slowing a few paces shy of her, though she appeared to be more frightened of the mountain lion than of the woman.

"It is all right, child," Saorla said, scratching the cat behind one of its ears. "She is gentle if I command her to be so."

Emmy took another step. "Can I pet her?"

"Of course you can."

The girl closed the remaining distance, and after hesitating for a second, lifted her hand and patted the puma's head, which was nearly as high as her own.

"You are a brave soul, I can tell. What is your name?"

"Emmy."

Saorla frowned. "Emmy?"

"That's short for Emelia."

"I see." Saorla scrutinized her, taking in her hair, her face. She took one of the girl's hands in her own and examined it, back and palm. "You are very beautiful."

"Thank you. So are you."

Saorla clapped her hands together and laughed, high and unrestrained, completely unlike the hard, mocking laughter I had heard from her in the past. "What a charming child." She looked past

Emmy to Gracie. "I sense the power in her. You have as well, I'm sure. She requires proper training. She can be so much. Surely you understand this."

"When the time comes," Gracie said, "I'll teach her what she needs to know."

"You are neither powerful enough nor skilled enough to bring her to her full potential. She needs more than you can possibly give her."

"Listen to what she has to say."

Gracie rounded on me. "Are you—?"

I cast a quick look Billie's way, just with my eyes.

"—kidding me?" she said, completing the question. But all the fire had gone out of her words. She knew what I wanted her to do.

"The difference between Saorla and her kind, and those of us who oppose them is that they'll force you to do as they wish. We never will. So listen to her. Decide for yourself what's best for you and the kids."

"That is most wise of you, Justis Fearsson, despite your false characterization of me."

Gracie took a step in Saorla's direction, and so positioned herself in such a way as to block me, at least partially, from the necromancer's view. "Would I be with you when you trained her?" She reached out a hand to her son, who walked to her and took hold of it. "And would you train Zach, too?"

I didn't listen for Saorla's response. I glanced at Billie who was watching me, her cheeks pale, determination in her emerald eyes. I wanted to send her back to her car, and tell her to drive as far from here as possible. But I knew she wouldn't leave us, and I wasn't sure that she could get by the mountain lion without drawing the animal's attention. And that might well have been enough to break the spell that had rendered her invisible to Saorla.

She moved her hand deliberately, raising it so that I could see. She had out the key fob from her car, and her thumb rested on the red "panic" button that would set off her car horn.

Another smile passed between us.

CHAPTER 17

For all her power, Saorla was neither immortal nor immune to pain. She might have thought herself Namid's equal, and certainly her powers rivaled those of the runemyste. But she was more vulnerable than he to attacks from ordinary weremystes. I knew this because on more than one occasion during our previous encounters, I'd managed to wound her. Bullets from the Glock, an ashtray I'd thrown at her head with a spell, a crafting that thrust a magical blade through her heart: I'd used all of these against her with varying degrees of success. I had even managed to use a transporting spell to get her away from Billie, though in order to make that work, I'd had to grab hold of the necromancer and transport myself with her. I didn't expect she'd allow me to get that close to her again.

In fact, that was the problem with all of these assaults. Saorla was as canny as she was strong; I wouldn't have been surprised to learn that she remembered each of my attacks, and had already warded herself against them. Which meant I needed something new, a spell that would allow me to take advantage of the distraction Billie's car alarm would provide, without harming Gracie and the kids, who remained uncomfortably close to Saorla and the werecat.

I considered another transporting spell. As long as I didn't lunge for her or try to touch her in any way, she might not expect me to make the attempt. I could send her to the bluff where Billie and I had intended to meet. Or just beyond it. I liked the idea of sending her to a fall of a few hundred feet. If we got lucky the impact would kill her.

But transporting spells were tricky, and we were only going to get one chance at this. If the crafting failed, we were all screwed.

She would be warded against any direct attack spell, and even if she wasn't, whatever I might try—fire, a blade, even a chasm in the ground that would swallow her—would put the kids at risk.

When at last I came up with a spell that might work under these circumstances, I almost laughed at the simplicity of it. Saorla would call it crude, and so might Namid; it would be one thing they could agree on. But I thought it would work, and I couldn't imagine that she was warded against it.

I recited the elements in my head, and on the third go-round nodded to Billie.

She pressed the button. Her horn blared. Saorla straightened and spun, all in one elegant motion. And I released my spell.

I had thrown objects at her in the past. And ideally this time I would have transported her. So why not combine the two. Three elements: Saorla, the bluff where Billie and I watched our first sunset together, and a giant hand to throw her beyond that point.

The air around us sizzled. Saorla soared into the sky, flailing and screaming

"Bind the cat!" I shouted at Gracie, who was staring after the necromancer, her mouth hanging open.

I cast again, jailing the coyotes once more.

"The cat's secure!"

"Back to the cars then! I've got Zach."

Gracie grabbed Emmy by the hand. I swept Zach into my arms as I ran by. He let out a giggle. Again I thought that it must have been nice to be five years old.

Billie had thumbed the panic button again, to stop the horn. And in the relative quiet that followed, I heard the rhythmic thump of an approaching helicopter.

"Crap!"

Gracie looked back at me. "What—?" Her gaze shifted skyward; she'd heard it, too. "Damn it!"

Emmy scowled. "Quarter."

"They know the truck," I said. "And my warding is still on Billie's car. It'll be tight, but we leave the pickup here."

"We need our things."

"Right. Make it quick."

The helicopter was still some distance off, but the chop of its rotors grew louder with each pounding beat of my heart. I followed Gracie to the truck and almost walked into her when she stopped and turned. Her scowl reminded me of Emmy.

"Out of my way."

"What are you doing?" I asked.

"Buying us time."

I stepped away from her, watched as she closed her eyes and held a hand out, her wrist cocked much the way Fitzwater's had been the other day when he attacked us. Magic purred in the ground beneath us and an instant later that distant helicopter engine coughed and sputtered. I still hadn't spotted the chopper, and though I listened for an explosion or crash I heard neither.

"You might have killed them," I said, "and we don't know for certain who was in that helicopter."

"I wasn't going to wait to find out who it was, and if Fitzwater was in there I hope they're dead." She opened the door to my dad's pickup.

"I don't care if you kill Fitzwater, but there's a pilot in that chopper, and maybe other guys."

She wheeled, and before I knew it I had backed away from her. "I don't give a damn! They were coming after us, and there's only one road in and out of this place. I didn't like those odds. I can live with killing a pilot who agrees to work for Fitzwater. You should feel the same way."

I couldn't bring myself to argue. I stood there while she grabbed her bag and the kids' things from the pickup. When she was done, I retrieved my backpack and locked up the truck.

We climbed into the Honda, Billie behind the wheel, me in the passenger seat, Gracie and the kids in back. While Billie steered us toward the monument entrance, I scanned the sky, just in case they had found some way to overcome Gracie's spell. I had to resist the urge to cast my dad's glamour on Billie's car again. The magic was still working. Another casting would be superfluous and, more to the point, might draw Saorla's notice, or Fitzwater's. I knew all of this. But sitting in the car doing nothing was almost more than I could bear.

"Is everyone all right?" I asked, looking back at Gracie and the kids.

Zach nodded, his thumb in his mouth, the stuffed animal tucked under his arm. Emmy appeared none the worse for wear, but her cheeks were flushed and she glowered my way.

"She wasn't that mean," she said, sounding sullen. "You didn't have to hurt her." It took me a moment to realize she was talking about Saorla.

"I'm sorry, Emmy, but I did. She seemed nice, I know. She's charming and she's pretty, and I think she genuinely liked you. But she doesn't want what's best for you, or for your mom and brother."

"Do you?"

Gracie laid a hand on the girl's leg. "Emmy—"

"It's all right," I said. I shifted my gaze back to Emmy. "Yes, I do. That's why I've been helping you. Saorla and I are on opposite sides of what you might call a war, a magical one."

Zach removed his thumb from his mouth. "A real war?"

"Yeah, a real war. People have died. Men and women who work for Saorla have killed. That silver-haired man in the helicopter—the one who chased us in the desert the other day—he works for her."

I wanted to say more, but Saorla chose that moment to let herself back into my mind.

I grunted through the agony, was aware of Billie saying my name. But I could do nothing more than cradle my head in my hands. It felt as though the necromancer had poured gasoline into my skull and struck a match. Torment. The pain consumed me, blinded me, took away all other senses. I couldn't say whether I screamed or writhed or begged someone to kill me and end the anguish. I wanted to do all of those things. I have no idea how she didn't kill me with whatever magic she was using.

Apparently the thought had entered her mind, as well.

I ought to kill you for your effrontery. You dare to use such a spell against me? You deserve to die.

Then kill me, I thought back at her. I was incapable of speech, or I would have spoken the words aloud.

First you will deliver the woman and her children. Then you will die.

I've already told you I won't.

Aye, so you have. Three times now you have refused me. You have broken our agreement. Namid'skemu can protect you no longer. You are mine to do with as I please. So is your father, and the woman. I could hear the relish in her voice, could picture the triumphant gleam in her eyes. *You will suffer for what you have done. And in the end your defiance will be as meaningless as your promise, for I shall have the woman and her babes regardless. They will be part of a great army that will destroy the runemystes. You are powerless to prevent this. You always have been.*

In my mind, I shook my head. *As Namid would say, that has yet to be scried. And this seems as good a time as any to tell you that I know the real reason you're after them. I know what you're looking for, and you're not going to find it. Neither will Fitzwater. I'm going to get that blade before you do, Saorla, and I'm going to give it to Namid. He'll know how to destroy it.*

This last was a bluff. Namid had already told me that it couldn't be destroyed. But she didn't need to know that, and I didn't give her a chance to say more. Frankly, I was sick to death of listening to her. I didn't want to use blood for another spell. I hadn't forgotten Namid's warning—*Weremystes who use blood for spells soon find themselves relying on blood*—or his remark from the previous night about how I smelled of dark magic. I even entertained the idea of using the magic Gracie and I had discussed, of trying to draw upon some other source of power. But I didn't know how, and I wasn't sure this was the best time to experiment. I knew only that I had to end the pain and get her away from me, from us.

I bit down hard on my tongue, tasting blood. And with my last bit of strength, I cast a warding unlike any I had tried before. This was no simple shield spell. I pictured a steel wall around my mind, and I imagined it charged with power, like an electric fence. My brain, the barrier, the power coursing through it.

As soon as I released the magic, Saorla cried out, sharp, high-pitched, and abruptly cut off.

I exhaled, only realizing then that it had been some time since I last drew a breath. The pain was gone, though the memory of it was enough to make me keep my head perfectly still.

The car was moving. Good. Billie hadn't stopped.

"Are you all right?" she asked. It was a measure of how much we'd been through together that the words came out even and low. She hadn't panicked. She rarely did.

"I think so." My words, on the other hand, sounded raspy and weak, as if they had been spoken by the world's oldest weremyste.

"What happened?" Gracie.

"Saorla wasn't amused by my spell. I think she intended to kill me."

"So why aren't you dead?"

I shrugged, winced at the pain that lanced through the top of my skull. "I managed a warding that drove her away."

"I'm sorry, Jay," Emmy said in a choked voice.

I opened my eyes and found her gaze with my own. My vision swam and even that tiny bit of movement brought agony, but I didn't care. "You have nothing to be sorry for, Emmy."

Tears streaked her face. "I didn't know she'd hurt you."

"Of course you didn't."

"I shouldn't have . . . I'm sorry."

"It's—"

Gracie cut me off with a raised hand. "You shouldn't have what?" She asked, sitting forward so she could look her daughter in the eye. "What did you do, Emmy?"

Emmy wiped her face, but more tears fell. "She seemed so nice. I didn't think she could hurt someone like she hurt Jay. Really I didn't."

"What did you do?" Gracie asked again, biting off the words.

"She spoke to me. Not with her mouth. I heard her voice in my head. And she could hear me, too. She asked about Daddy, and where we lived. She wanted to know where we had been and where we were going next."

"And you told her."

"I thought it would be all right. She had a nice smile and she . . . she said nice things to me."

"What else did she ask? What did you tell her?"

"That was all. Where we lived, and where we'd been. I think she wanted to ask me more. We were still talking when Jay made her fly away."

Gracie exhaled, concern in her dark eyes.

"I'd rather she didn't know where we'd been," I said. "She might be able to learn more about your . . ." I faltered knowing that Emmy was weighing every word. "About your magic by visiting the motel. But they already knew we were at Organ Pipe. All things considered, it could have been worse."

Gracie nodded and turned back to Emmy. "You have to be more careful, Emmy. You saw that I didn't trust her, that Jay didn't trust her. You heard the things she said. You need to have faith in us. You have to recognize that we know what's best for you and Zach. Saorla might have seemed nice, but obviously we thought she was dangerous. You should have respected that."

Emmy nodded, tears still spilling from her dark eyes.

Gracie took a deep breath, then gathered Emmy in her arms and let her cry.

"So where are we going?" Billie asked some time later, breaking a long silence. Zach stared out the window, his thumb back in his mouth. Emmy had fallen asleep in Gracie's arms.

"We'll keep heading west," I said. "Toward Painted Rock State Park. There's some open desert there, and that's what we need right now."

"All right. Then I should probably get on I-8."

"No!" Gracie and I said at the same time.

Billie raised an eyebrow. "O-kay," she said, drawing out the word. "Care to explain that?"

"We think Saorla and her friends are watching the interstates. Magically. We've been doing everything we can to avoid them."

"Then I'm going to need directions."

"Right. Are there maps in the car?"

She glanced my way and shook her head in disapproval. "My phone's in my bag. And it's time you traded in your flip phone for something more suited to this century."

"Yes, ma'am."

We stopped for food outside of Gila Bend and then followed backroads to Painted Rock Road. It was a slow drive, but we didn't see Saorla or Fitzwater. Late in the afternoon, with the sun gilding the desert in shades of gold and orange, we reached the entrance to the state park. The quality of the road had deteriorated steadily, and it was now little more than a narrow strip of ancient asphalt, smooth enough, but desolate and empty.

"Keep going," I said.

Billie's brow creased. "But I thought—"

"I want open desert, and, if possible, no other people."

A few miles past the park, that asphalt road gave way to dirt and gravel, cut across some irrigated farmland, and crossed the mostly-dry bed of the Gila River. Just beyond the river bed, we came to a rutted dirt track that descended into an arid, shallow valley.

I glanced back and saw no one behind us. "Turn here."

Billie shot me a dirty look. "You're buying me new struts."

She drove us down the rutted road, keeping to about five miles per hour. I could hardly blame her; the road was bad, filled with huge potholes and washboard stretches. Even at that speed, we bounced and bucked like a supermarket kiddie ride.

After we had gone perhaps a mile and could no longer see the main road, I suggested that we stop and get out. The kids were a little green around the gills, and I didn't want to pay for the struts *and* an upholstery cleaning.

"What are we even doing here?" Gracie asked, stretching her back and surveying the terrain, which was pretty desolate, even for an inveterate desert lover like me.

"Lying low for a while," I said. A half-truth. I glanced at Billie across the top of the car. "Were you able to find all the stuff I asked you to bring?"

She nodded, though her expression soured. "One of your neighbors watched me like a hawk. I think she knew I didn't belong there. And you know I don't like having anything to do with guns."

"Don't worry about the neighbor. The glamour I cast shielded you from the people who can hurt us; the rest don't matter. And I'm sorry about the pistol, but we need it out here."

"Who for?" Billie asked. The unwitting straight man.

"You, of course."

She blinked.

I walked to her side of the car, and put my arms around her waist. "You told me during the summer, after all that we went through then with Saorla, that it was time you learned to defend yourself. Do you remember?"

"Yes," she said, speaking softly. "I didn't think you did."

"You were still recovering from the explosion, and more recently you've been contending with the PTSD. But I haven't forgotten, and I think it's long past time we got started."

"But does it have to be a . . . a weapon?"

"It should be lots of things. If I could teach you spells, I would. I'm not qualified to teach you self-defense, though I'll train with you whenever you want. But I can teach you to shoot. I'm good at that. And I have a feeling Gracie can help, too."

She didn't appear pleased, but she shrugged and said, "All right."

"I'm hungry!" Zach said, to no one in particular. Apparently his queasiness from the ride had vanished.

Billie grinned. "I guess we should break out the snacks first."

It soon became clear that Billie had taken to heart my instructions to raid my pantry. In addition to a half-eaten bag of chips, some pretzels, a jar of almonds, several bottles of juice, and a box of dry cereal, she had brought a loaf of bread, peanut butter, and my prized cache of chocolate-hazelnut spread.

While the kids feasted, Gracie kept her distance, her arms crossed, her gaze continually flicking in the direction of the main road.

"You hungry?" I called to her.

She shook her head. "Not really." But she wandered back in our direction anyway, still checking the horizon periodically.

"I don't think we were followed," I said.

"That doesn't mean they can't find us."

Billie approached her and held out a hand. "We haven't been formally introduced. I'm Billie Castle."

"The blogger?" Gracie said, her eyes widening a little.

"That's me."

Gracie turned my way. "You didn't tell me your girlfriend was a celebrity."

"Wait," I said to Billie, "you have a blog?"

She smirked.

"You're famous?" Emmy asked, chewing on a bite of peanut butter and chocolate sandwich.

"Just a little bit."

"It's nice to meet you, Billie," Gracie said. "I'm Gracie Davett. And you've met Emmy and Zach."

"Yes."

For a moment neither of them spoke and at last, lacking anything else to do, Billie took a pretzel from the open bag.

Gracie toed the dirt. "Look, I'm sorry for what I said back on the trail. I was scared and . . . I don't know how the weres found us, but I'm sure it wasn't your fault."

"Thanks."

"You can ask Jay; I'm not the easiest person to get along with, and I get downright mean when I'm scared for my kids."

"That's understandable. I'm certain I'd be the same way."

They lapsed into another silence, eyeing each other. I had the feeling they were never going to be best friends, but I also thought that they could work together if and when they had to.

"I'm going to teach Billie to shoot," I said. I pointed north, toward a section of the riverbed. "We'll go over there and obviously we'll aim away from here. But keep the kids close, okay?"

"Yeah, sure."

I took the .380 and ammo from the trunk of Billie's car and walked in the direction of that spot I'd pointed out. Billie walked with me.

"She's nice," Billie said, so that only I could hear.

"You think?"

She exhaled. "Not really, no. But from what you've told me, she's been through a lot." She peered up at the sky, which was deep blue and empty of clouds. "She doesn't seem to like me very much."

"It takes a while to get past her defenses."

"Have you?"

I shrugged. "Sometimes it seems like I have. Other times, not so much."

"She's beautiful."

I stopped, and Billie did, too.

"Something on your mind?" I asked.

She stared off to the side for a few seconds before meeting my gaze straight on. "She's *very* beautiful. Are you going to tell me you didn't notice?"

"No, I'm not going to tell you that. And I'll even admit that things got a little awkward between us last night, after she took her were form and then shifted back. Apparently the change leaves her a little . . ."

"Randy?"

"Good word."

"So what happened?"

"Absolutely nothing. And that's how I wanted it. I promise."

She blew out another breath. "Well, good."

"You believe me?"

"Yes, I do. Really." She kissed me. "Now, let's go shoot something."

I laughed.

We found what appeared to be a safe spot, and I began her first lesson. I named the various parts of the pistol and showed her how to thumb the safety on and off, put in a magazine, and chamber a round. I also taught her the basic commandments of firearm safety: always assume a weapon is loaded, keep the muzzle pointed in a safe direction, never put a finger on the trigger until ready to fire.

I could tell she was intimidated by the weapon, which I didn't want. Respecting a firearm is one thing; being afraid of it is quite another.

But to my surprise, once we started shooting, she did really well, better than I did the first time I shot with my dad so many years ago. At first, she was jerking the weapon each time she pulled the trigger, and she missed the crude targets I set up low and right. But once we corrected that, it turned out she had a knack for shooting. She couldn't have been more surprised.

I let her try the Glock, but she didn't like it. Too powerful, too loud. She loved the Sig Sauer, but I wanted to keep that one with me as a backup. And she seemed comfortable enough with the .380.

As we walked back to where Gracie and the kids waited for us, she still held the weapon. The magazine was empty, and I'd had her check to make sure there was no round in the chamber. She kept looking down, as if continually surprised to see a firearm in her hand.

"I enjoyed this more than I wanted to," she said.

"It's kind of fun, isn't it?"

"Yes," she said, making it sound like an accusation. "I have a progressive blog to maintain, Fearsson. How am I supposed to rail against the NRA after this?"

"That's easy. The guys who run the NRA are idiots. But that doesn't make the owners of firearms idiots. And it doesn't make all guns bad."

"You mean weapons."

I grinned. "Obi Wan has taught you well."

"You two done making noise?" Gracie asked as we drew close to the car. The kids were playing some game that involved throwing rocks at the lobes of a prickly pear.

"Yeah. Sorry we kept you waiting."

Gracie waved off the apology. "How'd she do?"

"She did well. We've increased our little army by fifty percent."

"Good. When do we get to fight something?"

I chuckled. "Not yet. We're going to get ourselves settled in a campsite, and then I have a couple of errands to run."

"No," Gracie said, shaking her head. "We're not splitting up."

"We have to. And you didn't mind sending me off for dinner last night."

"That was different," she said. "I hadn't met Saorla yet."

"I know. I won't be gone long."

"But—"

"Gracie, I'm heading to 620." In answer to her puzzled expression, I said in a hushed voice, "Phoenix police headquarters. Unless you want to be booked for a couple of magical murders, you can't come with me."

She eyed the kids, who hadn't heard what I said. "It was self-defense."

"I know that. My old partner knows that, too. But it doesn't change the fact that you're wanted. I need to talk to her, find out where her investigation is and what she might have learned about Fitzwater." I had other people to see as well, but I didn't think it would be such a good idea to mention my other errands.

I'd had enough of reacting and running. I felt like I was playing the weak end of a chessboard endgame, my king dodging and weaving, just trying to stay alive. That might work for a few moves, but eventually I was going to lose. The time had come to change the dynamic. I needed more information, and I was ready to stir things up a bit. But I couldn't do much of what I had in mind with Gracie by my side.

"Fine," she said, after chewing on what I'd said. "We'll keep busy. You play poker?" she asked Billie.

"A little. I take it you're good."

"I'm okay. Emmy will take you for everything you're worth. It'll be fun. We'll play for M&M's."

Billie smiled. "All right."

"Before we get to that," I said, "I need a few minutes alone with Gracie."

Billie simply nodded and said, "All right." But Gracie studied me, her scowl conveying a mix of fear and hostility.

I walked back toward the makeshift shooting range, knowing that she would follow, and purposefully keeping within sight of Billie and the kids.

"Billie seems nice," Gracie said, once we were out of earshot of the others.

"She said the same about you." I didn't bother mentioning that she had retracted the compliment as soon as I challenged it.

"She calls you Fearsson."

I stopped and faced her. "Yeah. What of it?"

"I did, too, at one point. The way you reacted, I figured you didn't like it. But you didn't want *me* calling you that."

"It's her name for me," I said.

"I get that. And you were afraid that things between us were straying into dangerous territory."

"This isn't what I wanted to talk about."

"No shit."

"How did you get the knife, Gracie?"

She eyed me for a breath, then scanned the horizon again, a hand raised to shade her eyes. "That's what you wanted to discuss?"

"I need to know."

"I'm not ready to talk about this."

"We're running out of time."

Her gaze met mine. "But we're not out yet. What else did you want to ask me?"

I shook my head. "I'm not letting you off that easy. What do you intend to do with it?"

"I've already told you—"

"*We are talking about this now!*" I shouted it at her, without regard for who might hear me. I didn't care if Emmy and Zach never spoke to me again because I was mean to their mom. I didn't care if Billie thought me a bully for speaking to Gracie this way. I'd had enough. "I have risked jail for you. I've put my life on the line. I've endured an attack from Saorla that nearly made my brain explode. And I've been willing to do it because I don't want any harm to come to those kids. But you *will* answer these questions."

She opened her mouth, and I stopped her with a raised finger that made her flinch.

"I swear to God, if you tell me that you didn't ask for my help, I'm leaving you here in the middle of fucking nowhere and taking your kids back to your parents."

I wasn't sure I could follow through on the threat—Gracie was as powerful a weremyste as I, maybe more.

It seemed, though, that the threat was enough.

"I promise you it's safe," she said, her voice low.

"Where?"

"I won't tell you that."

"What are you going to do with it?"

She squinted up at that sun. "I don't know. Honestly."

"How did you get it?"

Her cheeks blazed red. "I won't tell you that either."

A thought came to me, but for now I kept it to myself. "It should be destroyed," I said instead.

"A few days ago I would have said you were crazy for even thinking it. Something that old, that powerful? Destroying it . . ." She shook her head again. "I couldn't have even imagined it."

"And now?"

"And now I'm starting to think you might be right. I'm not there yet, but I don't think Saorla and her bunch should ever have it. And I don't want to spend the rest of my life running away from them, trying to hold on to it."

"I can help you with it," I said. "Together, we can destroy it." I thought of Namid. "Or maybe we can give it to someone who can keep it safe."

"I'll think about it. Really."

She wasn't ready to give in, and I didn't have the time to convince her. "All right," I said, sighing the words. I took a step back toward where we'd parked. "We should probably get going."

Gracie didn't move. "You already have helped. I know I'm a pain in the ass. But you've helped a lot, and I'm grateful."

"Thanks."

We walked back to where Billie was waiting.

"Everything all right?" she asked.

"Fine," I said. "Let's get going."

Gracie rounded up the kids and lured them into the car with a promise of snacks once we were back on the main road.

As we drove, Billie complained again about the abuse of her struts. I tried to tell her that the car would be fine.

"Yeah right," she said. "There's no way you would have done this in your car."

"Well, no. But that's different. The Z-ster is almost forty years old. It's vintage." Only as I said the words, did I remember my father saying much the same thing about his truck. His beloved truck, which was still sitting in Sonoran Desert National Monument. I hoped.

"I'm sorry," Gracie said from the back seat. "The Z-ster?"

I twisted in my seat to look at her. "That's my car. It's a 1977 280Z."

"The Z-ster," she said again. "That has got to be the stupidest name for a car I've ever heard."

"Thank you!" Billie said, in a way that made it sound like she'd been thinking the same thing forever.

"Hey, wait a minute!"

"Sorry, Fearsson, but she's right. It's a dumb name."

"It is not!"

"Yeah," Gracie said, "it really is. Why not name it something normal that starts with 'Z'? Like . . . Zelda."

Billie nodded. "I like that."

"I don't."

"Zana is nice," Billie said. I think she was pretending she hadn't heard me.

"Zoë," Emmy said. "That's a friend of mine's name."

"Zeeber!" Zach said, lifting his zebra and grinning ear to ear.

Even I had to laugh at that. I had a feeling that before the day was out, the Z-ster would have a new name.

We found an RV campground outside of Gila Bend that also allowed tent camping. It wasn't too expensive, the bathrooms were reasonably clean and included showers, and the tent sites were some distance away from the RV spaces. I would have preferred to be back in Organ Pipe, or somewhere in the Superstition Wilderness, but all things considered, it wasn't too bad a spot. And I liked the idea of staying in a mix of motels and campsites. Anything to keep Saorla and her friends guessing.

Still, as an added precaution, I decided to cast that glamour again, this time on Gracie and the kids. It had worked for Billie, and I hoped it might work for them, too. The complicating factors were Gracie's magic and Emmy's potential, which, to a being like Saorla, must have been like beacons on a dark night. I didn't know if any spell I cast would be enough to hide them. I had to try, though. I told Billie and Gracie as much.

"You're going to cast it on yourself, as well, right?" Billie asked.

"Actually, I'm not."

"Fearsson—"

"Why not?" Gracie's question cut across whatever objections Billie had intended to raise.

"Because the spell as I cast it on Billie would keep you from being seen not only by Saorla, but also by Fitzwater and other weremancers." I paused searching for the right words, trying to keep what I had to say as vague as I could. "And it's possible that I'll need to speak with a few of them to get the information I need. They have to be able to see me."

I watched Gracie for her reaction to this, but she seemed to have moved on already, which was fine with me.

"I've never used a glamour like this on a person," she said. "If it works, the kids and I will be invisible to Saorla and the rest, like Billie was on the trail?"

"That's the idea. The effect won't last forever; this isn't a permanent solution. I'm one weremyste, and a limited one at that. Saorla will find a way past my crafting eventually. But for right now it does seem to be working."

"All right. But you should cast it on all of us, not just the kids and me. Or better yet, teach me to cast it and I'll do it myself." She grinned, dark eyes dancing. "It could be a handy spell to know."

"Billie's already protected, and like I said, I don't want to be. At least not yet. And I think I have to be the one to cast it. My dad put a glamour on me, and I put an even stronger one on Billie. They both worked. I'm not as convinced that I could cast the spell on myself and have it be as effective."

"But you don't know that for certain."

"No. I'm guessing, and this isn't the time to test alternate theories. I need to get going. I won't cast the spell without your permission, but I'd like to do it."

Gracie shrugged, nodded. "Yeah, sure. Go ahead."

She called the kids over and I cast the spell, reciting the elements to myself exactly as I had when I crafted Billie's warding, so that Gracie and the kids would be completely concealed. It took less than a minute. When I had finished, the kids ran off to play once more, and Gracie moved away, perhaps sensing that Billie and I wanted time alone.

"I wish you'd let Gracie put that same spell on you," Billie said, wrapping her arms around me, and putting her head to my chest.

"I can't."

"So you said. But you were keeping something from us."

"Only from her," I said, dropping my voice. "I'm going to see her husband, and I need to be able to question him. The problem is, I don't know if he's working for Saorla, so I can't make myself invisible to her servants."

CHAPTER 18

I helped Billie set up our tent, then left to drive back into the city. I had only been away from Phoenix for a couple of days, but it felt much longer. Already I had grown accustomed to life without smog and bumper-to-bumper traffic. The car was too quiet. I missed the kids' chatter, which was as ridiculous as it was true. I'd grown attached to them; I'd have given my life to keep them safe. After two days. It made me a bit more understanding of Gracie's combativeness. If they were mine, I'd have behaved exactly the same way.

I was driving against the worst of the early rush-hour traffic and reached downtown Phoenix before the mass exodus from business and office buildings began in earnest. I parked a couple of blocks from 620, and walked to the building, keeping an eye out for weres and unnaturally good-looking weremancers. I didn't go inside, but dialed Kona's number while standing out front.

"Hey, stranger," she said. "Where are you?"

"Downstairs. Let's talk."

She told me she'd come right down and ended the call. Minutes later, she and Kevin emerged from the building. Kona spotted me right away, but she didn't raise a hand in greeting or call my name. Instead, she and Kevin walked away from me, and at the nearest corner turned, vanishing from view. I followed.

They were waiting for me halfway down the side street.

"I feel like I'm in a bad movie," I said.

227

Kona's expression didn't change. "Yeah, well, this is your fault, not mine."

"What did I do?"

"Where's Gracie Davett?"

When I didn't answer, she nodded. "That's what you did. You're harboring a fugitive, Justis. You're an accessory after the fact. I should take you in now."

"If all that's true, you should. But since you can't prove a damn thing, we both know you're not going to. And since you believe as I do that she was acting to protect herself and her kids, you're just as glad. So cut the shit, Kona."

She pursed her lips, staring down at the sidewalk. "Are they safe?"

"Who's asking? You or the PPD?"

"We're asking," Kevin said. "Off the record."

"Yeah, they're safe. We had a run in with the silver-haired gentleman who killed Merilee Guilford and Burt Kendall. We were lucky to get away. And earlier today we had to fight off Saorla and a couple of her werepets."

"Saorla?" Kona said. "You mean that crazy woman who destroyed your father's trailer last summer?"

"One and the same. You're not the only ones trying to track down Gracie and her kids. By the way, the vampire's name is Lionel Fitzwater. At least that's the name he gave me. It could be an alias."

"Well, it's more than we had. Man's like a ghost; there's no record of him anywhere. So, thanks."

"What about the husband?"

She lifted a shoulder. "What about him? He's still anxious to have his kids back, and we still have no clear evidence to support a domestic violence charge."

"You won't. I was wrong about that."

Her eyebrows went up. "Kevin, make a note of the time and day; Justis has admitted to being wrong about something."

I looked away, grinning. "Gracie is a were," I said. "I'd bet good money that her injuries have coincided with the full moon. The change takes a toll, and running wild through the desert brush will leave some cuts and scrapes."

"Again, thank you. This why you came in today? To help us with our investigation?"

I met her gaze again. "I came in to tell you that I don't like us being on opposite sides of a case, and yes, to give you what little information I have."

"I don't like it either. But at some point I have to pick up my badge again and be your former partner instead of just your friend. She might have killed in self-defense, but you and I don't get to decide that. Judges and juries make those determinations. And in the meantime, you're helping a woman who's wanted for a double homicide."

"The minute she's arrested, her kids lose the only chance they have of staying free. Gracie's parents can't protect them, and I'm not sure which side of this Neil Davett is on."

"Then you might want to find out."

I nodded. "I was already planning to. But before we get to that, let me tell you what I've learned about Burt's murder." I described for them my encounter with Lucas Quinn's widow and granddaughter.

"What is it these people are after?" Kona asked.

"It's an ancient stone knife." I gave them a description of the *Sgian-Bán*, though I didn't think there was much chance they'd ever find it. "It's imbued with magic, and in my circles it's about as powerful a weapon as you can imagine."

"Do you have any idea where it is?"

"I don't. But I'm sure Gracie knows, and maybe Neil, too. That's one of the reasons Saorla and her bunch are after her."

"One of them . . ."

"Gracie's powerful, and her daughter shows signs of being something really special."

"So you're going to talk to the husband?"

"That's my plan. Gracie's parents, too. Do you happen to have an address for them?"

She twisted her mouth. "Am I on your payroll now?"

I said nothing. Since leaving the force, I'd done plenty of free work for the PPD on cases involving magic. Kona knew this.

She dug her notebook out of her blazer pocket, found the Trejos' address and read it to me. It turned out Marisol and Eduardo lived in Chandler, not all that far from my place. I jotted the address down in my own notebook, so much like Kona's it was scary, and started to walk away.

"Thanks, Kona. I'll share with you anything more I find out about

Burt, and about the rest of this as well. If you learn anything of note about Fitzwater, let me know, all right?"

"Officially? No way. Unofficially, of course I will."

"I appreciate it. And stay away from him. He's not someone you want to mess with."

"Him and Saorla both, huh?"

"Welcome to my world, partner."

I hurried back to Billie's car, satisfied that Kona and I weren't completely at odds. I knew that she couldn't stop looking for Gracie, and she seemed to understand why I wasn't ready to turn the woman in. We weren't on the same side, but at least we weren't working at cross purposes.

I drove down to Chandler and soon found the Trejos' home, a modest ranch house in a solidly middle-class neighborhood. I put on the blinker and started to pull over to the curb, but as I did, all kinds of alarms went off in my head. I pulled away from the curb again and drove on, scanning the street more closely. It took me a few seconds to spot them, but once I did, I was amazed I had missed them in the first place.

The street was being watched by Jacinto Amaya's men. How else could I explain the presence of three Lexus sedans on a single city block, in a part of town where the average homeowner made less in a year than each car cost?

I pulled over a block down, wondering what to try next. I had a feeling Amaya's men wouldn't let me anywhere near the house, but I wasn't sure why they would be guarding the Trejos' home in the first place. Did they think Marisol and Eduardo were in danger, too?

Or does Amaya think the Sgian Bán *is here?*

I got out of the car and walked back to their house, expecting at any moment to be accosted by Rolon and Paco, or some other pair of guys every bit as huge and menacing. But no one stopped me, which told me all I needed to know.

I approached the front door, wary, the back of my neck itching, and rang the bell. Marisol answered, the aroma of cooking onion, garlic, and cumin wafting out onto the front landing.

"Yes? Can I help—?"

She broke off, narrowing her eyes as she stared at me through the screen door.

"Jay Fearsson, Missus Trejo. The private detective Jacinto Amaya hired—"

"Have you found them?"

"I know they're safe. I don't wish to say more right now."

"But why—"

"Please. You have to trust me. I'm sorry to show up unannounced, but I have a couple of questions for you."

"Yes, of course." She pushed open the screen. "Please come in."

I stepped into the house and was enveloped by the aromas. My stomach growled, even though I wasn't hungry. Or hadn't been. "Whatever you're making smells incredible."

Her smile was forced, but still I saw Gracie's face in hers. "Thank you. If you don't mind speaking in the kitchen, I'm in the middle of making dinner."

"That'll be fine."

I followed her through a small carpeted dining room to the kitchen, which was small as well, with red Formica counters, a stainless steel sink, and an oval table in the corner. A pot and several pans sat on the range.

She crossed to the stove and stirred whatever was in the pot. "Please tell me about my daughter," she said, her back to me.

"As I said, she and the children are safe. I don't know yet when they'll be able to come home, but I hope you won't have to wait too much longer."

"You can't tell me where they are?"

"I don't think that would be wise."

She glanced my way and nodded. There were tears in her eyes.

"Has Neil come by since last we spoke?"

"Neil? No, why would he? He knows how we feel about him."

"Has anyone else come by? Have you heard from Jacinto Amaya, or from anyone who works for him? Have friends of Gracie's come around asking for her?"

She shook her head, appearing truly perplexed by my questions. "No, no one. But Gracie only stayed with us for a short time before leaving. I don't know if many of her friends knew she was living here."

If this was an act, it was a damn fine one. I was betting she didn't know Amaya's men were watching the house.

"Have you had any trouble with break-ins?"

"Break-ins?" she repeated, incredulous. "What is this about?"

"I'm still trying to figure that out. Can you show me the room in which Gracie stayed while she was here?"

I thought she would refuse. I wasn't giving many answers, and my reticence had to be frustrating her. But after regarding me for a few seconds, she shut off the burners and led me through a corridor to a cramped bedroom. A twin bed along the far wall was flanked by two sagging air mattresses. Stuffed animals and picture books were strewn on the floor.

"I haven't straightened up since they left. I keep hoping they'll come back so I won't have to."

"May I?" I asked.

She hesitated before letting me pass. I would have preferred to search the room without her watching me, but I didn't have the nerve to ask her to leave. I checked under the mattresses and in the bedding, and made a quick search of the closet and dresser.

"If you tell me what you're looking for, I might be able to help you."

If Amaya thought the knife was in the house, would he send men in for it, or would he be content to guard the house and make sure it remained hidden? The answer seemed to be the latter. But it begged another question: did he know it was here, or was this merely a guess?

"Mister Fearsson?"

"Telling you what I'm after could endanger your life." I tried a spell. Three elements. My hand, the knife, wherever it was, and the distance in between. I released the crafting on the third repetition of the elements. Nothing happened.

"What was that?"

"I tried to summon what I'm looking for."

"So perhaps it's not here."

"Perhaps. Or maybe the spell failed."

I returned to the doorway. "I'm grateful to you for speaking with me," I said. "I'm sorry to have disturbed you."

She glared at me, but then led me back to the front door. "You're a rather exasperating man."

"Gracie thinks so, too."

Her expression softened a bit.

"She's brave and smart as hell," I said. "And her children are adorable."

Marisol smiled. "Thank you. And thank you as well for keeping them safe."

"I'll be in touch as soon as I can. You have my word on that."

I left her and started back up the block toward Billie's car. As I walked by the first of Amaya's sedans, however, I slowed and, making up my mind, stepped to the passenger side window and knocked on it.

A few seconds passed and then the window rolled down, revealing two guys I didn't know. They were dressed in suits and both appeared to be Latino.

"You can tell Jacinto I'm on my way to his place next. He'll want to know."

I didn't wait for a reply, but continued to the car, got in, and drove away.

I didn't expect that Amaya would be amused by the stunt, but I also didn't think it a great idea to show up at his place unannounced. A few months before, I had made the mistake of doing just that. Amaya had been pissed, and his army of bodyguards had been twitchy as hell, which is not something you want in guys carrying MP5 submachine guns. I wasn't about to repeat the mistake. It was bad enough I would be showing up without having been invited. With this in mind, the next time I found myself idling at a red light, I warded myself against the attack spell I thought Jacinto would be most likely to use.

I drove up toward North Scottsdale, still avoiding the interstates, and in fact, all the major highways, including the Pima. I didn't know if whatever mojo Saorla had used on the roads would counteract the glamour I'd put on Billie's car, but I wasn't about to chance it. The drive took far longer than it should have and even knowing that the car was protected, I spent way too much time checking my mirrors to see if I was being tailed.

By the time I turned into Ocotillo Winds Estates, the sun had set and the Western sky was on fire with yellows and oranges and reds. I asked the uniformed security guy in the subdivision's front guard house to call ahead to Amaya's house and tell him I was here.

Despite taking this precaution, as soon as I steered the Honda into

Amaya's driveway, I was surrounded by armed men calling for me to exit the car with my hands up, turn, and brace myself against the car door. They knew me; I'd been to the house often enough that I recognized several of them. But Amaya didn't make a habit of welcoming folks who happened to drop by, and I was driving a strange car. If I had been in their position, I'd have done the same thing.

As they frisked me, I told them they'd find my Glock in the shoulder holster and a second weapon in the ankle holster. They took both pistols, of course, and made sure I wasn't carrying anything else. At last, one of them said that I could lower my hands.

I faced the guards and saw Rolon standing with them, my weapons in his hand, the dim glow of the twilight sky illuminating his face.

"What the hell, Jay?" he said by way of greeting. He wasn't smiling, which was unusual in and of itself. He also gave no indication that he was about to escort me into the house. After all we'd been through together during the summer, fighting Saorla and other dark mystes, I had come to think of him as a friend. But clearly friendship only went so far when a person worked for Jacinto Amaya.

"It's good to see you, Rolon."

"I wish I could say the same, *amigo*. Jacinto is not too happy with you. He says you reneged on an agreement, didn't do what you were hired to do. You even hung up on him. And now you show up here uninvited, unannounced." He gave a small shrug, the gesture strange on so large a man. "He's not sure what to make of this, you know? He doesn't know if you're a friend or what?"

That was a hell of a thing to say. Either I could assure him that I was Amaya's friend, which would allow Jacinto to demand all sorts of favors from me, starting with the delivery of Gracie and the kids to his "protection." Or I could refuse to rise to the bait, in which case I was all but declaring that I didn't think of Amaya as a friend. That was bound to go over well with his armed guards.

As for the rest, between Amaya saying that I'd failed to do what he'd hired me to do, and Saorla complaining that I had failed to give her a promised boon, I was in danger of gaining a reputation in the magical community as a man who couldn't be trusted. True, she was an evil wack-job, and he a murderous drug dealer. But still, people took trust issues seriously, particularly in an isolated and stigmatized community like ours.

In the end, I chose to punt.

"The nature of my relationship with Mister Amaya hasn't changed," I said. "And I haven't reneged on anything or failed to do what he hired me to do. In fact I've done most of it already, and might well finish the job very soon. I did announce that I was coming, both at the gate to the subdivision, and to the guys Jacinto has watching the Trejo house. As to showing up uninvited . . ." My turn to shrug. "I really didn't have any choice in the matter. If you'll let me in, I can explain all of this to him."

For a few seconds he didn't move. At last, a short burst of amplified static sounded from something in his other hand. I hadn't realized he was holding a walkie talkie.

He lifted the receiver to his mouth. "You heard?" he asked.

"Yes." Amaya's voice. "Send him in."

"Roger that."

He lowered the device and flashed me a smile. "Looks like you talked your way back into his good graces."

I doubted it would be quite that easy, but I was glad to see the grin on Rolon's face.

"Thank you, my friend."

"That's kind of a lame car you're driving," he said, walking me toward the front door.

"That's my girlfriend's car."

"My point exactly. You should have borrowed Paco's lowrider, or that Lexus Jacinto let you drive during the summer."

"This was a last-minute choice. And I notice you didn't say I could have borrowed your new lowrider."

He shook his head, his expression growing serious. "No, way. Too much car for you." He smiled again and I had to laugh.

Rolon led me through the foyer and into the grand living room where I'd met with Gracie's parents and Jacinto a few nights before. It seemed like years ago.

Amaya sat in a leather arm chair near the window, the glowing skyline of Scottsdale and the dying embers of the sunset at his back. He didn't get up, or say anything to me. He didn't even crack a smile.

"Thank you, Rolon," he said with a glance at his man. "You can go."

Rolon nodded and turned. Once Amaya could no longer see his

face, he glanced my way and raised an eyebrow. I think he meant it as a warning.

The echo of his footsteps was still fading when Amaya's spell hit me. I'd expected that he would attack with the same conjuring he had used the last time I showed up uninvited, and I wasn't disappointed. Then it had felt like a fist, or a pair of them: one to the jaw, the other to the gut.

This time I was warded. The force of the casting knocked me onto my heels, but otherwise it had no effect on me. If anything this appeared to piss him off even more, and for a second I feared that I had miscalculated.

But instead of throwing a more powerful spell at me, he glanced away, a small smile curving his lips. I let out a breath I hadn't known I was holding.

"I'm getting predictable."

"Not really," I said. "But I was figuring—hoping, really—that you wanted to make a point more than you wanted to actually hurt me. And so that spell would have been the natural choice."

"Like I said, predictable."

I conceded the point with a shrug.

He indicated a chair near his. "Sit down. If you want a beer, there's one in the fridge by the bar."

I thought about it for half a second and decided that I really did want a beer. "Can I get one for you?"

"Sure," he said.

I took two Bohemia Stouts from the refrigerator, opened them both, and handed one to Jacinto before dropping myself into the other chair.

He took a long swig and said, "You didn't do what I hired you to do. I told you specifically that I wanted her brought here."

"Yes, you did. And I told you I might not be able to. She's still wanted for murder, and we've had run-ins with dark sorcerers, weres, and Saorla. It's not safe to bring her here, not for her and the kids, not for me . . . and not for you. You don't want to be arrested for harboring a fugitive."

"How is she?" Amaya asked. I took the question as a measure of acquiescence.

"She's a pain in the ass, if you want to know."

"That's not—"

"Did you know that she's a were, as well as a weremyste?" I wasn't going a very good job of keeping Gracie's secret, but Kona and Kevin weren't going to tell anyone, and I had a feeling Amaya knew already.

"I had some idea," he said. At least he was being honest with me.

"And did you know that the silver-haired gentleman's name is Lionel Fitzwater?"

"Yes. He and I have had dealings before. How did you learn his name?"

"He introduced himself, right before I kicked his ass."

That earned me a broad grin. "I wish I'd seen that."

"What do you know about the knife?" I asked.

The smile vanished as quickly as it had come. "What do *you* know about it?"

"It's called the *Sgian-Bán*. It's a stone blade infused with the blood magic of necromancers, and it was used to kill Saorla and her kind and thus give them eternal life."

None of this appeared to come as a surprise. "What else?"

"Fitzwater is trying to find it, no doubt on Saorla's behalf. He's already killed several people, including an *Akimel O'odham* named Lucas Quinn, a pawnshop owner named Burt Kendall, and Burt's assistant. I think he also broke into the Davett house, but I'm sure he didn't find it there. And you expect him to show up at the Trejo place as well, which is why you have your men watching their street."

"About that," he said. "I don't recall giving you permission to approach them."

"And I don't recall asking you."

He had been raising the beer bottle to his lips and he paused now, eyeing me over the brown glass. "Fair enough," he said, surprising me. "The truth is, if we'd known about the knife sooner, we might have gotten to it first, and a lot of this could have been avoided. I knew Lucas. I liked him. He and I did a good deal of business, all of it on the up-and-up, two collectors trading goods. If he'd trusted me enough to tell me about the knife, he might still be alive."

"Maybe he thought it was too powerful for you to have. I think Lucas was smarter than all of us."

"Meaning what?" I heard a warning in the question and knew I was pushing up against the limits of what Amaya would tolerate.

"If everything people have told me about the *Sgian-Bán* is true, it could do incalculable harm if it fell into the wrong hands."

His nostrils flared. "And you're saying I'm—"

I held up a hand. "No, I'm not. You and I are on the same side in this war. When it comes to magic, I know where your heart lies. But however noble our intentions might be, and as powerful as we both would like to think we are, Saorla and Fitzwater might well be stronger. Wielding that knife would be a terrible mistake, because if we're beaten, and they take it, everything we care about could be lost.

"To be honest this is the same reason I didn't bring Gracie and the kids here when I found them. I was afraid you wanted to use them much the way Saorla does. And if you're defeated they'll be taken."

"You don't trust me to keep them safe?" Amaya asked.

"I know what they're worth, the same way I know what the knife is worth. I don't want them being treated as bounty in a magical war, and I don't want them being used as warriors, either."

"And you believe I intend to do just that."

"Don't you? Hasn't that been your intention all along?"

"You say we're on the same side in this war. You claim me as an ally. But you treat me as an enemy. That's not very smart, Jay."

"I've never treated you as an enemy, and you know it. Your problem with me is that I refuse to treat you like a general. I'm not in this to follow orders. I don't want those kids within a thousand miles of this war. And I'm willing to let Gracie choose sides for herself."

Amaya sipped his beer, his gaze fixed on me.

"You didn't answer my question," I said.

"I'm aware. Annoying, isn't it?"

I started to ask another question, but thought better of it. I didn't know if Amaya had considered what I wanted to ask him about, and I wasn't sure I wanted to put the idea in his head.

"Marisol didn't seem to know that I'd found Gracie and the kids," I said instead. "I'm a bit surprised you didn't tell the Trejos right away."

"Now you're questioning my judgment?"

I stared back at him, saying nothing.

At last he took another swig of beer, at the same time allowing his gaze to slide away. "I didn't want to tell them until I could arrange a reunion. Bring her back here and my first call will be to Marisol and Eduardo."

"If you promise me that you'll turn Gracie and the kids over to her parents, I'll bring them here tonight."

He scrutinized me with those impenetrable dark eyes, and I had a sudden, unsettling flash of what it would be like to have the man as a true enemy. "Are you trying to dictate terms to me, Jay?"

"Yes, sir."

My candor seemed to put him at ease. "It's an empty offer anyway. The Trejos can't protect them. The safest place for them is here with me, and you know that. But I'll tell you what I will do: I can bring Marisol and Eduardo here, and let all of them stay together in one of the guest villas. Engracia and the kids would be safe, *and* with her parents."

"I'll think about it," I said. "But to be honest, I'm not sure they'd be safe even here. Saorla is more powerful than both of us."

He didn't argue the point. "How did you beat Fitzwater?"

"I had a little help from Gracie, and I fought dirty."

Amaya laughed. "Good for you. At some point I'll want details." He stood. "But tonight I have a dinner and fundraiser to attend, so I'm afraid I have to cut our conversation short."

I stood as well and gripped Amaya's proffered hand. He maintained his grip, his other hand on my shoulder, his eyes boring into mine.

"You're playing a very dangerous game, Jay. I hope you know that. I like you. What's more, I respect you. But don't push me too far. I don't respond well to defiance, and I don't like it when people show me up."

I didn't flinch from his gaze. Maybe that made me foolish, but I didn't think that he wanted to hurt me so much as scare me. And, I realized, I wasn't as easy to scare as I used to be.

"I swear to you, Mister Amaya, I'm not trying to show you up. I'm trying to find a weapon of incredible power and at the same time do what's best for a young woman and her children. And though you might have *instructed* me to bring them here, you *hired* me to find them and to keep them safe. I've done the first part, and I'm trying to do the second."

"I'd like to believe you, but I won't wait forever."

I drained my beer and placed the bottle on a coaster. "Then it sounds like I have work to do. I should be on my way." I crossed to the arched entryway to the living room. "Before this is over, I'm going to have to fight Saorla again," I said, pausing on the threshold. "She wants Gracie and the kids even more than you do, and at one point I promised her a boon."

His eyebrows went up. "A boon? What the hell were you thinking?"

"I wasn't thinking. It was this past summer, a few hours before we faced her and her friends at my dad's trailer. I was just trying to keep Billie alive."

"So, what are you going to do?"

"I'm defying her, too, and she's even less pleased about it than you are. But at some point, I'm going to have to kill her."

"Or be killed by her."

"Right, but I'm choosing to be an optimist."

He looked skeptical.

"Anyway, if it comes to a battle, will you stand with me again?"

"Name the time and place. *Mis hombres* and I will be there."

My smile was no less genuine for being grim. "Thanks."

I had hoped to see Rolon and Paco before I left Amaya's estate, but they weren't in the driveway with the other security guys when I left the house. One of the men returned my weapons to me, but Jacinto's guards didn't say much. They opened the iron gate, waited for me to drive back out onto the street, and shut the gate behind me. It all struck me as a little too abrupt.

So almost from the moment I left the mansion, I was checking my mirrors for a trailing car. I spotted it about a minute after I pulled out of the subdivision. Late model sedan, dark color; the driver kept his or her distance, and, once we were on well-traveled streets, even allowed a car or two to pull in between us. I changed lanes a couple of times, testing the other driver as I guessed who it might be. He—they, really; if I was right, there were two of them in the car—didn't match my changes right away; they were too good for that. But as we approached intersections, they would drift into my lane, in case I intended to turn. By the time we drove past the entrance ramps for the 101 Loop, I knew beyond a doubt that they were following me.

Last time I'd been followed, Neil Davett was in the pursuing car, which was ironic, since I was on my way to his house now. But I didn't want to arrive there with company. Our first encounter had been difficult enough with just the two of us. Bringing an audience, be they Amaya's muscle or Saorla's magical soldiers, would only complicate things.

I'd put plenty of wardings on Billie's car already; one more probably wasn't going to make much difference. But I cast the spell anyway, taking special care to protect the tires. Once I knew that I was safe, I led my shadow onto a quiet residential street and crafted the spell I used as a standby in such circumstances. Their car, the driver's side front tire, and a nail.

I heard the blow out, watched in my rearview mirror as the car veered and then stopped about half a block behind me. I pulled into a driveway, turned around, and drove back to the other car, slowing as my window pulled even with theirs.

"Having trouble?" I called.

After a few seconds' pause, the driver's window glided down, revealing Rolon, red-faced and wearing a fearsome scowl. Paco sat in the passenger seat.

"Hey, I know you two."

"Shut up," Rolon said.

Paco laughed.

Rolon twisted in his seat. "You shut up, too. You think Jacinto's going to find this funny?"

"I didn't mean to get you in trouble, *amigo*," I said. I pitched my voice higher and made it a bit nasal, trying to do my best Bogart imitation. "But I've got a job to do, too. Where I'm going, you can't follow. What I've got to do, you can't be any part of." I looked from one of them to the other, waiting for at least one of them to laugh. Nothing. "Seriously?" I said. "Not even a grin?"

"What are you talking about?" Rolon asked. Before I could answer, he opened the door, climbed out, and slammed the door shut again. He squatted beside the flat tire and cursed.

"It's from *Casablanca*. Haven't you ever seen it?"

Rolon glared back at me.

"Don't you guys like movies?"

"I don't like anything in black and white," Paco said.

"I really am sorry, Rolon. But I can't have you trailing me tonight."

He straightened and crossed to my window. I half-expected him to drag me from the car and kick the crap out of me. "Jacinto is going to be even more pissed at you than he was."

"I'm willing to take that chance. You have a phone or do you need to borrow one?"

He pulled a phone from his jacket pocket and dialed a number. "You'd better go, Jay. You don't want to be anywhere near here when help arrives."

I nodded, rolled up the window and left them there. I didn't envy Rolon the conversation he'd be having with Amaya, and I wasn't looking forward to my next encounter with either of them.

CHAPTER 19

The Davett house sat in a quiet neighborhood, much like the one in which I'd left Paco and Rolon. Nice houses, neat yards, clean streets. None of the homes here compared to even the most modest of those in Ocotillo Winds Estates, but judging from the late model SUVs, minivans, and sedans I saw in most of the driveways, people in this area did all right.

Neil's metallic green Hyundai—with a brand new front tire—was parked outside a ranch house that wasn't much bigger or smaller than its neighbors. Most of the lights in the house were off, but I could see that some of the back rooms were lit. He was home.

I eased out of Billie's car, closed the door quietly, and approached the house, wondering if I should draw a weapon. My last conversation with Neil hadn't gone well, and I didn't expect this one to start off much better. A dog barked in a yard across the street, and I slowed, not wanting to draw attention to myself.

It never even occurred to me that the dog might be barking at someone else. Stupid.

Spells hit me from both sides. The wardings I'd cast before going to Amaya's house were still in place; they probably saved my life. But that much power directed at me from two angles was enough to put me down. I collapsed to the sidewalk as if I'd been bludgeoned with a sledgehammer, which is essentially how it felt.

I heard footsteps—the scrape of men's dress shoes in front of me,

243

the click of a woman's heels behind. GQ and Vogue. What were the odds?

"Look who we found," GQ said. I could picture the grin on his disturbingly handsome face. I didn't open my eyes though. Better to let him think I was too dazed and hurt to do anything.

I remembered the spells I'd used on them last time, outside the Casa del Oro, and assumed they would have wards in place to block similar attacks. I needed something new.

I hadn't split the ground open under Saorla out on the trail earlier in the day, because I had tried something similar in a battle with her during the summer. But these two hadn't been there.

Three elements: the sidewalk, GQ, and a giant crack in the cement. The ground opened beneath him with a roar that promised to rouse the entire neighborhood. His shout of surprise and alarm ended with a sharp grunt.

"Butch!"

Another spell hit me. My wardings blunted the worst of this one, too, but it felt like someone had kicked me in the back. Vogue ran toward him as fast as her stilettos would allow, giving me a wide berth.

I conjured again. Vogue, the street where she was running, and a magical wire about neck high. She hit it hard and fast, and went down in a heap, like a running back who'd been clotheslined.

I scrambled to my feet. As far as I could tell, GQ hadn't moved or made a sound since tumbling into the chasm. Vogue, on the other hand, was already trying to get up. One of her shoes had fallen off. I grabbed it and tossed it out of reach. I pulled the other shoe off of her, and threw it away, too. Then I hoisted her to her feet, and wrapped my forearm around her neck.

"His name's Butch? Seriously?"

She tried to pry my arm off, but I was stronger than she.

"You're going to answer some questions for me," I said. "And then I'll decide whether or not to throw you down into that hole with your friend."

"I'm not going to tell you anything." Her voice sounded strained, and she struggled to break free. Without the heels, she was a couple of inches shorter than I was, and, more to the point, she couldn't shatter my foot with a well-placed stomp.

"Where's Fitzwater?"

"I don't know what you're talking about."

"Did his helicopter crash today? Did he survive?"

She went still. Apparently she hadn't yet received news of the mechanical problems Gracie conjured for the chopper.

"No answer? Fine. Are you following me, or have you been watching Davett's house?"

"Who's Davett?"

I tightened my grip on her. Little did I know, that was what she'd been waiting for me to do. She threw an elbow, catching me in the gut. I didn't let go of her, at least not that time. The second elbow loosened my hold. She slipped out of my grip, grabbed my arm with both hands and flipped me so that I landed hard on my back and smacked the back of my head on the asphalt. Just like you see in the movies.

For good measure, she kicked me in the temple. Good thing I took her shoes.

"What the hell is going on out here?"

I tried to see who had spoken, but I couldn't focus. I had an idea, though, I was pretty sure my situation was on its way from bad to worse.

"Go back inside, Davett," Vogue said.

"Who are you?"

"A friend. I was sent to keep an eye on you, to keep people like this guy from bothering you."

"And who's that?"

Footsteps on the path leading from the house to the sidewalk.

"Hey, I know him."

"Yeah? Well, I hope you're not too attached."

I could hear her walking around, and a moment later her steps clicked again; she'd retrieved her heels. I guess there was a dress code for killing me. No shoes, no shirt, no murder.

"Not attached at all. What happened to the sidewalk?"

"He did that," Vogue said, clearly meaning me. "My partner's down there. Can you give me a hand?"

"Yeah, sure."

I forced myself up, but my head throbbed viciously, and I was dizzy as hell. If I could make it back to the car, I might get away, but I wasn't sure I could walk that far.

Another spell stirred the air, and Vogue cried out. From my knees I saw Neil straighten and walk in my direction.

"Can you walk?"

"What the hell?" I managed.

"Should we close that up, trap them in there?"

"I thought you were . . ." I shook my head, which turned out to be a bad idea. I squeezed my eyes shut, hoping that would stop the world around me from spinning. It didn't.

Vogue let out a low groan from within the split pavement.

"I don't want to be here when she gets out," Davett said.

"If we close it up, they'll die."

"Would that bother you?"

I looked at him—the middle one of the three. "Believe it or not, it would."

"I can knock her out again."

"She's warded. In fact, how is it possible your first spell worked?"

Neil held up his hand. Blood still oozed from a cut across the back of it, below the knuckles. "I find that blood spells work well against wardings."

He cast again—the air practically shimmered with his magic—and another grunt came from within the chasm.

"You'd think she would have known that."

"They were probably after you," he said. "I don't think she expected you to use blood, and I don't think she expected me to attack her at all." He reached out his unbloodied hand. I stared at it, and then at him. At last I gripped it and let him help me to my feet. "Come on inside. We'll put some ice on that bruise."

He led me into his house and to the kitchen. I sat on a stool by a granite counter and he brought me a glass of water and then a baggie filled with ice. I drained the glass and put the ice to the lump on the back of my head, wincing at the first touch of cold.

"Why are you helping me? The last time we met, we didn't exactly hit it off."

"No, we didn't. But I'm no friend of those guys." He jerked a thumb toward the street out front. "And I'm hoping that if I help you, you might be willing to help me."

I thought about this for all of two seconds before nodding.

"I'll start by apologizing," I said. "Last time I accused you of abusing Gracie. I know better now. She swears you never hurt her or the kids, and I know that she's a were. I'm certain that all her injuries have coincided with phasings."

"So you have found her."

"Sorry. Should have led with that. She and the kids are fine."

He closed his eyes, rubbed a hand over his mouth. "Thank God. Where are they?"

"Someplace the two in the sidewalk and their friends won't think to look for them, with someone I'd trust with my own life."

"You're not going to tell me."

"Not yet, no. I appreciate your help, but I'm afraid it's going to take more than that to win my trust." He took a breath to say something, but I stopped him with a raised finger. "Think about it for a minute. Would you really want me to be so quick to trust, with the safety of your wife and kids on the line?"

I could see that he was ticked off, but he didn't argue. "Has she talked about me, other than to say that I didn't hurt her?"

"We've been busy with other things," I said.

He raked me up and down with his gaze. I sensed that in that moment he saw me as a potential rival rather than as an ally. "What the hell does that mean?"

"It means we've been attacked by weremystes using dark magic, and by weres turned before the phasing for the express purpose of tracking us down. And we also had to deal with Gracie being forced to shift, which scared the crap out of your kids, especially Emmy."

"You were there when she changed?"

"I was in the next room. We were at a motel—Gracie and the kids in one room, me in another—and Emmy came and got me."

"What about when she shifted back?" he sounded sullen, like a jilted teenaged boy, and he was still watching me like he blamed me for the jilting.

I remembered what Gracie had told me: *Sometimes after changing I'm . . . hungry, in more ways than one.* She also said that Neil might not know about the talent Emmy had already exhibited. I needed to watch my every word.

"Did I mention that the person she's with right now is my girlfriend?"

He shook his head.

"Nothing happened between us, Neil. And I should tell you that Emmy would have kicked the crap out of me if something had. She still isn't crazy about having me around, and she goes out of her way to remind me—and Gracie, too—that I'm not her father. Not that either of us needs to be reminded, but she's eight, and she misses you."

He swallowed and nodded, his eyes bright with tears.

"I'm sorry if this is abrupt, but those two outside are going to wake up soon. They're going to be pissed off and they're going to want to take it out on me. I need to ask you a few things."

"Yeah, all right."

"Do you know of a woman named Saorla?"

"I've heard the name."

"Where?"

His cheeks flushed.

"Dark sorcerers," I said.

He gave a reluctant nod. "Yes. Who is she?"

"She's the one who's after your wife and kids. What did these weremystes say about her?"

"Not much. But from the way they spoke her name, I could tell that they answered to her, and that they were afraid of her."

"I don't doubt it. You know what a runemyste is, right?"

"Of course." In about a second his cheeks went from flushed to ashen. "She's a runemyste?"

"Not quite. The runemyste I know calls her a necromancer. But she's nearly as old as the runemystes, and the power she wields is almost on par with theirs."

"Shit."

"Saorla is gathering an army. She wants to destroy the runemystes, because she believes doing so will leave her and her kind as the most powerful magical beings in our world."

"How many of her kind are there?"

"That's a good question. I don't know. But I sense that she's their leader, whatever their numbers. She's trying to lure weremystes to her cause, using blood magic and the promise of enhanced power. She'll enlist those who agree to follow her, and she'll kill the rest of us. She wants Gracie on her side. She probably wants you, too. But she wants Gracie more."

"I'm sure she does."

"How long have you been working with these dark sorcerers, Neil?"

"I haven't been." Seeing the skepticism on my face he frowned. "What did Gracie tell you?"

"She thinks you're jealous of her spellcraft, of the power she possesses. And she thinks that jealousy drove you to start playing with blood magic."

He didn't deny it. "I was never one of them. I dabbled, nothing more. And I haven't dealt with them for a while now, since Gracie left. Truth is, blood magic scares me. She's right, I guess. I am jealous of what she can do, but I'm also afraid of it. I'm not sure I could control power like hers. The dark sorcerers you're talking about . . ." He shook his head. "They use a lot of blood. Not little cuts and scratches like the one I gave myself tonight. They do sacrifices. Actual sacrifices. And not just animals, either. How fucked up is that?"

"Did you talk to them about Gracie?" I asked. "Is that how they first became aware of her?"

His brows knitted in a way that reminded me of Zach. I hadn't noticed it until then, but the kid was the image of his father. "Is that what she told you?"

"I haven't asked her." I lied, but I didn't think this was the time to tell him I already knew the history of his failed marriage.

The truth is, I'm not sure my denial convinced him. He narrowed his eyes and didn't speak for several seconds. "I turned to blood magic because I wanted to be as powerful as she was. And I tried a bit of it around the house. She didn't like that at all."

That much at least, she had told me.

"But it made her curious. So one night we got a babysitter, and once the kids were settled, she and I drove out to South Mountain Park. Sometimes folks gather there to do magic, play around with blood spells. Some of the stuff that happens there I really don't understand. I think they're trying to make themselves stronger."

I didn't doubt it. South Mountain Park was one of the places where the Blind Angel Killer murdered his victims, and I'd seen enough of what Saorla's weremancers did to know that they were constantly looking for ways to enhance their power.

"Anyway, Gracie tried a few blood spells." He shook his head again, though this time he wore a faint smile. "You should have seen it. Blood magic, with the power she already has? She summoned a wind that literally blew people over. *That's* how she got on their radar. It wasn't anything I did. Not directly at least. We left that night, and she never came with me again. But every time after, when I went alone, they asked about her. 'When's your wife coming back?'" He laughed, dry as the Gila River bed. "They didn't give a damn about me. They wanted Gracie."

"Was Fitzwater one of the ones you used to see in the park?"

He tensed visibly at the mention of the name. "How do you know him?"

"He's one of the ones who's after Gracie. You know about what happened at the burger place, right?"

Neil nodded. "That was Fitzwater?"

"Yes."

"Did he kill all of them?"

"No. Just the one outside. I'm afraid Gracie killed the other two. She did it defending herself and the kids, but she's in a lot of trouble."

"That much I've figured out."

"One more question," I said. "And then I really have to go. Did you tell the others that Gracie is a weremyste *and* a were?"

He pressed his lips thin, his gaze sliding away. There was my answer.

"It was after that night she came with me to the park. They were asking questions about her, probably trying to figure out where all that power of hers comes from. I guess I was bragging, making myself seem more important because I was married to her. Of course, I didn't let on that our marriage was tanking. I just talked, and, yeah, I'm sure I mentioned that phasings in our house tend to be pretty interesting."

The phasing. It would begin tomorrow night, and I had no idea how to keep the kids safe, from Gracie and from me.

"What did you do with Emmy and Zach during the phasings? When you and Gracie were still together, I mean."

"My parents live in Avondale," he said. "And you know that Gracie's folks live near here as well. Sometimes, the kids would spend the phasings with one set of grandparents or the other. Or they used to. I don't know what Gracie has done the last few months. Other times, I'd keep the kids with me. Compared to what others go through, my phasings aren't all that bad. I get scattered and imagine things. But the advantage of my magic being weaker than hers is that my reaction to the full moon is mild by comparison. I worry about her shifting into her cat and hurting the kids, or running off into the wilderness and leaving them alone."

"I'll make sure they're safe, and Billie—that's my girlfriend—she'll stay with them."

"Thank you. It was never easy dealing with her phasings. And of course it got a lot worse after she started changing into a cat at other times."

I had been gathering myself to stand and leave, but those words immobilized me as if a spell. "When did that begin?"

"Not long after she came with me to the park. She didn't go with me again, but as I found out a while later, she wasn't done with those dark sorcerers I knew. It's not like she had an affair or something. But someone contacted her. A woman. And they met. Gracie told me that the woman cast a spell on her that would make the phasings easier. She wouldn't have to shift if she didn't want to. That's what she thought. But the reality was different, and things wound up getting a lot worse."

That much didn't surprise me. In gathering weres to their cause and bending the unwitting to their purposes, Saorla's legions had done the same to lots of people in the Phoenix area. I was reasonably sure that most of the weres I'd encountered over the past few days—the wolf by the Casa del Oro Motel, the owl in Billie's living room, the mountain lion and coyotes on the trail at Sonoran Desert National Monument—were conscripts rather than volunteers.

"They were turning her at will," I said. "Their will."

"Exactly. It would start without warning, and she'd take her cat form and run off into the night, or even the day, one time. It scared us both, but by then we weren't talking that much. And then right before she left me, it happened one last time, and she vanished for more than a day. When she finally came back, she was hurt, covered with bruises and cuts and bites from another animal."

There it was, the connection I'd been looking for and hadn't imagined I would find.

"When was this?" I asked, trying not to sound too eager. I had some idea of what he would say, though.

"A couple of months ago. Late in August, I think. Why?"

To this point, I had avoided any mention of the *Sgian-Bán*, but I wasn't sure I could go on that way. Not now.

Combining what Neil had told me with what I already knew, I thought I could piece together a plausible explanation for what had happened to Gracie that night. Sure, it was a guess, but I was confident that it was a good one. In her bobcat form she had gone to the Gila River Community, to Lucas Quinn's shack, where she was supposed to find and steal a stone knife that she would then hand over to Fitzwater. She did as she was told, not knowing that she would find more than just an old *Akimel O'odham* collector. Lucas's widow was there, and when her territory was invaded by another were, she shifted to her wolf and fought Gracie off.

I didn't know how the old woman had gained the ability to shift at times other than the phasing. Maybe someone had given her that power with a spell. Maybe she came by it some other way. But I was sure she had inflicted those wounds on Gracie. And I was also sure that though she drove Gracie away, she didn't do so until after Gracie found the knife.

Neil's question still hung between us. He watched me, waiting for an answer, maybe wondering if I would refuse to tell him this, too.

"Is that when the knife came into your lives?" I asked.

The way he gaped at me, you would have thought I'd turned his kitchen table to solid gold. "How did you know that?"

"Educated guess. Saorla has been using weres as servants, sending them on errands she'd never think to assign to weremystes like Fitzwater." I paused, thinking it all through. "That's why you didn't file a report on the break-in, because you knew exactly who had come and what they were after. Did you realize then—with the break-in—that Gracie had taken it when she and the kids left? Or did you think it was stolen that day."

He shook his head, his expression clouding. "I already knew she had it. She thought that it was worth a lot of money, and that it might be her ticket out of the marriage, and out of this place." I assumed he meant Phoenix.

"So she wanted to sell it back to them."

"Something like that. We weren't really talking, so I'm not certain. But that would be something she'd try to do. She's fearless."

"That's one word for it."

"You think they're after her for the knife."

"I know they are. They want her, too, for the magic she wields, and because she's both were and weremyste. But as valuable as she might be to them, the knife is more important. Saorla is determined to have it."

"I tried to warn her about it," he said. "I didn't want it in the house, but she wouldn't listen."

I hardly found that surprising, but I thought it best to keep that sentiment to myself. Besides, it was past time for me to be leaving. I stood. My head still hurt, but not nearly as much as it had. The dizziness had passed.

Neil didn't move. "So maybe she was right, and this was all my fault after all." He met my gaze but couldn't hold it for long. "It started with my blood magic. And then I told them Gracie's a were—if I hadn't done that, the knife never would have come into our lives."

"Neil—"

"Her being a were is unusual, I know it is. That's probably what also clued them into Emmy's power, isn't it?"

"You know about Emmy's power?"

The look he gave me made me feel like an idiot. "Of course I do. She's my kid. It's not something I'm likely to miss. Gracie and I never talked about it, probably because it scared us both. But she's not casting spells yet, is she? I mean, she wouldn't mean much to Saorla's army. She's only eight years old, for God's sake."

"Saorla has lived in her present form for centuries," I said. "She's practically immortal, though I'm determined to kill her. Years don't mean as much to her as they do to you and me. She can afford to be patient. And if she can get her hands on Emmy now, if she can train her in the use of blood magic from the moment Emmy crafts her first spell . . ." I let the thought go unfinished.

"I'd like to help you kill her. I understand why you're reluctant to trust me. I haven't handled any of this very well, and with all that Gracie has told you, you probably think I'm either evil or the dumbest guy on the planet. But I have a little power, and I'm not afraid of a fight, especially if it means keeping my kids safe."

I was torn. I wasn't sure I trusted him. I was certain, though, that Gracie would be good and pissed if I returned to the campground tonight with Neil in tow. In that moment I wasn't sure I cared. We were two weremystes against all of Saorla's weremancers. Amaya and his guys would help us if I managed to get word to them in time, but that was a big if. By the same token, Neil could only help us so much; increasing our numbers from two to three wouldn't make a lot of difference if Saorla came at us with twenty of her closest friends.

Before I could decide what to do, destiny took a hand—I seemed to have *Casablanca* on the brain today.

An explosion from outside shook the house and drove Neil to his feet.

"What the hell was that?"

But I think we both knew: GQ and Vogue.

And friends, as it turned out. Four of them stood in front of the house. GQ and Vogue stood on the small lawn. Their clothes were rumpled, and Vogue bore a nasty bruise on her forehead, but otherwise they looked little the worse for their time underground. A weremancer I didn't know stood with them, a man in jeans and a dress shirt. I couldn't make out much of his face for the blur of magic that obscured his features.

Lionel Fitzwater stood on the path leading to the house. A dog lay crumpled at his feet, no doubt the latest victim of his magical blood letting. What kind of twisted, evil conjurer kills a dog for a spell? I would have liked to pull out my Glock then and there, and shoot the bastard, but I figured he was warded against bullets and just about anything else I might throw his way. Including cracks in the sidewalk.

Neil's front door had been blown in, and lay smoldering on the oaken floor of his living room. I assumed that the house had been warded. Otherwise, a blood-fueled spell this powerful would have caved in the entire front of the structure.

"Mister Fearsson and Mister Davett," Lionel said, his accent making him sound like the narrator of a nature documentary. "It's unfortunate that you've decided to work together. I believe Saorla would have preferred you remain at odds."

The moon hung low in the sky behind him, a shade shy of full, its weight on my mind enough to make my thought process sluggish and disjointed.

"What do you want to do?" Neil asked under his breath.

"You mean aside from kill him?"

"If you can, be my guest, but I'm guessing you're no more capable of that than I am."

Fitzwater made a small motion with his hand. GQ and the new guy started toward the open door.

I cast a quick spell; an attack spell designed to knock them back. I didn't expect to break through their wardings. I wanted to stagger them, make them think twice about simply marching into the house and taking us. I succeeded in the former, but they kept coming.

I cast a second spell, a warding this time. I tried to do what Gracie had described: I attempted to twine my magic with the electricity in the house, and for a moment I thought I had it. But maybe my surprise at almost succeeding was enough to keep the spell from working. I didn't have time enough to make a second attempt. With another apology to Namid, I bit down on the inside of my cheek and cast my protective spell, exhaling hard as I did, the power torn from my chest. I wasn't sure I'd ever tried a shield spell of this magnitude and strength. But as soon as the magic left me, with a charge that made the air pop and my skin tingle, a gleaming wall of blue-green magic took form outside the house, not only where the door had been, but all around it, along every wall and window.

"Nice," Neil said.

"That'll hold them for a minute or two. But we can't stay here."

The third spell I intended to try would require more elements, not to mention quick action on my part once it took effect. That last crafting had taken a lot out of me and I wasn't sure I could pull it off.

The house shook again and Fitzwater's friends went down like duckpins. The old man kept his feet, but even he reeled back a couple of steps. Whatever spell he'd thrown at my barrier had rebounded without doing any damage to the house. He frowned and readjusted his fedora.

"Butch, be a good lad and come here a moment, would you?"

Butch and the new guy eyed the older man, but Butch made no move in his direction. Apparently they weren't eager to lend their blood to the great cause.

"Now!" Fitzwater said, his voice like the pealing of a church bell.

Butch took one halting step toward him. I could see he was fighting whatever magic Fitzwater had used against him.

"Butch, no!" Vogue ran to him and grabbed his arm, trying to pull him back.

Tired as I was, I knew that this was the best chance we were likely to have.

"Be ready," I said, keeping my voice low. At the same time, I reached into my pocket.

Neil glanced my way, but I was too intent on the elements of my spell to meet his gaze. Seven elements this time: the living room where we were standing, Billie's car, me, the driver's seat, Neil, the passenger seat, and the distance we'd have to travel. I let the images swirl in my mind as I repeated the words six times. On the seventh go-round, I released it.

Cold and darkness swallowed me, like some great ravenous beast. I heard Neil cry out in surprise, his voice sounding flat and muffled, and yet nearby. It was the only sign I had that he had made the jump with me.

Transporting spells always seemed to take longer than they actually did. It probably had something to do with the lack of air in that inky, frigid in-between, the growing pressure in my chest, the panic that clawed at my mind. I'd done a good number of these castings, and enduring them was no easier now than it had been the first time.

But just when I thought I couldn't last another heartbeat, I emerged from the blackness and found myself sitting in Billie's car, Neil beside me, eyes wide, mouth agape. My hand was still in my pocket and I pulled out Billie's key, shoved it in the ignition and started up the car.

Checking the mirrors, I saw Fitzwater and his friends whirl toward the sound. Fitzwater strode forward, intent on Butch, who stared at the car, blissfully unaware. Vogue screamed Butch's name, but by then I had the car in drive and was peeling away from the curb.

Eyeing the mirrors again, I saw Fitzwater grab Butch, and hold out a hand toward the Honda.

"Ward us," I said, shouting the words.

To his credit, Neil didn't hesitate. He muttered a spell, and the thrum of his magic filled the car. At the same time, I swerved to the other side of the road, hoping the glamour remained on Billie's car and that Fitzwater was aiming his attack by sound rather than sight

An instant later the spell hit. Despite the warding and my efforts, the car shuddered at the impact and the rear wheels lifted off the pavement. For one terrifying instant I thought we would flip over. And still Fitzwater hadn't hit us with the full force of his spell. The rear of an SUV parked along the curb caved in, the rear windshield exploding in a shower of glass. The SUV's alarm blared. Billie's car righted itself and I floored the gas, refusing to give the weremancer a second chance to attack us. The last thing I saw as we turned the corner, tires screeching, was Fitzwater removing his hand from the back of Butch's neck, and Butch dropping to the ground like a stone.

CHAPTER 20

We drove a good distance without saying a word, my hands gripping the wheel so hard my fingers ached, my gaze drawn repeatedly to the rearview mirror as I tried to determine which of the myriad sets of headlights behind us might belong to weremancers. I hoped that whatever magic Fitzwater had tried to use against us hadn't removed the glamour from Billie's car, but of course, I couldn't be sure.

Neil stared straight ahead, holding himself perfectly still, his tension thickening the air in the car like a fog. I couldn't tell if he was still recovering from what had happened at the house, or was already thinking about his coming reunion with Gracie, Emmy, and Zach.

"She won't want to see me," he said, an answer to my unspoken question.

"The kids will," I said. "Zach talks about you all the time."

He looked at me. "You just saying that?"

"No. Every time we're about to encounter someone new, he asks if it's going to be you."

He nodded, faced forward again. "Still, Gracie won't be happy."

"She'll deal with it. I wasn't about to leave you there."

"Thanks." A pause, and then, "Look this is kind of weird considering all that we've been through in the past hour, but I can't remember your name. Fitzwater called you Fearsson."

"Yeah, Jay Fearsson." I offered my hand, and he gripped it. "Pleasure to meet you."

259

"You're the guy who killed the Blind Angel Killer."

I was famous in this town for exactly one thing, but it certainly was a big deal. "That's right. I'm a private detective. I used to be a cop."

"That much I remember from our first conversation."

We fell silent again and I steered us back toward Gila Bend, by way of Buckeye. Once we were clear of the city, the traffic thinned and we made good time. Still, I avoided the interstates and highways and after a while I sensed Neil growing impatient.

"Where are we going?" he asked.

"A campground in Gila Bend."

"Gila Bend? We're driving to Gila Bend? Do you have any idea how far out of our way you've taken us?"

"Yeah, I do. But we're avoiding highways and interstates."

That brought him up short. "Why?"

"Gracie and I believe Saorla spelled them. I'm afraid that if we use them, she'll be able to track us, despite the glamour I put on this car." I cast a look his way. "I'm a pretty smart guy, Neil. I promise, I wouldn't have taken this route without a damn good reason."

He nodded.

I pulled out my cell phone and dialed Billie's number.

"Where are you?" she said, skipping right past "Hello."

"On our way back."

"'Our?'"

"You might want to prepare Gracie for the fact that I've got her husband with me. Do it quietly. Let her be the one to tell the kids."

"Okay. Everything go all right?"

"Not really, no. I'll fill you in when we get there. It shouldn't be long now."

"All right. Bye."

I closed the phone and dropped it back in my pocket.

"Nice phone."

I laughed. "Yeah, when you're in the PI biz you use nothing but state-of-the-art equipment. It's a requirement of the job."

"I can see that." He fiddled with his seat belt, eyes on the road. "You think warning her was the right thing to do?"

"It was for me. I can see where you might have preferred to surprise them all, but it's taken a while for Gracie and me to figure each other out. Our personalities don't mesh that well. One way or another, she was going to be pissed at me. But I think it would have been much worse if we'd simply shown up. I'm sorry."

"No, it's . . . I understand. She's not the easiest person to get along with."

"In her defense, neither am I."

We entered the campground about ten minutes later. Neil looked around as we drove in, his forehead furrowing more and more.

"This is the safe spot where you left them?"

"Yes. They're warded in several ways, and Saorla has no particular reason to look for us here."

I pulled into the site. Gracie, Billie, and the kids were sitting at a picnic table, still playing cards. Gracie stood as we pulled in, but the kids barely took notice of my arrival. Apparently she hadn't told them who was with me.

"Where are they?" Neil asked. "There's no one here."

I had my Glock in hand almost before the last word crossed his lips.

"If you so much as blink, I swear I'll blow your head off."

"What the hell—"

"Don't say a word."

"What are you doing, Jay?" Gracie called to me.

"He can't see you."

I watched her process what I'd said. It took her a few seconds, but when at last it hit her, she sat back down again, stricken, open-mouthed.

Neil stared out the windshield, squinting. "I heard her!" He grabbed at the door handle. "Where is she?"

"Don't touch it!"

"Would you please—"

"You're working with them," I said, my voice climbing. "The glamour I put on Gracie hides her from Saorla and her weremancers. Which means you're one of them."

"I'm not!"

"I don't believe you."

"I helped you get away from Fitzwater and the others!"

"That's what I thought, too. But really you did very little. You claimed to cast a spell on the woman when she was down in that hole in the sidewalk, but I never saw what your spell did. The only other magic you used was a warding on the car, and I'm not convinced that did much for us."

He looked like he wanted to cry, which only confused me more. "You really think I'd turn on my own family?"

"I can believe you'd turn on Gracie. And you might just be fool enough to believe that Saorla intends to take good care of the kids."

"Jay, it's all right. Let him out." Gracie had stood once more and stepped around the table toward the car, so that she was fully illuminated by the headlights. She had on her jeans and fleece, and she held her Ruger loosely in her right hand.

"I'm not removing the glamour," I said. "I don't care what excuses he gives."

Gracie nodded. "That's fine."

I looked at Neil again. He was staring in the direction from which Gracie's voice had come. "I can kill with you with this," I said, gesturing with the Glock. "I can kill you with a spell. Gracie is armed, and so is Billie. I'm going to be watching your every move. So will they. Don't do anything stupid."

"I'm here to see my family. I know you don't believe that, but it's the truth. Now, can I get out?"

I nodded, but I also cast a spell, warding myself from assaults and transporting spells. The last thing I wanted was for Neil to magic away my Glock.

He opened the car door, and at the sound, the kids turned to look. "Daddy!" Emmy said.

And then they both were saying it. "Daddy! Daddy! Daddy!"

They jumped up from the table and flew to him, wrapping themselves around him, shouting all the while. Neil still couldn't see Gracie or the kids, but he could feel them, and he gathered them in his arms, kissing their cheeks. Tears shone on his face. Why would the glamour work against him if he wasn't working with Saorla? I'd been careful with the wording of the spell.

The truth was, from the moment I first saw him outside his house until now I hadn't sensed any deception in him. And the whole time he and I were in the car, it never occurred to me that he might not be able to see his family. Not that I had some magical lie detector in my head, but I had been a cop and a PI for a long time. I'd always had a knack for judging people's intentions.

Billie came to me and put her arm around me, but both of us watched Neil as he talked to the kids and hugged and kissed them. It was like a scene from some holiday television tearjerker, except I had an attack spell ready to fly, and Gracie watched her husband like a mama cat eyeing a rival.

"What do you think it means?" Billie asked.

"I don't know. The glamour I cast was very specific. I worded it in such a way that it should only work on Saorla and those who are working with her. Which means he's been lying to me. But . . ."

"But what?"

"He didn't seem to be lying," I said. "I know that sounds stupid, but I've learned to trust my instincts."

"Do you trust them as much as you trust your magic?"

It was a fine question, one for which I had no answer.

Gracie sidled closer, though like me she didn't for a moment take her eyes off Neil and the kids.

"You shouldn't have brought him."

"You might be right. It seemed like a good idea at the time, but things happened very fast and I really didn't have long to think it through. For all I know this was their plan all along."

"Whose plan?"

"Fitzwater and a few of his buddies, including two weremancers I've had dealings with before. I think those two were watching your old house, either because they thought that Neil might lead them to you, or because they anticipated I'd show up sooner or later. They attacked me when I got there, and Neil helped me out. At least it seemed that way at the time. But while we were inside talking, they called for reinforcements."

"How did you get away?"

"Transporting spell to the car. I thought I was saving both of us. Now I wonder if it was some elaborate scheme to get him here."

Gracie offered a vague nod, but she was watching the kids, her expression hard to read.

"The kids are happy to see him," I said.

She shrugged. "He's a good dad. I've told you that. I was thinking that he looked happy, too. Happier than I've seen him in a long time."

"Maybe we should give you some time alone," Billie said. "All of you."

"No." Both of them looked at me. "I'll keep my distance, but I'm not letting him out of my sight until I know for certain that he can be trusted."

"I have more power than he does," Gracie said. "And he can't see us. I think we'll be fine." To Billie she said, "Thanks. A little time alone would probably be a good idea."

I started to argue, but Billie took hold of my arm and tugged me away, her touch gentle but insistent. "Come on, Fearsson. You're probably hungry."

Against my better instincts, I followed her, glancing back in their direction several times. Gracie had approached Neil and the kids and apparently said something to him. I couldn't hear what. He looked up, but I could tell he was having trouble locating her by the sound of her voice. It was nice to know my glamours worked so well.

"Give them some privacy," Billie said.

I faced her. "You're right."

She raised a hand to the bruise on my temple. "That doesn't look so good. I wish we had some ice."

"I'll be okay." I pulled her to me and kissed her. "I don't think I gave you a proper greeting earlier today."

We kissed again. "You didn't," she said. "You were too busy fighting off mountain lions and coyotes."

"It's been a day."

"Well, you should have some dinner. Do you want cheese and crackers or a peanut butter sandwich?"

"Wow. What choices!"

She grinned. "Shut up. It's the best we could do."

We dug out the peanut butter and bread, and I made myself a sandwich. As I did, I considered again all that had happened at Neil's house, searching for some memory that might tell me whether he had been deceiving me. Once again, I found myself thinking that I would have sensed the lies, the dissembling. During our previous encounter, the night he followed me from Amaya's, I hadn't found it difficult to read his emotions or his intent. He was a weremyste, a dad. I wasn't sure what he did for a living, but he didn't strike me as an international man of intrigue. He was a white-collar working stiff who had gotten himself caught up in magical goings-on he didn't quite understand and didn't have the power to influence. That was how he struck me then, and right up until the moment I realized he couldn't see Billie, Gracie, and the kids, that was how he had struck me tonight.

"What are you thinking?" Billie asked.

"I'm trying to decide if Neil is the best actor I've ever seen or just a guy who's trying to get his wife and kids back."

"Come up with an answer yet?"

"Not really," I said around a bite of sandwich.

"Couldn't he be both?"

I stopped chewing.

"I mean not both," Billie went on, "but couldn't he be a good guy and still have gotten mixed up with the wrong crowd?"

Somehow I was on my feet.

"Fearsson?"

"That's exactly what happened," I said. "We have to get out of here."

She stood as well. "You mean now? We have to take down the tents?"

I'd already left a tent and sleeping bag in Organ Pipe, but those had been cheap ones bought the day before at a sporting goods store. The tent and bag she'd gotten from my house were much better and way more expensive. But I wasn't sure we had time to break everything down and pack the car.

"Tell me what's going on," she said her voice tight.

"Come with me," I said, starting back toward Gracie and Neil. "I'll tell all of you."

They were sitting by the fire. Neil seemed to be telling a story, and the kids stared up at him, practically sitting on top of him. I sensed they couldn't quite believe he was here. Gracie sat nearby, though noticeably separate from the others.

She looked up at my approach. "What is it?"

"They're tracking you," I said, speaking to Neil.

"What?"

"That's why the glamour is working against you. You're with them in a sense; you're helping them. You just don't know it."

He kissed each of the kids, set them on the ground on either side of him, and stood. "Then get me the hell away from here. We'll get back in the car, and you and I will just drive. We can lure them into the desert."

It was the type of thing a devoted father would say, one who hadn't been lying and plotting against his family. Despite the danger I knew we were in, I was glad. The truth was, I wanted to trust him. Moreover, his idea wasn't half bad. Except . . .

"I'm not sure we have that much time. And the glamour on Billie's car won't work at night. They might not see the vehicle itself, but they'll see the glow from the headlights."

"Right. That's what we want, for them to follow us."

"I think Jay's point," Gracie said, "is that you might not last long out in the desert with Fitzwater and his friends. And even if you do, it means more running for the kids and me. Without a car, this time." She looked at me across the fire. "Is that about right?"

"Yeah. I was thinking of trying something new."

"Oh, boy," Billie said in a whisper. She knew me well.

"Emmy will know when they're close," I said to Neil, "and when they are, I'll put the same glamour on you that I've put on the others. All of us will be hidden. But the weremancers will be close enough that they won't retreat. They'll come looking for us, and while we're hidden by my spells, we'll take them out one at a time."

"What about the kids?"

"Billie and the kids will stay hidden in her car, which also has a glamour on it. Worse case scenario, she drives them away from here, and we do whatever we can to disable Fitzwater's car."

Neil pondered this for a few seconds before asking Gracie, "What do you think?"

"I'm tired of running away," she said. "And I think what Jay's suggesting might work."

"I'm not crazy about it," Billie said. "You're making me the last line of defense for the kids, and I don't have access to magic."

"They want me alive," Gracie said. "The kids, too. I can't say what they'll do to you, but they're not going to hurt the three of us. I don't know if that helps or not."

"It does, actually." Billie looked at me. "Okay, let's do this."

I handed her the key to her car. "Where's the pistol you were using earlier."

She pulled it from the pocket of her jacket and held it up for me to see.

"Is the magazine full?"

"Yep." She pulled back the slide and released it with a chiming of steel, like an old pro. "And now I've got a round chambered. You do what you have to do, Fearsson. We'll be all right."

Okay, I wasn't proud of this, but I don't think she had ever done anything that turned me on more. Not that this was the time.

"What if you're wrong?" Neil asked me.

"What do you mean?"

"What if they're not tracking me? What if they're not on their way here after all?"

"I'm not wrong."

As if on cue, the sound of approaching cars reached me. This was open desert; there weren't any buildings or mountains around to deflect the sound. The cars were coming from the east, their engines purring, most of the noise emanating from their tires. Late models, if I had to guess, I would have said they were sedans or SUVs. Probably two of them. I hoped it was only two.

"Mommy?" Emmy said. It came out half as a question, half as a warning.

"We hear the cars, sweetie. Is it them?"

She nodded. "It's him."

I was sure she meant Fitzwater.

"These guys have to use cars?" Billie said.

"Not always. Saorla could transport them here if she wanted. But she still can't find me. And we're not in the middle of nowhere, or out at my dad's trailer. We're near a town, and so they're choosing to be cautious." I faced Neil. "You ready?"

"I guess."

I cast the glamour once more, putting it on both of us, and again making certain that it rendered us invisible to Saorla, as well as Fitzwater and the rest of the weremancers. I knew that the sorcerers in those cars would feel the spell, but that was all right: more bait for the hook.

As soon as the pulse of magic touched the air around us, Neil's eyes widened. He was looking in Gracie's direction, and now, it seemed, he could see her. He faced the kids, and the smile that lit his face couldn't help but make me smile as well.

"There you two are," he said, breathless, his eyes shining again.

"Well, yah," Emmy said, sounding more like a jaded teenager than an eight year old.

I hated to rush the moment, but we really didn't have time for this now.

"Kids, come with me and Billie."

We led them over to Billie's car. The kids climbed in the back with their blankets and stuffed animals, and huddled down in the footwells. Billie positioned herself on the back seat, the .380 still in her hand. I handed her the Glock as well.

"Don't you—?"

"I have a back-up weapon," I said. "And the Glock has more firepower."

She eyed the Glock. "I don't like this one."

"I don't care," I said. "They'll probably be warded against bullets. If you fire, aim low or high. The shot may rebound, and if you aim center it has a better chance of hitting you."

"What's the point if they're warded?"

"It gives them something else to think about. And it may be that they won't be warded after all. The other thing, which I learned in my battle with Cahors, is that wardings against bullets don't work nearly as well at close range. If you're close enough, the power of the weapon might overwhelm the power of the spell."

She nodded, taking it all in.

I kissed her. "You'll be fine. Hopefully they won't even know you're here." I looked down at the kids, who were staring back at me. "You two have to be completely silent, okay? Not a sound. No matter what you hear from outside, you keep still. Do you understand?"

They both nodded, solemn and clearly frightened.

"As soon as it's safe, we'll come and get you."

I closed the car door as gently as I could while making sure it shut all the way.

Gracie and Neil waited for me near the fire.

"What now?" Gracie whispered.

"First thing we do is move away from the flames. Our shadows will give us away."

We crept away from the blaze toward my tent.

"We should spread out, try to force them to do the same. And then wait for an opportunity. Be patient. They'll be warded against most attack spells. Go for less direct assaults. And if you can kick the crap out of them with your hands, that might be best of all."

"Unless it's Fitzwater," Gracie said.

She started to move off.

"Wait," I said. "Where's the knife, Gracie?"

Neil eyed us both, but Gracie ignored him, watching only me.

"It's hidden."

"I know that, but—"

"This isn't the time. They're not going to find it. That's all that matters."

"You'd better be right." I didn't know what else to say. "Good luck."

We separated, Gracie, slipping off toward the other tent and seeming to melt into the night. I left Neil near my tent and crept closer to the road, intending to keep myself between the weremancers and Billie's car.

A pair of SUVs rolled toward us along the campground loop road, brights on, windows open. They stopped briefly in front of another campsite, but then drove on, much like travelers in search of an empty site. But I sensed their power, and I hoped that my glamour dampened ours.

Apparently it didn't. They stopped at our site, and after a few seconds and some whispered conversation I couldn't quite make out, the doors opened. Fitzwater, Vogue, and the other weremancer from Neil's house got out of the first vehicle. I assumed that Butch's body still lay on Neil's front walk. Four more weremancers got out of the second SUV, and my heart sank. Seven against three. I didn't like those odds.

Two of the newcomers were women, and two were men. Their faces were blurred with magic, and though none of them appeared to be as powerful as Fitzwater, they were all plenty strong.

I decided on a change in strategy. Instead of trying to stay near the car, I'd be better off leading a few of them deeper into the desert. Or, to be more precise, Billie and the kids would be better off. I eased away, moving deliberately, making no noise. Yet.

I kept an eye on the weremancers, and frowned in the darkness when I saw Fitzwater, accompanied by the man from Neil's, head off in the same direction Gracie had gone. I would have altered my course to follow, but three of the sorcerers were coming my way: Vogue and a man and woman from the other car. Three for me, while Gracie and

Neil each got two. I was just lucky, I guess. I paused long enough to pull my Sig Sauer from the ankle holster.

This late at night the moon was almost directly overhead, and it shone brightly enough to illuminate the desert. The shadow it cast was short; they'd have to be right on top of me to spot it. I could see all three of my pursuers clearly, my one advantage. Of course, they could see each other, which meant that if I took down one, the others would know. I'd have to get around that somehow.

At a gesture from Vogue, they fanned out, although they continued in my direction. I kept moving, keeping some distance between us, and trying to think of the best way to separate them so that I could take them on one at a time.

It didn't take me long to realize that not only was there no way to do this, but it also wasn't necessary. I slowed and shifted direction so that I could intercept the woman from the other car, who walked to Vogue's left.

When I was close enough to attack her, I cast the glamour spell again. She felt the magic, of course, as did her companions, but that couldn't be helped. The casting also allowed her to see me, because now we were both concealed from Vogue and the man walking with her. At the sight of me, all of three feet in front of her, her eyes about bugged out of her head, like she was a character from *Who Framed Roger Rabbit?* She opened her mouth to shout a warning to her friends, but before she could make a sound, I pistol-whipped her. The first blow knocked her to her knees. The second put her out.

As I've said before, I don't like to hit any woman. I also don't like to use my pistols as blunt force weapons, mostly out of concern for the pistols. But outnumbered three to one, and eager to make certain that Billie and the kids were safe, and that Gracie and Neil could handle their pursuers, I saw no better alternatives.

Vogue and the man with her were already heading in my direction, drawn by my spell, the sudden disappearance of their friend, and the sound of the blows I'd landed.

"Susan!" the man called.

Vogue glared at him. "Shut up."

They walked fast, making no effort to keep quiet, which allowed me to use their footsteps to mask the sound of my own. I circled them, drawing nearer to the man.

They halted near to where Susan lay, unconscious and still invisible. Vogue scanned the terrain, turning a tight circle as she did.

"Damn it!" she muttered. She pointed to her right.

With obvious reluctance, the man walked away from her, placing his feet with care again, and looking far more nervous than he had moments before. As it happened, he walked right toward me.

I waited until he was close before throwing the glamour spell at him, too. As soon as he was invisible to Vogue, I swung at him, landing a blow with the hand holding the pistol. His knees buckled, but he managed to keep his feet. A conjuring hit me in the gut, nearly doubling me over. Before I could recover, he dug a fist into my side and then caught me on the chin with an uppercut that rattled my teeth.

I fell back several steps, and he advanced on me, convinced that he had the advantage. Vogue, was coming this way, too. She couldn't see either of us, but she'd heard enough to know where we were.

He was almost on top of me when I cast. I went back to an old favorite, opening a hole in the desert floor just where he was about to place his foot. It seemed Vogue had warned him about this one, because he reacted fast enough to avoid falling in. But he couldn't keep from stumbling, one leg sinking into the sand. I cast again, closing the hole I'd conjured so as to trap his leg. And while he was still snared, I planted my foot like an NFL placekicker and kicked him in the side of the head.

He collapsed to the side, with a sickening snap of the bone in that trapped leg.

Magic hummed in the cool night air, and a conjuring slammed into me with the force of a pickup truck. I flew backwards, hit the ground, rolled, and came to rest against a prickly pear cactus, which might well have been the most pleasant part of the experience.

I didn't know what spell Vogue had cast, but I had a feeling that it would have killed me if not for my warding. She was close now, and though I was still concealed by my glamour, she seemed to have a fix on my location.

I spotted another cluster of prickly pear a few feet away, in between us. What the hell. Three elements: her, the needles on the lobes of the cacti, and the distance in between.

The spines flew at her, stabbing into her face, her hands, her neck.

She screamed, and swatted at them like they were hornets. And as she did, I cast the spell a second time, using a different knot of cacti.

I got to my feet and retrieved my weapon. Every muscle and bone in my body hurt; I'd already been through a lot this night. But I had enough left in me to close the distance between us and knock her senseless with the Sig Sauer.

I removed the glamour I'd put on the man and Susan; I didn't want them being able to see us if they woke too soon. Then I went in search of Gracie and Neil.

This fight was still far from over.

CHAPTER 21

I walked back toward the campsite, watching for Fitzwater and his other friends, placing my feet with the care of a hunter. Before long, I spotted that familiar shock of silver hair.

Fitzwater walked one step behind the guy I'd first seen at Neil's. They didn't know it, but Gracie was following them, her Ruger held before her. I hoped she was smart enough not to fire it even from that distance. These guys were warded, and any bullets shot in their direction might hit her.

I didn't envy Fitzwater's companion. The silver-haired weremancer had only to reach out for the guy, and he'd be able to grab hold and draw blood. The other weremancer would have no chance to defend himself.

Neil and the two weremancers who had gone after him were nowhere to be seen. I closed on Fitzwater, glancing repeatedly at Gracie.

When she finally saw me, she stopped and swung her weapon in my direction. Only then did she realize it was me. She rolled her eyes and started after the weremancers again.

A ripple of magic from closer to the road made all of us turn. I couldn't tell what kind of spell had been cast, or who had cast it. But after sharing a look, Fitzwater and the other weremancer started in that direction. Gracie and I followed, both of us matching our footsteps to theirs.

Another spell stirred the air, and a yowl of pain tore through the silence. The weremancer with Fitzwater broke into a run, and the older man followed, clearly trying to keep up with him. They were near their SUVs, and an idea came to me.

There were two ways to do what I had in mind, and either one—the Sig Sauer or a spell—would give away my position. A spell, though, seemed the safer choice. Still pursuing them, I waited until the younger weremancer was beside the SUV, and then I cast. The elements were fairly simple: my hand, a ball of fire, and the gas tank of the nearer vehicle.

The result proved even more spectacular than I had anticipated. The SUV exploded, flames momentarily bathing the desert in golden yellow light. The force of the blast knocked the younger man off his feet. Fitzwater stopped and threw up his arms to shield his face.

It was so much fun, I blew up the second SUV as well.

By now Gracie and I were close enough to Fitzwater that if I'd wanted to I could have charged him and thrown a punch. Gracie seemed to read my intent, because she grabbed hold of my arm. At my look, she shook her head.

And then she did something I had never seen before. I knew it was possible. I had asked her about such spells the other day. But knowing it could be done was one thing; seeing it was enough to steal my breath.

Standing so close to her, I felt her magic brush against me, like a passing stranger in a crowd. Both SUVs continued to burn, but now the flames in the second vehicle diminished almost to nothing. And at the same time, the SUV rose into the air and flew toward Fitzwater, as if thrown at him by some giant angry child.

It should have killed him, but at the last minute, he dove out of the way. The SUV hit the ground and rolled over several times.

Still prone, Fitzwater grabbed his companion by the ankle. The younger man tried to kick his hand away, but to no avail. The silver-haired man cast; between my castings and Gracie's, he knew where we were now.

I had time to shout a warning, but that was all. A wave of fire crashed over us with the strength of an ocean breaker and the heat of flowing lava. Gracie howled in agony, and I think I did the same.

Again, our wardings saved our lives. But even after the strength of Fitzwater's spell spent itself, I was too dazed and hurt to move. By the time I opened my eyes, the old weremancer stood over us, holding both of our pistols in one hand and dabbing at a bloody gash on his forehead with the other. The man whose leg he had grabbed, and whose blood had fueled that last spell, lay unmoving on the ground.

Fitzwater seemed to know in a general sense where we were, but I could tell that he couldn't yet see us; the glamour still worked.

"Enough of this, Engracia," he said. "Show yourself."

Even before I looked her way, I knew Gracie wouldn't answer. She was already watching me, a question in her eyes.

"We've got one of them."

Fitzwater turned. I forced myself up into a sitting position, as did Gracie.

The two remaining weremancers walked toward us, Neil held between them. He had a cut on his head much like Fitzwater's and he appeared unsteady on his feet. But at least he was alive. For the moment.

I didn't think that Fitzwater or his friends could see Neil, but it didn't seem to matter. They had him, and Fitzwater could do with him what he wanted, including use him as a blood source for yet another spell.

"Is this Mister Fearsson?" he asked, glancing back in our general direction. "Or perhaps your husband, Engracia. The father of your splendid children. In either case, I imagine you value his life. So I will keep him alive, and in repayment for this mercy, you will reveal yourself. Right now."

Gracie said nothing, but she did look at me again, her expression pained.

"I can kill him in any number of ways. You know that I can use him to cast a spell that will hurt you as much as that last one did."

I wanted to cast a transporting spell to get back our weapons, but I was sure he would respond by killing Neil, and right now the pistols wouldn't help us much.

On the other hand, transporting Neil would help us a lot. I glanced Gracie's way and whispered, "Be ready," much as I had to Neil earlier.

Seven element spells took a good deal more power than did the simpler ones, and already tonight I had done a lot of magic and absorbed a lot of abuse. But there was no way I would end this night by telling Emmy and Zach that I'd allowed their dad to be killed and their mom to be taken.

Neil, the two weremancers holding him, Fitzwater, where they were standing, where we sat on the sand and stone, the distance in between, and the blood on Fitzwater's head, just in case they were expecting the spell.

I knew Namid wanted me to stay away from blood spells. I could almost hear him berating me. But again this wasn't the moment to get hung up on scruples.

I didn't dare take too much time to let the spell build. I gathered the elements in my mind and the let the magic fly.

Neil vanished from view, and Gracie let out a gasp. But she recovered and cast again. Neil reappeared a few feet from us and upon doing so, collapsed to the ground. Gracie's spell lashed at Fitzwater, driving him to his knees. But she spat a curse, and I knew she'd hoped it would do more.

"Where the hell did he go?" asked one of the other weremancers, no doubt speaking of Neil.

Fitzwater looked up at them. "You've lost him? Damn it!"

I cast a second transporting spell—a simpler one—and an instant later held the pistols in my hand.

The silver-haired man stood and turned, but he remained where he was, probably wondering what spell we'd try next. Gracie crawled to where Neil lay and checked him for a pulse. She looked my way and nodded; he was still alive.

"What now, Fitzwater?" I asked. "You came with six other weremancers. Now there are three of you. If you kill another of your friends for a spell, you'll be outnumbered."

"Mister Fearsson," he said. "What a pleasure to speak with you again. Would that I could see you."

"I think I'm just as glad you can't."

A car engine started up nearby. Billie's car, which was also protected by a glamour. Fitzwater glanced in that direction, but quickly turned back to me. "We do seem to be stalemated, don't we?"

"We do. So maybe it's time you left." I wanted to keep him talking. He didn't know Billie was with us. He assumed the three of us were the only adults here, which probably meant he hadn't considered the possibility that the car he heard was ours. I hoped that Billie would drive the kids far from here.

He opened his hands. "In what should we leave? Thanks to you, we have no cars to drive. Perhaps you care to lend us yours."

"We don't have one either," I said. "We were dropped here."

Fitzwater's brow knitted. "And the children?"

"What about them?"

He knew better than to ask where they were, but I could see that I'd confused him.

"You're lying. You have a vehicle, and you have the children with you." Again he glanced in the direction of Billie's car, perhaps putting it all together. "They could be in one of those tents, or in the car that started up a moment ago. But they're here. Engracia wouldn't allow them out of her sight. For all I know, they're right in front of me, protected by the same magic that hides you."

I didn't answer.

"I'll take your silence as confirmation. Good." He closed his eyes. I could see his mouth moving and I assumed he was about to cast again. All of us were warded, but I thought about casting another protective spell anyway.

A moment later, I realized that he hadn't been crafting a spell, but instead had done something far worse: he had summoned Saorla.

She winked into view beside him, moonlight gleaming on her lovely face, her hair twisting in the cool desert breeze.

I struck fast and hard. Seven elements: Saorla, Fitzwater, a giant blade, the distance between the two of them and me, their wardings, which I wanted to overcome, my magic, and the flames burning on the second SUV. I'd tried something similar at Neil's house, and failed. And the elements for this conjuring were almost more than I could keep in my head. But I felt the magic building inside me. So did Saorla. I didn't think she could see me, but she glared in my direction anyway. I didn't wait a full six repetitions to release it. As soon as she looked my way, I let it go.

I knew as soon as I cast that the spell had worked, at least in one sense. The flames on the burning vehicle diminished, and magic suffused the night air. Saorla doubled over with the impact of the crafting, grunting softly. Fitzwater flew as if swatted, landed on the road, and rolled once.

But the spell didn't slice them in half, as I had hoped it would. Saorla straightened after a few seconds, and Fitzwater let out a moan before pushing himself up onto his hands and knees.

You have learned nothing, Justis Fearsson. The words echoed in my head, my only warning of what was to come.

Anguish. It spiked through my skull, as sharp and unrelenting as a steel blade. I think I screamed. I know I clawed at my scalp, trying to pull out whatever she had used to impale me. But of course, there was nothing I could grab, nothing I could remove, and the pain went on and on for what seemed an eternity.

"Stop it!"

Gracie's voice came from a great distance, through agony and fatigue, and Saorla's soft laughter.

"Leave him alone."

"Will you let me see you?"

"Yes."

"No," I said, croaking the word. "Our . . . only . . . advantage."

"The glamour will die with you," Gracie whispered. She was far closer to me than I had thought. Her hand rested on my shoulder. "Either way she's going to see us. This way we still have a chance."

"All right," I said. And then I repeated it, loud enough that the words would reach Saorla. "All right."

The pain didn't stop, but it diminished. I could open my eyes. Finding myself flat on my back, I sat up, a groan escaping me.

"You will remove the glamour?" Saorla asked.

"Yes." I cast the spell, unsure in that moment of whether I had the strength to make it work. It should have been a simple three element crafting, but only if I was willing to expose all of us, including Billie and the kids. So I made it more complicated than it needed to be. Saorla, Fitzwater and the other weremancers, my glamour, Neil, Gracie, and me, and the removal of the spell.

I released the magic, knew from the way Gracie glanced my way that she felt the spell on her skin, just as I did.

"Much better," Saorla said. She started to say more, but then stopped and stared off into the night. I felt magic purr in the ground.

"A glamour of my own, Justis Fearsson. Whoever blew up those vehicles attracted the notice of the local fire department. They won't find us now. You'll not have any help from them." The smile that curved her lips was short-lived. "Now, where are the children? Where's the girl I met earlier today?"

"Far away from here," I said.

"I do not believe you."

Footsteps rustled the dirt behind us. Turning my head—the motion painful enough to make me suck air through my teeth—I saw Vogue and her two companions stumble into the light cast by the burning SUVs. The man whose leg I'd broken was limping, but it seemed that he or his friends had healed the break. Great. Neil had yet to wake, but even if he did, we were outnumbered again. Not that it mattered. With Saorla here, numbers were the least of our concerns.

"Search the tents," Saorla said. "Find those children."

Gracie lifted her chin. "You won't."

Something snapped, and Gracie cried out. She dropped the Ruger and clutched her mangled hand.

"That was but one finger," Saorla said, walking toward us. "I can break them all, and will if you do not tell me where you have hidden the children."

"You know that won't work, Saorla," I said. "Earlier today you claimed to know what it was like to bear children. Have you forgotten what it means to be a mother? She'd rather die than tell you anything. And she'd endure any pain to keep them safe."

She halted and scowled down at me.

"And before you try one of us, I assure you the father would do the same, and so would I. I'd gladly die if it meant keeping you in the dark, and keeping those kids safe."

"Very well," she said, in a tone that was entirely too sanguine for my taste. "Perhaps she would care to tell me where the *Sgian-Bán* is hidden." She spoke the blade's name in an accent I had never heard, and though loath to admit it, I couldn't help thinking that she made it sound beautiful, powerful, even magical. "Will she endure the same pain to protect a blade, an object no more alive than that automobile? Is she willing to watch you die in order to keep it hidden?" She stepped around me to where Neil lay. "Would she allow me to kill the father of her babes?"

"No," Gracie said. Tears streaked her cheeks, shining in the light of the moon and the fires.

"Tell me where it is."

Gracie glared up at her, her lips pressed thin. I sensed that she was bracing herself, and I knew what for.

Bone broke again, and she shrieked, bending over until her forehead rested on the desert floor.

"Tell me!"

It had been an act. Gracie had wanted the necromancer to break another of her fingers. It was the only way to make Saorla believe the lie she was about to tell. I'm not sure I could have done it. I knew a lot of brave people—Kona, my dad in his own way, Billie. In that moment I thought Gracie more courageous than all of them.

"My parents have it," she said, panting out the words. "They don't know. But it's in their house. Hidden, safe."

"You will take me there. You will find it and give it to me." She glanced back at Fitzwater, but he was still on his hands and knees. She sneered, turned to Vogue. "Watch them," she said. "If they attempt to escape, kill them. And take their weapons. We may be warded, but I prefer they not have any means of creating mischief."

Saorla grabbed a handful of Gracie's hair and hauled her to her feet, drawing a sob.

I opened my mouth to object, but before I could, the two of them vanished.

Vogue stalked toward me, her eyes narrowed and shining with firelight. I had no doubt she intended to kill me. Over the past few days, I had knocked her around quite a bit. She wanted revenge. Her companions—Susan and the man whose leg I'd broken—trailed behind her. I had a feeling that they wanted a piece of me, too. But before Vogue could kick me in the head again, or put a knife through my heart, or light me on fire, Fitzwater said, "Leave him."

His voice sounded weak, but it stopped her. He remained Saorla's must trusted servant, even if he did look and sound like a beat up old man. He stood, though it seemed to take a great effort.

"We've got the woman," Vogue said. "What does he matter?"

"Saorla wants him alive for now." He flashed a weak smile my way. "Apparently he still owes her a boon. And since we have the woman, and will soon have the blade, she'll have to think of some other way to use him. Take his gun, and the woman's, but don't do anything else to him."

Vogue's expression curdled, but she did as she was told, stooping to grab Gracie's weapon off the ground and then looming over me, the Ruger aimed at my forehead, her free hand outstretched. I couldn't remember if I had warded myself against bullets, and I wasn't sure I trusted my other wardings to withstand a gunshot from point-blank range. Despising her, and hating myself a little, I handed her the Sig Sauer.

She eyed it, and I could tell she was remembering the pistol-whipping from earlier. But she didn't hit me or blow my brains out. She pocketed my weapon, but held on to the Ruger, and she stepped back, putting a bit of distance between us.

Unsure of what to try next, weary beyond words, I stared at the spot where Gracie and Saorla had been.

Maybe I should have been relieved to hear that the necromancer wouldn't be killing me immediately upon her return. But knowing that Gracie had lied to her, and knowing too that eventually Saorla would find the blade anyway, I wasn't sure death wouldn't be preferable to what was coming.

It is the one weapon in your world that can be used to kill runemystes.

She would find a way to force me to summon Namid, and then she'd kill him while I watched. I knew it wouldn't be as easy for her as that made it sound. But I also was familiar enough with Saorla to know this was her intent.

I glimpsed movement out of the corner of my eye, and it was all I could do not to turn my head and draw the attention of Vogue and Fitzwater. Allowing my eyes to roam the moonlit landscape in a way that would seem natural, I saw that Neil was moving the index finger on his right hand. He remained motionless otherwise, his eyes closed. In every respect he appeared to be unconscious still. But his finger moved with the regularity of a windshield wiper blade. It had to be intentional, an attempt to get my attention.

I braced my hands on the ground and started to stand.

"Stop it!" Vogue said, holding the Ruger with both hands. "What do you think you're doing?"

I did stop, and I raised one hand: a placating gesture. "I just want to stand up," I said. "My legs and back are killing me."

"Stay where you are."

"I'm not trying to get myself shot," I said. Moving ever so slowly,

I got to one knee and held up both hands for her to see. "And I know that you and Fitzwater can pummel me with spells if you want to. But sitting on the rock and sand isn't as comfortable as it sounds."

"I don't give a crap! Don't move!"

I stayed as I was on one knee, my hands raised. I had her full attention now, which was what I wanted.

Susan, though, proved herself a bit more observant.

"Hey," she said, "I think this guy is moving."

I wanted to shout at Neil that now was as good a time as any to do something—anything. To his credit, he didn't need to be told. Magic hummed in the ground beneath my knee. I watched Vogue for some sign that the spell had hit her, but saw none.

Puzzlement knitted her brow. "What was that?"

"Hey!" Susan said, voice rising.

A knife flashed in Neil's hand; I knew it hadn't been there before. That first crafting had been a transporting spell. He slashed at his other arm and cast almost in the same moment, blood appearing on his skin and vanishing as if wiped away. The second spell resonated like a drum, far more powerful than the first.

And Vogue burst into flame.

It wasn't the attack I would have used, but Neil had admitted to me that he wasn't the most accomplished of weremystes, and fire spells were easy.

Vogue's shriek skirled upward. The Ruger went off—I think in her agony she pulled the trigger. An instant later it dropped to the ground. She took two writhing steps, her arms flailing, before dropping to her knees.

I grabbed the Ruger and aimed it at Susan and her friend.

Another spell swirled through the air, and the flames burning on Vogue went out. After the brightness of the blaze, my eyes needed time to readjust to the night. I assumed I wasn't alone in that regard, and cast a crude camouflage spell. Three elements instead of seven: the night, the desert, and me blending with both.

I sensed another spell and dove, as if avoiding a gunshot. I hit the ground, rolled, and came up with the Ruger trained on Susan again.

"Where the hell is he?" said the man standing with her.

I'd only get one chance to strike at them, and I knew the pistol was the worst of my options.

Vogue was no longer burning, but her hair and clothes were essentially gone, and even in the dim light of the moon and smoldering SUVs I could see that her skin was blistered and melted in some places.

"He's close still," Fitzwater said. "And if he values Mister Davett's life—"

I didn't wait to hear more. There was more blood on Neil's arm, but I hoped that he would cast again and use it himself. He needed it more than I did. More to the point, I knew what Namid would say about me resorting to more blood magic. I had already used the flames from the SUV. I could do these enhanced spells. But my last crafting had diminished the fires too much.

And in that scintilla of time, I remembered what Gracie had told me a couple of days before. *There's power everywhere . . .* Namid had said much the same thing to me in Billie's dining room.

Desperate times and desperate measures.

Heat from the day's sun still radiated from the ground, and so I drew on that, hoping to God it would work as well as it had for Gracie the other day. I wanted to incapacitate Susan and the guy with her, and I didn't give a damn about being gentle. I envisioned a block of cement falling on their heads. Them, the block, and the energy from that heat to enhance the spell.

The magic I felt flowing up through my legs was like nothing I'd ever drawn upon before. I half-expected lightning to fly from my hands. At the touch of that conjuring, Susan and her friend collapsed with such finality, I wondered if I'd used too much power.

But I didn't hesitate, whirling toward Fitzwater and the two remaining weremancers, I drew upon that power again.

I didn't get the chance to cast.

Neil let out a whine that built slowly to a scream of such anguish, I could do nothing more than stare at him. He held his head in his hands, the knife beside him on the ground, all but forgotten.

"Cast another spell and he dies," Fitzwater said over Neil's cries. He was still in the roadway, but from what I could see, he had recovered from the spells we'd thrown at him earlier. He stood straight-backed, his fists clenched at his side.

"Show yourself," he demanded. "Or he dies."

Between us, Neil and I had evened the odds a bit. But I couldn't take out Fitzwater and the two with him without costing Neil his life, and that wasn't a trade I was ready to make.

"Easy, Fitzwater."

I cast again to remove the camouflage spell. Fitzwater's eyes found me right away. I still held the Ruger, and, to be on the safe side, I laid it on the ground and kicked it away a few feet.

Neil continued to wail.

"Now, stop hurting him."

"And if I don't?"

"I'll crush you like a bug."

I meant it. On this night, with that last spell I'd cast, I had taken to heart the lessons Namid had been trying for so many years to impart to me. He was right: I didn't need blood. It wasn't just that I understood what he meant when he told me that power was all around us. I could feel that power, and somehow I had discovered the means to access it. Maybe it was the product of new-found wisdom, born of Gracie's advice and Namid's teachings. Maybe my frustration at having been held back for so long by my own ignorance and limitations had reached the tipping point. Maybe it really was the product of that desperation. Or perhaps it was some combination of all three. Whatever the cause, I finally got it. For the first time in my life, I believed I was worthy of being called a runecrafter.

If it came to a battle between Fitzwater and me, I knew I could beat him. My fear, though, was that he would kill Neil or someone else before I could do so. That was the only reason I didn't try to destroy him where he stood.

He must have heard the confidence in my voice, because seconds later, Neil's cries subsided to a soft whimper.

"You shouldn't have done that to my friends," Fitzwater said. "You and Davett have made things much harder for yourselves."

"I suppose you expected us to sit here, waiting to die. I didn't try to kill those two," I said, waving a hand at the unconscious weremancers. "That's more consideration than they deserved. It's more than you gave to Burt Kendall and his assistant."

His smile could have brought snow. "I don't know what you're talking about."

"You're a liar."

The smile slipped, leaving him looking as angry as I'd seen him. "Watch your mouth."

"No, I don't think I will. What do you plan to do about it?"

I wanted him to attack me. I wanted him to see for himself what I already knew.

He threw a spell. I didn't know what it was, nor I did I care. I warded myself, drawing on the heat in the sand and the moonlight on the brush and cacti, the fires burning low and the wind carrying the smoke eastward. His casting passed over me like the gentle swell of a wave on a calm morning.

Another grin had crept across his features, but now his face fell.

"That wasn't very good, Lionel," I said. "My turn."

I drew on those same sources and added three elements: my fist, his gut, and a solid blow.

He doubled over with a retching grunt. I would have liked to make him throw up, but he managed not to.

"That's how you do it," I said. "Maybe it's time for you to take blood from one of your remaining companions."

Fitzwater glanced over his shoulder at the two weremancers. They backed away from him.

He faced me again. "Or I could simply kill Davett."

I cast another spell. Moments before I had been exhausted almost to the point of collapse, because I realized now, I had been fighting my magic even as I used it. With the understanding of how magic ought to work, came an ease of runecrafting I had never imagined was possible. I didn't even sense that headache Gracie had warned me about. Namid would have been proud.

An aqua shell of power appeared over Neil, glowing like bioluminescent algae in the sea.

"Go ahead and try," I said.

For the first time, Fitzwater appeared frightened. And I wanted to revel in his fear, to repay him for the terror he had inflicted on Gracie, Emmy, and Zach, to avenge Burt and Tommy and Lucas Quinn.

But at that moment, Saorla winked into view again, her fist entangled in Gracie's hair.

Gracie could barely keep herself upright. Her face was damp with sweat and tears. Her hand appeared mangled beyond repair, and she had a welt on her jaw and another on her temple.

Saorla looked at me, and then at Neil and the glowing shield I had created.

"Well, we can't have that."

She snapped her fingers, and the warding vanished.

CHAPTER 22

Saorla pushed Gracie away from her. Gracie stumbled and fell to the dirt, using her injured hand to break the fall, and then sobbing.

"She lied to me," Saorla said to no one in particular. "The *Sgian-Bán* was not there."

"What did you do to her parents?" I asked.

The necromancer cast a sidelong glance my way, a sly smile curving her lips. "What do you think I did with them? Do you expect me to say that they are dead? That they tried to interfere and so I punished them as they deserved?"

"Is that what happened?"

She continued to watch me, that maddening smile lingering.

I squatted beside Gracie. "Are your parents all right?"

"Yes," she said, whispering the word. "They're totally freaked out, but she didn't hurt them."

"Again, Justis Fearsson, you expect the worst of me, only to be disappointed when I prove myself something other than a creature of pure evil. Namid'skemu has twisted your mind."

I stood once more. "All right, Saorla. You can prove Namid wrong right now. I have questions for you. Answer them honestly and allow me to see that you're something other than the wicked hag I believe you to be."

She narrowed her eyes, though whether out of curiosity at what I would ask, or anger at the "wicked hag" thing, I couldn't say. "What would you ask?"

287

"Nothing terribly complicated. Why do you want the *Sgian-Bán*?"

Saorla stilled, like a wolf on the hunt.

"I'm sorry. Is that one too hard for you?"

"It is the knife that made my people," she said. I could tell she was choosing her words with care. "As such it is a powerful weapon."

"An honest answer, Saorla. Or does that lie beyond your meager talents?"

"Why are you trying to provoke me?"

"I'm trying to get you to own up to what you are. Why do you want the knife?"

"You already know, don't you?" she said. "He has—"

She stopped herself.

"Warned me against you?" I said for her. "Yes, he has. And he's right, isn't he? You want the blade so that you can use it to kill Namid and the other runemystes."

"This is a war!" she said. "And yes, I seek a weapon that will allow me to defeat my enemies. That doesn't make me wicked or evil. Any warrior would do the same."

"You're right."

She blinked. "What?"

"You're right. It's not your quest for the knife that makes you evil. But that leads to my next question: why do you want to destroy the runemystes?"

She recognized the trap, but only after I had sprung it. She wished to destroy the runemystes precisely because of all Namid and his kind did to protect our world against dark magic. She wanted to make slaves not only of weres and weremystes, but also of those who possessed no magic at all. If she succeeded, she would make herself the most powerful and brutal despot the world had ever known.

She couldn't say this of course, not in front of those who served her cause. Fortunately for her, though, she was free to ignore my question and there wasn't a damn thing I could do about it. I might have mastered enough magic to make myself a match for Fitzwater, but I wasn't yet a threat to Saorla. At least I didn't think I was.

"Enough of this foolishness," she said. "Where is the Pale Knife?"

"I have no idea."

I smiled, grateful to Gracie in that moment for having refused to answer my questions earlier in the day. Saorla would have known if

I was lying; I could tell that she was listening for any hint of deception in my words. She appeared genuinely surprised to have heard none.

She waved a hand, indicating Gracie and Neil. "One of them knows. Perhaps they both do."

"If so, they haven't told me."

"But perhaps they will. You still owe me a boon. You shall fulfill your obligation to me by extracting the information from them. You are free to choose how this might be done."

"And if I refuse?"

She glared at me, light from the flames burning in her eyes. "It would be a meaningless gesture, and likely a fatal one." She spread her hands wide. "You did not wish to hand over the woman to me, and despite your efforts she is mine anyway. All that you did to protect her, all that you endured, has been in vain. Have you learned nothing?"

"I kept the kids from you."

"I have the mother and the father. Do you truly believe the children will elude me for much longer? Now, fulfill your oath."

"And if I do?" I asked, stalling for time. I needed inspiration, some way to fight Saorla. I sensed that Gracie had nothing left, and I didn't know how much I could expect from Neil.

"You seek to bargain with me over something I was already promised?" she asked, her tone silken and dangerous.

"I want to know what will happen to me, and to my friends. Say I do as you ask, and I find out where the *Sgian-Bán* is hidden. Once you have it, do you intend to kill me, to kill them?"

"You deserve to die. You have defied me, attacked me. Even now, I sense that you seek to deceive me. I would be justified in killing you, and I would feel no remorse at all after doing so. But I find you most interesting. You have courage, misplaced though it may be. I believe you could prove valuable in what is to come, if only I can cure you of your blind devotion to Namid'skemu. I wonder, though, if that is even possible."

Before I could answer her, my phone buzzed.

"What was that?" Saorla asked.

It would have been ridiculous for me to interrupt such a perilous exchange with a centuries-old magical being who could kill me with a thought in order to respond to a text message. Yet, that's exactly what I intended to do. Like I said, I was stalling. And the only two people who ever texted me were Kona and Billie. At that moment, I would have welcomed word from either of them.

"What was it?" she asked again.

"My phone."

"You have received a communication from someone."

"That's right."

"From whom?"

"To check, I have to reach into my pocket."

She laughed. "There is nothing you could hold in your pocket that I might fear."

I shrugged, pulled out the phone. The message was from Billie. Two words. "Make noise."

She could have had in mind any number of sounds, but I thought I knew exactly what she was after.

"Who has contacted you? What do they say?"

"It's from Billie," I said.

"Your woman."

"Yes. She has the kids and they're far from here."

"Tell me where!"

I smiled. "No."

And I cast. My first R&B crafting: I pulled power from the earth and the fire, and I used them to enhance the wind. Magic surged through me. Gracie gave a small gasp, but I kept my eyes on Saorla. She watched me, clearly perplexed. At first, the effect of the spell was barely noticeable. What I was attempting was like trying to push a car. My magic needed to gather momentum. I maintained the spell, feeding it with more power. The breeze strengthened into a wind, which gathered into a gale, which began to howl like some wild beast summoned from the desert.

I directed the tempest at Saorla and her weremancers. Dust flew from behind me, clouding the night. Saorla's hair whipped around her face, but she stood utterly still, otherwise unaffected.

"You are wasting your power, Justis Fearsson," she shouted over the roar of the wind.

I didn't answer. Let her think I intended this as an attack.

Fitzwater anchored his hat to his head with a rigid hand, and he leaned into the gale, refusing to give an inch. The man and woman standing with him did the same. That was also fine with me.

Old Lionel never saw Billie's car as it flashed into view, its headlights off. More to the point, he never heard it.

The Honda slammed into him. He somersaulted into the windshield, flipped over the roof, and bounced onto the rear of the car, before crashing to the pavement and moving no more. I think he was dead before he hit the road.

Billie kept driving.

Saorla spun to see what had happened and upon spotting her pet vampire, let out a scream that spiraled into the night.

I released my spell, allowing the wind to die away.

"What did you do?" the necromancer demanded, whirling to face me once more. She looked back at the pair behind her. "What did he do? What just happened?"

They appeared to have no better idea than she. Billie's car was still protected by the glamour, and of course, no one had heard it coming or going.

"Is Namid'skemu with you?" Saorla asked. "Is that how you have done this? Show yourself, Runemyste!" she called, raising her voice over the abating wind. "You are not to interfere! You know this!"

"It wasn't Namid," I said. "It was me. I'm not as weak as you think I am."

"No, you are every bit as weak—"

She broke off, turning her head slightly, her ear tipped upward. I heard it, too, and I cursed under my breath. The crunch of gravel under a car's tire, the whisper of an idling engine.

"Of course," she said. Her spell rode the wind like smoke and a moment later she let out a cry of triumph.

Damn it!

"Find the car," she said to the two remaining weremancers. "Bring them here. Do not harm the children." Her eyes found mine. "I would prefer you did not harm the woman, either, but if she resists in any way, do what you must."

"They know you're there, Billie!" I called. "Don't fight them!"

Saorla nodded. "That may be the most intelligent thing I have ever known you to do."

I didn't answer. My mind raced. I didn't dare attack Saorla directly.

I didn't have the power to penetrate her wardings, and I expected her punishments for any such attempt to be extravagant. And now that she had the kids and Billie, the risks were too great. So often in my dealings with the necromancer, I had sensed that she and I were engaged in a magical game of chess. Right now, as pleased as I was that Fitzwater was dead, as proud as I was of what Billie had managed to do, I couldn't help feeling that I had sacrificed my queen to take out a rook. The cost had been too great.

I could do nothing but stare into the darkness and wait. Gracie and Neil gazed in the same direction, tense and silent. Before long we heard footsteps, and then shouts of, "Mommy! Daddy!"

"Hey!" The man's voice.

"It is all right," Saorla said. "Let them come."

Emmy and Zach flew to their parents, Emmy to Gracie, Zach to Neil. Like to like.

Billie followed, flanked by the two weremancers. She didn't appear to be injured in any way, but I wondered how long that would last. With a glance at her escort, she hurried toward me. I took her in my arms and kissed her brow.

"You all right?" I asked.

"Yes. I'm sorry. I thought I could . . . I wanted to do more."

"You did great."

"Yes, yes," Saorla said, cutting across us. "This is all quite heartwarming. But my tolerance for these games has run out. Where is the *Sgian-Bán*?"

No one answered.

She eyed each of us, her gaze coming to rest on me. Of course. "There is still the matter of our arrangement. You have refused me again and again, and have managed to keep me from exacting a measure of revenge for your effrontery. No longer. You offered me a boon in exchange for the life of your woman. You have reneged, and so her life is mine."

"No!" Gracie said it before I could. She climbed to her feet, her attempts to cradle her broken hand making the motion awkward. "I have the knife. This isn't Jay's fault, or Billie's. Or anyone else's for that matter. I have it, and I'll give it to you if you let the rest of them go."

"You will give it to me. It is mine, and this is *not* a negotiation."

Gracie glared back at her.

"You would prefer I killed them one by one, until you acquiesce? The girl has value, and so do you. Perhaps Justis Fearsson does as well. I have yet to decide. But the boy? Your husband? The woman? I will kill each of them in turn, starting with the youngest. Is that what you wish?"

A tear slipped from Gracie's eye. She shook her head. "No. Please."

"*Then give it to me!*"

"I have to cast," she said. "A transporting spell."

"Have a care, my dear. I will know at the first touch of your magic if you attempt any other crafting, or if you try to send something from here rather than summon it to you. Your spell will fail, and their lives will be forfeit. Do you understand?"

"Yes." Her tears fell freely now. She glanced at me. "I'm sorry."

"Live to fight another day," I said.

She nodded. An instant later, I felt the frisson of a spell. And an object appeared in her hands.

My first impulse was to laugh. My first thought was that Gracie was either truly brilliant or completely nuts.

"Zeeber!" Zach cried. He released Neil and reached for the stuffed zebra.

"You'll have him back in a minute, kiddo," Gracie said. "I promise."

She held it out to Saorla, but the necromancer didn't move.

"What is that . . . thing?"

"It's my son's stuffed animal. A toy. The knife is inside it."

"If this is a ruse—"

"It's not. I swear."

"Very well. You will give it to Justis Fearsson. He can deliver it into my hands, as he should have long ago."

I had an instant to prepare. I knew what Saorla would do, what her kind always seemed to do. Once more I delved with my magic into the ground beneath me, the light and air all around me. And I cast a warding.

Saorla laughed, and her spell fell upon me with the weight of the full moon.

"You still believe you can ward yourself against me? You are a stubborn fool. You cannot resist my magic; you are mine to control."

She regarded Billie. "Do you see how weak he is, this man of yours? He is nothing. Take that thing from her," she said to me.

I held out a hand. Gracie searched my eyes, hoping, I suppose, to see some spark of my spirit, of my independence. Seeing none, she placed Zeeber in my hand.

"Is it in there?"

I gave the animal a squeeze, from the sides first, but I felt nothing. I tried again, compressing it top to bottom. Still I felt nothing.

"Is it? Answer me!"

"I don't know."

"It is," Gracie said. "I swear. It's wrapped and protected. I had to make sure Zach wouldn't hurt himself. But I swear on the lives of my children, it's in there."

This seemed to convince Saorla. She smiled, exultant. "Bring it here!"

I turned and carried Zeeber to her. She grabbed it from me—I made no effort to stop her—and felt it the way I had, her smile faltering. So close to her, I caught a whiff of decay, of putrescence and corruption: the essence of her, the cloying residue of her malign origins.

She pulled a knife from the belt at her waist and sliced into the toy. Zach cried out; I heard Gracie murmur something to him.

Saorla reached a hand into the toy. After a moment, that triumphant smile returned. "Yes! I can feel the magic of it. You tried to dampen it, didn't you?" she said to Gracie. "To make it easier to hide. But a mere mortal, even one as skilled as you, cannot conceal such power entirely."

She pulled something from within the animal—a small wrapped parcel—and allowed Zeeber to drop to the ground. The object she held was wrapped in cloth, which she cut through with her blade, then a layer of bubble wrap, and another of cloth. But at last, as these fell away, she pulled the *Sgian-Bán* free, the pale stone catching the moonlight.

It looked just as Namid had described. It was a warm, milky beige from hilt to tip, with runes carved in the honed edge and a dark red streak, the color of ancient blood, running through the blade. There was a crudeness to it, and yet it seemed to pulse with power. If I could have done so, I would have reached out and touched it.

"Glorious one," Saorla whispered. She held it in her palm, gazing down at it like it was something beloved. With a finger that might have trembled, she caressed that dark red streak within the blade, and traced the runes. "I have sought you for centuries."

After a moment, she appeared to remember the rest of us. She clasped the knife by the hilt and held it up over her head. "Behold!" She turned to look at the weremancers before facing Gracie and the others once more. "The *Sgian-Bán*. The Pale Knife."

"It's beautiful," I said.

Her eyes snapped to mine. "You—"

Three elements. Her hand, the knife, my hand.

She had warded herself against attacks. She thought herself immune to any spell I might throw at her. She thought me firmly under her control. But my warding had worked. And it had never occurred to her to protect herself from a spell as simple as this one.

The blade vanished from her hand, and reappeared an instant later in mine. I didn't hesitate. If the knife possessed the power she believed it did, no protective conjuring could shield her from its bite. Still, I knew I would have only the one chance to get this right.

My thrust caught her just below the sternum. Her eyes went wide and her mouth opened, though no sound escaped her. Searing heat shot through the blade and into my arm, tearing a roar from my throat. But, I gritted my teeth against the pain and pressed the blade in farther, feeling its edge grate against bone.

A luminous glow poured from the wound, bright—almost blinding in its intensity—as if the sun itself had burst from her chest, and yet dark, baleful, the color of ancient dried blood.

Saorla's hands closed over mine, her fingers cold, but her grasp still powerful. She tried to peel my hand away from the hilt of the *Sgian-Bán*, but I held on. Heat still flowed like lava into my hand and arm, advancing toward my shoulder. My fingers felt as though they were soldered to the stone, and I feared what might happen if that radiating fire spread into my chest. But right now, I feared Saorla more.

She pulled back her hands, and with a wail of torment, of disbelief and outrage, of terror at the thought that she might actually be mortal, she shoved me. Magic surged through both of her hands, and I flew backward, hit the ground and rolled like a tumbleweed.

But though dazed and hurt, I managed to look back at her, fearing that even now she might find a way to cheat the death that should have been hers a thousand years ago.

She stared down at the jutting hilt of the knife, which I had left buried in her flesh. And then she gripped it with both hands, clearly intending to pull it free.

But upon touching her hands to the stone, she screamed again, and that same heat I had felt lit her fingers ablaze. She grabbed at the knife once more, despite the flames, but appeared unable to pull it free.

Still that bloody light poured out of her, but now the torrent began to ebb, the radiance of the glow to diminish. She dropped to her knees, her eyes finding mine.

"You," she said again, her voice strained.

I forced myself to my feet and staggered toward her.

"Jay!" Gracie called.

"It's all right." I eased closer.

"There are others," Saorla said, breathing the words. "I shall be avenged."

I stood over her and offered no reply. For another few seconds, she stared up at me. Then her eyes rolled back in her head and she toppled over onto her side, light still seeping from the wound.

The last pair of weremancers had watched all of this, their mouths hanging open. Now they shifted their gazes to me.

"Get out of here," I said. "Don't ever let me see your faces again."

I heard footsteps behind me: Neil and Gracie. One of the weremancers—the woman—nodded once, and the two of them backed away from us. Eventually they turned and began the long walk back to the city.

Gracie stared down at Saorla's body. I thought she might prod the corpse with a toe, but she didn't. Rather, she surveyed the area around our campsite. Fitzwater's body was still sprawled in the street, near the man whose blood he had used for a spell. Vogue, Susan, and the other man lay in the dirt near the tents, alive and needing care.

"You told me they could be beaten," she said. "I didn't believe you."

"I know."

"Did you believe it?" she asked me. "Or were you saying it to keep me from giving up?"

"We'll go with the first option."

A wan smile touched her lips.

"We should heal that hand," I said.

"I'll do it," Neil said, perhaps a little too quickly.

Her smile lingered. "Yeah, all right."

I left them there and walked to Billie, who had stayed back with the kids.

She put her arms around me, her eyes searching mine. "Are you all right?"

"A little sore. But otherwise I'm fine." I flexed my right hand. My entire arm felt like it had been barbecued, but while my skin might have been a little pink, there were no burns, no blisters. I'd been lucky.

"That was amazing, Fearsson. I thought she had . . . I don't know what I thought. But you had me fooled, along with everyone else."

I smiled. "It's nice to know I can still surprise you."

"Well, don't make a habit of it. I think I've had my fill of surprises for a while. I'd like things to just be normal."

"Normal?" I said. "Have we met? I don't do normal."

"So I've noticed." Her grin faded. "What did she say to you at the end?"

"Saorla?"

Billie nodded.

I wanted to lie to her, to reassure her, but she deserved better, and she was strong enough to hear the truth.

"That she wasn't the last, and that others of her kind would avenge her death."

"Cheery."

"Yeah, no shit."

"That's a bad one, Jay," Emmy said from nearby. "Two quarters for each of us."

CHAPTER 23

Neil did a decent job of healing Gracie's hand, and as soon as he finished, Gracie was ready to leave.

I insisted that we call ambulances for the injured weremancers. I wanted to call Kona, too. She would have to take Gracie in, but I trusted her to take into account all the mitigating circumstances and to do her best to get the charges against Gracie dropped or at least lessened.

I knew I wouldn't be able to convince Gracie that this was the wisest course, and Neil didn't have much more success than I did. To my surprise, though, Billie did, and before Gracie changed her mind, I put in the call.

I told Kona where we were and gave her the *Reader's Digest* version of what had happened.

"You're way outside my jurisdiction, Justis."

"I know that. But Fitzwater and Gracie are your murder suspects, and Saorla's been on PPD's radar for a while now, too. You need to pull some strings, or get one of the higher-ups to do it."

"You say Billie ran down Fitzwater?"

"That's right."

"Well, she might be in a bit of trouble, too."

"I hadn't thought of that. Hold on." I walked to where Billie had stopped her car. It was dark, of course, but the moonlight was bright enough for me to see that there wasn't a mark on that little blue

Honda. Nothing. No dents in the bumper or hood, not even a crack in the windshield. Those had been some powerful wardings.

"It's not a problem," I said into the phone. "You'd never know that her car touched him."

"So who are we going to pin it on?"

"It was a hit and run, Kona. The driver never even slowed down."

"I don't like this at all. If it was anyone but Fitzwater, I wouldn't go along."

"If it was anyone but Fitzwater, she wouldn't have hit him."

She couldn't argue with that.

We ended our call and I rejoined Billie and the others to wait for Kona, Kevin, and the state police to get there. I heard the ambulance approaching, and braced myself for what I knew would be hours of questioning. The glamour Saorla had placed over us had died with the necromancer. Maybe the fire department would finally show up, too.

"What do we tell them?" Gracie asked, her voice low.

"As much of the truth as we can," I said. But I stepped back to Saorla's body. No more light came from the wound, and already the stench of rot, a hint of which always clung to her, had become almost too strong to bear. I hesitated, but then stooped and gripped the *Sgian-Bán*. The hilt was as cool as, well, stone. I pulled on it, expecting resistance, but the blade slid free. It was as clean as it had been when first Saorla pulled it from Zeeber.

I carried it back to where the others waited, watching me.

Gracie held out her hand for it, but I looked her in the eye and slipped it into my coat pocket.

"It's not yours," I said. "It's not mine, either, but I'll find a place for it."

I could see she didn't like this at all, but she held her tongue.

It was a long night. Kona met the State Police near Gila Bend and drove with them to the campground, which meant that we didn't have to answer questions from anyone but her. Just about every one of us, except Billie and the kids, sported injuries from our battle, which made piecing together a coherent narrative that would allow the police to assign blame that much more difficult. It was a tangled mess, but I knew that those dark sorcerers had no interest in pressing charges against us. Any court proceedings would shine too much light on their activities. For my part, I wouldn't have minded sending them all to prison, but there wasn't a jail in the state that would hold the weremancers if they didn't want to be held.

Kona knew all of this as well, of course. And though she masked her reactions, I could tell she was glad to see the corpses of Fitzwater and Saorla. Still, those of us who didn't need hospital care, all wound up going back to 620 for further questioning.

Billie and I didn't get out of there until well past dawn. Kona and Kevin were still interrogating Gracie when we left.

Margarite, Kona's life partner, drove us back out to Gila Bend to retrieve Billie's car, and Billie then drove me to the national monument so that I could get my dad's pickup. I was eager to swap the truck for my 280Z, whatever the hell I was going to call it now.

Billie and I parted there, with me promising her that I would see her later in the day.

I headed back into the city, and as I drove, I placed a call to Jacinto Amaya.

He answered on the first ring.

"What's happened?" he asked.

"Gracie and the kids are safe. The kids are with the husband, who turned out to be a pretty decent guy, and Gracie is answering questions at Phoenix Police headquarters."

"What about Fitzwater?"

"He's dead. And so is Saorla."

Amaya was silent for a long time. "How did you manage that?"

"I had some help," I said.

"I would expect. But killing Saorla? I didn't think that could be done."

"I used the *Sgian-Bán*."

Another long pause. "So you have it?"

He sounded too eager, and I knew I could never allow him to get anywhere near that knife. "I did," I said.

"And now?"

"It was destroyed when I killed Saorla. There was a lot of light and flame, and when it was over and she was dead, the knife was gone."

"Damn."

"Yeah, it's a tough break."

"It certainly is," he said, in a tone that made we wonder if he believed me. "But at least we know that it will never again fall into the hands of dark sorcerers."

"That's right," I said. "I assure you it never will."

"All right. Come by the house later today, and I'll pay you for the work you did."

"How about tomorrow? It's been a wild few days and I'm wiped."

"Sure, tomorrow's fine. Thank you, Jay. I'm glad Gracie and her children are safe. I know Marisol and Eduardo will be relieved."

I closed the phone and dropped it back into my pocket, my gaze never leaving the road. But I was aware of the bright gleaming eyes fixed on me from the passenger seat.

"You have something you want to say to me, ghost?"

Namid rumbled like desert thunder. "You lied to him, Ohanko. The Pale Knife cannot be destroyed."

"You could do it."

He shook his head. "It is not our place to interfere, even in this."

"That's what I figured. So, yes, I lied. I don't want him to have it."

"You believe it is safe in your care?"

"No, I have something else in mind."

"Very well. I will trust in your judgment."

I glanced his way. "Thank you. Before Saorla died, she told me that there were others of her kind, and she made it clear they'd be coming for me."

"I have no doubt this is true. There were as many necromancers as there were runemystes. Perhaps more. You must continue to tread like the fox. And you must train."

"Right. About that, I think I'm ready to learn some new spells. I figured a few things out last night. I'm not the weremyste I was yesterday. I'm a runecrafter now."

"I believe I will be the judge of that."

"Yeah, you will. And you'd better bring something more than the weak-ass shit you threw at me in Billie's dining room the other day."

"Is this trash talk?"

I grinned. Namid always sounded funny using modern phrases. "Yes, it is."

"Very good. I will look forward to our next meeting, Ohanko. Watch your ass."

I was still laughing long after he disappeared.

I returned the truck to my dad and sat with him for a little while. He was unusually coherent this day, especially considering that the phasing would begin at sundown. We sipped beers, and I told him all about the past few days and my final confrontation with Saorla. He interrupted me a few times to ask questions, sounding very much like the cop he must have been in his heyday. When I finished, he patted my leg and nodded.

"Sounds like you did good work."

"I think I did." I finished my bottle and set it on the ground by my folding chair. "Did you enjoy being a dad?" I asked. "When I was young, I mean."

He shrugged. "Sure. Being a dad is a lot of fun. I was working hard then, and of course I had the phasings to deal with. But you were a good kid, and your mom and I were still doing okay then. So yeah, I enjoyed it. Why?"

I shook my head. "Just wondering."

"Why don't I believe that?"

"I liked being with Gracie's kids, and it made me wonder . . . I'm young still, and . . . I don't know. It has me thinking."

"Well, there's nothing wrong with thinking. But remember that any kids you bring into this world are probably going to be weremystes, too. That's not a deal-breaker, obviously. It wasn't for me and your mom. But it's also nothing to take lightly."

I left him a short while later and drove my car to Billie's. In all the time we had been together, I still hadn't stayed with her during a phasing. In part I feared that I might hurt her. But I also had been reluctant to let her see me in the depths of my monthly psychosis. I knew, though, that if we were to have a future together, I'd have to let her see what my phasings were like.

Apparently she knew this, too.

"I think you should stay here tonight," she said as we ate a late lunch.

"Tonight's—"

"I know what tonight is. I don't care. I want you here with me."

I nodded, feeling both frightened and relieved. "All right."

Those words seemed to throw every clock in the world into overdrive. I would have gladly sold my soul for a spell that would slow down time. Before I knew it, the sky had begun to darken and the full moon, not yet risen but lurking like a demon just below the horizon, had settled its weight on my mind.

Billie remained by my side, but I shrank from her, fearing the coming insanity, terrified of what she would see in me. Until at last, she took both of my hands and forced me to look her in the eye.

"I'm not going anywhere," she said, whispering the words with such intensity, I knew she meant it not only for this night, but for all the phasings to come.

It was my last coherent thought. The moon rose. My grip on reality loosened, slipped away altogether. The delusions and hallucinations crept in. Most were fleeting, here and gone like a desert wind. Others proved more stubborn. I remember seeing Saorla's face, watching as she killed Zach and then Emmy. I'm sure I screamed and wept.

But Billie stayed with me. And more significant, I remained aware of her the entire time. She didn't morph into some ghoul, or my dead mother, or—thank God—Saorla. She was just Billie. Solid, real, unchanged despite the maelstrom of confusion around me. At some point she must have led me to bed and tucked me in, because I awoke the next morning with her beside me, watching me, a smile on her lovely face.

"How are you doing?"

"I feel hungover," I said, croaking the words. "But that's normal." I watched her. "You didn't run away screaming."

"I told you I wouldn't." She kissed me lightly on the lips. "I'm hungry. How about some breakfast?"

I nodded, not entirely sure what to say. I'd never thought of treating a morning during the phasing as if it were the start of just another day—normal, routine. Maybe she was on to something.

"I'm supposed to see Amaya today."

She shook her head. "You're not going anywhere. You're staying with me."

"But—"

"He's a weremyste, too, right?"

"Yes."

"Then he'll understand."

Hard to argue.

Breakfast consisted of pancakes and sausage. Normal, routine.

We spent much of the day on her couch flipping the channels on her television. She was more subdued than usual, and I began to worry that maybe the first night of the phasing had freaked her out after all. She'd gotten a glimpse of our future, of what life with me would really be like, and she'd come to realize that she didn't want any part of it. Already she was dreading this second night, afraid that it would be even worse than the first. That was my fear, at least.

Turns out, I was just a bit off.

Late in the afternoon I finally worked up the courage to say something. "Maybe I should go."

She eyed me as if I was nuts. "Go where?"

"I don't know. Home?"

"Don't be stupid. You're staying here." She switched the television back to a channel that was airing reruns of an old detective series. She liked to watch PI shows with me and ask what was real and what was BS.

"Last night really didn't scare you off, did it?"

"Clown. Of course not."

"Then why so quiet?"

She shrugged, but suddenly she wouldn't look me in the eye.

"Billie?"

"It's nothing. I was just . . . I've been wondering. Do you ever think about having kids?"

Namid had been telling me for years that as my runecrafting improved, and I learned to better control my magic, I might ease the effects of the phasing on my long-term sanity.

I had no doubt this was true. What I hadn't expected was that the giant steps I had taken with my spellcraft in recent days might make this first phasing itself less severe. I suppose it was also possible that being with Billie, having her there to keep me at least somewhat grounded, helped me through the worst of the full moon. Whatever the reason, the next two nights were no more harrowing than the first. This proved to be the easiest phasing I'd ever endured.

The morning after the third night, I went to Amaya for my check and then drove out to see Gracie, who had been placed in the Estrella Jail west of Sky Harbor Airport. She looked tired and pale, but she seemed to be in good spirits.

"Detective Shaw thinks the charges will be dropped eventually," she said. "Maybe as soon as the end of next week."

"That's great," I said. "Kona wouldn't have told you that if she didn't think she could get it done."

Gracie nodded, studying her hands. "I miss the kids."

"I'm sure. They with your parents?"

"No, Neil."

"I think that's good, too. There a chance you two could get back together?"

"I don't think so. We're good at the parenting thing, but we kinda suck at the marriage thing."

"So where will you go?"

"I'm thinking about Sedona. I can get a job at the hospital up there, and Mister Amaya has told my mom that he might be able to help me out with a small loan. Interest free."

Smart. Really smart. Amaya had found a way to give Gracie and her kids as much freedom as they could possibly want, while making certain they were more closely tied to him than ever. Why wasn't I ever that smart?

Of course I kept all of this to myself, saying only, "Sedona sounds perfect."

"It does, doesn't it?"

"Well, I'll check in with Kona about the charges. But I want you to be in touch before you leave, all right?"

"I will," she said. "I promise."

From the jail, I drove back out to the Gila River Indian Community. I parked the car at the base of that rough, narrow dirt track that led to Lucan Quinn's shack, and started the long walk up the hill. The 280Z would have been eaten alive by that road, and I was in the mood for a hike.

I walked slowly, enjoying a cool, clear morning, listening for the buzzy calls of Black-throated Sparrows, and watching the skies for Swainson's Hawks.

When at last I crested the top of the rise, I found the shack empty. I sensed, though, that I wasn't alone.

"I'm looking for the granddaughter of Lucas Quinn," I called, my voice swallowed by the desert wind as it rushed over the scrub and dirt.

I waited for several minutes and finally opened my mouth to call for her again. But at that moment, there came a soft rustling of brush. Turning toward the sound, I saw a huge wolf pad into view, her amber eyes bright in the sunshine.

"Hello, Grandma," I said.

I licked my lips and glanced around hoping the girl was nearby.

The wolf growled low and deep, but she didn't bare her teeth.

"I have something for you," I said. I held up my hands for her to see, reached into my jacket pocket, and pulled out the stone knife. "This should be yours. It can't be destroyed, and I think it would be dangerous for anyone else to have. But it can't be allowed to fall into the hands of the people who killed your husband. It has to remain hidden. Forever. Do you understand?"

For a moment, she merely stared back at me, and I wondered how much of what I said had reached her. But then she threw back her great, beautiful head and howled, the sound penetrating the same wind that had muted my voice.

This wasn't the first time I had heard a wolf howl in the wild, but I'd never seen one do it or been so close. I could feel the note in my chest, mournful, pure, haunting, a cry of love and grief and, dare I hope it, expiation.

I listened as her howl went on and on, my throat tight, my pulse racing at the sheer beauty of what she had shared with me. And when at last she finished, I whispered, "Thank you."

I knelt and held out the *Sgian-Bán* to her. She walked to me, her eyes never leaving my face. And she licked my fingers just once, before taking the knife between her teeth and trotting away.

The wolf headed toward a line of low hills lying to the north, her head held high, her steps quick and nimble. She didn't look back at me, and I didn't stay to see where she took the blade.

Acknowledgements

✳ ✳ ✳

As with the previous books in the series, I wish to thank Karen Kontak and Jeri F. of the Phoenix Police Department's Crime Analysis and Research Unit, who gave me valuable information about life in the PPD and in Phoenix's various police precincts and beats, and Gayle Millette, of the Phoenix Medical Examiner's Office, for her help with details about the OME. I owe a great debt to Michael Prater, for his expertise on firearms, and for his bravery in actually taking me out shooting. I also received valuable feedback on firearms from a reader, William Cawthon, to whom I'm deeply grateful.

Faith Hunter, A.J. Hartley, Elyse Poller, Laura Willis, Michael Thompson, Patrick Dean, Virginia Craighill, April Alvarez, and Megan Roberts offered feedback on various elements of the story and manuscript. I'm grateful to all of them.

Huge thanks as always to my agent, Lucienne Diver, for her close reading of the manuscript, her wisdom and professional advice, and her friendship.

I am deeply grateful to Jim Minz, for his editorial feedback on the manuscript, which improved the finished product immensely. Thanks as well to Toni Weisskopf, Tony Daniel, Gray Rinehart, Danielle Turner, Carol Russo, Christopher Cifani, Marla Ainspan, and all the great folks at Baen Books.

Finally, as always, I am grateful to Nancy, Alex, and Erin, for their support, their silliness, and their love.

—D.B.C.

About the Author

✹ ✹ ✹

David B. Coe is the Crawford Award-winning author of nineteen novels and the occasional short story. Under his own name he has written three epic fantasy series, as well as the novelization of Ridley Scott's *Robin Hood*. As D.B. Jackson, he is the author of the Thieftaker Chronicles, a historical urban fantasy. *Shadow's Blade* is the third book in the Case Files of Justis Fearsson, after *Spell-Blind* and *His Father's Eyes*. David's books have been translated into a dozen languages. He lives on the Cumberland Plateau with his wife and daughters.